Praise for INDIGO

"Remarkable reading. Jenkins is a scholar,
which brings a depth to her writing
that few romances achieve."
Detroit Free Press

"Jenkins once again lifts readers into a love story
that is smart and sassy as well as fascinating and
informative. Her star continues to climb."
Romantic Times

Praise for VIVID

"Beverly Jenkins brings to living color a rarely
read piece of Americana—the lives of Black
Americans just after the Civil War. All her
characters are first class and the romance
is top of the line . . ."
Affaire de Coeur

"Jenkins weaves relevant Black history throughout,
which makes the novel an informative
and entertaining read."
VIBE Magazine

Praise for NIGHT SONG

"Hooray for new author Beverly Jenkins . . .
this passionate romance is a definite winner."
Rendezvous

"Heartbreaking drama that will hold you
enthralled. Not to be missed."
Affaire de Coeur

Other **AVON ROMANCES**

DECEIVE ME NOT *by Eve Byron*
DESTINY'S WARRIOR *by Kit Dee*
EVER HIS BRIDE *by Linda Needham*
GRAY HAWK'S LADY *by Karen Kay*
THE MACKENZIES: CLEVE *by Ana Leigh*
STOLEN KISSES *by Suzanne Enoch*
WILD IRISH SKIES *by Nancy Richards-Akers*

Coming Soon

CAPTAIN JACK'S WOMAN *by Stephanie Laurens*
MOUNTAIN BRIDE *by Susan Sawyer*

And Don't Miss These
ROMANTIC TREASURES
from Avon Books

THE COURTSHIP OF CADE KOLBY *by Lori Copeland*
FALLING IN LOVE AGAIN *by Cathy Maxwell*
FLY WITH THE EAGLE *by Kathleen Harrington*

TOPAZ

BEVERLY JENKINS

AVON BOOKS ◆ NEW YORK

This is a work of fiction. Names, characters, places, and incidents either are the product of the author's imagination or are used fictitiously. Any resemblance to actual events, locales, organizations, or persons, living or dead, is entirely coincidental and beyond the intent of either the author or the publisher.

AVON BOOKS
A division of
The Hearst Corporation
1350 Avenue of the Americas
New York, New York 10019

Copyright © 1997 by Beverly E. Jenkins
Published by arrangement with the author
Visit our website at **http://AvonBooks.com**
Library of Congress Catalog Card Number: 97-93015
ISBN: 0-380-78660-5

First Avon Books Printing: September 1997

AVON TRADEMARK REG. U.S. PAT. OFF. AND IN OTHER COUNTRIES, MARCA REGISTRADA, HECHO EN U.S.A.

Printed in the U.S.A.

WCD   10 9 8 7 6 5 4 3 2 1

To my sisters Lorraine and Marji, who let me tell them stories when we were very young, and to my late grandfather Richard Coklow Sr.

"We come here not to tell a lie, but to tell the whole truth. . . . "

John Horse
Black Chief of the Seminole Nation, 1873

Topaz

Chapter 1

Chicago
May 1884

Under the cover of the darkness, Katherine Love stood with her back pressed closely against the outside wall of the warehouse, hoping she couldn't be seen. The night watchman was on the far side of yard, and she was waiting for him to pass. She could see him walking and swinging his lantern in and out of the shadows. He was whistling cheerily as he checked a few doors to make certain they hadn't been tampered with, but he gave no more than a cursory look to most of the sheds and buildings along the route.

This was the third night Katherine had come here hoping to rendezvous with a man hired to assist her in her plan, but for reasons unknown, he'd never shown. She hoped this third night would be the charm.

As the watchman came closer to her, she hunkered down behind a large trash bin filled with lumber and discarded crates. Her five-feet seven-inch frame made it difficult for her to appear small, but the black axle grease she'd smeared over her brown skin, coupled with her black shirt and men's trousers, made it easier for her to blend into the shadows, as did the black knitted fisherman's cap hiding her short curls.

The watchman approached, then passed by her so closely, that she could have reached out, grabbed his pant leg, and probably frightened him half to death. But she wasn't here to pull silly pranks.

He moved on. She waited for the sounds of his whistling and footsteps to fade into the distance before releasing her pent-up breath; she'd hurdled the first obstacle. Once her contact appeared, they would have a little under an hour to complete the night's work before the watchman returned to this portion of the warehouse yard. Plenty of time—if the contact showed.

Silence resettled, and a cautious Katherine waited without moving. The distant bark of a dog floated in on the May night air. She stood silently and watched. Minutes passed; then, from out of the darkness, came the faint flickering light of a match. It disappeared so quickly that she thought she might have imagined it. She peered closely, tensely waiting to see if it would appear again. When it did, she offered up a silent hallelujah. The light was the agreed upon signal. Katherine peeled her tall body away from the shadows of her hiding place. Keeping herself low, she quickly crossed the open yard and headed for the person who'd struck the match.

She didn't know his name; she had no reason to. They would probably never meet again once that night's job ended, yet he greeted her with a smile from behind the burnt cork covering his light-brown face. "You're the *Globe* reporter?"

"Yes," she whispered.

"They didn't tell me you were a woman."

She dearly hoped her gender would not be a problem because she did not have the time to educate a man on the fine points of what a woman of the nineteenth century could achieve. "Does my gender matter?" she asked.

He took a moment to scan her clothing and face, then shrugged. "Not to me."

Katherine was glad. "Are you ready?"

He nodded yes.

"Then let's go rob us a safe."

Katherine and her accomplice rapidly covered the short distance to the main building. The safe she'd alluded to belonged to Mr. Rupert Samuels, a wealthy Chicago businessman and a pillar of the city's Black community. He had many storehouses on this large plot of land on the far edge of the city, but only one held his business office.

When they reached the door, her companion whispered, "They said you had a way in?"

It was her turn to nod yes as she reached into her trouser pocket and withdrew a small thin box. Inside were a set of lock picks given to her for her twenty-fifth birthday by a wily old gentleman burglar she'd met during her stint as a newspaperwoman back in Virginia. Katherine inserted one of the gap-toothed picks into the door's padlock, and it opened. She sensed the surprise emanating from the man at her side, but she didn't pause to acknowledge it. Men were surprised by her unconventional ways all the time.

They tiptoed inside cautiously. Katherine was fairly certain no one would be about, but she knew better than to take that for granted. The solid silence made her breathing sound like a train engine, and her heart beat as loud as a drum. She reached back and softly closed the door. "The safe's hidden behind that Bannister painting on the far wall," she told her accomplice quietly.

The man replied, "I'll need a bit of light."

She heard the scratch of a match and then saw the lit wick of a candle stub. He cupped his hand around the dancing finger of flame to prevent the light from casting too well. He looked around, spied the copy of the prize-winning Bannister painting *Under the Oaks*, and told Katherine, "Keep watch."

Katherine slid back into the darkness, by the door. She was glad for his help because she couldn't've gotten into the safe alone. Thanks to her old burglar friend, she could easily spring the locks on doors and some strong-boxes, but her abilities did not extend to wall safes. It had taken her editor, Geoff Pratt, weeks to find a man who could be trusted to discretely carry out this en-deavor. The long search had cut so deeply into the time frame she and Geoff had allotted for this investigation that if tonight's burglary proved unsuccessful, her six long months of hard work would go for naught.

Her companion called out softly, "It's open and we've struck gold."

The announcement filled Katherine with excitement, but she kept her wits about her. She opened the door a crack to make certain no one was approaching from out-side before going over to see what the safe held.

The candle provided just enough light to illuminate the area around Samuels's large oak desk. The inside of the safe was filled with shadows, but they weren't thick enough to hide the three printer's plates stacked against the back wall. With a satisfied smile, Katherine reached inside and lifted them out. Rupert Samuels had printed hundreds, maybe thousands, of counterfeit railroad stock certificates using the plates Katherine now passed over to her companion. At first glance, the Samuels scheme appeared to be very beneficial: How better to circumvent the jim crow laws than to have a rail line that would cater only to members of the race? The hoodwinked investors, mostly pensioners and widows, had willingly let themselves be led to the slaughter by the well-dressed and seemingly sincere young men selling the stocks. After the bank drafts of the victims cleared, the salesmen vanished, and the investors were left holding worthless pieces of paper.

Katherine reached back inside the safe and pulled out a stack of fraudulent stock certificates and a large ledger. She held the ledger toward the light and hastily scanned the entries. There were page and pages of names, each one adjacent to addresses and dollar amounts. She came across the name of Sally Dotson, an old friend of her Aunt Ceil's and Katherine's landlady. Sally and many of the members of her church had been fleeced by the stock sharps. When Sally told Katherine what had happened, Katherine wrote to her editor, Geoff Pratt, in New York hoping he had an idea as to how they could recoup their savings. Geoff could offer no immediate solution but wired back that he had been approached by a man in New York claiming to be a disgruntled ex-employee of a similar scam being run there. The man was angry because he hadn't been paid what he'd been promised and wanted to expose the leader of the ring, Rupert Samuels of Chicago. Katherine and Geoff set this plan in motion to get at the truth. Katherine assumed the other names chronicled in the ledgers were also victims. With this ledger in hand, the authorities could indict Samuels and his cronies for fraud as soon as luncheon tomorrow. She wondered if he would enjoy languishing in a prison cell? Knowing Rupert Samuels the way she did, she was quite certain he would not.

Katherine gave the ledger and the phony stocks to her accomplice, who slipped them into a canvas bag along with the plates. He would be taking the evidence to her editor, Geoff, in New York. Geoff in turn would hand them over to the federal authorities. Katherine's job then would be to disappear. When the authorities swooped down on Rupert, she planned to be on a train to Boston for a much needed holiday. Left behind would be the woman she'd posed as for the past six months: Katherine Lane, a meek seamstress's assistant. Also left behind would be Katherine Lane, Rupert Samuels's fiancée. She and Rupert were slated to be wed tomorrow in what the society papers were calling the "wedding of the year."

Katherine did not love Rupert. Becoming his intended had not been part of the original plan, but he'd fallen in love with her over the course of her assignment and proposed marriage. She'd been flabbergasted at the irony at first, then decided to take advantage of her position in his life to advance her investigation. Katherine wished she could be a fly on the wall tomorrow when he had to explain to all his well-heeled guests that the bride had flown the coop. But his missing bride would be the least of his worries once the authorities arrived in a week or so, and he had to explain to them about the ledger, the phony stock certificates, and the counterfeit plates. Rupert Samuels was a predator who fed upon the old and feeble of the race. She harbored not a whit of guilt over being the catalyst for what probably would be the most humiliating day of his life—it was a fate he richly deserved.

Katherine and her accomplice placed everything back the way they'd found it, except for the incriminating items in the bag. This done, they turned to head out of the office when the sounds of approaching voices carried in through the closed door. Before either of them could draw a breath of alarm, it opened. The pair stood wide-eyed in the light of a hand-held lantern.

Never one for meekness, Katherine grabbed up a lamp from the desk and hurled it. Her true aim shattered the light. Chaos erupted. Men shouted in the darkness. She tried to make a dash for the door, but it slammed closed, effectively cutting off her exit. Someone grabbed her from behind. She instinctively jabbed back hard with her elbow. Her captor let out a sharp groan and released her all in one motion, but her satisfaction quickly died as he snatched her by the arm and forcefully bent it behind her back. Pain screamed in her shoulder. He continued to apply pressure until the agony forced her to her knees.

The fight continued on the other side of the office, and the sounds of furniture being bumped around and items crashing to the floor mated with the sounds of men breathing heavily and groans of pain.

Then came silence.

The man holding on to Katherine called out in his all-too-familiar voice, "I got one, Mr. Samuels."

The voice belonged to Joe, Rupert's driver and hired thug. His short, muscular body had always reminded Katherine of a caged gorilla she'd seen at a fair in Washington a few years ago.

Katherine was dragged roughly to her feet. The force of his hold on her arm kept her firmly in place.

Another familiar voice, sounding winded, echoed from close by, "All set here, too, Mr. Samuels."

Rupert's other thug, Frank.

A lamp was lit.

When her cool eyes met Rupert's, he barked with astonishment, *"Katherine?!"*

He hastened over and snatched the cap from her head. His eyes seemed to widen even further.

"Good evening, Rupert." Katherine was amazed at how calmly she'd spoken. In truth, she was scared to death. The gun in Rupert's hand did not help matters. Its silvery cast gleamed sinisterly in the light.

Her companion, though subdued, stood defiantly. Apparently he'd been able to put up more of a fight than had Katherine. His split lip appeared minor when compared to the blood running from Frank's nose and the gaping cut above his brow.

Rupert continued to stare at her attire and the grease smeared on her face with a wonder usually reserved for a person who'd suddenly sprouted another head. "You're supposed to be at home resting for the wedding. What is the meaning of this?"

Katherine toyed with lying to him but doubted even she could fabricate a believable explanation under such damning circumstances.

When she did not immediately reply, Rupert turned his attention to the tense man at her side and said easily, "The cat seems to have Katherine's tongue, so let's see if I can get an explanation from you. You are . . . ?"

"Just a friend."

Rupert looked to Frank and nodded calmly. Frank threw a punch into the man's abdomen that doubled him over.

Rupert's voice was sympathetic. " I need a more detailed reply, I'm afraid."

Katherine stiffened with outrage, but Joe's firm hold on her arm checked her.

Rupert gestured to Joe. "Let her go, and see if you can determine what they've been doing in here."

Joe released her and began searching around the desk. It took him but a moment to find the canvas bag. His startled voice rang out, "Mr. Samuels, look at this!"

Rupert's dark eyes settled on the plates, and his jaw visibly tightened. The gaze he turned on Katherine spoke his anger, but his voice remained low and controlled. "Katherine, you either tell me what this is about, or your friend here will have to suffer the consequences."

The last thing Katherine wanted was for her accomplice to be hurt. "He isn't really involved, Rupert. Let him go and I'll tell you everything."

Rupert leaned close to her and said, "You're in no position to bargain, Katherine. Either tell me, or he'll be dead before he draws another breath. Now, start from the beginning. Where were you taking those plates?"

"To Washington."

He studied her face a moment as if the answer surprised him. "Why?"

"Some people I know are interested in them."

He leaned close and whispered, "Why?"

She tried not to let him see her fear. "I've seen the certificates you printed from the plates. You swindled an old friend of mine."

He chuckled patronizingly. "I've never swindled anyone."

"Are you saying the Banneker Railroad is a legitimate business enterprise?"

"No one in my employ ever coerced anyone to invest."

"You lie so prettily. The great Mr. Banneker is undoubtedly twirling in his grave, knowing his name is being used to fleece his own race."

He smiled. "All part of my charm. How'd you know the plates were in the safe?"

"I saw them one evening when we stopped here so you could place some papers in the safe."

"Who's helping you, besides him?" he asked pointing the gun at her accomplice.

"No one."

Rupert again gestured to Frank, who punched Katherine's accomplice a second time. When he retched in reaction, Katherine yelled, "Stop it! Don't hit him again!"

Rupert grabbed Katherine's chin and forced her to meet his angry eyes. "Or what, you'll tell me the truth? Frank will beat this man to death if I order him to. Now, again, who's helping you?"

"Mr. Joseph Pulitzer."

Rupert appeared to stiffen a moment. "Pulitzer?"

"Yes," she lied proudly.

Rupert observed her a moment as if trying to glean the truth from her eyes. He released his hold, then asked "Why would Pulitzer help you?"

"Because I work for his newspaper."

"He doesn't employ Blacks."

"Are you certain? He doesn't make it known, but there are a few of us hidden in the back."

Katherine told the lie because Pulitzer and his paper were a force to be reckoned with. She hoped it would make Rupert think twice about bringing that power down upon his handsome head should Katherine or her companion come to serious harm.

Evidently, Rupert was not buying it. "Pulitzer has better things to do than meddle in the sordid affairs of Black folks. What's your real name?"

"Victoria Lewis." It wasn't really, but she had no intention of telling him the truth unless it became absolutely necessary.

He then spoke to Joe and Frank. "Get him out of my sight."

Katherine made a move to intervene, but Rupert raised the gun. The sight of it and his mocking eyes kept her in her place. Her accomplice tried to make the task difficult for the two thugs, but they hustled him out just the same. The departure left the grim Katherine alone with the man she was due to marry tomorrow. "Where are they taking him?"

"Oh, I don't know, but I'm certain they'll inform me

when they return. Until then, I'm just going to stand here and look at you."

Rupert leaned back against the desk and folded his arms. He was a very handsome man, educated, and possessed impeccable manners. She was wondering how much of the investors' savings had gone toward the purchase of his expensive suit when he spoke.

"Mother Pearl kept telling me there was something about you she didn't care for."

"Your mother never cared for me because I was a seamstress."

"There was that, but she insisted there was something else she sensed. I ignored her, of course, but it appears she was correct. A pity, because as you know, I truly fancied myself in love with you."

Guilt flowed through Katherine for the tiniest moment. She had harbored mixed feelings over leading him on. Maybe, had the circumstances been different—and had Rupert not swindled hundreds of old people in three states—she might have welcomed him as a suitor. He was charming, witty, and loved the theater as much as she. But Rupert was also a snake. To send him to prison, she would have posed as Mr. Lincoln himself.

Rupert's voice cut into her thoughts. "So, do you have anything to say for yourself?"

"No."

"Well, you should. Over a hundred guests are coming to see us marry tomorrow."

"Tell them you finally came to your senses and decided not to wed out of class."

"No, I've a better idea. The wedding will go on as planned. After that, we'll have a long talk."

"But I don't wish to marry you."

"I know, but it hardly matters what you want at this point, does it?"

She could see Rupert studying her and her attire yet again before hearing him ask, "Is this what we men have to look forward to if we give women the vote—a gaggle of women running amok in trousers and axle grease, burglarizing the property of the men they profess to love? I knew you were clever and far more intelligent than most women, but never in my wildest dreams did I suspect you were not the woman you claimed to be."

"Coming from a man like you, I consider that a compliment."

"And it is. A woman with your mind could go far with a man like me."

"Yes, she could, Rupert. She could go straight to prison."

"I do admire your wit, Katherine. Your meddling has upset me, however. I prefer my females uncomplicated, biddable. It seems you are neither."

"Another compliment. I wonder how many you would have bestowed had I succeeded in leaving you at the altar."

Her words appeared to catch him off guard. "What do you mean?"

She thought it made little difference now, so she told him of her plan to deliver the evidence to the authorities and vanish.

He stared, and for the first time the mask fell away from his smooth-skinned face, and the anger rose to the surface. "You would have made me a laughingstock."

"Among other things, yes."

"You would have left me to explain to the cream of this city that my bride was nowhere to be found?!"

Katherine thought he looked properly outraged. "Yes, but humiliation is good for the soul, Rupert. At least I didn't swindle you out of your land or life savings as you did those pensioners."

Katherine had a tendency to speak first and weigh the consequences afterward. Belatedly, she realized taunting him might have been unwise. As always, though, it was too late to retract her words.

He grabbed her by the chin again and forced her eyes to meet his own, saying threateningly, "The only thing keeping your dead body from being found by some rag picker in an alley in the morning is the fact that I don't know who else you might have told about those plates."

"I've told many many people," she promised without flinching. "Many people."

He let her go. In reality, only a few people knew about Rupert's true nature, but the knowledge that he wouldn't dispose of her right away gave Katherine hope that she'd live to fight another day. It also gave her one whole night to figure a way out of her mess.

Frank and Joe returned and Joe came over to whisper something into Rupert's ear. While Katherine looked on tensely, Rupert smiled her way as he listened. Then when Joe was done, Rupert said to her, "Come, Katherine, we can leave now."

Her voice was thick with suspicion. "What have they done with him?"

"Nothing that will concern you ever again. Now, I'm taking you back to my town house so I can keep an eye on you until tomorrow's festivities, but first we're going to pay a visit to your dress shop. I want Frank and Joe to make certain you haven't hidden any secrets there."

He snatched her by the arm and forced her from the office. While Katherine tried not to let her fear rise any higher, she prayed her father, Bart, would not be at the shop waiting for her. There were already too many people in danger. She didn't want him to become embroiled in this, also.

Chapter 2

B art Love glanced up from his cards. He was losing again. An extra ace lay hidden inside the cuff
of his new frock coat, but he didn't know the other players well enough to chance cheating. Back home in Indian
Territory everyone knew he cheated. Hell, they expected
no less. But he wasn't back home. He'd only been in
Chicago a few months. He didn't want to end up shot
or taken to jail.

In the end, it didn't matter much, because when he
looked over to the door and saw Deputy Marshal Dixon
Wildhorse stride in, Bart's eyes widened in terror. His
heart began to pound. He became so short of breath, he
actually thought he might faint. *Wildhorse was supposed
to be dead!*

Yet the Black Seminole lawman stood very tall and
very much alive. As he approached, his blazing dark
eyes told of his anger, an anger directed solely at Bart—
an anger Bart knew he'd better try and defuse or suffer
the dire consequences.

Dixon Wildhorse ignored the shocked silence that
greeted his entrance into the small, dimly lit drinking
establishment. Since coming east, he'd become accus-

tomed to being gawked at like a caged cougar at a fair. When he reached Bart's table, he leaned down to the prey he'd been tracking for the past six weeks and asked him quietly, "Is there someplace we can talk—privately?"

Bart could not stop his shaking. He very slowly placed his cards facedown on the table. The other players and patrons continued to stare at the big, dark-skinned man standing over Love. His large, gray Stetson, his high-heeled boots, and the brilliant, topaz gemstone in his ear told them he wasn't local. His attire conjured up the tales of the Wild West being so prominently reported upon in the newspapers.

Someone called out, "Hey! Are you one of them cowboys?"

Dix turned. He held the questioner's eyes just long enough for the man to begin to squirm before redirecting his attention to Bart.

Bart's voice shook as he said, "Um, let me just settle up here." His trembling hands removed his purse from the inside pocket of his new coat. "How much do I owe you, boys?"

At first no one uttered a sound, seemingly for fear of drawing the attention of the cowboy's unnerving stare. To move things along, Dix singled out the man seated next to Bart and asked him in a voice just loud enough to be audible, "How much?"

The man responded haltingly, "Uh, two—two dollars."

Dix nodded his thanks, then told Bart, "Pay them."

Bart wouldn't meet Dix's eyes as he nervously counted out the amount. He was so nervous, in fact, that he dropped a few coins on the sawdust-covered floor.

The lawman bent to retrieve them, then slowly and soundlessly placed them back on the tabletop. The pre-

ciseness of the lawman's movements gave Bart an even
worse case of the shakes.

Bart finished counting out what he owed. That done,
he made a move to pick up the purse and put it back in
his pocket, only to have Dix's big hand slam down and
cover it. Bart looked up into Dix's cold black eyes and
gave him a sheepish grin. Dix did not grin in reply;
instead, he picked up the purse and stuffed it into his
own shirt pocket. Then, employing the same soft yet
powerful voice, he told Bart, "Let's go."

Bart pushed his chair back from the table. His fear
was so great, he prayed his legs didn't fail him.

Dix followed Bart up to his rented room. As soon as
the door closed behind them, Bart took a seat. Dix stood,
silent.

Bart ran a finger around his shirt's starched collar.

Dix asked, "What's the matter, Bart, collar too
tight?"

Bart nodded. "A mite."

"Rope's going to be tighter than that, you know."

Bart Love blinked. "It was just a misunderstanding
Dix. A silly misunderstanding."

"Then you have my money?"

Bart blinked again. "Well, I . . ."

Dix answered for him. "You don't have my money."

Bart shook his head as if deeply saddened, but before
his gray-haired head stopped moving, Dix dragged him
up to match his own towering height and spoke directly
into his cinnamon-colored eyes. "Bart, you better have
my money for the two hundred head of cattle you stole
and then sold—or do you know what I'm going to do?"

Bart hastily intimated his ignorance.

"I'm going to bury you so deep in the Territorial
prison, it'll take a mole to bring you breakfast."

Dix eased Bart back down to earth.

Everyone in Indian Territory knew Bartholomew Love had absolutely no shame, and he proved it by throwing himself down onto Dix's boots to beg for mercy. "Please, Dix, don't send me to prison! I'm an old man! I'll die there!"

"Yes, you just might."

"I'll do anything, Dix—I'll clean the stables, mop your office. I'll shovel pies out of the street if you say to, but don't send me to prison. I only sold your cows 'cause I thought you was dead."

"That's an *excuse?!*" Dix's husky voice was sharp.

Bart shook his head hastily, scrambling to his feet. "No, Dix, it ain't, but try and see it from my side."

"You don't have a side," the lawman voiced pointedly. "Plenty of folks in town thought I might be dead, but only you stole my property."

Bart hung his head.

"How much of my money do you have left?"

Bart swallowed, confessing, "Just what's left in the purse."

Dix shook his head, filled with anger and disgust. Back home, he had a reputation for being fair in his dealings with folks and slow to anger. When he did get angry, even grizzlies knew to give him a wide berth— or so the legends went—and right now Dixon Wildhorse was the most riled man east of the Rockies. It took all the discipline of his varied ancestry to not pound Bart Love into meal.

Bart scrambled to find some way to soothe the big lawman's wrath. "Please, Dix, let me make it up to you!"

"How? You can't sell me back my own cows like you did that Boston greenhorn last year."

The folks in the Territory had gotten a big kick out

of that prank. Bart had stolen the greenhorn's cows, then sold them back to the Bostonian as new stock, making himself a tidy profit. No one alerted the 'horn to the sleight of hand because he'd been a back-East pain in the rear since the day he came to town. Selling Dix's stock was an entirely different matter, however.

Dix asked again, "How do you aim to repay me?"

"How about my daughter? Everybody in the Territory knows you've been looking to marry up."

Dix's black eyes widened. "*Your daughter?!*"

"Yes, she's uh, educated, clean. She's no beauty, mind you—way too tall—but she's respectable."

Dix could not believe what he'd heard. "Let me get this straight. In exchange for the hundreds of dollars you owe me for those cows, you want to give me your daughter?"

Bart nodded.

"Bart Love, you are truly without a soul. Where is this too-tall daughter now?"

"Right here in Chicago."

"How old is she?"

"Nineteen or so."

"And what do you suppose she'll say when she's told you're giving her away?"

"She won't say nothing. She's looking to marry up, too. She'll be right pleased."

Dix shook his head. "Bart, I don't believe you for a minute."

"I know, Dix, but I'm telling the truth. Hear me out."

Dix knew that Bart couldn't be trusted to give the real color of grass, but he let him keep talking.

"After my wife, Jenny, died, I left Katherine here in Chicago to be raised by my wife's sister. Outside of my own late Jenny, her sister, Ceil, was the finest woman on this earth. Ceil's gone now, too, bless her memory. . . ."

Bart paused as if waiting for the lawman to be moved by the revelation, but when Dix's grim expression did not change, Bart stumbled on. "Uh, as I was saying, I know Ceil raised my Katherine to be a soft-spoken, biddable woman because I've been spending a fair amount of time with her in the three months I've been here. She'd make you the perfect wife."

In reality, Dix *had* been searching for a wife. He'd reached the point in his life where he felt secure enough to take on the responsibility of a family. In order to have the sons he desired, he needed a wife. He had no illusions of falling in love. He simply wanted to marry a woman he could be comfortable with, a woman he didn't mind coming home to in the evenings. But Bart Love's daughter? Dix eyed the old schemer. He had no way of knowing if he even *had* a daughter.

In spite of Bart's sins—and his own anger—Dix didn't really want the old con man to die in jail, but the debt had to be paid. For more than a decade, Dix had chased outlaws to hell and back in order to accumulate the money needed to build that herd. Thanks to Bart's scheming, the herd had been sold to the army, and now Bart wanted his daughter to pay the price.

It was not such a far-fetched idea; arranged marriages were still very common. In fact, in some clans it would have been tantamount to disrespect for Dix to refuse to consider this attempt at making amends, especially since the girl was the only thing of value Bart claimed to possess. Dix grimly assessed the look of hope shining in the old man's eyes. He could feel the vestiges of the old ways rise in his blood, pulling at him. Even though he didn't want to, he knew he had to at least meet the girl. He asked Bart skeptically, "Is she truly educated?"

Bart nodded enthusiastically. "Yep. Respectable, too. She's a seamstress, just like her ma was before she died."

To Dix, choice of occupation meant little in determining a person's character. He'd known seamstresses both prim and chaste. He'd also known a few who should have been working in cathouses. But Bart's claim that she was educated meant much. Dix wanted his sons to grow up with the written word. The railroads and homesteaders were rapidly changing the West. Sometime in the very near future a man would need more than a strong back and a quick gun to make a living. He wanted his children prepared to walk in that new world; having an educated mother would help them along the path. "All right, take me to her. If she's acceptable and *willing*, we'll see. If not, I'm taking you back to the Territory to stand trial for rustling."

It was nearly midnight by the time they hailed a hack and took the journey across town to the shop where Bart's daughter worked and rented a small room. The streets were quiet and deserted. Her workplace was off the main thoroughfare, nestled between a printer's shop and a dry-goods store. They found the shop door unlocked and the darkened interior in shambles.

An anxious Bart called out his daughter's name while Dix drew his Colt. No one answered. The damage appeared extensive. Tables were turned over, joining other pieces of furniture like drawers and full-length mirrors that had been shattered and tossed aside. Spools of thread, buttons, and dressmaker pins littered the floor. Bolts of fabric lay twisted and torn, and every dress form had been slashed open.

Bart and Dix shared equal looks of concern as they maneuvered their way through the dark shop aided only by the light of the moon outside. Dix found an unbroken lamp in the rubble and lit it with a match from his pocket. Light made the damage appear even more stark. Dix swung the lamp Bart's way and saw the fright on the older man's face. The lawman's husky voice broke the silence, "I assume the place is usually kept neater than it is tonight."

Bart didn't answer. Instead, he took a seat on the floor and placed his head in his hands.

"Where's your daughter, Bart?"

Bart looked at Dix and whispered, "I don't know."

"Do you know why anyone might have done this?"

He shook his head slowly. "No."

Dix looked around. His lawman's instincts said the destruction appeared too thorough to be a random robbery. The mutilated dress forms and the dumped out drawers made him believe someone had come here looking for something. "You said your daughter rented a room here?"

"Yes," Bart answered quietly. "Back through there."

Dix had the feeling Bart knew far more than he was letting on, but Dix didn't press. Instead he waded his way through the mess to the daughter's room, which had been given the same trashing. The mattress had been slashed open as had the bed pillows and the cushions of two old stuffed chairs. Clothes he assumed to be hers were strewn about. Dix could almost imagine the intruder tossing the garments aside while pawing through the dresser and wardrobe in the search. But what had he been after—and where was Bart's daughter?

He rejoined Bart, who'd found another lamp and placed it upon a table. He stood before the light, studying something in his palm.

Bart looked up. "I found Katherine's pendant. It was given to her by my late wife, Jenny. Katherine would never have taken this from around her neck unless she were in trouble.''

Dix asked, ''So, are you going to tell me what this is all about, or do we walk out of here right now and head to the train back to Indian Territory?''

As Bart hesitated, Dix almost wished the old man would choose to remain mum. All he truly wanted to do was go home. He hated back east cities, especially large, back east cities and Chicago fit both descriptions. He found the crowds oppressive, the air foul, and the constant noise deafening.

But as Bart began to speak, Dix knew his wish for a speedy return to the western side of the divide would not be granted. ''My Katherine is not really a seamstress.''

Dix sighed. The truth be told, he didn't find the revelation surprising—after all, she was Bart's cub. ''What is she really?''

''A newspaperwoman.''

Dix ran his hands over his tired eyes. A newspaperwoman. ''And what is this all about?'' he asked, gesturing at the torn-apart shop.

Bart spent the next few minutes telling Dix as much as he knew about Katherine's masquerade as a seamstress's assistant and of her newspaper's interest in Rupert Samuels and his business affairs.

''Do you think Samuels is responsible for this?''

''Maybe.'' Then he said, ''Dix we have to find her.''

''We?''

''Please, Dix. You're the best lawman in the Territory. If anyone can find her, it'll be you.''

Dix knew better than to succumb to Bart's flattery. He also knew he couldn't just walk away; the code he lived by would not let him turn his back on the troubles of folks he knew—not even folks like Bart Love. "Do you know where this Samuels lives?"

"Yes."

Dix didn't really want to become involved with this, code or no code; with the Love family involved, things were only bound to get worse. "How old is this too-tall daughter really?"

Bart looked guilty. "Twenty-eight, maybe as old as twenty-nine."

Dix shook his head. "You'd lie to St. Peter, Bart. Let's go."

Bart ran out of the store in order to catch up to the marshal's long strides. "This mean we're going to look for her?"

Dix didn't slow as he answered, "Against my better judgment, yes."

"Dix, I'll never forget this. Never!"

"Neither will I, I'll bet."

While he and Bart stood hidden in the shadows across the street, Dix noted the size and structure of the fashionable Samuels town house. In spite of the late hour, a few lights were burning in various rooms, but it appeared to be just another wealthy home.

Dix asked quietly, "If this man is such a swindler, why haven't the local constables hauled him in before now?"

"No evidence. My Katherine saw some printer's plates in his office about a month ago. Tonight she planned on burglarizing his office so she could get them."

Dix turned and stared. "She planned to do *what?!*"

"Rob him of the plates."

"How?"

"By going into his safe. It was the only way to get

her hands on something the authorities would believe. Samuels is a big man, you know.''

Dix did not believe this. How meek and biddable could a safe-robbing woman be? *She'd make a perfect wife,* he thought sarcastically. ''Did it ever occur to you that that mess back at the shop could be tied to her meddling?''

Bart took immediate offense at Dix's tone. ''She isn't meddling. Samuels swindled a whole passel of old folks. One of them happpened to be a dear friend of Katherine's, and she took it upon herself to put Samuels in jail for what he's done. My Katherine is real loyal.''

Loyal and obviously in need of a keeper, Dix thought dryly. He turned to Bart to ask what else he had failed to divulge but held on to the question when a fashionable coach came to a halt in front of the Samuels house.

Dix and Bart slid farther back into the trees as Bart whispered, ''That's Samuels's coach.''

Two men stepped out, follwed by a third. ''The one in the fancy suit is Samuels. The other two are hired hands.''

Dix sized up the men and their employer. ''How many men does he usually keep with him.''

''Seen only these two. Katherine said they're thugs.''

Dix watched the thugs peer up and down the street as if on the lookout for someone or something. After a few moments they seemed satisfied with whatever they had or had not seen, and only then did Rupert reopen the carriage's door. Dix heard Bart gasp as a tall figure in black was pulled from the coach and forced in the direction of the house by Samuels's propelling hold on the arm. ''That's my Katherine!'' Bart whispered.

Dix surveyed the woman. She was indeed quite tall and dressed like a man in a black shirt and trousers. Her face had been blackened by what appeared to be grease or cork. He could see her short hair under the soft light given off by the lamps lining the walk.

She did not appear to be pleased to have Samuels as her escort. She did her best to delay entering the house, but Samuels was stronger and forced her ahead.

"He's taking her inside! Dix, do something!" Bart whispered, panicked.

"Not a good idea. They outnumber us. If I rush them, they'll have all three of us. Do you think he'd harm her?"

"I don't know, but he probably won't harm her before tomorrow."

"Why not?"

"Because they're marrying up tomorrow afternoon at two."

"What?!"

Bart lowered his head. "Didn't I tell you that back at the shop?"

Dix answered through gritted teeth, "No, you did not. How in the hell am I supposed to get her out of there if she's going to marry the man?"

"They weren't supposed to really marry up. But things got a tad complicated. She planned on getting the plates tonight and disappearing. Something must have gone wrong."

"Obviously."

"So, how are you going to rescue her?"

Dix answered truthfully, "I've no idea."

"But, Dix, you have to have a plan."

"Bart, I am tempted to let that she-cub of yours stew in her own safe-robbing juices."

"But I know you won't," Bart replied confidently. "If you did, you'd have trouble sleeping at night knowing you left my Katherine in the hands of someone like Samuels. You're too decent a man, Dixon Wildhorse."

Dix sighed. Somehow he wished he'd never tracked Bart to Chicago. "Come on. We'll head back to your place. A plan is bound to show up before the wedding rolls around."

Or at least he hoped one would.

Chapter 3

❧

It was now the day of the wedding, and Katherine paced the confines of the small attic room for what seemed the thousandth time. The pacing helped her think, and at this juncture she needed all the options her quick mind could muster. She'd been locked in there since shortly after her arrival at the town house the night before. Initially, she'd been ushered into a bedroom in the main wing of the house, but when Rupert's mother, Pearl, happened across Katherine preparing to climb to freedom via one of the windows, an angry Rupert escorted her here. According to him, the attic space had once been a hiding place for fugitive slaves during the volatile abolitionist years. It had only one window. The tiny, triangular pane allowed in the light of the day but would never allow escape by a woman of Katherine's size.

Her worries over the fate of her accomplice had not diminished. No matter how many times she'd asked Rupert to reveal the man's whereabouts, he would not. She wanted to believe Joe and Frank hadn't committed murder, but deep in her soul she knew they had. Even when she had to stand by last night and watch Rupert's thugs destroy the dress shop in their search for incriminating evidence against her, her thoughts had centered on the man Geoff had hired to open the safe. Did he have a family? Children who would tearfully grieve over his absence? Geoff had also been on her mind. He had no way of knowing the burglary attempt had failed. In a few days, when he didn't receive the plates or any word from her, he would realize something had gone awry, but by then who knew where she might be.

When Katherine had first approached Geoff with the idea of looking into the Banneker Railroad stock swindle, he'd had many misgivings—not because he questioned her ability to succeed, but because he worried for her safety should the ball begin to unravel. At the time, Katherine had taken his concerns to heart and agreed with the need for caution. To ease his fears, she'd given him every reassurance she could think of, promising not to place herself in harm's way. Katherine rarely lost an argument or let herself be swayed away from a stance, so after a few more rounds of wrangling, Geoff had surrendered and let her proceed with the assignment.

She hated to admit it, but he'd been right to worry; here she stood, despondent over her accomplice's death and embroiled in more danger than she could have ever imagined. She also thought about the dress shop. Poor Mrs. Tuttle had worked all of her life to build up her shop's clientele. In the thirty-five years she'd been in business, she'd become both wealthy and the modiste of choice to the elite Black women of Chicago. Now, thanks to the extensive damage done to the place by Rupert's employees, Mrs. Tuttle's dream had been turned into a nightmare.

Katherine sighed sadly. So far she'd been responsible for a man's death and the wrecking of a very kind woman's livelihood. And in a few more hours she was going to have to marry Rupert Samuels.

A knock on the door sounded, and Katherine waited tensely as the lock turned. The door opened to reveal Pearl Samuels. She entered smiling, dressed in the beautiful, pale-rose gown Katherine and Mrs. Tuttle had created especially for the groom's mother. However, neither Katherine nor Mrs. Tuttle had designed the dainty lady's derringer held in Pearl's gloved hand.

Mother Pearl closed the door behind her, saying, "It's good to see you are still with us, dear."

"I haven't had much choice."

Pearl nodded her understanding. "You present quite a dilemma, Katherine—if that is indeed your name."

"In what way?"

"Rupert and I were at our wit's end on how to proceed with you. I told him in the beginning not to pursue you. Now he wishes he'd listened."

Pearl was a very influential member of Chicago's representative society. She'd been aghast at the idea of her wealthy son marrying a common seamstress. The initial gossip that greeted the wedding announcement had driven her to her bed. "Were it up to me, you would simply vanish in much the same fashion as your accomplice. But our guests are expecting a wedding, and they shall have one."

"I'd rather not."

"What you'd rather is not at issue at this point. I'd rather you had never entered our lives. No woman of breeding would stoop to being a journalist."

"Tell that to Mary Shadd, Pearl."

"Who?"

Katherine waved her off. "Never mind. You said you and Rupert *were* at your wit's end over what to do with me. Does that mean you've come to a decision?"

"It does," Pearl proudly announced. "After the ceremony you will be taken to a sanitorium owned by a physician friend of Rupert's. We want you under lock and key while we determine your true identity and how much you know."

"I have friends who will question my sudden disappearance."

"I'm sure you have, dear, but they won't bother looking for you if they believe you are dead."

A chill grabbed Katherine's heart as she looked into Pearl's emotionless eyes.

Pearl spoke kindly. "In a few days, you and my son are going to be involved in a staged carriage accident. Rupert will tell everyone that you were killed. My son will publicly mourn your tragic, untimely passing as they lower your closed casket into the grave. No one will ask the whereabouts of a woman known to be dead."

Geoff would, Katherine knew. Because the marriage was never to have taken place, news of the wedding would raise questions in his mind. Katherine had to admit, however, it was a clever plan. Too clever.

Pearl smiled. "Until we know who you are and what information you may have passed on, you will remain under the doctor's care. Who knows, you may need his care for the rest of your life."

Katherine's eyes closed.

Pearl moved elegantly back to the door. "Now, hurry and dress, dear. Rupert and the guests will be waiting. And remember to smile. It's your wedding day."

After Pearl's departure, Katherine walked over to the cot and stared down at the dress lying across it. Not even her present distress could make the dress any less exquisite. Made by her own hands out of white Chinese silk Rupert had sent away for, the close-fitting, high-necked dress was plainly designed, but elegant. When she first began creating the dress, she looked upon it as a prop in her charade, nothing more. She'd sewn on the seed pearls and added the bits of lace, confident that the gown would never be worn—at least not in a wedding with Rupert Samuels. She'd been certain that Rupert would be indicted long before her becoming his wife turned into a reality. Now, she had very little confidence in anything.

Sighing, she dashed away the uncharacteristic tears stinging her eyes and began to dress. Rupert had not searched her person last night, probably because he didn't believe it necessary, her being female and all. In his mind, the man with her had undoubtedly been in charge of the breaking and entering. As a result, she still had her lock picks. Not knowing where else to hide them, she very carefully slid them one by one into the hem of her wedding gown. One never knew when she might need them again.

The parlor downstairs had been grandly decorated for the event. Vases of exotic lilies had been set about, and pure-white ribbons streamed across the high ceilings above the heads of the very select group of guests. At the far end of the expansive room stood a bower adorned with embroidered white draperies caught back by strips of gold satin. Were Katherine really Rupert's intended, she would have been touched, knowing he'd spared no expense in making this day a memorable one; however, she had never intended to be his bride. Never. Yet here she stood, preparing to say vows with a man planning to fake her death and then lock her away, maybe for the rest of her natural life.

Katherine walked with measured steps down the length of the lily-white runner but did not smile as she joined the elegantly attired Rupert and the preacher standing before the bower. If the guests were curious about her tight face, she doubted they would attribute it to anything other than nervousness. No one knew of her plight. As far as the guests were concerned, the groom was a prize catch; any woman lucky enough to land him was to be envied.

Katherine didn't want to be envied. As the preacher began reciting the opening words, she wanted only to put as much distance as possible between herself and Pearl's son. A veiled glance to the door showed men lounging nearby who could only be Rupert's employees. Even if she did somehow manage to get to the exit, they most certainly would not let her leave.

Outside, the sky was a glorious May blue. Dix, wearing his gray dress Stetson and a newly purchased dark suit, walked up the winding stone path to the Samuels town house. He was stopped midway by one of the men he'd seen last night with Samuels.

"Invitation, please."

Dix offered him a winning smile, then made an elaborate show of patting the pockets of his suit coat and trousers. "Must've left it at home on the bureau. Sorry."

He made a move to pass, but the man stepped purposefully in his path. "You can't go in without an invitation," the man stated. "Mr. Samuels's orders, cowboy." The word *cowboy* was spoken with a mocking sneer.

Dix looked down upon the man who stood at least six inches below and said quietly, "I think you'd better step aside before someone gets hurt."

"Oh, really," the man replied skeptically.

He then called to a companion standing on the porch.

"Hey, Joe. This one says I'm gonna get hurt if I don't step aside and let him in."

Joe stepped off the porch, saying with a grin, "Naw, Frank, he didn't tell you that. Did you mister?"

Dix sized up the approaching Joe and then Frank. Although both men were muscular, neither was large enough to stop anyone from going anywhere—at least where Dix hailed from. He tried to be nice one more time. "Now, boys, I'm going in there whether you like it or not, so let me pass, and you'll both keep your teeth."

Mocking him, Joe knocked his knees together. "Oh, we're so afraid."

Frank laughed uproariously.

Dix pushed them aside and headed up the walk.

When the thugs took exception to his actions, the fight was on.

Inside, in the parlor, the preacher asked Katherine for the third time to repeat the line he'd just read to her from the vows. Because of her hesitation, Rupert's face held a forced, tight smile. Katherine's eyes pleaded with the preacher, but he simply smiled indulgently, saying, "We all know you're nervous, Katherine."

The guests tittered in response to the preacher's kindly quip; then suddenly, a woman screamed as three whirling dervishes came crashing through the parlor door into the room. Katherine recognized Frank and Joe but not the dark-skinned giant at the center of the storm. Fists were flying, guests began to scatter, and Frank and Joe were thrown from the big man's back like they were Lilliputians. As chaos erupted and women screamed, Katherine thought it an ideal time to lose herself in the bedlam, but when she took a step forward, Rupert's hand closed tightly upon her arm. He smiled at her knowingly, then barked to his employees, "Get that man out of here!"

Easier said than done, Katherine noted. She watched as more of Rupert's thugs waded in, only to be dispatched by fists that broke jaws and sent teeth and men sailing in all directions.

When the dust settled, only the giant remained standing. Every last one of Rupert's men were prone on the floor and out cold. Katherine still had no idea as to the victorious man's identity, but she wanted to cheer.

Apparently Rupert did not share her enthusiasm. Still holding Katherine tightly by the arm, he snapped, "Identify yourself!"

The giant took a moment to survey his prone opponents. Evidently pleased, he smiled crookedly around his split and bloodied lip. Only after he retrieved his hat did he begin his approach to the bower.

The guests scurried out of his path, but not a one of them headed for the exit. They all stared on as riveted as Katherine at the man with skin the color of a black panther and eyes to match. He walked as if he owned the earth beneath his polished boots, and strode with the proud bearing of a Dahomey king. He was as handsome as he was tall, and although he wore the eastern cut suit seemingly comfortably, the brilliant topaz stud in his earlobe stamped him as the most exotic man Katherine had ever encountered.

Over the excited buzzing of the guests, Rupert barked again, "I demand that you answer me!"

When the giant stopped before Katherine and stared down into her eyes, her heart began to pound. He appeared even taller up close. His nose bore the proud lines of his heritage, and his jaw was strong and firm. His shoulders were so wide that both sleeves of the suit had been split in the melee.

Katherine saw concern in his black eyes, a concern so strong that her own eyes welled up because she knew at once that he'd come here to save her.

He spoke in a voice meant only for her. "Sorry I had to be so disruptive."

"Quite all right," she replied just as softly.

He offered a small smile, seemingly pleased by her response. He then reached out a finger and slowly brushed away the lone, joyful tear escaping down her cheek. "Has anyone harmed you?"

She trembled from the contact, then shook her head no.

"Good. Let's get you out of here."

Rupert stared at the two of them and yelled, *"What the hell is going on here?!"*

Dix forced himself to look away from the beautiful tear-bright eyes of Bart Love's daughter and at the peacock still holding her tightly by the arm. "Let her go."

Rupert opened his mouth to say something, but Dix was in no mood for any more debating. The Black Seminole lawman threw what he hoped would be his last punch of the day, hitting Rupert squarely on the jaw. Rupert crumpled instantly and joined his minions prone on the floor.

Then Dix politely tipped his hat to the wide-eyed preacher. "Forgive the ruckus, Padre."

The preacher could only nod as Dix took Katherine by the hand and led her past the gaping, gasping guests and out of the house.

He hastened her to a coach parked a ways up the carriage-lined street. Dix helped her in, then followed her as he hollered to the driver to head out.

Inside the fast-moving coach, Katherine's cinnamon-colored eyes shone with happiness as she sat with her head back on the seat, savoring the exhilaration of freedom. "Thank you so much," she sighed genuinely. "Another second or two and I might have had to actually marry that bounder."

"You're welcome."

Katherine wondered if Rupert had come around yet. She smiled at the memory of him crumpling to the floor like wet linen. He'd gotten no more than he deserved. Still filled with mirth, she turned to her rescuer and spied the split lip he'd received for his trouble. She felt responsible for the injury and the raw knuckles he sported on both hands. "Your lip is bleeding," she informed him, moving across to where he sat on the opposite bench. "Do you have a handkerchief?"

Dix surveyed her for a moment.

Katherine said, "I don't bite. I simply wish to fix your lip. It's the least I can do after what you did for me back there."

Dix reached into his coat pocket and handed her the clean linen. He'd been prepared to be unmoved by Bart's daughter but instead found himself fascinated by her scent, her beautiful white gown, and her nearness. His eyes lingered over the short, glossy hair and her lovely full mouth, then closed as she applied the soft cloth to his split lower lip. She dabbed gently but firmly, and each touch hit him like the kick of a mule. He finally had to ease the handkerchief from her hand. "I can handle it from here."

He held her gaze as he pressed the cloth to his mouth. What kind of woman was this? he wondered. He couldn't ever remember being around a woman whose very presence seemed to charge the air. After a moment he drew the cloth away so that she could see his injured lip, then asked, "Is that better?"

Katherine somehow managed to drag her attention away from his compelling, brilliant eyes and settled it on his mouth. Unable to speak for a moment, she finally gathered her faculties, then stammered just the same, "Uh, yes. It seems to be. I–I think I'll sit back over there."

Dix nodded slowly, hiding his amusement. He watched as she put up a honey-brown hand to peel back the window drape and peer out as if to judge their progress. When she seemed satisfied, she let the drape drop, saying, "I'm assuming Geoff sent you after me."

Katherine couldn't wait to see Geoff. He was more than just her editor, he was a dear friend. She planned on giving him a big hug for staging such a rousing rescue.

"Don't know a Geoff."

His reply gave Katherine pause until she realized her rescuer might not be personally acquainted with her editor friend. More than likely, Geoff had hired the handsome giant through an intermediary as a precautionary measure. "Then do you know if I'm to go on to Boston as planned or return to New York?"

"You're going to Indian Territory."

Katherine's face showed her confusion. "Why Indian Territory?"

"Because that's where I live."

Katherine thought that maybe she hadn't made herself clear—this mountain of a man obviously had more brawn than brains. "No," she said slowly as if speaking to a small child, "not where *you're* going, but where *I'm* going."

"Indian Territory," he said again.

Katherine shook her head. How did she explain to him what she needed to know? Looking over at him while the rattling coach kept up its steady pace, she wondered why he had that odd smile on his face. It was almost as if he were harboring some sort of secret. "Who are you?"

"Dixon Wildhorse."

"Didn't someone hire you to rescue me?"

"Nope, your daddy sent me after you."

"Oh, that explains it. He must have found my pendant at the shop and knew I was in trouble."

"Yes, he did."

"Are we going to meet him?"

"Yep. Then the three of us will be heading back to Indian Territory. Your daddy has something to settle back there."

"Is he in some sort of trouble?"

"You could say that, yes."

"What has he done?"

"Wrangled somebody out of two hundred head of cattle."

Katherine sighed with relief. "Oh, is that all? I thought he'd done something serious." Katherine noted the decidedly cool look that entered her rescuer's eyes on the heels of her statement, and she wondered what she'd said. Then she remembered the day her father had showed up at the shop two months ago. She hadn't seen him more than twice in the past fifteen years, so the visit was quite a surprise. When she'd recovered from the shock of his sudden appearance, he explained that he'd sold some cows for a friend and had made quite a profit. Could these possibly be the same cows? She was almost afraid to ask the question on the tip of her tongue. "Who did these cows belong to?"

"Me." And he didn't appear to be pleased.

Katherine brought her hands to her mouth and stared. "But he told me he sold them for a friend."

"He lied."

Katherine felt her own guilt rise over the actions of her wayward parent.

Dix added, "Your daddy does it lot."

"Steal cows?"

"No, lie."

Katherine took immediate offense. "That's a fairly harsh assessment, Mr. Horse."

"No, Kate, that's truth. I've known him going on fifteen years. For ten of those years, we folks in the Territory weren't even sure Bart Love was really his true name. He'd lie about the sun shining."

"Oh, come now. My father is a character, but you make him sound like some terrible pariah. Am I needed in Indian Territory for a trial of some sort?"

"Nope."

"Then why?"

"You're needed because your daddy decided you'd make me a good wife."

Chapter 4

Katherine couldn't help herself. She began to laugh and laugh until the interior of the carriage rang with the sound. "Oh, wait until I see that Geoff," she said. "He put you up to this, didn't he? I'd make you a good wife. That's funny." She wiped the tears of mirth from her eyes, then asked, "Now, truthfully, why am I needed in Indian Territory?"

He simply sat there, arms folded across his massive chest. When she received no ready reply, her smile faded. She leaned forward and searched his face. The hairs on the back of her neck stood up with warning. "You can't be serious."

Silence.

"Mr. Horse, I am extremely grateful for your assistance back there, but why would you believe I'd wish to marry you?"

"To keep your daddy out of territorial prison."

Her cinnamon eyes widened. "Prison?! *For cows?!*"

"It's a hanging offense."

The staggering implications put her back against the seat. She sat absolutely speechless for a moment. When

40

she found her voice again, she asked, "But why am I involved?"

"Your daddy's using you to pay the debt."

"In what manner?"

"He gave me your hand."

"What?!" Katherine couldn't believe her ears. "But why would you agree to such an outrageous proposal?"

"Because I need a wife."

"And any woman will do?"

"No, not any woman."

Katherine ignored the implications in his soft, rough voice. "Mr. Horse, my father can't just give me away."

"Do you want him to go to jail?"

"Of course not," she replied. "Granted he hasn't been much of a parent since mama died, but she loved him. She wouldn't want him locked away, and neither would I."

"How long has it been since her passing?"

"I was thirteen at the time, so it's been fifteen years."

Dix did some quick arithmetic. Twenty-eight. Her age made her a bit long in the tooth as new brides went, but he found maturity in her favor. He didn't need an addle-brained young'un. He could have had his pick of that type of female back home.

Katherine found his unwavering scrutiny very unnerving. She had no trouble accepting him as her personal cavalry, but as a husband? Granted he was far more handsome than any man had a right to be, and a woman would have to be dead inside not to feel the raw, male power he emanated, but she had vowed long ago never to marry, and she had no plans to change her mind—not even for a man as overpowering as this one. "Mr. Horse, I am not going to marry you."

"Wildhorse," he said.

"Excuse me?"

"Wildhorse. The name's Wildhorse. One word."

"Pardon me," she said genuinely, then said, "It sounds Indian."

Dix took a moment to assess her before he formed his reply. Some women ran screaming into the streets from anything even remotely associated with the Native people. Was she such a woman? "Would it bother you if it were?"

She shook her head. "No."

"I'm Black Seminole."

She waited for him to say more and when he didn't, she decided that any woman he did marry would need to carry around a set of pliers just to pry answers from his full, mustached lips.

Dix said, "Tell me about you and Samuels."

"There isn't much to tell except the wedding was never supposed to take place."

"Do you love him?"

"No."

Dix doubted she would elaborate further, and he was correct. He didn't press. He'd hear the full story soon enough.

Katherine looked over at him and said, "Mr. Wildhorse, again, I understand your wish to be compensated for my father's theft, but surely there are far more suitable women back home for you to marry."

"Haven't found one yet."

"Well, what are you looking for in a wife?"

"The usual—can she give me sons, companionship? Will she be the type of woman I don't mind coming home to in the evening?"

Those last words were spoken directly into Katherine's eyes. She fumbled to find her voice. "And you believe I am such a woman?"

"Yes, I do."

"Why?"

"You're clean, educated. Virgin, too, by the look of your mouth."

Katherine's heart took off like a runaway train. She didn't realize she'd brought her hand to her lips until she noticed the faint amusement glowing in his eyes. She quickly put her hand in her lap, saying, "Suppose I admit having taken numerous lovers—would you still find me suitable?"

"Nope, but since you haven't taken *any* lovers, the point is moot."

"You can't possibly know if I've taken lovers by my–my mouth."

Silence.

Katherine felt absolutely mesmerized by all that he was—his low, husky voice; his presence; his compelling onyx eyes. She wondered if she had unknowingly ingested a strange mind-numbing potion, because under normal circumstances she would have sent a cowboy like him crawling off into the sunset with his six-gun tucked between his legs; instead, he had her acting as if she'd never met a man before in her life! "I don't plan on marrying anyone, Mr. Wildhorse."

"Why not?" Dix asked as he slowly surveyed what he could of her physical form in the smooth fitting, high-necked white dress. She was not as skinny as most city women, a fact he found pleasing. And her bosom looked awfully sweet.

Katherine's voice brought him back to the present. "Mr. Wildhorse, are you listening?"

"Sorry, I was a bit distracted. What did you say?"

"I said, I won't be marrying because my career as a newspaperwoman will always come first."

"Oh, are you one of those newfangled women who think men are only good for carrying packages?"

"No," came her denial. "Some of my best friends are men. I simply don't care to marry one."

"You sound pretty set on that."

His words gave Katherine hope that maybe he was beginning to understand. "I am quite set. Frankly, I find nothing intriguing about the so-called institution of marriage. I believe any woman who enters into it willingly should be placed *in* an institution."

"Strong words from a woman who's never been properly kissed."

"I've been kissed, Mr. Wildhorse, believe me I have."

"Your face says you didn't care much for it, though."

"Truthfully, you are correct." The few kisses she'd shared with Rupert had not moved her in any way. In fact, her limited experience with the whole ritual made her wonder what all the hubbub was about. She could see him watching her with that smile hiding just behind his eyes. "I suppose you're now going to say your kisses will change my feelings."

"Nope," he denied, shaking his head. "When the time comes, you'll let me know how you feel."

Katherine's heart began to pound anew in response to the look in his eyes.

Then he asked, "Are you scared of marriage?"

Katherine was so glad for the change in subject that she replied truthfully. "I am afraid of turning my life over to a man, yes."

"Why?"

"Have you ever had your every move and breath controlled by someone else, Mr. Wildhorse?"

Dix thought back on the bittersweet history of his people. "Yes, I have."

"Is it a situation you'd wish to relive?"

"No."

"My point is made."

Dix decided then and there that no other woman would do. She had fire, spirit: their sons would be proud and strong. "All marriages aren't that way."

"An example?"

"Ours won't be."

That got her attention. "What will make it different?"

"Me."

His eyes were unveiled, serious. For a moment he let her peer into the depths of his soul, revealing an intensity that mesmerized her. Her voice came out a whisper, "But you know nothing about me."

"No, and you know nothing about me. But I will pledge to keep you safe and stay faithful to my vows. I don't expect your love, just your companionship."

Katherine had to draw in a calming breath. Even if she were to break her own vow and marry, Dixon Wildhorse was not the type of man she'd envisioned as a life mate. She preferred men of brain, not brawn—or at least that's what she'd always believed—men who liked the theater, men able to hold her attention with their knowledge of the world. Dixon Wildhorse might know cows, but did he know anything else? To her chagrin, a little voice reminded her that he knew she'd never been properly kissed, but Katherine chose to bury that fact and concentrate on more tangible attributes, such as—could he even read? "Mr. Wildhorse, please understand, regardless of my father's debt to you, I simply cannot marry you."

"You'd rather I took you back to your friends, then?" he asked quietly. "I'm sure Samuels will be pleased. The guests probably haven't even left yet."

He pounded his fist against the wall of the coach and it halted almost immediately.

In the quiet that followed, Katherine stared over at him with wide eyes. "You wouldn't!"

Silence.

"You cannot make me marry you."

At that moment the carriage door opened, and the driver peered inside. "Problems, Dix?"

The man was tall as Dix but not as muscular. Katherine would need a panel of experts to decide which man was handsomer.

Dix made the introductions. "Kate, this is my good friend Jackson Blake; Blake, Bart's daughter, Katherine Love."

Blake nodded politely, "Pleased to meet you."

"Kate wants to go back to her friends."

Blake grinned, "Can't convince her to marry you, huh? Did you tell her you were a deputy marshal? Works for me sometimes."

Katherine stared. "You're a lawman? My father stole cows from a *lawman?!*"

Blake said, "Unbelievable, ain't it. Your pa is one of a kind."

Katherine, speechless, could only cast her eyes downward in embarrassment.

Dix said, "Well, Kate, it's me or Rupert. Which shall it be?"

Katherine looked from Blake to Dix, unable to believe this was happening. "How much were those cows worth? Maybe I can make restitution."

The steep figure he quoted made her stomach churn with distress.

"That much?" she asked weakly.

He nodded.

Blake said to Katherine, "Personally, I wouldn't marry him, either. He doesn't drink, smoke, or even dance for that matter. You'll never have a good time with him."

Dix said quietly, "Close the door, Blake."

Blake grinned in reply, then inclined his head Katherine's way in a polite good-bye. "Nice meeting you, Kate." The door closed.

"Your decision?"

"I'd like to speak with my father first."

She was stalling. He knew it and she knew it. So she finally said, "This is no way to start a marriage."

Silence.

She wanted to throw up her hands. "I'll escape first chance I get."

His eyes mirrored his amusement. "I'll consider myself warned, but I'm still waiting on your decision. Do I tell Blake to turn this rig around and head back?"

"You know I don't want that, so let's go before Rupert catches up to us."

Dix pounded twice on the wall, and the coach resumed rolling. "So, we haven't seen the last of him?"

"Probably not. Are you truly a deputy marshal?"

Nodding, he reached into his coat pocket and handed her his badge.

Katherine looked at it a moment, then ran a slow finger over the small topaz in the center. She raised her eyes to his, "Do all western lawmen have gemstones in their shields?"

"As far as I know I'm the only one."

"Why a topaz?"

"This stone and the one in my ear belonged to my grandfather. I wear them to honor him."

She did not tell him, but the topaz was her lodestone also. A small polished piece had been given to her by her mother on the night she died. Her mother had worn it all her life because she swore it had brought her good luck and kept her safe. Katherine wore the golden stone on a slim chain beneath her clothing, but to tell him that would only encourage him to believe she was indeed the woman he should be seeking as his wife.

Katherine handed back the shield, and Dix slipped it back in his pocket, feeling the heat of her hands lingering on the metal star.

"If you're a lawman then you must let me go to New York. Rupert is a swindler."

"Any evidence?"

"In my hands, no."

"Then we go home."

"But they killed someone. The man Geoff—he's my editor—hired to help break into the safe."

"And if you go to New York alone, who's to say you won't be killed, too? How would you protect yourself?"

Admittedly, she hadn't thought about that.

"Why is Rupert after you?"

Since he was a lawman, she saw no reason not to tell him the story. "He's the head man in a fraudulent stock scheme. He wants to know who I really am and who else I may have told about him. Now that it's all unraveled, I must get to New York. Geoff is going to be frantic with worry when he doesn't hear from me."

"I'm going home. You can wire Geoff on the way to the Territory. I'll wire a friend of mine in the army. He has friends in Washington who'll look into Rupert."

Katherine did not care for his simple dismissal of her woes. "Are you always so stubborn?"

"You're no wilting flower yourself, *chica.*"

She found herself smiling at him in spite of their wrangling. "Thank you, I'll take that as a compliment. Very few men consider a spirited woman very womanly."

"Women with spirit are to be treasured."

His voice made her insides teeter. She brought her hand to the base of her throat to calm her pounding pulse and forced herself to draw in a steadying breath.

Dix witnessed the slight tremble in the hand she held against her throat. He remembered how firmly the hand had grasped his own as he led her from Rupert's town house. Bart's daughter possessed strength and passion— though from the looks of her now she was far more comfortable with the former than the latter. He asked, "Something wrong?"

"No. Why?"

"Thought maybe you were having palpitations or something."

The flash in her eyes would have made a less secure man run for the hills, but Dix shrugged innocently. "Just asking."

Katherine wished she knew why he affected her so strongly. Palpitations indeed.

The coach halted in front of the small boardinghouse where her father rented a room. It was in a section of the city famous for its crime and vice. Katherine had tried to persuade Bart against living there, but he insisted that among the gamblers, petty thieves, and women of questionable reputation was where he felt most comfortable, and no amount of arguing from Katherine could change his mind.

Dix reached over and opened the door. As he raised his big body up to leave, he told her, "Wait here. It shouldn't take but a moment to collect Bart. He said he'd be waiting."

After his exit, Katherine pulled back the window drape and watched him enter the boardinghouse. The voice in her head told her that this would be a perfect time to escape. Katherine ignored it, though, even as she longed to put as great a distance between herself and

Wildhorse as she'd wanted to place between herself and Rupert. But escape meant getting past the driver Blake; it also meant her father would either hang or waste away in prison. She knew she'd never sleep another peaceful night should either scenario become a reality.

Quite suddenly the door opened, surprising her, especially since Wildhorse returned alone. He did not appear pleased.

"Where's my father?"

"You tell me."

Katherine swallowed guiltily. "He isn't there, I take it."

His eyes answered, his voice did not.

Defensive, Katherine pointed out, "None of this is my fault, you know."

"No, it's your daddy's, and I'm about a horse's eyelash from strangling him when I do find him." Dix figured it wouldn't be long before Samuels began scouring the city for information concerning his runaway bride. They didn't have time to waste trying to find Bart. "Where could he be?"

Katherine shrugged. "Gambling, visiting—who knows?"

Blake spent the better part of an hour driving Katherine and Dix around to various gambling dens in search of Bart Love. With each unsuccessful stop Dix became grimmer and grimmer, especially since they were no closer to gleaning Bart's whereabouts than they were when they'd begun. After a few more unsuccessful tries, Katherine suddenly remembered the widow her father had been paying court to since his arrival in town three months ago. Katherine could sense the lawman's patience unraveling, and for her father's sake, she prayed he would be with the widow when they arrived.

Luckily, he was. The widow, a plump cheery woman,

led Katherine and Dix into her small kitchen where they found Bart seated at the table enjoying a plateful of chicken and dumplings. His face widened with pleasure at their entrance. "Ah, Katherine, you look so much like your mother in that beautiful dress, you bring tears to these old eyes."

Katherine shook her head at his blarney. "Thank you, Papa, but weren't you supposed to be waiting back at your room?"

He glanced over at the stern-looking Dix and apologized genuinely. "I'm sorry, Dix, but I couldn't leave without one last sampling of Lolly's chicken and dumplings, now, could I?"

Lolly smiled. "Bart's told me all about the gold."

Katherine tried not to stare but failed. "Gold?"

"Yes," Lolly said looking down at Bart with loving eyes. "Hasn't he told you? The government surveyors have found a very large gold deposit on your father's spread out in Colorado. I must say, I've never met a cattle rancher before. He's promised to send for me once everything settles down."

Katherine's eye widened. She turned to Dix only to find his face unreadable.

Lolly continued, "Of course, it may take me a while to get accustomed to all the cows he has on his land. I—"

Katherine interrupted, "Papa, we have to leave."

"But, I'm not done here. Lolly's made mincemeat pie for dessert."

With a brittle smile Katherine turned to Lolly. "You'll have to excuse us, but we have a train to catch. Come, Papa, we mustn't be late."

"Aw, daughter, have a heart. . . ."

Dix had had enough. He strode over to the table, and without so much as a howdy-do, he lifted Bart up from the chair, tossed him over his broad shoulder, and exited, leaving both women speechless and stunned.

Since Katherine could not think of a word to say in the wake of such an emphatic exit, she mumbled something she hoped sounded like good-bye, then hastened after the men.

Inside the coach, Bart appeared wounded as he straightened his clothing. "You could at least let a man leave his lady love with dignity."

Dix drawled huskily, "Be glad I let you stay as long as I did."

Katherine had a few bones of her own to pick. "How could you tell that woman all those lies, Papa?"

"Katherine, it made Lolly feel good thinking she was being courted by a wealthy cattle baron. There was no harm in that."

"She's expecting you to send for her."

He appeared to think a moment. "Yes, that could be a problem, but I'll simply have you write her a letter saying I was killed in a stampede or something."

Katherine couldn't believe her ears "With all the trouble cows have brought you, I would think you'd not want to even think about them."

He dropped his head solemnly. "Dix told you, huh?"

"Yes, and he also told me about this ridiculous arrangement you expect me to honor."

"You're all I have, Katherine. What was I supposed to do?"

"You had no business taking his cows in the first place. The man's a lawman, for heaven's sake. And how could you promise my hand without consulting me?" Katherine knew this was neither the time nor place to be having this conversation, what with Wildhorse looking on, but it couldn't be helped.

"He's a good man, Katherine, one of the best the West has to offer."

Katherine looked over to Dix and said, "No offense intended, Mr. Wildhorse, but, Papa, I don't care if he is an Egyptian pharaoh. I've no desire to marry him."

"Katherine you must, otherwise I might hang."

"And therein lies the rub. You know I won't let you come to harm, but now I understand why Mama couldn't live with you."

Guilt grabbed her right away when she saw him drop his head. She hadn't meant to rail at him, but she was not a thing to be bartered away, like a sack of yams; she was a dream-filled, hard-working newspaperwoman. Her hopes of one day owning her own newspaper now seemed as far away as the moon, all because she wasn't hard-hearted enough to let her father suffer the consequences of his own, cow-rustling actions.

The carriage came to a stop at the train station, which was bustling with passengers, porters, and hacks for hire. They'd missed the four o'clock train west, thanks to the search for Bart. The next one would be at ten o'clock the next morning, according to the schedule Dix pulled from his pocket.

Dix said to Katherine, "Pull that shade back real easy and tell me if you see anyone out there you recognize."

"You believe Rupert may have someone watching for us?"

"Were it me, I'd have someone at the station and on every main street."

Katherine eased the shade aside as carefully as she could and hazarded a look around. Dix was correct. A man pushing a broom over by the ticket counter bore a startling resemblance to Frank. She spotted Joe dressed in a porter's uniform, hauling a dolly piled with trunks. A disheartened Katherine led the shade drop back.

"They're out there. Joe's posing as a porter, and Frank is sweeping the ground over by the ticket agent's booth."

Rupert employed many of Philadelphia's domestics, sweepers, and porters. He could have his people looking for them all over the city for as long as it took Katherine and Dix to surface.

Katherine turned to Dix. "What do we do?"

"Has Samuels or his men ever met your father?"

She shook her head no in response. Her masquerading as the seamstress Katherine Lane had begun months before her father's surprising arrival in Chicago. Once she explained to Bart the purpose behind the deception, both daughter and father agreed that having Rupert meet Bart would only complicate matters. "Why do you ask?"

"Because Bart's going to take my ticket and use it to get home. Since he isn't someone Rupert's people are looking for, he should have no trouble boarding the train."

Katherine had to admit it made sense. "But what about us? You and I can't simply stroll up to the train agent's booth and purchase our passage with Rupert's friend about."

"You're right. That's why you and I will take another way west."

Bart asked, "If you have another way home, why not take me with you?"

"Because I'm not going to spend the entire trip trying to keep you out of trouble. This safe-robbing daughter of yours will be plenty for me to handle, I'm thinking."

Katherine responded confidently, "I'm thinking you are correct."

Dix smiled inwardly. She challenged the warrior in him. He found the prospect of sparring with her surprisingly desirable, more desirable than he could have imagined when this whole drama began less than twenty-four hours ago.

Bart spoke up, "If my Katherine's going with you, Dix, I want to see her married before I get on that train."

Katherine gave her father a look that clearly stated her feelings on the matter, but he held her eyes with a firmness reserved for a truly caring parent. "I won't have your name sullied, Katherine. I owe it to you and to your mother to make sure this is done proper."

Katherine sighed bleakly. Evidently there was not going to be a way out of this mess. She would actually have to marry Dixon Wildhorse. She knew women were oftentimes forced to accept the marriage contracts forged by their parents, but she'd never considered herself subject to such medieval practices. She'd been given a liberal, forthright education by her mother and Aunt Ceil and raised to believe she could accomplish anything. She was certain both women were spinning in their graves at the notion of her agreeing to be the wife of a stranger because of her father's shenanigans.

Katherine was angry but resolved when she told Dix frostily, "Mr. Wildhorse, I will agree to marry you, but I do hope you realize you are taking on a very recalcitrant bride."

His answer came out quietly. "And you are taking on a warrior who knows that a prize is rarely achieved without struggle."

His eyes were like dark, eddying pools into which she sensed herself spiraling downward.

He spoke, "If you find that you still cannot abide me after our child is born, you will be free to return east and resume your life. You may even retake the many lovers you spoke of, as long as you are discreet, because we will remain married until death do us part. Agreed?"

Chin raised, Katherine nodded her acceptance of his

terms. She did appreciate him being astute enough to know that she didn't care to spend her life with him.

With the agreement now sealed, Bart smiled happily. Katherine did not.

Chapter 5

When Katherine stepped out of the coach, she was surprised to see that they'd stopped in front of a small farmhouse in the country. Having lived in large cities all her life—Chicago, New York, Boston—she'd grown accustomed to the ever present noise that accompanied the movement of so many people. The silence felt strange, almost as if she'd stepped into a foreign land. Behind her, Dix, Blake, and her father were speaking in hushed tones. She had no idea what they might be discussing since they hadn't bothered to include her, but she didn't much care. She'd know soon enough.

While she waited for them to conclude their confab, she gazed out over the furrowed fields and the tree-filled landscape that stretched as far as the eye could see. The air was thick with quiet. She wondered if Indian Territory would be as peaceful. She turned her mind away from the thought; she was not supposed to be speculating on his home. Her mind would be better served trying to come up with a way to wiggle out of this impending marriage noose.

The men ended their summit, and Dix motioned her toward the farmhouse's walk. "This way, Kate."

Katherine had never liked being called Kate; she thought Katherine far more distinguished. "I prefer, Katherine, Mr. Wildhorse,"

"And I prefer Dix," he replied, looking down at her. "I won't call you Kate if you don't call me Mr. Wildhorse."

Katherine thought that no man had the right to be so devastatingly handsome, especially a man she was determined not to like. Feeling herself getting dizzy from just looking at him, she sensed that if she wasn't careful, she could lose her wits around him most any time. With that in mind, she pulled herself away from the veiled amusement sparkling behind his eyes and said, "That is agreeable."

The outside of the house gave off a rustic, bucolic air. Katherine expected to be greeted by a kindly old farm woman, but the woman who ushered them inside looked like no farm woman Katherine had ever seen. Her bright gold dress was far too elaborate and low cut for such a remote location, and the heavy makeup on her aging face made her appear as if she'd just stepped off a theater stage.

When she spied Bart, her yell of glee pierced Katherine's ears. "Bart Love, is that you?! Get over here and give me a kiss!"

A grinning Bart did just as she asked, while Katherine stood there wondering just where they were and who this woman might be.

After ending the embrace, Bart grabbed Katherine's hand and pulled her forward. "Katherine, I want you to meet Miss Sunshine Collins. Sunshine, this is my Katherine."

"She's a pretty girl, Bart. This the one you're marrying, Dix?"

Dix nodded.

Sunshine said to Katherine, "Treat him good, darling. He's the best man in the Territory. I'd marry him myself if he'd have me."

Dix's eyes mirrored his pleasure, but Katherine missed his response because as Miss Sunshine led them into the parlor, Katherine was too busy staring around at the room's furnishings. She took in the plush red drapes and matching furniture, the risqué murals, and the equally shocking pieces of nude statuary placed about the premises. To that she added Miss Sunshine's overly made-up face, and she realized she had been brought to a bordello. Katherine wondered if this day could possibly get any worse.

It could.

Bart spoke up, "Miss Sunshine, do you know a preacher? We want to have the wedding here at your place, tonight."

Katherine stiffened. He couldn't possibly be serious about having her wed in a house of ill repute!

But Miss Sunshine's eyes took on a glow of excitement. "Tonight? Here? Why, sure. Me and the girls would be honored. Katherine and Dix, follow me. Since you're going to be married tonight, I'll put the two of you in my best room. Blake, you and Bart go on into the kitchen and have Cook start rustling us up a small spread. I'll be back to join you directly."

Katherine looked to Dix, hoping beyond hope that he would put a stop to this madness.

He simply gestured her forward. "After you."

An overwhelmed Katherine had no other choice but to follow Miss Sunshine up the red-carpeted stairs.

The upstairs decor was even more eye-popping. Wall-size murals, painted by someone with a true talent, graced the circular hallway. More statuary of nude and entwined couples struck myriad poses in a variety of pedestaled pieces. The journalist in Katherine should have been excited over being allowed this opportunity to tread the carpets of a place normally forbidden to women such as herself, but the woman in Katherine—the woman who had never seen a fully nude man until setting eyes on one of Miss Sunshine's highly erotic nude murals—stumbled at the sight.

Dix placed a steadying hand on her back and said, "I can lead you by the hand if you want to close your eyes."

Katherine was in no mood for Dixon's teasing. "That won't be necessary."

But in reality, it was a lie. In tandem with the numerous other shocks she'd suffered that day, all she really wanted to do was close her eyes and wake up back in her bed in New York.

Miss Sunshine turned back and said, "Come on in here a moment. I want you to meet my girls."

The girls were dressing and having their hair done by a woman stationed before a mirror on the far side of the room. There were at least ten of them of various sizes, shapes, and hues, and all greeted Dix's entrance excitedly. Some smiled temptingly, a few called out outrageous invitations, and one, half dressed in a wrapper that suggested she had nothing on underneath, sidled over and boldly kissed him on the cheek. "Hi, Marshal. . . ." she whispered.

"Melinda."

Katherine raised an eyebrow as Melinda blew Dix a kiss and slid away.

Miss Sunshine said, "Girls, I want you to meet Katherine Love."

"She isn't Bart's wife, is she?" one of the women asked.

Another said, "If she is, Lilah's the one she's got the

bone to pick with. It's her fault he ain't been coming home nights.''

Over the laughter, a shocked Katherine stared at the woman in question. Lilah, with her red hair and dusting of freckles, appeared to be no older than Katherine.

Lilah met Katherine's eye without shame, however, saying, ''You're Bart's daughter, aren't you?''

Katherine nodded, or she thought she did.

''Pleased to meet you. Your pa talks about you all the time. He's real proud of you being a newspaperwoman.''

Miss Sunshine said, ''Katherine's going to marry the marshal this evening.''

Groans of protest and cries of denial followed the announcement.

Miss Sunshine scolded, ''Now, girls, be nice. Where are your manners? Not a one of you city canaries would last a week in the territory, so set your caps elsewhere.''

The woman who'd given Dix the kiss on the cheek, cooed, ''With a man like that, I'd last until he begged me to stop.''

Heat burned Katherine's cheeks. The girls laughed.

Miss Sunshine waggled a finger. ''Melinda, that's enough. Save it for the customers.''

Katherine glanced over at Dix. His eyes were unfathomable.

Leaving the girls, Dix and Katherine were ushered into a large suite on the back side of the house. Miss Sunshine promised she'd send for the preacher right away, then left them alone.

Katherine stood by a bay window, which faced out over the countryside. She hoped this day would soon end because she didn't know how much more of these shocks she could take. Her father and Lilah?! She turned to Dix and asked. ''Why did we come here?''

"I doubt Rupert will look for you in a place like this."

As the silence thickened in the room, Katherine tried not to stare around at the nude statues and the shocking frescoes painted on the walls. One, a particularly vivid rendering of a nude man and woman entwined in a position Katherine was convinced had to be physically impossible, stretched from ceiling to floor. She tilted her head to try and deduce just how the couple were joined. When she glanced up and found Dix watching her, she started guiltily. To cover her embarrassment, she said the first thing that came to mind. "How do you know Miss Sunshine?"

"She lived in the Territory at one time, then moved back here about five years ago."

"Is Sunshine her true name?"

He shrugged. "Has been for as long as I've known her. When she was younger, she toured the mining towns in Colorado with a stage act. The old-timers said she would bring the sunshine when she performed. The name stuck to her, I guess."

Katherine didn't think she wanted to know what type of act Miss Sunshine performed. "Do you really believe my father has been keeping time with Lilah?"

"The girls say he has, and they've no reason to lie." Then he asked, "Does it bother you?"

"I'm not certain. I am shocked, though. She appears no older than I."

"You already know what a character your daddy is— after stealing my cows, nothing he does would surprise me."

She supposed he was right. Katherine further surveyed the room. The big brass bed positioned on the far side of the room had to be the largest she'd ever seen. Its presence, in tandem with the erotic surroundings, brought to mind something she felt they needed to discuss.

But a knock at the door delayed further conversation.

Dix opened the door to Blake, who informed them that the preacher awaited them down in the parlor.

After Blake's departure, Dix could see Katherine staring out of the window with distant eyes. As she stood there looking as if she were preparing to face a noose instead of a preacher, Dix doubted she'd understand the code of the West. Bart's stealing made this union a necessity. Period. If Dix could accept this madness, so could she. Luckily for her, Bart hadn't stolen someone else's herd because if he had, the old swindler would already be on his way to the hellhole that passed for the Territorial prison—or to a grave. Admittedly, this was not the way things were done in the civilized East, but life was different west of the Mississippi.

To be truthful, he had his misgivings about this union, too. From the moment he'd set eyes on Katherine Love, his mind and gut had been at war. His mind said he had to be loco to take a woman like this as his wife; he'd spend as much time keeping her out of trouble as he would had he married her father. But his gut said differently. On the trail a man, especially a lawman, lived and sometimes died by the feelings and instincts in his gut, and at this juncture, those senses said the marriage, given half a chance, could survive an unorthodox beginning. He knew it wouldn't be smooth—she had the fire and determination to face a grizzly if someone challenged her to—but even if they never saw eye to eye, being married to her would never be boring,

For the second time in a day, Katherine—still in her wedding gown—entered a parlor to become someone's wife. Ironically, she'd been right about the gown never being worn in a ceremony with Rupert; however, she'd had no idea the fates had been saving it for a dark-eyed giant wearing a marshal's star.

The preacher was standing by the piano, Bible in hand. Beside him, seated on the piano bench, Miss Sunshine played a beautiful waltz. Spread around the room were the girls, Katherine's smiling father, and Blake. Lilah stepped forward and pressed a bouquet of fresh spring flowers into Katherine's shaking hands and earned a watery, grateful smile. As Katherine took her place beside Dix, it seemed the only person in the room not smiling was the preacher.

In a moment she found out why.

He stared at Katherine out of fire-and-brimstone eyes set in a dour, brown face, then turned to Dix and said, "Young man, even though you are aware of this fallen woman's past, do you still wish to take her as your wife?"

Katherine's eyes widened. Fallen woman?! He thought she was one of Miss Sunshine's girls! She could hear a bit of tittering coming from the girls, and she opened her mouth to correct the preacher's mistake when she heard Dix say, "I do."

The preacher jumped in right behind Dix's words and said to Katherine in a stern voice, "And you, young woman, do you promise to obey him and take his advice in all things, now that he has become your salvation?"

After the day she'd had, the last thing Katherine needed was to have some man telling her to obey another man, as if she were too addle-brained to make up her own mind. However, she gathered herself, thought about her father's fate if she didn't agree, and lied with a smile. "I do."

The preacher said, "I pronounce you man and wife."

Dix could sense his new wife's temper simmering.

She obviously hadn't appreciated being called a fallen woman even though Dix thought the honest mistake amusing. To distract her and to keep the preacher from saying anything else that might result in Katherine flattening a man of the cloth, Dix pulled her to him and kissed her slowly, until the anger melted away and only wonder remained.

When he finally turned her loose, Katherine had the vague sense of folks clapping and cheering, but she was too woozy to ascertain where the sounds were coming from. She stared up at Dix in awe. He said for her ears only, "Now you can say you've been properly kissed."

She wanted to sock him in the eye.

Her father came over and gave her a big hug. There were tears in his eyes as he whispered, "Thank you, Katherine. Thank you."

Considering the way she felt about this whole madcap affair, Katherine didn't believe saying "You're welcome" to be an appropriate, nor truthful, response, so she just hugged him in return. She hoped she'd be able to forgive him someday.

After her father stepped away, a few of the girls came over to wish the couple well. Some even hugged Katherine and offered sincere sounding congratulations.

Melinda, however, chose to be frank. She walked up to Dix and said, "When you tire of ice in your bed, give me a holler. I'll warm you up real nice."

Katherine had had quite enough of Melinda and so told her quietly, "Melinda, I am a very jealous woman, and if you ever even *look* at my husband again, you will wish you'd contracted syphilis instead."

Melinda's eyes widened.

Katherine asked in the same flat tone, "Do I make myself clear?"

Evidently she had, because Melinda left the room in a huff.

Dix couldn't help his smile. "I think we've seen the last of her."

Katherine was just glad to be able to vent some of her temper on someone.

Finally, Miss Sunshine came over. "I saw Melinda stomp out. I'm assuming someone put her in her place?"

"Guilty," Katherine said, raising her hand.

Miss Sunshine smiled. "Good for you." Then she said to Dix, "She's going to be just fine, Dix, just fine."

He didn't reply, but Katherine thought he appeared pleased.

Miss Sunshine gave them both a strong hug. "Well, you two go on up. Cook's sent up your dinner. I've got to get the preacher a friend for the evening; then I have to open up."

Katherine looked at her curiously. "A friend?"

"Yes, a friend—one of the girls."

Katherine stared.

Miss Sunshine laughed. "Aw honey, don't be shocked. The preacher's one of my best customers."

The table in the room had been set with a snow-white linen cloth, and the smells of the food beneath the covered dishes fragrantly scented the air.

"Hungry?" Dix asked.

"Extremely."

He helped her with her chair. Katherine could feel the heat of his body surrounding her before he moved to his side of the table. His nearness brought back the memory of his potent kiss.

They ate in silence for a while. Then Katherine brought up the subject she had wanted to discuss earlier.

"Do you plan on exercising your marital rights to-night?"

Dix looked up from his plate. Her eyes were frank. He liked her frankness just as much as he did her plain speech. He picked up his napkin from his lap and wiped his mouth. "No, you aren't ready."

"Ready for what?" she asked, pouring herself a cup of coffee.

"The passion a man can light in a woman."

Katherine scanned his face. She saw neither arrogance nor conceit, simply truth. She set the pot back down. "And that means what, exactly?"

"Just what I said," he stated simply. "If I were to take you tonight, you'd wake up in the morning mad at me and mad at yourself."

"Why?"

"Because you'd want more."

Katherine snorted. "You're pretty damn confident, aren't you, Marshal?"

"I'm pretty damn good."

Katherine blinked. She surveyed him as he cut into the thick steak on his plate. Once again she saw not an inkling of boast. In his own mind he was stating fact. "Your skills aside, I doubt I'd be pining for more. I'm not one of the women on these murals."

"No, you're not."

Katherine didn't think she liked his tone. "What are you implying?"

"Nothing."

"Then why the tone?"

There was a muted sparkle in his eyes as he chewed his steak. "Just agreeing with you, is all."

Katherine sampled some of the well-prepared chicken on her plate. "Why do men always believe they wield some magical power over women?"

"Because in our own limited ways we do."

"Hogwash. Some women are simply weaker than others."

"Passion can make the strongest woman weak; a man, too, for that matter."

"Once again, hogwash."

"Just as I said, you're not ready."

Katherine countered easily, "Whether I'm ready or not, I'm certain I won't go to pieces in the end. In fact, I'd wager my freedom against it."

He set his fork down and sat back. "Meaning what?"

"That if I can run the gauntlet of your self-declared expertise and remain unmoved, I win. We dissolve this marriage, my father goes free, I go back New York, and you return to Indian Territory."

Dix saw the challenge flashing in her cinnamon-colored eyes and wondered where she'd inherited her courage. It certainly hadn't come from that daddy of hers. She exuded a strength of purpose he rarely saw in women, east or west. He also noted amusedly that she appeared extremely confident for a woman who'd never known a man. "And if I win? What do I get besides your promise to honor your daddy's word?"

Katherine shrugged. "I don't know. I suppose you may choose your own boon, as long as it is within reason."

"You're going to lose, you know that?"

"I know no such thing."

"Katherine Wildhorse, you're going to bolt like a filly from a burning barn before I even get that dress off you."

The heated words set her heart to racing. She tried to ignore it. "If wishes were horses, beggars would ride."

"Riding is just what I had in mind."

"You've a quick wit."

"And an even slower hand."

Katherine hadn't an inkling as to what that meant, but his eyes left her so warm, she assumed it had to do with his bedding skills. No eastern-raised man would be so bold as to speak so frankly; eastern men were wary of causing a lady distress and always solicitous of a lady's feelings. But this western man? If all western men were as arrogant as this Seminole lawman, all the more reason to try and extricate herself from this exasperating situation.

Dix had absolutely no doubt she would bolt, and it would be before he removed her dress. A woman like Katherine had no idea how powerful desire could be, nor how much heat it could generate with the right man. He guessed that she'd be as passionate in bed as she was in life. He also guessed that she wouldn't like being shown that fact—at least not in the beginning. "These numerous lovers you claimed to have taken, they ever kiss you until your eyes closed the way they closed for me?"

She had to admit the truth. "No."

"So, you've had nothing but simple pecks on the lips?"

"Yes. Where else would a man kiss a woman but on the lips? I thought you were an expert on this subject?"

He slowly sipped his coffee. "You'd be surprised where kisses can be placed."

His watchful presence set the pulse at the base of her throat to beating fast.

He told her plainly, "If this marriage is consummated tonight, know that you'll be going to Indian Territory. No child of mine will grow up east of the Mississippi."

Katherine thought to set him at ease. "Believe me, there will be no going to Indian Territory."

He leaned across the table and replied, "What I believe is that you're going to be mad as a wet hen in the morning. That's what I believe.''

Katherine, buoyed by her own inner confidence, quipped, ''We'll see,'' then returned her attention to her dinner.

However, as the meal drew to a close, the temperature in the room seemed to rise, or at least it felt much warmer to Katherine. Night had fallen during the course of things, filling the candlelit room with a soft darkness. She glanced Dix's way and found him watching her with the same quiet gaze he'd worn most of the evening. She had no doubt she would be free to leave here later tonight after she won this contest, but a small voice cautioned her to admit to the possibility of failure. Dixon Wildhorse was an exceptionally handsome man. The sparkling ebony skin, the vibrant eyes, and the godlike physique added up to a man few women could resist. Every one of Miss Sunshine's girls had greeted his arrival with a purring smile and made no show of hiding their disappointment at the news of his imminent marriage. Katherine admittedly had little experience with the physical sides of life. Her aunt had explained the basics of men and women the night before she died, belatedly equipping Katherine with only the barest of facts. Could this Seminole lawman really be as good as he claimed? And what did that mean, exactly?

In hindsight, she realized she may have placed herself in a potentially untenable situation, but she clung to her position with all the determination of a cat on a windswept branch.

''Problem?'' he asked.

''No,'' she lied.

''You can always back down.''

''I have no intention of altering my position.''

"Then come on over here. Let's see how far we can get before you bolt."

Katherine stood stiffly, then walked around the table to where he sat. She hoped her features didn't betray her truly nervous insides.

To Dix she looked as stiff as one of Miss Sunshine's statues. The new Mrs. Wildhorse was not ready for a wedding night, but because she was too stubborn for her own good, the only way to convince her would be to prove it. He gently took her hand and eased her down onto his lap. "Just sit a minute," he told her softly. "We've plenty of time for you to get comfortable."

Katherine drew in a steadying breath. The heat of his nearness surrounded her like the heat of an August day.

He asked once more, "Are you certain you want to do this?"

Katherine found it too unnerving to meet his eyes, so she kept them lowered. "Yes. I've no desire to go to Indian Territory."

"No?" he asked softly, tracing his finger over the silken skin beneath her ear.

Katherine shook like she'd never shaken before. "No."

"That's too bad, *chica*. I think we could have fun. . . ."

He ran a caressing finger over her trembling lower lip, then whispered, "Kiss me, Kate. . . ."

She turned her head slightly, and his lips met hers. She pressed her lips together firmly.

He drew back slowly. "You have to play fair."

"This isn't a game."

"Ah, but it is. Indian Territory or New York. Or are you conceding?"

"I'm not conceding."

"Then relax. You're stiffer than a new pair of shoes."

This time when their lips met, hers were softer, less firm, and because they were she began to better understand the definition of *good*. The pleasure began with fleeting brushes of his full lips over her own: gentle, coaxing whispers that flooded her with sensations, that dimmed her will. His mustache tickled her upper lip. As he nibbled gently on her bottom lip, she trembled, then trembled again as his big hand slid up her back to bring her closer. Her determination to remain unmoved faded as her virgin's body savored this first, sweet drink from passion's cup. Her lips parted, encouraging him to let his tongue play against the soft corners of her mouth. When it slipped inside, Katherine swore that sparks ignited beneath her skin.

Dix thought her kisses were a mixture of honeysuckle and wildfire—sweet and hot. Even though she possessed little skill, he found the passion lurking beneath her nononsense exterior a joy to explore. Bart Love's daughter had a mouth lush as desert spring, a mouth meant for his kisses, a mouth that drew him to nibble and taste and want to brand as his own. She smelled sweet, too, he noted as he brushed his lips over the soft perfumed skin above the high collar of her wedding dress. He bit gently at the lobe of her ear, then circled his tongue around the small pearl stud fastened there. Her answering soft intake of breath sent a fire through his blood.

Katherine's mind felt blanketed by clouds. Each touch of his lips thrilled her so much, she realized that if she wasn't careful she could indeed go to pieces. The thought made the alarms sound in her head, and she gently broke the seal of their lips and pulled away. She fought to calm her breathing so that she could think.

His eyes were quizzical, amused. "Problems?"

"I . . . just need to catch my breath."

He smiled inwardly. "I suppose that is allowed. . . ." Dix liked the way she filled his lap. He preferred his women tall, statuesque. "Conceding?"

"No," she said, feeling caressed by the heat flowing from his gaze.

"Good . . . because breath-catching time is up. . . ."

He recaptured her mouth, tempting her with short, lush kisses until she melted back against his bracing shoulder. Katherine had never felt so surrounded by a man, so sheltered, so dazzled. His hand was slowly sliding up and down her gown-covered back, fairly scorching the skin inside. When his palm moved lazily over her breast, she stiffened and clamped her hand over his wrist. "What are you doing?" she asked warily.

The quizzical amusement returned to his eyes. "What comes naturally between a man and his wife."

"But why would you want to touch me . . . there? I thought it was simply kissing and . . . and cleaving," she said trying not to let her shock and embarrassment come through in her voice.

"When it's done right, there's nothing simple about it. There's a whole lot of territory to cover between the kissing and the cleaving."

Katherine didn't know what to make of this decidedly surprising turn of events. "I was told I just had to lie there, let you do what you needed to do, and count to fifty."

"What?" He chuckled. "Who told you this?"

"My Aunt Ceil. She said that's how long it takes for a man to do his business."

Dix wanted to laugh until he cried, but didn't want to chance hurting her feelings. Count to fifty?! "Katherine, not all men are the same. Granted there are probably men who can find peace in fifty seconds, but a man worth his salt will spend much more time because the lady should find pleasure, also.''

Katherine ran her hands over her eyes.

"What's the matter," he asked, as if he hadn't known.

"I have to concede," she confessed looking up at his mustached face.

He asked softly, "Why?"

"I'm not ready for the parts that come after the kissing and before the cleaving.''

"I know . . ." he told her.

"I don't like to lose.''

"I know that also, *chica*.''

Frustrated, she turned away. He reached out and gently turned her stiff chin back so that he could see her face. "There is no dishonor in admitting you'll have to return to fight another day.''

"Now that I've lost the wager, what prize do you claim?''

"No more talk of not going back to the Territory with me.''

She looked away and sighed in surrender. "Agreed.''

Her body still pulsed with the fire ignited by their kiss, but she had no idea what to do with it. "When does it stop?''

"When does what stop?''

"This . . . warmth?''

He smiled at her innocence. "It will fade in a while.''

"You think this is funny, don't you?''

"It is pretty interesting, I have to admit.'' He swatted her gently on the behind. "Stand up. Time for bed. We've a long day ahead of us.''

Katherine stood. Because of her humiliating defeat, she couldn't look him in the eye. "I—I need to have someone help me out of this dress.''

"I can do it, turn around.''

"No, I—I'll find Miss Sunshine or one of the girls. I'll
. . . be back."

"Katherine—" he called.

She fled the room before he could say more.

Chapter 6

Miss Sunshine must have opened the house for business because as Katherine rounded the hall, she could hear music, voices, and the sounds of folks having a good time. Once again, the journalist in her should've been excited over the opportunity to explore life in a place like this, but the woman in her had other things on her mind: mostly Dixon Wildhorse. Was there truly more to it than kissing and cleaving?

Downstairs, Katherine had trouble finding Miss Sunshine in the crowded parlor. The business was brisker than Katherine would ever have imagined. Through the press she could see some of the girls flirting and laughing with the drinking, smiling customers who appeared well-to-do and were of all races. In a corner chair her father sat with Lilah on his lap; Katherine could see the devilment playing in his eyes from where she stood.

As she continued to scan the room, a slightly inebriated man, mistaking her for one of the girls, grabbed her by the wrist as she passed his chair.

"Hey, I've never seen you before."

Katherine smiled down at him through her irritation and said, "You're correct. Now excuse me."

But he didn't release his hold. "Not so fast," he said easily. "What's your name?"

As always, a lie came easily from her lips. "Phoebe."

"How much is Miss Sunshine charging for a night with you, Phoebe? I can afford whatever it is, especially if that white dress means you're a virgin."

Before Katherine could even begin to form an answer to such an outrageous request, Lilah came to her rescue. She sidled up to the man and said to Katherine, "Now, you know I'm not going to let you have this handsome man. I've been eyeing him all night."

Lilah worked her way onto his lap, draped her arms around his neck, and told Katherine, "I think I saw Miss Sunshine looking for you, she's in the little office in the kitchen."

Since the man now seemed to have eyes only for the red-headed Lilah, Katherine gave her a silent thank you and hightailed it to the kitchen.

Miss Sunshine, sitting behind her desk engrossed in a ledger, appeared surprised.

"Katherine? Honey, what are you doing down here?"

"I need someone to help me unhook my dress."

"Unhook your dress? Did something happen to Dix?"

Katherine shook her head no.

"If you're down here needing help getting out of that dress, something must have happened to Dix."

"He's fine."

Miss Sunshine searched her face, then said quietly. "Then it must mean *you're* not fine. Pull up a chair and tell old Auntie Sunshine what's wrong."

So Katherine took a seat. "It's really nothing. I–I simply went into my wedding night dreadfully unprepared."

Sunshine gave Katherine a smile filled with affection.

"Dix said you were a plain talker. He likes that. I do, too. How dreadfully unprepared?"

"I was told about kissing and cleaving . . . but none of the parts in between."

"I see. Did you like the kissing?"

"It wasn't unpleasant—a bit overwhelming in ways, but not unpleasant."

"Well, that's a start. My advice to you is to give yourself time. Once you do, you might be surprised at how nice the parts in between can be."

"Really?" Katherine had never considered that.

"Trust me." The older woman's voice then became serious. "I know all about Bart's rustling and why you and Dix had to get married. You're probably still trying to get used to the idea, but like I said to you earlier, you won't find a better, more decent man than Dix. He'll make a fine husband and a fine father to your kids."

"I'd rather he and my father had come up with another solution."

"If they had, you might be married to that Rupert Samuels."

"You know about that, too?"

"Dix's been staying here since he came east. He told me the whole thing last night after he took Bart back to his place. Bart filled me in on the rest a little while ago. Samuels is a big man. Nobody's gonna believe he's a swindler without solid proof."

"I know, that's why I—"

Miss Sunshine interrupted Katherine to say, "What can I do for you, Melinda?"

Katherine turned to see Melinda standing in the doorway. Katherine had not closed the door behind her when she first entered the office, so she had no idea how long Melinda had been standing there or how much she might have heard.

Her brown eyes were cold when they met Katherine's. "I just stopped in to say I'm heading into town with one of the customers. He'll bring me back later."

"Be careful," Miss Sunshine cautioned.

"I plan to."

After Melinda's departure, Miss Sunshine and Katherine spent a few more minutes discussing Rupert and his scheme. Miss Sunshine offered to send a telegram to Geoff on Katherine's behalf so he wouldn't worry. When they concluded, Miss Sunshine said gently, "Now, you go on back upstairs before Dix has to come and find you. *He's* supposed to help you with your dress, not me. Okay."

Katherine nodded.

"Good. The girls and me rustled you up some clothes to get you through until Dix can take you shopping. Can't have you wearing nothing but your wedding dress. The clothes are there."

A small pile of gaily colored clothing was lying over a chair. Katherine picked up the garments and draped them over an arm. "Thank you, Miss Sunshine."

"You're welcome, Katherine. Just one more thing."

She opened a drawer in her desk and pulled out a small pearl-handled derringer. "Do you know how to use one of these?"

Katherine grinned. "Sure do."

"Then take it, it's yours. In the Territory a woman doesn't always have her man near when some joker needs to be put in his place, so it's always smart to carry your cavalry in your handbag. Be sure to plug them good the first time, though. Sweetie Pie doesn't hold but three shots."

Katherine picked up the lady's derringer and turned it over in her hand.

"And promise me, you'll never turn her on Dix."

"I promise," Katherine said, smiling. "Is it really named Sweetie Pie?"

"Yes, and if you keep her clean and dry, she'll keep you safe."

"Thank you again," Katherine declared, taking the small box of shells. "How will I ever repay you for the clothes, the advice, and Sweetie Pie?"

"Just be good to Dix and name one of your girls Caroline after me."

Katherine nodded. "I will."

When Katherine returned upstairs, she found the room shadowy and silent. The candles had burned low in her absence and were now barely able to keep the darkness at bay. Dix stood with his back to the room, looking out the bay window at the night. As she softly closed the door, he turned her way. They faced each other in the darkness, neither speaking for a moment, until Dix said in a voice quiet as the surroundings, "Welcome back. Thought I'd have to send a posse after you."

Katherine exhaled her nervousness. "I apologize if I worried you. I ended up talking with Miss Sunshine."

The view from the window reclaimed his attention. "Nice night. Makes me anxious to get home."

"When do we leave?" Katherine asked. She placed the clothes on the floor beside the bed and tucked Sweetie Pie inside. She thought it best to hold off on telling him about Miss Sunshine's gift. Being a man, Dix would probably try and take it from her, for her "own good."

"Tomorrow. We're going west with Blake and a wagon train he's heading."

"A wagon train?"

"He's leading some folks to one of Pap Singleton's colonies in southern Kansas."

Katherine knew that many Blacks in the south were still fleeing the terror being meted out by the Redemptionist Democrats. Thousands of the race had set up their own towns in places like Kansas, Nebraska, and other points west. Pap Singleton took credit for being the catalyst behind this mass migration, a movement the newspapers had dubbed the Great Exodus.

"How long will it take?"

"Depends on the weather, the pace we're able to maintain—a lot of things. More than a month for sure, though." He turned and looked over at her. "Think you can handle living in a wagon? You don't impress me as the outdoor type."

"I can adjust."

He smiled at her in the dark. "Not much scares you, does it?"

"So far, not much."

The parts between the kissing and the cleaving scared her, but neither of them brought it up. Instead, Katherine said, "Miss Sunshine and the girls gave me some clothes so I'd have something to wear besides this wedding dress. Everything I own is back at the shop."

"Don't worry about it. We'll do some shopping before we head out for Kansas."

"My money's at the shop, too."

"I have money."

"You can't pay for everything."

"Why not?"

"I'm accustomed to paying my own way."

And she was. She did not want to start out this marriage in debt to him. There would be enough problems to face without money adding to it all.

Once again he said, "Don't worry. If you want, I'll keep tabs, and you can repay me when you can."

It was a compromise she could live with. "That's agreeable."

He moved away from the window and silently doused the few remaining candles, plunging the room into darkness. "Time for bed, Katherine."

Katherine threw the bed a panicked look. "Where are you going to sleep?"

"In the bed."

"But . . ." Did he expect her to sleep in the bed with him?

"But what?" he asked in his soft, rough voice. "For the next six to eight weeks, you and I will be sleeping on bedrolls either on the ground or in a wagon. I'm not missing what may be my last chance to wake up in a real bed."

Upon hearing his explanation, Katherine relaxed. He'd already judged her not ready to be made his wife in bed, so she really had nothing to worry about. Or did she? "Can you help me with my dress, please, then?"

He crossed the room so silently that she didn't know he was behind her until she felt the heat of his body and the first faint whisper of his touch.

"Thought you wanted someone else to do this for you."

Katherine swallowed. "Miss Sunshine said it's my husband's job."

Silence.

She asked nervously, "Will you need a light?"

"No."

And he didn't. He undid her dress gently, slowly, expertly. He seemed to have little trouble unfastening the tiny buttons, while Katherine had a fair amount of trouble ignoring the sensations of his fingers brushing against her skin. By the time he worked his way down to the base of her spine, she had trouble breathing because of his touch and the knowledge that there was nothing between him and the skin of her back but the thin ivory-colored camisole she had on beneath the dress.

"Where's your whalebone?" he asked, tracing his finger softly up her spine.

His touch was so potent Katherine couldn't answer for a moment, but she finally managed to say, "Still in a whale somewhere. . . . I'm certain my mother is spinning in her grave knowing I'm walking about without a proper corset, but I can't abide the things."

Dix couldn't either. They left women short of breath and oftentimes scarred, but he knew few women with the gumption to buck convention and choose comfort instead. "Never wear a corset. . . ."

Katherine trembled under his voice and touch. She wondered if the way he was touching her now had anything to do with the parts between kissing and cleaving. If so, she might not mind it as much as she had imagined.

"There's a screen over there you can undress behind. Get into your night things so we can go to bed; otherwise neither of us is liable to get any sleep. . . ."

The moon broke through the clouds, bathing the room with a pale light and partially illuminating them. Katherine's eyes held all the wonder she felt as she searched Dix's face.

He told her softly, "Go to bed, Katherine."

Heeding his words, Katherine forced herself to move away from his mesmerizing presence and sought refuge behind the screen.

A yawn escaped her lips as she sorted through the things Miss Sunshine had provided, a task made difficult by the darkness, but she managed to find a wrapper that fit. She shrugged it on over her thin underthings, tied the belt, and crawled into bed. Her worries over where Dix would sleep never materialized because after the day she'd had, as soon as her head settled onto the pillow, Katherine Love Wildhorse promptly fell asleep.

However, she awakened in panic when a strong hand covered her mouth and no amount of struggling could move it away.

Then she heard Dix's harsh whisper, "Kate! It's me."

She went stock still, her fear genuine. Dix put a finger to his lips, motioning for her to remain quiet, then slowly removed his imprisoning hand.

He told her softly, "Someone is fiddling with the lock. I want you to lie here real still. I'm going over there by the door. Okay?"

When she nodded, Dix left the bed silent as a leaf falling on snow and took up his position. Katherine remembered placing Sweetie Pie among the clothes beside the bed. Hoping she was moving as silently as Dix had, she wiggled down to the floor to retrieve it, then slid back beneath the sheets.

Dix called softly, "What are you doing?"

"I had to get something."

The sound of the door opening silenced them both.

Katherine heard a voice that sounded suspiciously like Rupert's henchman Joe say quietly, "You get the cowboy. I'll get the girl."

Frank replied in a harsh whisper, "No, *you* get him, and *I'll* get the girl. I had my share this afternoon."

Then amazingly, Katherine heard Melinda snap, "Hurry up and get her out of here before you alert the whole house."

Evidently it was all Dix needed to hear, because after they tiptoed into the room, he lit a lamp.

Joe and Frank tried to scamper back out of the room only to find the door closed. They reminded Katherine of rats.

''Evening, boys.'' Dix drawled, his gun drawn. ''Melinda.''

Then he said to Katherine, ''Kate, light a couple more lamps. I want to see them clearly when I shoot them.''

Grinning, Katherine slid from the bed and did her husband's bidding. When the room was fully lit, Katherine stared at Dix with shock-widened eyes. He didn't have a stitch of clothing on! He was magnificently made, as if he'd been chiseled from onyx marble.

Melinda seemed to enjoy the view, too. ''Marshal, you're a well-made man.''

He ignored her.

Katherine couldn't ignore him, however. While Dix held his big Colt on the intruders, she stared, dazzled by the strength and power exuding from his body. When her vision innocently brushed his thighs, her eyes opened even wider. He could have been a model in one of the room's murals. Her heart racing, she settled her attention high on his face as he said to Joe and Frank, ''This is my wedding night, boys. Do you know what we do in Indian Territory to someone fool enough to intrude on a man's wedding night?''

On their faces, Frank and Joe still bore the cuts, scrapes and contusions they'd received earlier at the hands of the lawman. They quickly intimated their ignorance.

''Well, we certainly don't let them live.''

Neither Frank nor Joe appeared too pleased by the surprising turn of events. Both men were shooting daggers at the angry-faced Melinda.

Dix turned to Katherine, and his eyes widened as he got his first clear look at how she was dressed. His attention was caught between staring at the transparent wrapper encasing his wife's thinly clad body, and keeping his gun trained on the ugly mugs of Rupert's henchmen. Finally Dix told her, "Get beneath the covers, Katherine."

A bit puzzled by the command at first, Katherine looked to the leering eyes of Frank then down to herself. Seeing that her underwear was displayed through the shadow-thin wrapper for all to see, her eyes widened. She got back into the bed without argument and pulled the covers up to her chin.

Dix, no longer distracted by the lure of his semi-bare wife, bellowed for Blake, then motioned with the Colt for the intruders to stand away from the door.

Blake entered a few minutes later, dressed only in his trousers, but he had his gun, a twin to the one Dix carried. "What the hell's going on?"

"Varmints."

Blake looked them over. "Her, too?" he asked, indicating Melinda.

Katherine answered, "Especially her."

Dix told Blake, "March them downstairs. I'll pull on my pants and join you directly."

After Blake escorted them out at gunpoint, Dix closed the door. Katherine tried not to peek at him as he pulled on his pants, but failed.

He said, "I'm not trying to embarrass you. This is the way I sleep. I didn't have time to find my clothes in the dark."

"I understand," Katherine replied over her racing heart.

"I'll be right back; stay put."

When he returned more than an hour later, he stopped at the sight of her in the bed with a drawn weapon in her hand. It was a small weapon, but a weapon just the same. "Steal that off a squirrel?" he asked.

While relieved it had been him at the door, Katherine

gave him a look, then smiled as she lowered the weapon. "This is Sweetie Pie. She's a gift from Miss Sunshine."

"Do you know how to use it?"

"Yes."

Before he could quiz her further and maybe begin a male lecture on why she shouldn't be armed, Katherine quickly asked, "What happened with Melinda and her friends?"

"Evidently she heard you and Miss Sunshine talking about Samuels this evening. She knew his name, and being the conniver she is, she hightailed it to town to make a deal to deliver you. He promised her quite a sum of cash, it turns out. He sent Frank and Joe to bring you back."

"Why would she do something like that?"

"Sunshine says Melinda's always been an opportunist, and she doesn't really care for you all that much."

"I see."

Dix came over and sat on the bed. Katherine, still in the transparent wrapper, eased the covers back up to her chin.

Dix held her eyes. He'd have trouble sleeping from now on after getting a good look at her in that dressing gown. "We have to leave here."

"Now?"

"Now. We don't know if Samuels is on his way or what. Blake and I agree someone could be killed if shooting starts here, so we'll head out."

"What did you do with Frank and Joe?"

"Sent them back to town."

Katherine stared. "Why? They're just going to run back to Rupert."

"Not naked and covered with honey and feathers, they won't."

Katherine gasped. *"What?!"*

"Miss Sunshine's idea. While Blake and I held them at gunpoint, Sunshine and the girls had a grand time pouring honey on them. Miss Sunshine slit open a couple of pillows, shook the feathers over them, then sent them on their way."

Katherine began to laugh at the pictures his words conjured up. "My goodness, how are they going to get back to town?"

"It'll be dawn soon. If they have any sense, they'll hole up somewhere until tonight. If they travel during the day, some constable is liable to haul them away for public indecency."

Katherine's amusement made her shake her head. "What about Melinda?"

"Sunshine said she'd take care of Melinda. I've never seen Sunshine so angry."

"So, we're leaving now?"

"Soon as you get dressed. Blake's bringing the coach around."

Katherine searched his face. She was about to embark on an adventure that would change her life. She felt excitement in spite of her inner trepidation.

Dix asked her softly, "Ready?"

A confident Katherine answered, "Yes."

And so it began. Under the pearly light of dawn, Katherine, Dix, and Blake said their good-byes to Bart, Miss Sunshine, and her girls. Bart promised Dix he would board the afternoon train and be in Wewoka, waiting, when Dix and Katherine arrived. Dix promised Bart jail if he wasn't. Katherine hoped her father would keep his word.

With the men taking turns driving, it took them most of the day to reach the rendezvous with the wagon train. Once they arrived in the small town west of Chicago,

Blake gave Dix the directions to the church where he would be, and Dix promised to seek him out later. Blake went on ahead to see about his homesteaders while Katherine and Dix went off to shop for the clothing and toiletries she needed. She kept her purchases to a minimum, not certain how much money he could spare. She selected two skirts, a few shirtwaist blouses, and a pair of sturdy shoes. She added a bar of soap and a pair of cotton stockings.

When she brought her goods to the counter, Dix took one look at the paltry pile and said, "We can afford more."

She shook her head. "This will do."

He assessed her a moment, then counted out the coins for the clerk.

After leaving the store, they ate a hearty dinner in a boardinghouse dining room, then walked over to the church where they were to meet Blake. The longer days of late May meant dusk would not descend for another few hours, but Katherine hadn't gotten much sleep the night before, and she'd been yawning on and off all day. She dearly hoped she'd have the opportunity to relax sometime soon.

"Ever drive a wagon?" Dix asked as they walked.

Katherine, having a time keeping up with his fluid, long-legged stride, said, "No."

"Well, you're smart; you'll learn."

The clearing behind the church was filled with wagons. Atop the wagons were women of varying ages, colors, and sizes. The women were all driving back and forth, but not doing it very well, or so it appeared to Katherine. She saw two wagons nearly collide, while across the clearing more near accidents occurred. In the center of all this stood Jackson Blake, yelling at the top of his lungs, "A line, ladies! Can't you make a simple line?!"

From where Katherine stood, Blake appeared highly agitated. The women appeared to be trying their best as they yanked on their reins to pull the teams around, but the more Blake yelled, the more chaotic the scene became. One woman finally hopped down from one of the wagons and advanced upon Blake with such blazing eyes, Katherine thought she would attack him. Instead, the two began a heated debate of their own, complete with more yelling. Katherine clearly heard Blake being called a stubborn, cow-brained, jackass.

Katherine asked, "Do you know who she is?"

Dix chuckled. "Nope, never seen that red-haired hellion before, ever."

The woman's red hair and freckles reminded Katherine a bit of Lilah. She had obviously spoken her piece, since Blake threw his hat into the dust. Katherine watched her march back to her wagon, climb aboard, and slap the reins to get her team of horses moving again.

Blake could be seen glaring at her exit, but when he spotted Dix and Katherine, he came over to greet them.

Dix asked, "Who's the redhead?"

Blake said tightly, "She has the nerve to be named Grace. Nothing gracious about her as far as I can tell. Who'd ever thought a woman that small could yell so loud."

Dix looked out over the yard. "Where are the men?"

"There aren't any."

Dix stared at his old friend, then said, "What do you mean, there aren't any?"

"There aren't. It's going to be a train of nothing but women. They're mail-order brides."

"*What?!*"

"I didn't tell you when I asked you to be scout because I knew you'd say no."

"You know me well."

"Well, you can't back out now. You gave me your word."

Katherine thought this journey would be far more interesting than she'd originally thought. "Is Grace one of the brides?" she asked.

Blake laughed. "Grace? Not even the devil himself would be fool enough to stand up with her. No, Grace Atwood is the woman who put this train together."

Katherine knew mail-order brides had become fairly common now that more and more men were moving west, but she'd never heard of a group of women of the race undertaking such an endeavor. Her hands itched for a pen and paper to capture this story for her readers.

Dix asked, "Have any of them driven a team before?"

"A few, but most as you can see are green as spring grass."

Collisions and near misses continued to occur. Grace abandoned her own wagon to give as much help and encouragement as she could to the other women.

Observing the chaos in the yard, Dix asked, "Do you know how hard this is going to be?"

Blake nodded. "That's why I asked you to come along. Every other man I asked declined. Not even Grace's gold moved them."

Dix sighed. He already had one potentially troublesome female on his hands; now he had a wagon train full. Would he ever get back home? he wondered wistfully.

"Blake," Katherine asked, "who are the men?"

"Cavalry veterans who've started a colony in southern Kansas. One is Grace's cousin. He wrote to her and asked if she knew any women willing to make the trip and be wives. She didn't at first, but after placing a few notices around the area, over a hundred women showed up to be one of the thirty-five wives she needed. The men sent her the money to outfit the trip, and to hire someone to lead them out. Come, I'll show you where everything is stored.''

They walked a short distance to a rise above the clearing. Spread out below them lay a small tent city. "This is where we bunk until we pull out."

Katherine surveyed her unorthodox new home. She counted twenty tents. There were clothes hanging on lines, cooking fires, and women milling about. Katherine and Dix followed Blake down for a closer look. As he led them through the maze, the women greeted them with friendly smiles and nods. Katherine even saw a couple of them elbowing each other with appreciative grins as they got a good look at Dix.

One woman called from the opening of her tent, ''Is he one of the husbands, Mr. Blake?''

Blake replied, ''No, Loreli, this is Dixon Wildhorse, our scout, and his wife, Katherine.''

"Welcome aboard Katherine. He's a fine man!''

Katherine, feeling the friendliness of the woman, yelled in reply, ''Thanks!''

When Katherine looked up, Dix was studying her. She asked, ''What was I supposed to say, 'No, he's not. He's as ugly as a mule?' ''

Blake laughed.

Dix simply shook his head.

The supply tent was much larger than the others. Its interior resembled a well-stocked general store. There were harnesses and blankets, oil slickers, rifles and tarps. Around the walls were crates stacked high as Katherine's shoulders labeled DRESS GOODS, COOKING IMPLE-

MENTS, and FEED. There were axles, spare wheels, and all manner of tools. One corner held nothing but reins and large empty barrels.

Dix strolled through the merchandise. He fingered a few harnesses and tested the construction of a few of the large barrels.

"What are the barrels for?" Katherine asked.

"Water."

He randomly selected a couple of the rifles, checked the sights and chambers, then set them back with the others. He turned to Blake. "Your Grace didn't spare any expense, did she?"

"No, she didn't. The husbands sent her enough gold to buy only the best, and that's what she's done. She's a hellion, but she's an efficient one."

After Dix finished his cursory inspection, Blake led them back out into the sunshine.

"Is there a tent for Katherine and me?" Dix asked.

"Sure is. The ladies should have it up by now."

"The ladies?"

"Yes, Dix, the ladies. We don't have any men to do the work, remember? The women do everything. Grace's orders."

Katherine thought Grace's orders to be sound thinking. If they were to reach Kansas successfully, the women would have to learn to do everything on their own. There'd be no men to turn to when they crossed the plains when a wagon needed repairing or the horses had to be shod. Yes, Katherine thought, this would be a truly adventurous journey, indeed.

The women raising the tent were just about done when Katherine, Dix and Blake strolled up. There were ten in the crew, and all were variously occupied— pounding in support stakes, pulling ropes taut, and carrying supplies inside. It was a warm May evening, and the sweat of their labor glistened on their brows.

Blake said, "Ladies, I want you to met our scout, Deputy Marshal Dixon Wildhorse. This is his wife, Katherine."

A number of women greeted them kindly.

Then Grace stepped from inside the tent.

Blake made the introductions, after which Grace said, "Glad you could join us, Mr. and Mrs. Wildhorse. If you're friends of Mr. Blake's, I'm sure he's been filling your ears with plenty of lies about me. Don't believe him."

Katherine grinned.

"We have your tent ready. Hope you don't mind that we put you over here a bit from the main camp. Mr. Blake says you're newlyweds, so we thought you might like whatever privacy we could manage."

Dix tipped his head politely. Katherine chose to ignore the faint light of amusement in his eyes.

Grace then introduced Katherine and Dix to the other women. Katherine tried to remember which name went with which face but soon gave up, reasoning she would have plenty of time to get to know everyone on the long trail ahead.

After receiving a sincere thank you from Dix and Katherine, the ladies and Grace departed.

Blake said to Dix, "We'll go over the maps later this evening. Right now, I have to get back to the beehive. Dinner is usually a community affair, so you're welcome to join us if you've a mind to."

He tipped his hat to Katherine and went on his way, leaving a very awkward-feeling Katherine to stare up into the mustached face of her dark-skinned husband. She thought she saw him grin, but before she could puzzle over its cause, he swooped her up into the cradle of his arms and carried her to the opening of the tent.

"What are you doing?" she asked.

He stopped and looked down. "We're married. This is a threshold."

Katherine had to admit he was dazzling. "I didn't think it applied to tents."

"It applies to wherever we are, *chica.*"

She had no ready reply for that.

She let herself be carried in while trying to ignore the rousing cheers that rang out from the women. Dix set her on her feet again, leaving the faint heat from his arms against the backs of her thighs.

He told her, "Hope I didn't embarrass you. If I did, I apologize."

She shook her head no. She was simply a bit shaken. "You're a tad overwhelming, Marshal, that's all." When she looked up into his dark eyes, all the sweet trepidation she felt whenever they were alone came flooding back.

"Is that good or bad?" he asked quietly.

His gaze was so moving, Katherine felt as if she were being caressed by his hand. She finally answered by admitting, "I'm not certain."

Dix could feel himself being drawn to her in spite of everything. He realized he wanted to kiss her when her eyes slid closed and her lips parted passionately. He didn't, though. She was like a newly corralled filly; she needed to trust, and he needed to let her come to him at her own pace.

In order to gather herself and to escape his compelling eyes, Katherine took a look around the small, clean tent. Two rolled up pallets were lying side by side on the grassy floor. Close to the bedding stood a crate with a lantern on top. All the stacked crates ringing the interior resembled the ones in the supply tent.

"I've never lived in a tent," she said, trying not to

dwell upon the idea of sleeping with him in such intimate quarters for the rest of their stay.

"It's not bad unless its cold or raining."

He could see her trying not to glance at the pallets. "Sleeping arrangements bothering you?"

"No," she denied hastily, "of course not."

He noticed that she wouldn't meet his eyes, and so he declared, "I'm not the type to force a woman, Kate. When you're ready you'll let me know, but you will be sleeping by my side."

They were the words of a man confident in all that was male. She didn't argue, nor would she admit that his powerful presence befuddled her senses more than a little bit.

He said, "I've some planning to do with Blake over at the supply tent. Why don't you join the women? I'll look for you later."

She nodded, then watched him go.

That evening, after meeting with Grace and a few of the others on what they might expect on the long journey ahead, a very weary Katherine made her way back to the tent. She took a moment to light the lantern, then admitted to being relieved at not finding Dix inside waiting. She wanted to be asleep when he returned. She'd had more than enough of his dark eyes and compelling presence for one day. In her mind all she needed was a good night's sleep to replenish her inner reserves. Once rested, she would be better able to fight off this unfathomable attraction to Dixon Wildhorse. Although she'd kept the thoughts buried most of the day, she still felt the sting of last night's failed challenge and could not believe how naive she'd been. Circumstances very rarely forced her to eat crow, but last night she'd eaten tons of it—feathers, beak, and all—because she hadn't known the first thing about being with a man.

Now she knew one did not toy with passion.

Katherine sat on one of the crates and dug into her carpetbag in an effort to find something suitable to wear to bed. But the only garments available were the transparent wrappers and gowns given to her by Miss Sunshine. Belatedly she realized that she should have added a nightgown to the items she'd purchased at the town store. Now it was too late because the store was more than likely closed until tomorrow. She would either have to choose one of the gowns or sleep in her clothes, and neither choice held much appeal.

Keeping an eye on the tent opening, she hastily removed her blouse and skirt then drew on one of the filmy black nightgowns over her camisole and drawers. The matching wrapper was trimmed with bouncy black feathers. She was on her knees struggling with the knots on the rope around the rolled up bedding when her husband strode in.

"Evening, Kate." Dix smiled inwardly at the sight of her turned-up hips.

Katherine met his gaze. She could see him taking in her attire. "I'm not trying to tempt you. It was either this or my clothes. I neglected to buy a nightgown at the store earlier."

"I understand," he replied, tempted by her just the same. "Do you need help with those knots?"

When she nodded, he came over and hunkered close. Too close. As he made short work of the knots and then unfurled the pallets, all Katherine could think about were his fiery kisses.

Dix looked over at her parted lips and said, "Thought you said you weren't trying to tempt me."

"I'm not. . . ."

"That's not what your mouth is saying. . . ."

Katherine blinked. Her heart began to pound and she stammered, "I . . . you're mistaken."

The topaz in his ear caught the light from the lantern, twinkling like the faint amusement in his eyes. "My apologies, then."

Katherine dragged the edges of the feathered wrapper closed and sat down on her pallet. It had become so warm inside the tent she longed for a fan so she could cool herself.

Relief came a few moments later when he doused the lantern and darkness settled over the interior. She could hear the rustle of clothing and assumed he was undressing. To keep her mind away from the heated images those thoughts conjured up, she slipped down beneath the blankets and tried to get comfortable. To her surprise, she felt her bedding—and herself with it—begin to slide across the grass. "What are you doing?" she asked.

"Bringing you closer. You'll need my body heat, and I'll need yours."

She sat up in the dark. "And suppose I wish to sleep over there."

"But you don't."

He's right, said a taunting voice in her head, but the independent woman inside wanted to take issue with his assumptive arrogance and argue. However, they were no more than a whisper apart; Katherine could sense his heartbeat as surely as she felt her own.

To both her dismay and delight, he reached out and softly rubbed his thumb over her bottom lip; then, while she sat there trembling, he leaned in and kissed her just faintly enough for her to experience the sweet warmth of his mouth before he withdrew.

"Go to sleep, Kate."

Once again struck dumb, she finally managed to whisper. "It's *Katherine*. . . ."

His soft chuckle floated on the silence, followed by the sounds and feels of him settling in beside her.

Having little mind for an argument now, Katherine settled in, too. She offered not a word of protest as he covered them both with a large blanket.

When Dix first awoke the next morning, the sun had yet to rise. The sight and feel of his sleeping wife cuddled into his side made for a pleasant surprise. She was lying facing him, her head on his chest and shoulder, her leg sprawled across his own. She appeared so peaceful he didn't rouse her—no man in his right mind would. Since the hour was still early, he moved her just a bit so he could get comfortable enough to return to sleep. The slight change in position made her snuggle closer. She settled down after a second or so, but her hand came to rest perilously close to a very dangerous part of his anatomy. His manhood rose as her body's heat penetrated his defenses while she slept on, oblivious to the havoc she'd set off. Were he a fancy back-East dandy, he'd be obligated to remove the hand as discreetly as possible, and in that way save the lady a severe case of the embarrassments. However, Dix operated only under the constraints imposed by guns and the law, so he left the hand, enjoyed the feel of it and closed his eyes to await morning.

Katherine awoke rested but still half asleep. She stretched like a feline, then nuzzled against the soft, firm warmth beneath her cheek, content to sleep a bit longer. Suddenly an alarm bell sounded in her head, making her open her eyes and survey her surroundings. She raised her head and looked straight into the mildly amused eyes of her husband. Stunned into paralysis she took stock of where she was. The "pillow" had been his chest, she realized, and her hand . . . ! Scandalized, she hastily moved away, dragged a blanket over herself, and sat up. Her back to him she said tightly, "I'm sorry."

"No need to apologize. You were asleep and comfortable."

Too comfortable, she thought to herself, appalled. *Entirely too comfortable.* Her heart was pounding. She doubted she'd ever be able to face him again.

He eased himself behind her, then gently turned her chin his way so he could look into her eyes. "Don't be embarrassed. Touching is a natural occurrence when you sleep with someone."

Katherine could not help her feelings. How in the world had she ended up sleeping so snug up against him in the first place? She knew he had the ability to set her senses to flaring while awake, but now it seemed as if he had the ability to affect her even in her sleep!

"I'm not going to lie to you and say I didn't enjoy it."

As far as Katherine was concerned, his amused tone did not help matters, and the feel of him so warm and strong behind her made it hard to think.

Dix slid his finger gently over her hairline. "I think I like waking up with you at my side . . ." His touch made her quiver responsively as he added, "It's too bad you're not ready."

Katherine had trouble deciding which held more potency, his lulling voice or his touch. "Ready for what . . . ?" she asked.

"The pleasure a husband can give his wife." With that, Dix brushed his lips across her ear, then backed away.

Katherine's eyes were closed as he withdrew. She wanted to deny his effect on her but could not. Who would have ever thought a man like him could rattle a woman like her. "I'm supposed to be meeting Grace this morning for my driving lessons."

He reached out and traced the soft skin behind her ear. "I'm not holding you here, am I?"

She thought his touch could hold a woman prisoner for a lifetime. Forcing herself to slide away from his tempting presence, Katherine stood and began to gather her clothes. Dix hadn't said a word, but he didn't have to. She could feel his eyes, boring into her back.

He finally said, "I'll head on over to Blake's so you'll have some privacy."

"Thank you," she managed to say.

He dressed without another word, smiled her way, then left her alone with her thoughts, her pounding heart, and her steadily growing attraction.

Chapter 7

❦

Katherine remembered Dix saying she would have little trouble learning to drive because she was a smart woman. Well, after concluding her first day behind the reins, she didn't feel very smart at all. Who'd've thought it would take such skill to get six horses to move in a direction that she wanted them to go? She and the other novices spent the entire day atop their wagons, coaxing, cursing, and pleading. There were more than a few collisions, a few tears and a lot of scolding from Jackson Blake.

By the end of the second day Katherine could at least get the team to head straight. But she still had trouble turning left and despaired over ever mastering the reins.

When she returned to the clearing after the third day's driving, her arms felt like lead, her back ached, and her neck and shoulders were on fire from the strain. Blake had cautioned her about doing too much so soon. He had advised she not try to match the accomplishments of the other women, because some had been behind the reins for over a week now and had built up the stamina necessary to command the six-horse teams.

Katherine hadn't listened.

Her muscles ached so fiercely that she could barely lift a spoon to feed herself dinner. Turning her head hurt. Raising her arms hurt. Walking hurt. Loreli, the woman who'd called out to her the first day in camp, now offered Katherine a tin of ointment she claimed would help relieve the stiffness and pain. Katherine graciously accepted the gift, took her dirty dishes to the clean-up area, then trudged back to the tent she shared with Dix.

He was inside, seated on the grass poring over some maps. He looked up when she entered. The concern in his eyes made her guess that she looked just as bad as she felt.

She told him emotionlessly, "Blake has already admonished me for pushing myself too hard, too soon, so I've no desire to hear it again from you."

Dix thought she looked like she'd been run all night and hung up wet.

After she collapsed onto her pallet, Katherine closed her eyes to the pain in her stinging limbs and confessed wearily, "Lord, I've never ached like this before in my life!"

Dix shook his head. He was finding she never did anything by half. She'd learn to drive or die trying. "You want me to get you something?"

"Yes, a tub large enough to swim in and a bed so filled with feathers, it floats."

"How about I take you down to the river instead?"

Katherine preferred a tub filled with hot water and soothing, aromatic bath salts, but she'd settle for the river if only so she could wash away the day's perspiration and grime. "It does sound appealing, but you'll have to bring the river to me. I couldn't walk there if someone paid me in gold."

And she couldn't. Having to handle the reins all day had left her with only the energy to breathe, nothing more. Her back and shoulders ached from just the thought of having to move. The next thing she knew, she was up in Dix's arms. Stunned, she looked into his dark face and asked the same question she'd asked the first time this happened: "What are you doing?"

"Taking you down to the river. You said you wanted to go, didn't you?"

"Well, yes. . . ." Katherine was not accustomed to being carried around. She was taller than most women she encountered and knew few men able to pick her up this way. Dix seemed to have no trouble; in fact, he lifted her as effortlessly as if she were tiny as Grace.

Dix spoke to the wonder he could see in her eyes. "Problems?"

"I'm not accustomed to being handled this way."

"About time you started, don't you think?"

She had no idea how to respond to that, so she didn't.

On the way out of the tent he lowered her so she could grab her night things and toiletries, then headed them toward the river.

They passed no one from the camp. It had been a sweltering May day, but now the cool night air blew gently across Katherine's hot and tired frame. She tried to ride stiffly in his arms to avoid contact with his sculpted chest, but that position hurt her already aching back and neck, so relaxing against him became a grudgingly admitted necessity.

When Dix felt her go soft in his arms, he smiled inwardly at her small surrender.

At the river's edge he set her on her feet, then took a moment to assess the surroundings. He neither heard nor saw anything that might disturb her nocturnal bath and so told her, "I'll be up there on the bank so you can have some privacy. If you need me, just holler."

Katherine, being a city girl, had never washed in a

river before. Since arriving at the camp she'd been using the crude showering facilities set back from the church grounds. She peered around, wondering if she should be concerned about animals or snakes scurrying about in the dark brush, then decided she was too damned tired to care.

Undressing took a frustratingly long amount of time due to the lack of dexterity in her stiff hands and fingers. Undoing the small buttons on her shirtwaist and the ones on the waistband of her black skirt were such a chore, she sighed with pleasure when she was done. She thought about Dix standing somewhere in the dark, watching. Under normal circumstances, modesty would have prevented her from taking off her clothes and washing in a river, but not tonight. Tonight, she didn't care if the world watched as she stripped down to her camisole and lacy drawers. All she wanted was to slip into the lulling arms of the water and let it soothe her weary bones.

Up on the bank, Dix's position offered him a good view of the surrounding terrain and anyone who might be approaching. It also afforded him an unhurried view of his new wife as she stepped out of the brush and walked down to the river's edge. Her attire surprised him into a grin. He ran his eyes over the curve of her shoulders and the curve of her lacy behind. *My, my*. She was tall, lush, and graceful. He remembered the night back at Miss Sunshine's and Katherine's ill-fated attempt at challenging him for her freedom. Her kisses had been virginal yet responsive, shy, yet fiery. That first, sweet taste hadn't been enough, he would admit. Not nearly enough.

As she slowly waded in, Dix took a cigar from his pocket and lit it. As he shook the match out, he heard her scream, "This water is freezing!"

"It's a river, woman!"

"I know it's a river, but we're not in the Yukon!"

It was too late for Katherine to dash back to the shore because she was certain she'd already been frozen alive.

She could hear Dix coming down the bank behind her, saying, "The faster you wash, the faster you can get warm again."

That made sense, so Katherine washed herself quickly with the rough lye soap, then came ashore. She was a mass of shivers until he wrapped her in the large flannel drying sheet she'd brought along; then he lifted her up into his arms again. Without a word he headed back to the tent.

On the way he asked, "Never had a man carry you?"

She shook her head. "No."

Once they returned to the tent, he set her on her feet, saying, "You should dry off, then get to bed. How do you feel?"

"I'm still thawing," she replied from within the damp confines of the sheet.

"The cold is good for you."

"Says whom? Why didn't you tell me it would be freezing?"

"You wouldn't've gone in."

"Probably true," she admitted.

She collapsed into a sitting position on the grass. The stiffness in her body had relaxed somewhat after her icy dip, but she still found it hard to move around with ease.

She looked up at him towering above her and said, "In the pocket of my skirt is a tin that Loreli gave me this evening. Would you see if it's still there?"

He found it and handed it to her, asking, "What's it for?"

Katherine managed to pry it open. The salve was clear

and smelled of violets. "She says it helps ease aches and pains. I'll put it on after I dry off."

Dix tried hard not to be tempted by the damp sheet clinging to her curves but failed. The outline of her nipples, still tight from the cold river, made him force his eyes back to her face. "Picked up something in town this morning for you."

Mildly surprised, Katherine watched him extract a folded garment from his war bag, which he handed to her. Two nightgowns, she discovered as she unfolded them. The cotton was thin and fine. One had long sleeves, the other none. There was just enough lace for Katherine's liking.

He explained, "One for hot nights, one for cold."

"Thank you," she said, touched by his care for her. "They're just what I need."

"You're welcome." He then added, "I'll leave you until later, then. Blake and I have maps and supply lists to do."

Katherine studied his unreadable face. For the past few nights he hadn't come back to the tent until long after she'd fallen asleep. When she awoke in the morning, she found him already up and gone to tend to the details pertaining to his job as scout. Initially she'd been concerned about sleeping in the tent with him, but so far his absences made the concerns unnecessary. She wasn't certain how she felt about that. "Have you been staying away nights deliberately?"

Dix didn't lie. "Yes."

"Why?"

"I want you to settle in first. Get comfortable." Absence also made the heart fonder, he knew. He wanted her to miss him a bit.

She found his consideration warming. "Thank you."

"You're welcome," he replied sincerely. "I'll be back later tongiht."

During the days that followed, Dix suggested that she attend the lectures Blake conducted each evening on subjects pertaining to their journey. Katherine and the others received lessons in such things as first aid, harness mending, and smokeless cooking fires. They practiced tying down canvas in wind storms, skinning rabbits—a task Katherine absolutely hated—and compass reading. She found the lectures informative and noted that Jackson Blake never laughed at any of the questions the women raised, no matter how asinine the questions seemed.

Katherine genuinely liked the women. They'd come from all over the East and South to journey to Kansas with Grace, and they welcomed her into their circle as if she were one of the brides. All were seemingly optimistic and eagerly looking forward to meeting the husbands they'd selected from Grace's portfolios of sketched portraits.

In spite of Blake's grumbling, Katherine liked Grace, as well. Katherine had never leaned toward friendships with diminutive women because they always made her feel like an awkward, gawky giantess. But Grace, with her uncommonly beautiful face, her full head of rich red hair, and her delicate stature was someone Katherine hoped to call friend before the journey ended. Grace was smart, witty, and very willing to take on Jackson Blake when no one else would. The previous night at dinner, Grace had approached him on behalf of one of the newly arrived brides who'd insisted upon bringing her piano along on the trip. Blake had denied the request because of the lack of space, the lack of men strong enough to lift the piano into the wagon, and the unnecessary strain the added weight would place upon the wagon's team. Grace had ceded him those points, but cited the piano owner's desire to bring culture to her new Kansas home and how relaxing the music would be on the lonely plains after a long day of traveling. Blake refused to bend. Grace had argued further, but to no avail. The piano would have to be left behind. Grace had put up an admirable fight even though she'd lost the war.

Katherine was losing a war, too—the war to remain unmoved by the presence of her husband. Dix spent most of the daylight hours seeing to the business of scouting: plotting maps, picking up last minute supplies, and wiring ahead to order perishables and fresh horses from some of the towns their wagons would be traveling through. At night he still came in after she was asleep, but now he would awaken her softly to let her know of his return, then send her back to sleep with a brush of his hand across her cheek. In the morning he would be gone before she awoke, but his whispering presence lingered throughout the day.

Yesterday he'd left wildflowers on her bed for her to discover at the end of yet another muscle-tiring day. She had been touched by his sentiment and planned to wait up for him to say thanks. Instead, she'd fallen asleep, fully dressed, the flowers still clutched in her hand.

When she woke that morning, the flowers were in a canning jar filled with water and sitting atop the crate near her pallet. The sight of them made her smile.

After getting dressed, Katherine had a quick cup of coffee and a biscuit, then went in search of her husband. She wanted to thank him personally for the flowers. She asked around. No one had seen him. She tried the supply tent. No Dix. She checked the animal areas. No Dix. She stuck her head inside the tent Grace used as an office and stood paralyzed by the sight of Jackson Blake kissing Grace Atwood like there would be no tomorrow. Stunned, she backed out as quietly as she could and went on. Grace and Blake! She had been under the impression that the two were like oil and water. Katherine supposed stranger matches had been made—she had only to look at herself and Dix—but Grace and Blake?! Shaking herself, she gave up on looking for Dix to do her chores. She told herself she wasn't disappointed at not being able to find him, but she knew it was a lie.

Katherine was due for laundry detail. The sun wouldn't reach its zenith for another five hours, so early day was the best time to get the washing done.

By noon the sun was hot, and Katherine and the others were drenched with sweat. In addition to washing the clothes of the women in the camp, they also took in laundry for pay from the nearby townspeople. The service helped Grace defray some of the costs of renting the camp's land from the church, and it put a bit of extra coin in the pockets of those women who needed it. The bulk of the washing was done by two that afternoon. The only item that remained was a large bed sheet. Katherine, in the midst of carrying it to the clothesline, looked across the camp and saw her husband mounted on a beautiful black horse. His eyes held hers with such intensity, she forgot where she was and what she was doing. The newly washed sheet slipped from her hands and dropped unnoticed into the mud, drawing groans from her fellow washwomen. Hearing them brought Katherine around. Her eyes widened at the sight of the sheet, and she scrambled to pick it up.

By then, Dix had wheeled his horse around and headed off toward the supply tent. Loreli Winters, having witnessed the whole thing, said to Katherine, ''Don't worry about it, Katherine. Each of us is hoping the men we've chosen will make us drop our laundry with just a look, too.''

Everyone laughingly agreed. Katherine smiled as she hauled the sheet back to the wash tub, but she wanted to box Dix's ears for being able to affect her so effortlessly. She spent the rest of the day thinking about him while doing her other assigned chores. They'd been in camp almost a week now, and as Dix had predicted, her muscles and joints were now at home with the unladylike work so necessary to the readying of a wagon train. But Katherine didn't feel any less feminine. The strength she'd acquired made her proud and helped restore her former self-confidence.

Dinner was, indeed, a community affair. The women took turns cooking, and the meal was eaten at two long trestle tables that were set up each night. As they took their seats, Katherine had to endure more good-natured ribbing for having dropped the sheet in the mud. She could only smile in reply. All thirty-five of the women Grace had chosen as brides were now in camp. Katherine rather enjoyed the camaraderie. She hadn't shared such lively female company since her Aunt Ceil died five years ago. Thinking of her aunt naturally brought on thoughts of her mother, Jenny. Katherine unconsciously touched her fingers to the small topaz amulet given to her by her mother. In spite of the complications it might cause with Dix, she'd taken to wearing it regularly again because the weight of it around her neck had become so familiar over the years, she felt a bit bare without it. Katherine was certain both her mother and Aunt Ceil would've applauded these women for their courage and spirit. And while what their opinions on Dix would've been was anyone's guess, Katherine was pretty sure Aunt Ceil would have fainted dead away at such an overpowering man.

The women making up the wagon train weren't fainting over him, however. In fact, more than a few had congratulated her on her choice of husband. Katherine thanked them, despite the reality that she didn't know him as well as a true wife should, but she was beginning to believe she wanted to.

Dix and Blake rarely joined the women for meals, preferring each other's male company. Katherine didn't mind. The men were old friends, and there was much to discuss before the wagon train headed west. Tonight, however, Katherine found Dix in the tent still huddled over his charts. She knew he hadn't eaten because the cooking crew had told her so, and she brought him a tray.

He looked up slowly. If the sight of the tray in her hands surprised him, he didn't let on.

"Would you like something to eat?" she asked.

"Yes. Thank you."

Katherine could feel his presence washing over her like a warm glow as she handed him the tray. He set it beside him on one of the crates.

Keeping her tone light, she said, "Thank you for the flowers."

"You're welcome."

"I *don't* thank you for making me drop that sheet into the mud this afternoon." Just recalling how potent his eyes had been made her dizzy all over again.

A hint of amusement came to life in his eyes. "Me?"

"You, Dixon Wildhorse."

"No idea what you're talking about."

"Oh, really?"

"No. Men don't hold any power over women. You said so yourself."

She never thought those words would come back to haunt her. She scrambled for footing. "All I'm saying is you surprised me. That's why I dropped the sheet.''

''Ah, that explains it.''

Katherine couldn't hide her grin.

Dix decided he liked seeing her smile. She'd done it so rarely in the beginning that he had tended to doubt she knew how. Granted, she hadn't had much to smile about recently, but she now seemed more accepting.

While he ate, she sat down on the opposite side of the tent, hoping she wouldn't disturb him. From the pocket of her skirt she took a quill pen, a small bottle of ink, and some paper given to her by Grace.

''What are you writing?'' he asked.

''Grace asked me to chronicle the journey. She thinks it might be helpful to future generations.''

''Future generations? Blake's hellion is a big thinker.''

''That she is, and I admire her.''

Katherine began her account by listing the women's names and their places of birth. After the day's chores, she'd begun the process of interviewing everyone. She'd hastily scrawled each woman's information on a piece of paper and now faced the task of copying her notes into a form that could be read. ''How's the food?''

''Not bad. Can you cook?''

Katherine looked over at him. She wondered if he wanted the truth or would be content with a vague sort of answer. She remembered he enjoyed her plain speech, so in plain speech she told him, ''No, I can't.''

She saw the look in his black eyes and became defensive. ''At least I'm telling you the truth now.''

A fleeting smile lifted his mustache. ''I can cook. We won't starve.''

Katherine thought that good. She couldn't bake an edible loaf of bread if her life were hanging in the balance.

When she glanced up again a few minutes later, she found herself under his scrutiny.

She asked quietly, "Something wrong?"

"You're not what I expected, Katherine."

She held his eyes. "What were you expecting?"

"Meek and biddable."

She laughed. "I'm neither."

"No, you're not."

"I'm going to take that as a compliment, you know."

"I'm beginning to think maybe you should. Yes."

"Even though I can't cook?"

"Even though you can't cook."

She met his smile with one of her own. "What's Indian Territory like?"

"Wild and wooly."

"Will I like it?"

He shrugged. "We'll be living outside a town called Wewoka. It's the governmental seat for the Seminoles."

"So are you African or Indian?"

"My ancestors were fugitive slaves. They and many other Blacks, both fugitive and free, lived with the Seminole when the Spanish owned Florida. When the U.S. Government forced the Seminoles to cede their lands and move to Indian Territory, the Black Seminoles moved, too. At one time the government recognized us as Negro Indians; now, they don't care what any of the Five Civilized Tribes call themselves as long as we let them retake the Territory and open it up to the settlers."

"Who are the Five Civilized Tribes?"

"The Creek, Cherokee, Choctaw, Chickasaw, and Seminole."

"Do any of the other tribes have Blacks?"

"Through either slavery or intermarriage, African blood runs in a good portion of nearly all the tribes."

Katherine knew about the terrible removal forced

upon the nation's native peoples before the Civil War, but it never occurred to her that members of the race had been removed with them.

"The history of the Black Seminole is rich," Dix told her solemnly. "Maybe someday someone will write our story for future generations."

Katherine opened her mouth to volunteer, but he had returned his attention to his maps. She assumed that meant the discussion was over, but his words made her curious about him as a man. How much of him was Black and how much Seminole, or could the two be even separated? Did he have parents, siblings? How long had he been a lawman, and what had propelled him to take up the star? Katherine had always possessed a healthy curiosity about people. She supposed that was why she'd chosen journalism as a profession: It afforded her opportunities to satisfy that curiosity. She'd known Dix long enough to know he only gave answers when he cared to, and getting his story would be akin to pulling teeth. As she went back to her notes on the brides, she wondered if Grace had any pliers packed away in the stores.

The next day Grace called a morning meeting to inform everyone that the scheduled departure date would be in two days' time. Blake felt confident that the women were now sufficiently trained and ready to handle the long trek to Kansas. Upon hearing the long-anticipated good news, the women let loose a shout of joy that filled the clearing.

That afternoon they began loading the wagons. Katherine joined Dix to inspect the prairie schooner they would be traveling in. The schooners were a version of the Conestoga wagons used for hauling freight before the advent of the railroads. Unlike the Conestoga, which had a curved bed to keep freight from sliding during transport, the schooner had a flat bed and lower sides.

As they toured the outside of the vehicle, Dix asked Katherine, "Are you familiar with Hiram Walker?"

Katherine shook her head.

"Thought you were a newspaperwoman."

She gave him a mock warning look, and Dix's eyes danced in response.

"Hiram Walker was a Black man who lived in Independence, Missouri," he explained. "Back in the days before the railroad, he built many of the Conestogas that the homesteaders used to open the West. Old-timers say he employed fifty men, had twenty-five forges in his smithy, and was known as the best wagon builder around."

Katherine was impressed. "You surprise me, Marshal."

"Why?"

"You're not what I expected."

It was a rehash of their previous conversation. A smiling Dix asked, "No?"

"No," she confessed softly.

"What were you expecting?"

"All brawn and no brain."

He grinned. "That's plain spoken enough. Do I take that as a compliment?"

"I think you should, yes."

"Then I shall. . . ."

His voice touched her like a hand.

Katherine could feel herself becoming dizzy, so she walked up the ramp leading into the back of the schooner, hoping she could collect herself. Once inside she peered around. Even though she and Dix were not going to fill their wagon with sideboards, bedposts, and the other household items the brides were traveling with, there would not be a lot of room.

Dix seemed to have read her mind. "It's going to be even smaller in here after we add the gear."

By gear she knew he meant food, extra harnesses, wheels, and the like.

He stood, arms folded, watching her. "You and I won't be able to have many secrets."

She understood that. After sharing the tent with him, she'd grown less apprehensive about where this journey would lead them as man and wife. Since the night of her ill-fated challenge, the subject of his husbandly rights had not been raised, making her wonder when or whether it would be.

She stated, "I think we should christen our schooner the Hiram Walker."

"Folks don't name schooners."

"Why not? Is there some western law forbidding it?"

"No."

"Then I christen this schooner the Hiram Walker. May he sail well."

Dix, his arms still folded, met her eyes, then shook his head with amusement.

The women worked late into the night loading their possessions. Katherine, taking her job as chronicler very seriously, walked the grounds in search of items to add to the journal. Tonight she wanted to smell the excitement and feel the anticipation so that she could express it in the journal's opening pages. She was certain Geoff would want his agents and subscribers to read about this unique journey. She planned on wiring him the first few stories once she thought it safe to do so. Thinking about Geoff made her wonder if Rupert was still searching for her. She hoped he hadn't gone to Miss Sunshine's establishment and caused trouble. She also hoped Miss Sunshine had contacted Geoff, because if she hadn't, her editor friend was undoubtedly worried sick over her whereabouts by now.

As Katherine walked past the numerous campfires, she saw women loading grandfather clocks and dressers, sewing machines and wash tubs, mirrors and cooking pots. She stopped to help one woman lash her water barrels to the side of her wagon. Jackson Blake, their ever-present inspector, came over to make sure the ropes had been done tightly enough and in the end Katherine and the bride were forced to tie the barrels to the wagon again, this time tighter.

Prairie schooners were named such because their big white-canvas covers resembled the sails of a schooner. Blake found more than a few canvases improperly tied, so he made the owners redo them, as well. The women, by now well accustomed to Blake's sometimes brisk manner, redid the tasks without complaint. Everyone knew the sooner they all passed Blake's exhaustive inspection, the sooner they could head for Kansas.

Many parents and other relatives had come along with the brides, but Grace had forbidden them to camp with the women. She thought it important that the women learn to work as one because they would only have each other to depend upon during the journey. To Grace's way of thinking, having relatives around and underfoot would make the cohesiveness of the group that much harder to achieve. Some of the relatives hadn't liked the idea one bit, but Grace had firmly and politely stuck to her guns.

Now that the departure date had been announced, these relatives were free to enter the camp so that everyone could say their good-byes. Over by the church, Katherine met the family of a bride by the name of Belle

Carson. Belle introduced her father, a preacher, and her mother, whose only response to meeting Katherine was a stiff nod. Belle was not one of the women Katherine knew well. She was one of the youngest women in camp and kept to herself during the free times, preferring to read her Bible to the company of the women. Belle and Loreli Winters were to share a wagon.

Belle's parents looked on disapprovingly as she and Loreli loaded Belle's goods into the wagon. Katherine gave Loreli a pointed look, questioning the tension surrounding the wagon. Loreli gave her a shrug in response and kept loading.

Belle's mother asked Katherine, "And why are you going along, Mrs. Wildhorse? Are you a widow?"

"No. My husband is the scout for our journey."

"Then you have no choice."

"No, ma'am. I don't."

Belle's father interjected in a bitter voice, "But Belle does. She's going gallivanting across the country to a man she ain't never met, for no reason."

Belle heard his opinion as she came down the ramp that led from the wagon to the ground and said, "No disrespect intended, Papa, but why did you come all this way just to complain? I've already made up my mind. I'm going to Kansas."

Her father turned to her mother. "Had you raised her right, she'd be listening. You and that damn sister of yours. If she hadn't left Belle that money when she died, none of this would be happening!"

The mother snapped, "Someone had to leave Belle money. You certainly don't have any to give her—or me!"

Poor Belle looked stoic and determined as she transferred crates from the bed of her father's flatbed wagon to the bed of her own schooner. Katherine helped her and Loreli carry a few more items into their wagon, then excused herself and moved on.

There were other families who came to see their brides off, and most seemed happier about the journey than Belle's folks. Katherine saw mothers and fathers embracing their daughters with tears of sadness in their eyes. She sensed some would not see their daughters again for some time, if ever.

By the time Katherine returned to her tent she had more than enough details to flesh out the beginning of her journal's journey.

Tonight, 35 women of the race prepare to embark upon a unique journey. They're bound for Kansas—not as Ex-odusters fleeing the madness in the South, but to become brides to men they have only seen sketched in a portrait. Some of their families are distraught over the idea of their beloved daughters and sisters traveling the vast plains alone to marry men they've never met, but the women are determined and resolute in their desire to go. There are only two men on this journey, the wagon master and the guide. While these men predict the journey would test the courage of even the strongest man, they are confident the women will succeed.

Your agent,
Brother K. Love

Katherine disliked the idea of having to pose as a man in order to be credible, but the times and narrow minds forced her to don the masquerade. The great newspaperwoman Mary Shadd, an abolitionist and the first Black woman in North America to edit her own newspaper, had initially posed as a man when writing. She feared the men of the abolitionist movement would not take her fiery, thought-provoking editorials seriously if she revealed her true gender. Katherine and her editor, Geoff, feared the same thing, so until more women were allowed to openly wear the mantle of newspaperwoman, she would continue to be *Brother* K. Love.

In reality, she didn't mind so much in this instance because the masquerade served another purpose. Rupert Samuels knew she worked for a newspaper, but he would never connect Brother K. Love to Mrs. Katherine Lane Wildhorse.

Chapter 8

Dix spent the entire day chasing after a mattress for Katherine. The ideal choice had to be small enough to fit comfortably inside the prairie schooner christened Hiram, and soft enough to ensure that Katherine didn't arrive in Kansas covered with bruises. She was a city girl, so she had no idea how sore one could become sleeping on a bedroll on the hard bed of a wagon for forty-five days or more. Why he was scouring the countryside for something so frivolous when there were a million and a half more important things to do was a question he couldn't answer. In a way it was like the flowers. He had never brought flowers to a woman before in his life, so it was still a mystery to him as to why he got them for Katherine. When he had come in the other night and found her fully dressed and asleep atop her bedroll, the sight of the flowers clutched in her hands had given him pause. He had gently pried them loose from her fist, then found a jar for them in the supply tent. After setting the jar beside her, he'd sat atop his own bedroll and simply watched her sleep. He remembered wondering if she knew she snored. Probably not, he told himself with a smile.

Dix hauled the mattress inside Hiram and set it upright against some crates. Tomorrow they would put it in its permanent spot. As he looked around at what would be their home for the next month or so, his thoughts returned to the woman who'd been taking up a lot of his thinking lately. In the two and a half weeks that they had been married she'd impressed him with her grit and determination. She and many of the other women had not done much manual labor prior to joining the camp, but he'd watched them all learn to chop wood, haul harnesses, and muck out the makeshift corral. They learned to command four- and-six horse teams, shoe mules, and right an overturned wagon. A few of the women hadn't been up to the physical demands necessary and had turned tail and run, thus forcing Grace to seek replacements, but Katherine, like most of the others, had held on. She'd shouldered the muscle aches, Blake's yelling, and the sun-up-to-sun-down chores—all without a peep. He had thought she would cut and run for sure during the rabbit skinning lesson, but under his guidance she'd swallowed her distaste and plunged right at it. Had he not known otherwise, he'd swear she had the blood of the Black Seminole in her veins. Even though this marriage had turned her world topsy-turvy, she'd spent little time moping or stomping around in anger. Only a fool would believe she'd come to embrace the situation fully, but she appeared to be looking forward, not back, and Dix viewed that as a positive step.

However, he hadn't taken any positive steps toward wooing her into his bed, Dix thought as he left the wagon and headed for their tent. Of course, that did not mean he didn't desire her; he did. Lord knew he did. Just the thought of finally being able to unveil her tall, lush beauty and teach her passion had been keeping him up nights. His male needs notwithstanding, though, he knew better than to equate desire with love. Dix had no intention of letting his emotions enter into this relationship with the reluctant Mrs. Wildhorse. While he loved the vast and oftentimes harsh beauty of the Territory, there was no guarantee she would. He was almost willing to bet she'd hightail it back East as soon as a child was born, and as long as he maintained his emotional distance, there'd be no chance of her taking his broken heart along on the ride.

Eventually, though, the two of them would have to come together as husband and wife in order to have the child. As determined as Dix was not to let his emotions come into play, he was equally as determined that the child be conceived in fire and passion, not obligation and duty. The child's spirit deserved to be created with intensity, fervor, and mutual respect. Katherine Wildhorse was a wellspring of passion, and he planned on tapping that spring gently and slowly until it flowed sweet and free.

Had Katherine been informed that she was about to be slowly seduced until she flowed sweet and free, she would have said, "Hogwash!" For the most part, Dix had been a gentleman. There'd been no talk of "slow hands," "passion planting," or the parts between kissing and cleaving, and because there hadn't, she was content. She'd gone from being angry, shocked, and overwhelmed by the whirlwind events of the past several weeks to accepting his presence, mainly because he'd been considerate, solicitous, and undemanding since their arrival.

Katherine set the inked pages to dry atop one of the many crates stacked around her, then prepared for bed. This would be the last night they'd sleep in the tent. The camp would be dismantled come tomorrow and by the time they reached Kansas, she supposed this little tent would seem like a palace when compared to the cramped interior of the Hiram Walker.

Katherine quickly undressed and donned her nightgown. It was June first, and the month had come in hot and muggy. The humidity had been building steadily for the last four or five days, making everyone wish for a good hard rain. The wish for rain was a double-edged sword, however; yes, everyone wanted the weather to break, but no one wished to begin the journey to Kansas hip deep in mud and soaked to the skin.

The thin cotton of Katherine's sleeveless gown let her take advantage of what breeze there was, but the humidity still pressed down like a hand. She unhooked her gown to her waist and fanned herself with one of the folded maps she found lying on a crate on Dix's side of the tent. With her back to the tent's opening, she fanned and fanned. The effort brought only minimal relief, but mentally she felt better.

Still fanning herself, Katherine turned. The sight of Dix standing so tall and silent in the tent's opening made her hand slow to a stop. She was so mesmerized, she forgot about her open gown until his gaze lowered and lingered. Her sanity seemed to return all at once and she spun around to right her clothing; her fingers clumsy in their attempts to redo the hooks.

Her gown finally closed, an overwhelmed Katherine turned back. When her eyes met his, that same sweet trepidation began to rise. His big body filled the tent as always, and as always she had to admit he was the most magnificent man she'd ever encountered. With the polished topaz twinkling in his ear, he looked more like a buccaneer than an officer of the law. For reasons unknown, the sight of him as he'd appeared that night at Miss Sunshine's came to mind. He'd worn his nudity proudly, unabashedly. She had no inkling how Frank and Joe had viewed his surprising lack of attire, but at the time, it had thrown her for a loop. Thinking about it now made her decide to think about something else. It couldn't be very ladylike to admit the view of him had been burned into her memory like a brand.

To break the thickening silence—and his hold upon her senses—she said inanely, "I finished my first piece of the story. I'm going to wire it off to Geoff when I get the chance."

She was babbling; she knew it, she was certain that he did, too.

"You're a little warm, I take it."

The huskily voiced question added to the heat around Katherine. She could only nod. His eyes were so potent, she still felt as if she were partially unclothed.

Dix could feel the blood throbbing in his manhood in response to her surprising welcome home. His discipline aside, he wanted to ease her gown open once more and pay passionate tribute to the twin beauties she'd displayed so provocatively. The slim silver chain hanging around her neck was one he'd never seen her wear before. Using his curiosity as an excuse to move closer, he crossed the short distance to where she stood.

Katherine trembled in response when he stopped before her. She did not know what to expect, certainly not the feel of his dark finger sliding gently over the chain around her neck. The fiery contact made her eyes close for a breath of a moment.

Without asking her permission, he gently raised the chain to see what it held. Katherine knew this would be another turning point. She had wanted to keep her secret a bit longer, but she couldn't move. She was a prisoner to the charged air, his eyes, and the feel of the small gemstone sliding over her skin as he raised it from within her gown.

He held it against his fingers and looked at it for a long time. "Topaz," he stated quietly.

She nodded slowly. "My mother gave it to me when she died."

Katherine thought she saw him smile knowingly for just the briefest moment, but she had little time to puzzle over the matter because the feel of his sure hands slowly undoing the top hook of her gown made everything around her go fuzzy. The second one he freed left her breathless. By the time he'd released the third hook she had trouble standing, especially when he replaced the amulet against her skin, then pressed his lips to the spot where it lay between her breasts. While she fought to breathe, he looked up into her eyes. "Why haven't you worn this before?

Filled with a rising heat, she couldn't lie. "I . . . didn't want you to think the stones connected us."

"Why not?" he asked.

"Because . . . when I've met my obligation to you, I wish to return to my life." Katherine wondered if a woman could be set afire by the heat in a man's eyes.

"Once I make you my wife, you may not wish to go. . . ."

The words pulsed within her, strong as a heartbeat. "Such arrogance can't be healthy."

He leaned down and kissed her. "Such a mouth has to be kissed. . . ."

His lips were warm as he slid them over her own. She kissed him back without a thought, mimicking the movements of his expertise until the embers of desire made her senses flare to life. In reaction, he gathered her in close, then ran a hand up to the back of her neck, deepening the enchantment. He murmured against her parted lips, "Maybe leaving is not really what you'll want,

Kate. Maybe, you'll stick around, just so I can do this. . . .''

His hands opened her gown to her waist. Her sharp intake of breath turned into a croon as his lips captured her breast. He feasted slowly and leisurely. When he transferred his attention to the other nipple, it was already ripe as a spring bud.

By the time he withdrew, Katherine was so dazzled, she couldn't recall her name. He, on the other hand, looked entirely too pleased. He gave her one last kiss that melted her like ice cream in the summertime, then refastened her gown. "Just thought I'd give you something to think about.''

As she stood there pulsing and breathless, he picked up his bedroll and silently left the tent.

Outside in the night air, Dix fought to keep himself from turning around and walking back inside. It was one of the hardest things he'd ever had to do in his life. By his estimation, Katherine was ready—very ready—and so was he, but back at Miss Sunshine's, his independent wife had declared herself immune to the heat of passion. If he recalled her words correctly, she'd said some women were simply weaker than others. Well, in a few more days, he promised himself, she'd be weak enough to initiate into the age-old games of sensual pleasures; but not tonight. He wanted her to simmer a bit, ripen a bit more until her inner passion took hold. Only then would she enter the marriage bed ready and unafraid. But the remembered sight and taste of her beautiful body were playing havoc with his discipline. He was hard as rock, and if he went back into that tent tonight, she was going to have her hands full, which was why he needed someplace else to sleep. The topaz amulet had been a surprising discovery. In the old days the knowledge that they wore kindred stones might have been interpreted as a sign of the rightness of their marriage, a joining brought about by the spirits. Right here and right now, joining was all Dix could think about.

In the end though, his need to find an alternative place to bunk was put aside as thunder rumbled up above and the skies opened up. The rain came down in buckets and his first priority became the animals over in the camp's corral. As the lightning and thunder cracked around him, he ran to the enclosure and found Blake, Grace, and some of the women already at work. While Blake shouted instructions over the rising winds, the women led the terrified animals into the camp's small makeshift stable. It was really nothing more than a lean-to, but it would give the animals shelter and cut some of the storm's fury.

When that task was done, everyone hastened back to their tents. Dix had no place else to go except back to his own. By the time he returned, he was soaked through to the skin and so was his bedroll.

His sudden entrance took Katherine by surprise. She sat up on her pallet as a flash of lightning eerily illuminated him against the night. Seconds later, thunder answered with a ground-rattling roar.

"I didn't think you were coming back," she told him. She wouldn't say it aloud, but she was glad he had returned. Katherine was deathly afraid of storms. At the age of nine she and her then best friend, Linda Hill, had been caught in a sudden storm on the way home from school. They ran beneath a tree. Lightning struck. The girls, standing no more than a foot apart were knocked out by the bolt's force. Linda never woke up and was buried the next day. Over time, Katherine recovered from the death of her friend, but a fear of storms took root. Now that she'd matured, she could control the anxiety a bit better, but only if she were indoors. Being within the thin, fragile walls of the tent did not help.

As she looked over at Dix stripping away his wet shirt, she realized she was hugging her knees and rocking slowly. The movement helped her keep a grip on herself as the storm continued to unleash its fury. A bolt of lightning struck so near, the force buffeted the tent. Katherine bit down on her bottom lip to keep from letting loose a scream.

Dix could see the terror on her face as the particularly brilliant flash lit the interior. "What's wrong?"

"I'm scared of storms," she offered simply.

He came over and sat behind her, saying quietly, "Sometimes a fear can be ridden if it's shared. How about I just hold you a minute?"

"Yes, that would help," she whispered.

Dix had never seen dignified terror before, but that was how she appeared—terrified yet determined to keep the fear from being seen. He eased her atop his lap, settled her in against his chest, and wrapped her in his arms as if she were the most precious woman in the world. He pressed his lips to her brow and whispered, "If you want to scream, go ahead and scream. If you want to jump when the thunder answers the lightning's call, go ahead. There is no shame in it, *chica*. . . ."

Katherine exhaled a ragged breath, glad for his understanding. "I am fearless in every aspect of life except this one. I hate not being able to handle myself better."

"It's all right."

"No, it isn't."

The tent began to leak under the deluge. To keep them from being soaked, Dix grabbed a tarp from one of the crates and covered them fully.

Katherine felt like a moth in a cocoon as she snuggled against his bare chest. She could hear his heartbeat. She wondered if this is what it meant to be married, being able to have someone help you along when the fears became too large. He hadn't taunted her or found any humor in her distress; he'd simply come to her and offered her help that was both unconditional and nonjudgmental. She could learn to like this man, she mused.

Dix held her close. He could feel her stiffen each time the lightning struck, then relax until the next strike.

The storm raged on. The wind ripped out one of the tent's anchoring poles and the interior became an eddying rush of wind and rain. Dix burrowed deeper beneath the voluminous tarp, and whispered against her ear, "It's just the tent pole. We're going to get a little wetter is all."

Katherine very much wanted to scream, but she refused to shame herself. Instead she bit down onto her lip until she could taste the coppery taste of blood. She prayed the storm would end soon.

In answer to her plea, the thunder's rumbling soon became fainter, less forceful, indicating it had passed on.

Dix threw back the tarp and looked down at the woman in his arms. "Are you okay?"

Katherine, suddenly ashamed of her frailty, wouldn't meet his eyes.

He reached out and gently lifted her chin so their gazes could meet. "There's nothing to be ashamed of, Katherine, not with me. . . ."

"A grown woman shouldn't be afraid of storms."

"But you are. It isn't something you asked for, is it?"

"No."

"Then your fear makes you human like the rest of us."

He was correct, she knew, but she still had little patience with her anxiety. His kindness had been a blessing, however. With all the sincerity she felt, Katherine told him softly, "Thank you."

"What for?"

"For your . . . understanding."

"Any excuse to hold you in my arms, Kate."

Before she could determine if he'd been teasing or serious, he patted her on the behind. "Up with you; snuggling time is over. Let's see how much damage we took."

No one got much sleep for the rest of the night. Katherine, wearing one of Dix's shirts over her nightgown, pulled on her brogans and slogged through the mud to the main encampment. Because the camp had been pitched in a valley, the swirling winds had toppled tents and snapped off trees like matchsticks. Luckily the wagons had been partially packed. The weight inside the beds enabled them to weather the storm without sustaining much damage. A few canvases were ripped loose, but nothing that couldn't be remedied before the departure scheduled for the next day. As long as the rains didn't return, there would be ample time to get everybody and everything dried out.

They finally slept, but because of the water and mud, they were forced to do so on the floor of the church. Out of respect for the ladies, Dix and Blake bunked in another part of the church.

Before leaving, Dix made certain Katherine was comfortable on the dry bedroll he'd taken from their wagon's stores. Hunkering down beside his muddy-faced little safe robber, he kissed her softly on the lips. "See you in the morning, Kate."

The kiss filled her with such sweetness that by the time she realized he'd called her Kate yet again, he was already gone.

The next morning, Katherine walked over to Grace's tent to see if there were any last-minute details she or anyone else could handle. Grace's tent was one the few in the encampment left untouched by last night's storm. She entered to see Grace pacing back and forth, a decidedly indignant look upon her face.

"Whatever is the matter?"

Grace shot her a look and said, "He makes me so angry I could scream."

"Who?" Katherine asked, though she was fairly certain she already knew the answer.

"Jackson 'pigheaded' Blake," Grace said tartly. "A more stubborn and arrogant man has yet to be born."

Katherine could only assume Blake must have just departed. Grace hadn't been ranting this way at breakfast a few hours ago. "What has he done now?"

Grace stopped her pacing, held Katherine's eyes a moment, and said, "He kissed me! Again! In his arrogance, he believes I enjoy it!"

Katherine asked chuckling, "Well, do you?"

Grace admitted slyly, "Just between you and me? Of course. His kisses make me see sunsets."

Katherine couldn't help her smile, and Grace continued, "Stupidest, damnedest experience of my life."

Grace was as plainspoken as Katherine in many ways.

"So what are you going to do?" Katherine asked.

"Pray I make it to Kansas without killing him or falling in love with him."

"He's a handsome man."

"Therein lies the problem. He's too handsome for his own good. Handsome men have roving eyes, and I doubt Blake's are any different."

Katherine had never thought about Dix in such terms. Lord knew he was handsome, but Katherine didn't know if Dix had roving eyes. She tended to think not. He had pledged to remain true to his vows, and she believed him to be a man of his word. "Grace, maybe he will be true."

"Ha! Do you have any idea where I had to meet him to ask about him mastering the wagon train?"

"No, where?"

"A whorehouse outside of Chicago known as Sunshine's Paradise. When I was shown into his room, he was drunk and half asleep. Mistook me for a whore named Lilah!"

Katherine smiled. She'd noticed Grace's resemblance to Lilah from the start. "Lilah's quite nice, actually. At least he didn't mistake you for that malicious Melinda."

Grace stared. "You *know* Lilah?"

Katherine nodded. "Sure do. Miss Sunshine, too. In fact, Dix and I were married there."

"You were married in a *whorehouse?!*"

"Yes. The preacher mistook *me* for one of the girls. I was horrified."

Grace put her hands to her mouth and stared at Katherine with widened eyes. "Katherine, I know it's improper to pry, but this sounds like a dime novel, and I can't wait for us to know one another better so I can hear the whole story."

Katherine laughed.

Grace said, "I'm serious. How long do we have to be friends?"

"I think you are just about as outrageous as I, Grace Atwood."

"And I think you and I are going to get along famously, Katherine Wildhorse."

The two women shook hands to seal their pact.

Grace then said, "You know, I always wanted to be tall like you, able to look a man right in the eye and sock him in it if need be. A good kick in the knee is about all I can give from down here."

Katherine grinned. "Well, truthfully, I've never wanted to be any shorter, at least not since becoming full grown. Though you tiny ones always make me feel clumsy, awkward. You take dainty little steps; we giraffes stride."

"But the carriage and the confidence—I envy that."

"Really?"

"Yes, you and that husband of yours complement each other well, both being so tall."

"He's the tallest man I've ever known. I'm accustomed to looking down at someone, I've never had to crane my neck up. It can be disconcerting at times."

"I've seen the way he looks at you."

Katherine chuckled. "What do you mean?"

"His eyes follow you a lot when he thinks you're not looking. Passion eyes, if I can be frank. It's the way Blake looks at me sometimes—makes me feel like my clothes are about to catch fire."

Katherine had to admit Grace was correct on that count.

Grace cracked, "Like I said, stupidest, damnedest experience of my whole life."

"Well, it's obvious he moves you. Do you love him?"

"Lord, I hope not. Do you love your husband?"

Lord, I hope not, she thought, but aloud she said, "I haven't known him long enough."

"What does that mean?"

"It means I never met him until the day we got married at Miss Sunshine's last month."

Grace stared.

"I wed Dixon to satisfy a debt."

Katherine then gave Grace a brief account of the how and whys of her marriage, leaving out the details surrounding Rupert.

When she was done, Grace stared in amazement. "Your father stole the property of a United States deputy marshal?!"

Katherine replied, "Yes, and I still find that unbelievable."

"And you had to marry him?"

"Or watch my father be thrown into prison or hung."

"My goodness, Katherine, and you agreed?"

"What choice did I have?"

"In reality, none when it comes right down to it—but, my, what a choice. Although it didn't hurt to have Dix turn out to be such a handsome specimen. If he'd had the face of a mule *my* father might have been up the creek without a paddle."

Both women chuckled.

Grace asked, "Is he as kind as he seems?"

"So far." It was the truth. He had been kind. She had only to remember the previous night and the concern he showed during the storm.

"Well, a man as magnificent as that shouldn't be too hard to love."

"Look who's doling out advice. What about Blake?"

"Jackson Blake has undoubtedly broken a lot of hearts in his lifetime, but his streak ends here."

"So you say."

"So I hope."

The two women spent a few minutes more visiting, going over duties for that day and the next. Then Katherine left to help Dix with the final loading of the Hiram Walker.

She found him inside the wagon. It was their first meeting of the morning. Katherine had fallen asleep last night with the memory of his fiery kisses. She'd awakened this morning the same way. Seeing him now brought it all back again—his touch, his eyes. Just see-

ing him made her nipples rise up in shameless anticipation.

"Morning," he said, moving a stack of crates from
one side of the wagon to the other. "Picked up a mattress for you yesterday. Trying to see if it will fit."

"A mattress?"

"You know, one of those things you sleep on, goes
on a bed."

She peered around the shadowy interior until her eyes
settled on a small mattress leaning on the wagon's wall
beside her. "Is this it?"

He nodded as he slid a barrel out of the way.
"Thought you'd be more comfortable."

Katherine observed him. "A bedroll would've suf-
ficed. You didn't have to do this."

"I know."

He moved a few more crates and boxes, then came
over to the mattress. He paused a moment and their eyes
held. Katherine could feel his vibrance washing over her,
bringing with it her own burgeoning attunement.

Without a word he grabbed the mattress and set it in
its place.

Dix wanted to tenderly lower her to the bed and ease
them both into the rhythm that would salve the ache of
his desire.

"Thank you again for last night."

"Are you talking about before the storm or during?"

She cut him a smiling look. "During."

"You're sure?"

"Are all the men in Indian Territory as arrogant as
you?"

"Some are, some aren't."

She shook her head. "It's a wonder your hat fits on
your head."

"You still haven't answered my question."

"Which was?"

"Are you certain about what you're thanking me for?"

"Yes. I am. The storm."

"Just checking," he explained, amused.

"I must admit to being made a little breathless last night."

"By the storm?"

Arrogant and *conceited*. "No, by your kisses."

"I think it was more than just a *little* breathless."

She stood with her hands on her hips, not knowing whether to laugh or sock him soundly. "Never mind."

Leaning back against a stack of crates, his arms folded casually, he gave her a grin that seemed to fill the interior with brilliant sunlight. "You've never had a man give back as good as he gets, have you?"

"No, I haven't."

"Bet you've run roughshod over any man who's ever had the nerve to stand in your way."

"Yes, I have," she stated proudly. "Women can't advance if they pick up their skirts and run every time a man growls."

Dix thought her fierce and fearless; a man couldn't ask for a better mother for his sons.

"So, do you still think passion only affects women who are weak?"

Katherine looked away. Once again her naive words had come back to haunt her. "I—"

"And don't you dare lie."

"Me?" she asked dramatically, pointing to herself. "Lie?"

"Yes, you, Mrs. Wildhorse. Don't forget, I know your daddy."

She grinned. Her eyes became serious, though, as she spoke, "I was naive and wrong."

He told her softly, "We're going to do fine, you and I. Just fine."

Chapter 9

The journey begins on the morning of June 3, 1884. The skies are cloudy. The women are cheerful and expectant after having been prayed over by the reverend from the local church and given a rousing send-off by the townspeople and a five-man band. In spite of the doubts expressed by some of the men in the crowd, the women appear to be well in command of their wagon teams and hold the reins expertly, if not proudly. The wagon master hopes to travel at least 16 miles a day.

Agent, Brother K. Love

The caravan made the first night's camp in a farmer's field about ten miles outside of the town of Aurora. When they arrived, Dix, who'd ridden ahead to finalize the arrangements, greeted them with hat in hand, waving from atop the black stallion and directing them to the field they were to use. The lead wagon rolled by him, and the others followed. When Katherine's passed by, she smiled his way.

The farmer's wife must have been cooking all day

because there were spitted hogs, corn pudding, and yams enough for everyone. Dessert consisted of strawberries and ice cream.

After graciously thanking their host and hostess for their generosity, the brides, Katherine included, returned to their wagons bone-tired. The day had been fraught with excitement, and now weariness had taken hold. They'd covered ten miles—a fair piece, according to Blake—but everyone knew they would need to pick up the pace if they wanted to reach Kansas City on schedule.

Katherine climbed slowly into the Hiram Walker. She lit a small candle to shoo away the darkness, then carefully set it atop the crates that bordered the front of the bed. She wanted a bath after the long day, but the water in the barrels lashed to the side of the wagon was not to be wasted on such frivolity. Blake and Dix had mapped out a route that would take them near fresh water as often as possible, but it was not an excuse to waste such a valuable resource, especially on the first day out.

Putting the thought of a bath out of her mind, Katherine prepared for bed. She'd seen Dix only briefly at dinner. No doubt he and Blake would be huddled over the maps and strategies until long after midnight. She peeled the quilt back from the mattress, then knelt to search through the small chest that held her clothing for a nightgown.

Dix walked across the dark field toward the wagons. He'd just spent the past hour arguing with the farmer over the fee for the use of the land. The agreed-upon price had been two dollars, but the beady-eyed little swindler later decided he needed to cover the price of the food. Grace had very firmly pointed out that no one had asked to be fed in the first place, and that they thought he'd fed them as a courtesy, but he held fast to his position. He wanted the five dollars or they'd have to get off his property. Grace the Hellion was ready to oblige him. She was all set to gather everyone and head back to the trail when the farmer's wife walked in. After Grace explained the problem to her, the wife took the husband aside and started arguing with him. A few minutes later the wife returned, apologized for her husband's greedy behavior, and that was that. Grace gave the wife the agreed-upon two dollars and tossed in one more for her good heart.

Dix chuckled. It was obvious who wore the pants in the farmer's family, and Dix was glad. He imagined if Katherine were in a marriage back East, she, too, would wear the trousers. In fact she'd been wearing a pair the first night he saw her being dragged into Samuels' town house. Back then he'd had no idea of the determination and fire she contained, nor how much he'd come to respect and admire her. He found himself still touched by the vulnerable woman he'd seen the night of the storm. In spite of her anxieties, she'd shown pluck, and ever since, he wanted to place her inside his heart and keep her safe. He had no business holding such sentiments, especially since he was determined to keep his emotions locked away, but that night she touched him in places he never knew he had.

Since the death of his grandfather a decade ago, Dix's life had been singularly consumed with dispensing justice. He'd had to be tough and impassive to be a successful lawman; the less emotion he carried within himself the better. Letting down his guard could get him killed in his line of work.

Now, he didn't know what was happening to him. He'd brought her flowers; he'd neglected his job to scour the countryside for a mattress; he'd held her close to assuage her fear of storms. These were not the actions of a dispassionate man, he grudgingly admitted. His growing desire for her had also muddied the waters. He'd planned to teach her passion so the marriage bed would be a pleasure for them both, but he hadn't planned on being so consumed by desire for her that she was now all he could think about. His eyes still burned from the sight of her fanning herself that night. Her lush curves had aroused him instantaneously. Yet he still believed once he had the opportunity to fully taste her virgin beauty, everything would be fine, and he'd no longer want to make love to her with every breath he drew. He'd revert to his true nature and desire her no more or no less than any other woman he'd desired in his past, even though she was his wife.

Inside the Hiram Walker, Katherine—now dressed in her sleeveless nightgown—sat atop the mattress, writing down the record of the day's journey. The light was poor and she was tired, but she wanted to pen her thoughts and reactions to this very special day before going to sleep. When the wagon rocked slightly from the weight of someone climbing aboard, she paused and looked up. It was Dix. He, like she, had to duck to enter the interior and to move around. "I thought you and Blake would be poring over maps until dawn."

"Nope. All done for tonight."

Katherine set aside her paper and pen. "We didn't do so bad on our first day out."

He unbuckled his holster and gun and set it aside. "No, we didn't. We need to cover more ground, though."

She agreed. Back in the early days of Conestoga travel, sixteen miles had been the daily ideal; however, due to uncharted roads and inadequate maps, the parties were lucky if they covered six or seven. Roads were better now, so although Blake hoped to average sixteen a day, he'd voiced a preference for traveling eighteen to twenty.

Katherine watched silently as Dix sat on one of the crates to pull off his boots. In his western clothing he seemed even larger than life. She'd seen him only briefly this morning, but that one quick look at him atop the beautiful black stallion made her heart pound. He sat the horse as if it were an extension of his form. The buckskin shirt he had on seemed to suit him better than eastern clothing he'd worn previously, and the Stetson pulled low over those glittering eyes made him even more distracting.

She'd never tell him, of course, but she'd thought about him on and off all day. What was he doing? When would he return? Her multifaceted marshal had begun to intrigue her more than a bit. More than a lot, if she were being entirely truthful about the matter. His kisses were as memorable as his name. The skin beneath her golden topaz still burned from the touch of his lips. Even now, thinking back on it made a sweet warmth invade her senses.

She watched from the shadows as he removed his shirt. Who would think a chest so strong and hale could shelter a woman so tenderly?

He pulled on a shirt to sleep in, then shook out his bedroll and placed it near the front of the wagon, saying, "Here's something for your journal. The farmer wanted us to pay him for dinner tonight."

Katherine's eyes narrowed. "I thought he fed us out of the goodness of his heart."

"So did his wife."

Dix then told Katherine the story. When he finished, Katherine was outdone by the man's greed but impressed by the honesty of his wife.

Dix sat down on the bedroll and leaned his head back

against the crates. To Katherine he appeared very weary. "Tired?" she asked softly.

He nodded. "Haven't set a horse in a while. My neck and shoulders are pretty upset."

"When my mother's back would ache from bending over a needle for hours at a time, I'd rub her awhile. She always said I had good hands. Shall I try with you?"

He turned his head, and their eyes met across the shadows. Time seemed to stretch. For a moment she thought he would say no, but he finally nodded his agreement.

Katherine crawled to the mattress's edge. "Come sit over here."

He complied and she knelt at his back. She began to knead the tight muscles in his shoulders, working slowly at first, moving from one side of his neck to the other. When the muscles began to soften and relax, she transferred her hands to his well-formed arms.

Dix wanted to purr. Katherine did have good hands— hands so good he didn't want to move. The fire in his neck and shoulders were being magically extinguished. He wondered if she were aware that men sometimes paid top dollar for such a pleasurable service—though they would expect her to massage much more than their necks and arms.

His thoughts faded as she began to apply sharp, short chops to his spine and the surface of his back. It felt so good he growled contentedly. The pounding loosened up the tightness from his hips to his shoulders and down his arms. He felt like a charmed snake as his spine and muscles responded to the beck and call of her hands. He asked huskily, "What do I need to do to get you to do this for me everyday?"

"Simply ask," she replied quietly.

She spent a few more minutes kneading here and

chopping there, then slowly ran her hands over his shoulders once more. Finished, she sat back on her heels. "Is that better?"

"Much," he breathed contentedly, then turned and held her eyes. "Thanks."

"You're welcome," she said almost shyly.

"Now it's your turn."

Her confusion showed on her face.

He said, "Trade places with me."

Still having no inkling as to what he intended, she came and sat in front of him. A heartbeat later, she felt his warm hands on her shoulders. He began kneading them gently. She purred just as he had earlier. She, too, had held reins all day. She'd taken it for granted she would awaken stiff and sore in the morning. Now she knew she would not. His hands worked her neck and shoulders with just enough pressure to melt the aches. She was liking this man more and more.

She mimicked his question, "What do I have to do to get you to do this every day?"

He touched her neck with his lips and said, "Simply ask."

Katherine's aches and pains had diminished immensely. She felt as light as a spring breeze. "That was simply wonderful. You have good hands, too. Thank you."

"You're welcome."

She turned and viewed him over her shoulder. Was this also part of marriage, having someone to be the balm when you needed salving?

"Are you ready for bed?" he asked.

She nodded, then gathered her courage and said, "This mattress is almost large enough for two. You don't have to sleep on the floor."

Dix said nothing. He watched her as if trying to figure out if she was sincere.

Katherine plunged on, "The floor has to be hard."

The floor isn't the only thing hard in this wagon, he thought. "I think it'll be better if I sleep over there."

"Why?"

A ghost of a smile crossed his face. "If I sleep with you, Katherine, we may not get any sleep."

His husky words trailed across her senses like raw silk. The frankness in his eyes touched her like a hand.

He asked, "You still offering?"

Not trusting her voice, she nodded yes.

He replied, "Fine, then. I suppose I have to get used to your snoring sometime."

"I don't snore."

Silence.

"I do *not* snore."

He gave her another ghost of a grin.

"Do I?"

He nodded.

She turned away from his glittering gaze, appalled by the revelation.

"It's nothing to be ashamed of," he said.

"No, but it isn't something a lady cares to be told, either."

"I understand. But the truth is, you snore."

"Thank you, Dixon Wildhorse."

He chuckled, then reached out and slowly dragged her onto his lap. He lifted her chin and looked right into her cinnamon-colored eyes. "Didn't mean to make you mad."

"Yes, you did," Katherine quipped knowingly.

He couldn't suppress the grin this time. "You'd've made a great woman warrior back at Fort Negro."

"Thank you," she said softly. She remembered the

last time she'd sat on his lap; then, as now, the heat of him surrounded her, dazzled her. "Where's this Fort Negro?"

"It was in Florida on the Appalachicola River. The government destroyed it back in 1816. I'll tell you about it sometime. . . ."

Katherine knew he was going to kiss her, and her heart began to pound.

When he raised a finger to trace the fullness of her lips, she began to shake.

"Your mouth is sweeter than strawberries. . . . I've been thinking about tasting it all day. Kiss me, Katherine. . . ."

She didn't have to be asked twice.

The kiss was gentle at first, a slow, heated reacquaintance. Then, as the passion began to glow, the kiss deepened. He gathered her in and pulled her close, coaxing her lips to part so he could taste the honeyed depths of her mouth. She breathlessly complied. She hadn't been ready for this that first night at Miss Sunshine's, but now she reveled in the feel of his lips searing her neck, thrilled to the touch of his hand slowly caressing her back and bare shoulders. She was ready to know where their passion would lead.

Dix brushed his lips over her ear and throat and cupped his large hand over the lush weight of her breast. She didn't bolt or protest. She simply let him linger at each point until she moaned. Through the thin cotton of her gown, he brushed his mouth over her nipples, making her ache for more. The passion was sharp, and she arched her back in response. All this was still very new. He bit her gently while his hand toyed with the other nipple. She was on fire.

It took all Dix had not to summarily strip her clothing away and take her as he so longed to do. She was virgin, untouched and untried; showing her the intense passion he truly harbored would undoubtedly result in a lot more noise than polite society allowed. The wagons were circled fairly close to one another and he didn't want her to start the trip as the subject of gossip.

But he wanted her in all ways a man could want a woman. The tiny trembles of her skin as his lips brushed over the long graceful column of her neck fueled his need. The sound of her short intakes of breath as he bit her gently on the lobe of her ear added more fuel. He had to touch her or die.

The feel of his hands opening the hooks of her nightgown set Katherine soaring. She felt brazen and shy all at once as she lay back against his bracing arm alternately being kissed and undressed. He parted the halves of the bodice, brushed his mustached lips against the brown expanse of her throat and asked, ''Are you going to bolt on me . . . ?''

Katherine couldn't answer; she was too busy melting. But she was given no time to think. When he flicked the tip of his tongue against her topaz, the heat rippled over her like the waves in a pond. He touched his lips to the bud of one breast and then the other before slowly raising his head and drawing back. In the shadows, he held her passion-lidded eyes. His fingers slowly cajoled her nipples to ripen and rise.

Katherine keened softly, hips rising. It was too sweet, too hot, too tempting. She didn't want his masterful mouth and hands to leave her. As if reading her thoughts, his big hand slid her gown up her thighs.

Dix could feel her long, firm legs trembling beneath his hand—legs smooth as silk, legs he wanted to slowly part and tease. She was as lush as an African goddess, and the urge to pay her erotic tribute pulsed like lightning through his blood. He moved his hand over the secret warmth hidden between her thighs and tempted her wantonly through the long slit in her lacy drawers.

Dix's manhood leaped as she parted her legs in surrender and he rewarded her with a kiss where she least expected it. He lazily explored the damp treasure until she flowed sweet and free, then whispered against her ear, "The next time we'll do this without your drawers. . . ."

The soft-spoken promise made her arch to the places his hands were tutoring. Desire was building inside her like steam inside a kettle. His hands were so deliciously brazen, the heat so overwhelming, that her virgin's body exploded with a forceful beauty.

He covered her scream with his mouth. His fingers continued to stroke her over the edge, leaving her twisting and mindless.

Dix wanted to proceed to the next logical step in the age-old dance of man and woman. The thought of her nude and rising to meet his heated strokes almost impelled him onward, but he held off in spite of his near-bursting need. He'd have her soon enough. Tonight she'd had her first taste of true passion; it would not be long before they'd get to savor the whole feast.

Only after the explosive passion diminished to tiny, pulsating tremors did Katherine open her eyes. He smiled down, a smile Katherine thought entirely too male. "Is that your legendary 'slow hand'?"

He grinned. "A bit of it."

She sat up straight. "A bit?"

Even in the faint light offered by the moon, his eyes were like black jewels—jewels that could enthrall her as easily as a wizard's spell. She didn't know if she wanted to be so susceptible to him and his bliss-filling slow hands. He didn't impress her as the type of man who'd be bowled over by a woman, any woman. She didn't want to come out of this marriage with a broken heart.

Her thoughts went up in smoke when he slid a finger over the soft undercurve of her breast, then the surface of her mother's topaz. The nipple ripened like a summer bud once more.

He whispered in the dark, "Next time, we'll do more. . . ."

He touched his mouth to the topaz and then the nipple, making her groan thickly. In the silence of the Hiram Walker he brought her to completion yet again. Only then did he let her go to sleep.

The train was now five days out, and things were going fine. But Blake's lectures let them know that this would be no easy trek. Many of the emigrants in the forties and fifties lost their lives journeying across the continent. Bad roads, cholera, and inadequate supplies added to the toll. Blake and Dix had passed along tales of deaths in river crossings, trails lined with graves and the newborn infants who rested in many of them.

Most overland travel by Conestoga had ground to a halt after the Civil War. Due to the rapid growth of the railroads, wagon travel was becoming a thing of the past. Grace had considered traveling by train, but with jim crow overtaking the country like an insidious disease, she knew the chances of everyone and everything arriving in Kansas unscathed were relatively low. She'd had no desire to have her brides travel in cattle cars or have all of their possessions summarily put down on the side of the tracks because of the bigotry of a narrow-minded passenger or railroad employee, so she opted for wagons. Though it would add more than a month to the trip, and there would be more risk of tragedy along the way, everyone would reach Kansas with their dignity intact—and that meant more, much more.

Katherine thought it an ideal way to see the country, even if she did have to do it while staring over the rump of a team of mules. The pace was slow enough so that one could get a good look at the endless horizon, the variety of fauna, and the birds flying above. The leisurely pace also placed little strain on the animals and on the skills of the drivers. The anxious excitement that had gripped everyone on the first day of the journey had finally dissipated; now everyone seemed to have relaxed and settled into the ride.

Katherine held the reins loosely as the wheels rattled over the terrain. In her mind she could hear Blake yelling, "Relax, relax! You're going to yank the poor mule's gums up into his ears!" He'd yelled at them so often about so many things, she hoped they would remember it all.

Ahead of her were nine wagons and behind her ten. They looked very much like a fleet of sailing schooners. Each wagon held two of the thirty-five brides. The wagon at the end was being driven by a widow named Yancey Fitzgerald. They'd come across the Fitzgerald wagon yesterday. She'd been on her way to Missouri unescorted. She and her three young boys had been turned out by her husband's relatives after her husband's untimely death. After meeting with Grace, she'd gladly hitched her wagon onto the train, volunteering to earn her way by being trail cook in the hope of finding a new father for her sons in Kansas.

Dix was scouting somewhere up ahead. Katherine thought back to that first night's camp. His touch had left her absolutely incoherent. She hadn't known kisses could make one dizzy, nor that a man's mouth could be so bold and masterful. His were not the delicate, innocent pecks of an eastern-raised gentleman, but the rushing, mind-fogging kisses of a man of power.

She decided she liked the parts between kissing and cleaving. She'd gone to sleep pulsing and throbbing and had awakened the next morning in the same condition. She wondered briefly if the pleasure made her a brazen woman. She certainly felt that way, and just between her and the mules, she couldn't wait to feel brazen again. He'd planted tiny seeds of attraction within her from the moment they met, and those seeds now knew where their sun lay.

They finally stopped for lunch a bit after noon. The heat from the June day had been beating down since breaking camp that morning. Katherine was so hot, her blouse clung damply to her skin. She, like the other women, had begun to feel the effects of the long days behind the reins in her stinging shoulders and stiff legs, but only a few women had been laid low. Loreli Winters's wagon mate, Belle Carson, was one of them. Loreli had been doing all the driving because Belle was ailing. Since the second day out, she had been so sick that she'd been unable to keep food down. Grace had been extremely concerned, until a tearful Belle confessed she was carrying a child. The news had taken the whole train by surprise. A few of the women had been outraged and wanted poor Belle taken to the nearest town and left there.

Grace would have none of it. Loreli, who over the past few days had emerged as one of the train's leaders, would have none of it, either. She declared Belle her responsibility, and anyone who had a problem with it would have to take it up with her. Standing with the others as the confrontation took place during that evening's meeting, Katherine noticed no one stepped forward to meet Loreli's challenge. The bright-skinned

Missouri native had made her living as a gambler before joining Grace's caravan. She was as intelligent as she was fearless. In Katherine's opinion, Belle couldn't have chosen a better champion.

Since no one seemed inclined to take on Loreli, Grace declared the meeting adjourned, and everyone went on to bed. In the aftermath, a few of the women made their displeasure known by cutting both Belle and Loreli. The issue had made the first tear in the quilt of women Grace had gathered for this purpose. Katherine hoped it didn't become larger.

Lunch consisted of beef jerky and a cup of leftover coffee. Yancey Fitzgerald and her boys cooked only at breakfast and at suppertime. As Katherine pulled on a piece of the jerky with her teeth, she fantasized about having real food in a real restaurant. Once they arrived in Kansas City, she planned on wiring Geoff and have him forward her enough funds to get a large hotel suite and a beautiful meal. She liked the adventure of this journey, but the food and accommodations left a lot to be desired. Katherine swatted at the mosquitoes. They, too, were becoming an increasing problem. Over the past few days the little beasties had left their red, itchy calling cards on everyone.

Katherine ate as much of the jerky as could be stomached, took a stroll around the wagon to check for breaks in her wheels and axle, then spent a moment making certain the mules hadn't picked up any stones.

They were back on the trail in another hour. There were many more days to go.

Chapter 10

~~~ੴ~~~

The caravan rendezvoused with Dix about three hours later. The fierce rays of the sun had taken its toll on humans and animals alike, so having to stop for Dix seemed like a godsend to the women. He greeted them with disturbing news, however. The land ahead belonged to a man who refused to allow the wagons to cross his property. Having to go around meant a thirty-five mile detour, a setback of two, maybe three days.

Dix then added, "He also holds rights to the water running about three miles north. We're forbidden that also."

Everyone groaned.

They'd been on the road for five days. Water had been used sparingly, but if they had to go another three days without, the supply could become very low. Katherine looked around at her sister travelers. Like Katherine, they were all in need of a bath; skirts and denims were stained with trail dust and soil. Because of the dust and heat, many of the women had given up on maintaining their coifs and had covered their heads with colorful bandanas. Katherine's short hair had been bound up since the third day.

Grace asked Dix, "Would my talking to the land-owner make a difference?"

Dix shook his head. "He's an old reb. He won't change his mind."

A disgusted Blake looked out over the horizon as if judging how much daylight remained. He then told everyone, "Then we go around. Let's head out."

The women climbed back onto their wagons to follow Dix and Blake leading the way.

By evening they were still traveling. The animals were tired, the women were tired, and all Katherine wanted to do was drop the reins and crawl into bed. Unlike some of the others, Katherine had no one to relieve her of the driving. Because of Dix's scouting responsibilities, she alone shouldered the responsibility of piloting the Hiram Walker.

By the time darkness fell, they'd covered nearly twenty-five miles, and now under the fickle light of a cloud-shrouded moon and lanterns attached to the teams and wagons, they traveled on. Just when Katherine thought she couldn't hold the reins a moment longer, the schooners ahead began to slow. She pulled back on her own team.

She wondered why they'd stopped. The night prevented her from seeing ahead with any clarity, but she clearly heard the voices of women rising in celebration. She wanted to get down and see what had happened at the front of the line, but her weariness took precedence; she doubted she'd have the strength to climb back up if Blake ordered them to move on.

The weariness faded, however, as Dix came thundering up out of the darkness. "What has happened?" she asked

"We met a farmer who'll let us make camp."

"Hallelujah!" Katherine breathed.

"He also has a stream where you ladies may bathe."

Bathe had to be the sweetest word she'd heard in days. "How far ahead?"

"Two and a half miles."

Katherine's arms and shoulders were so sore that she didn't want to spend another moment holding the reins; but rather than complain, she concentrated on how wonderful it would feel to to be clean again.

Dix could see Katherine's fatigue clearly by the pale light of the lanterns. The weariness in her eyes and posture pulled at his heartstrings. He told her, "You look dead. I'll drive the rest of the way. Slide over while I go hitch my horse to the back of the wagon."

"That isn't necessary."

He dismounted, ignoring her words.

"Did you hear—"

Too late. He'd disappeared around the side.

When he returned a moment later and climbed up, Katherine hadn't moved, mainly because she didn't want him to think her incapable of pulling her weight.

He met the stubborn set of her chin with soft words. "Kate you've been driving all day. Move over. You won't lose face if I drive."

"I can manage."

"You can either move over or ride the rest of the way in my lap. . . ."

Katherine met his eyes. He'd probably make good on that promise, she mused—not that she'd mind. The idea of being in his lap, getting kissed, intrigued her more than she'd willingly admit aloud.

She slid aside.

He shook his head with amusement. "Warrior Woman would be a good name for you."

She turned away from his dazzling smile to shield her own. "The last time you called me Warrior Woman you mentioned a Negro Fort? You promised to tell me the story behind it.''

As the wagon train slowly got underway, Katherine learned that Negro Fort was an earth-and-wood fort built on the Appalachicola River in Florida.

"Back then Florida was Spanish owned," he pointed out.

Katherine nodded. She knew that fact from her school lessons.

"Well, under Spanish rule it became a haven for fugitive slaves from the border states of Georgia and Alabama. Blacks had been slipping into Florida's swamps and disappearing since before the War of Independence. All along, the American planters kept demanding the return of their property, but the Spanish paid them little attention, and the U.S. government refused to get involved. The governor of Georgia finally decided to take matters into his own hands. He mustered up an army and sent them across the border into northern Florida to bring back any Blacks they could find.''

"Were they successful?"

"Nope. The combined forces of the Blacks, the Indians, and the Spanish citizens whipped their butts and sent them home.''

Katherine smiled.

"Of course, they didn't give up," Dix added.

"Of course not.''

While Katherine listened intently, Dix continued telling her a history she'd never known. After the remnants of the militia crawled home in defeat, they whispered about the fierce Black fighters they'd encountered and told of well-armed Blacks living in towns with Seminoles. They, like Katherine, were unaware that the two peoples had been coexisting and intermarrying for nearly three generations. The governor of Georgia demanded that the Seminole give up the fugitives, but the Seminole refused and continued to refuse for the next thirty years. The Americans saw the Blacks only as property. To the Seminole they were family and friends. Why the government expected that the Seminole would turn family members over to slave catchers was beyond Katherine's understanding. According to Dix, the great Seminole war chief Osceola himself had a beautiful wife named Che-Cho-Ter, or Morning Dew as she was called in English. Her mother had been a descendant of escaped slaves, her father a Seminole chief. She and Osceola had four beautiful children.

The war of 1812 temporarily placed portions of northern Florida in British hands. The British call for Indian volunteers to fight the Americans was answered by seven hundred Seminoles. The residents of the Black towns also allied themselves with Great Britain. Black towns already circled St. Augustine and had for many years. The Spanish governors of the past had encouraged the settlements because the Black citizens served as unpaid protectors of Spanish interests in exchange for freedom.

The combined Black and Seminole forces treated the Americans much as they had the Georgia militia. When the war ended and the British withdrew from Florida, the English agent at Blount Fort turned the impenetrable earthen fort over to some of the Seminole and Black fighters. They renamed it Negro Fort and many of their families came to live and maintain their well-manicured fields under the protection of the fort's formidable cannons.

"When was it destroyed?" Katherine asked.

"Two years later. July 26, 1816," he replied quietly.

"You know the date?" she asked softly, sensing his sadness.

"Every Seminole knows the date. The cry of Negro Fort fueled war with the United States government for the next thirty years."

In a clear, emotionless voice, Dix told the tale of Andrew Jackson, himself a slave owner and how he took up the planters torch after the 1812 war. Jackson found the idea of the hundreds of Blacks living free in Black and Seminole towns intolerable. He personally declared war on Spanish Florida. Under his orders, the fort was targeted for destruction.

"But wasn't it in Spanish Florida?"

"Yes. The ships and men he sent up the river were supposedly there to insure a safe supply route upstream to a U.S. outpost on the Florida-Georgia border known as Fort Scott, but Jackson had sent orders two months before, demanding the fort be destroyed at all costs. Any Blacks found were to be returned to their masters. The Seminoles were to be handed over to the Creeks."

"Why the Creeks?"

"The Creek claimed the Seminole in much the same way the planters claimed the Blacks. In 1716, Seminole chief Sacafaca split with the Creek Confederation and took his people and a few other tribes into Florida. The Creek never accepted the leaving, so they and the Americans became allies. Negro Fort had been well armed by the British. There was one brass five-and-a-half inch howitzer, two six-pound cannons, two nine pounders, three twenty-four pounders, and one thirty-two pounder. When the fighting began, the cannons on the American gunboats were unable to penetrate the walls."

"So what did they do?"

"They heated their cannonballs until they were red hot and sent them raining down onto the fort. One hit the fort's powder magazine, and it exploded. The firestorm killed two hundred and seventy, Blacks and Seminoles, men, women and children. Their charred and dismembered bodies were found strewn all over the fields outside the fort. My grandfather said the number of felled Blacks equaled nearly one-third of all the fugitives living in Florida at that time. The fort smoldered for days.''

Katherine whispered, ''Good heavens.''

''Sixty-two people survived but were too badly injured to offer a fight when the Americans came ashore. Those who lived were sold to slave owners who held no legal claims. The Seminoles were given to the Creeks as their reward for guiding the Americans to the fort. For the next thirty years my people fought to maintain their freedom and the Seminole fought to stay on their land.''

When the wagons finally made camp, Dix parked a bit away from the main circle. He then fed and settled the animals. He'd become so silent and introspective after telling her the story of Negro Fort, Katherine was reluctant to leave him when word came down the line of a bathing expedition. He shooed her on with a small smile, so Katherine joined the other women for the walk to the banks of the stream.

On the way, not one complained about the mosquitos or the roots they tripped over in the dark; they'd been on the trail for five days, and nothing mattered but the cleanliness offered by the night-black water stretched out before them like a ribbon.

Loreli Winters shocked the drawers off some of the primmer members of their party when she stripped herself naked, saying, ''I intend to get clean tonight, ladies. Lord knows when the next chance will come.''

Katherine and a few of the others agreed, so tossing

conventional modesty to the wind, they, too, discarded all of their soiled and sweat-stained garments and waded into the water. It was so cold, their howling and laughter filled the air. They wasted little time employing the soap, then hurried back to the bank.

Katherine entered the lantern-lit wagon to find Dix inside, drying his hair. Drops of water clung to the dark muscles of his bare torso. His mouth lifted in a smile at the sight of her. "How was the stream?"

"Cold, but glorious."

Clad in a fresh, clean nightgown she plopped down onto the mattress, weary but content.

"You took advantage of the stream also, I see," she said, trying not to stare at his well-formed arms and chest.

"Yep. Blake and I just returned."

Dix could feel himself being drawn across the room by her cinnamon-colored eyes. As she lay there clad in her thin robe and nightgown, he wanted to undress her and sample the sweet tastes of her clean, lush loveliness. Her tall, well-endowed form haunted his days and nights. His desire for her seemed to grow with each new dawn.

The air surrounding them thickened with tension. All the saints in heaven knew Katherine didn't want to be attracted to Dixon Wildhorse, but she was—very much so. Even though he was not the man she'd envisioned spending her life with, any future man would have a difficult time surpassing the standards he'd set not only in handsomeness but in deed. She found herself anticipating the way his lips would brush hers in a kiss.

His soft voice broke the silence. "You shouldn't look at me that way unless you want to be kissed. . . ."

The huskiness of his tone rippled across her senses. "I . . . think I do." She hadn't meant to voice her desire aloud. The words had come out without thought.

"Plainspoken as usual," he noted quietly.

He came over and joined her atop the thin mattress. He leaned over her so that his arms gently penned her in, then brushed his mouth warmly over her own. "I want you, Kate. . . ."

She wanted him too, even though she hadn't an inkling as to what that really meant. His mouth lowered to hers, and the whispery kisses were heated and enthralling. His large hand slid over her breasts, and her nipples perked up. He touched his mouth to her breast through the thin cotton, making her want to weep from the lightning he fostered. He had her gown off her shoulders and his mouth to her bareness a moment later. Only when both nipples were hard as jewels did he draw back.

"Is that enough of a kiss for you, Warrior Woman . . . ?"

Katherine, leaning back on her arms for support, couldn't answer. How he expected her to form speech when his hands were casting a spell on her body was beyond her knowledge.

He asked her again softly, "Do you want more kisses . . . ?"

He lowered his head, and soon his slow loving made her groan her pleasure.

Dix pushed the thin cotton gown up her legs to her waist. His manhood throbbed as he filled his hand with the firm ripe fullness of her hip and possessively caressed the smooth skin. He savored the feel of her in the loose drawers, then slid his finger over the brazen opening at her center. Her sharp intake of breath hardened him even more.

Dix played with her until she flowed sweet and free. Her legs were splayed deliciously, firing him, seducing him to explore her further, inviting him to kiss her mouth languidly. She returned his kiss with an equal fervor, nibbling on his bottom lip, flicking her tongue lazily over the corners of his mouth.

The feel of her warm hands running up and down his arms increased his desire. He wanted to take her with all the vigor he possessed, but for now he'd content himself with watching her eyes close as he circled her heat, hearing her soft hiss of pleasure as he bit her nipples ever so gently, and feeling her hips rise in wanton response as he branded her his and his alone.

Katherine could feel herself about to shatter, and a hot second later she did. Rapture rippled through her with such vibrating intensity, she had to fight to keep her sharp cries of completion from piercing the night as she rode out her pleasure under his glowing eyes.

He brought her back to earth with tender kisses and warm touches. The remnants of her pleasure echoed and throbbed like the soft beat of a drum. The still-dazzled Katherine wondered how he knew so much about her physical self? He seemed to know just what her body needed to satisfy its pleading and how to make her flow as if she were molten inside. On their wedding night, he'd told her he was "damned good"—and damned if he wasn't right. If she had any sense she would get up and never let him kiss her again; this liaison could only end in disaster. But it was too late to close the door; the filly had already fled the barn.

Emboldened by his sensual tutoring, Katherine leaned up and nibbled on his full lower lip. "I want to be yours. . . ." she murmured against his mouth.

He leaned down and kissed her for a sweet, silent moment. He could kiss her all night long, he was finding. He ran his hand over her soft hip, savoring the warm skin, cupping her roundness. "I love the way you fill my hands. . . ."

Katherine had never had a man whisper to her this way. Few men in her past had ever seemed to fully appreciate her statuesque height and proportions. Dix seemed pleased by them both.

She could feel the fire beginning to catch again. "I want to be your wife. Teach me. . . ."

"Your first time should not be in the back of a cramped wagon."

"I don't care where it is, as long as it is with you."

Her fevered words were the most thrilling he'd ever heard.

"Teach me. I promise I won't bolt."

His eyes were as potent as she'd ever seen. Anticipation made her heart pound and her senses bloom.

"Let's see if that's a promise you can keep. . . ."

When he cupped her bare breasts, she trembled. When he kissed them in heated reacquaintance, she trembled even more. When he eased her onto his lap, she lost track of time, herself, and all that had gone before as the loving began again. His wizard's hands and spellbinding caresses took her once more to passion's door, and she entered the rarefied realm without inhibition. Her drawers were taken from her with fiery slowness, and she gasped as his hands wantonly explored. Her soft sighs of response filled the dark silence. She'd no idea if it was proper to enjoy herself so vocally, but at this juncture she didn't care; she just didn't want him to stop, not his kisses, not his whispers, not any of it.

He spent an inordinate amount of time torridly stripping her of her gown. Nude and throbbing, Katherine lay there waiting as he removed his pants. Never in her life had she imagined such passion was possible.

He soon rejoined her and then knelt at her side. He ran his large hand over the flat plane of her belly and brushed the soft, dark triangle. When he leaned down and kissed the whorl of her navel, she shuddered and tightened, hips rising off the bed. His fingers sought her dampness, making her twist and croon.

"Are you ready . . . ?"

She answered by rising lustfully against his blazing hand.

"I think you are . . . let's see. . . ."

He eased a finger into the pulsing, flowing cove and heard her give a strangled, pleasure-filled cry. "Was that a yes, Kate . . . ?"

He could feel his self-control fading. If he didn't have her soon, he'd explode. He withdrew his finger and touched his lips to her mouth. "Open for me, *chica,* let me teach you the way. . . ."

Katherine felt the hard, blissful entry of his manhood and closed her eyes with the rapture it instilled. All of her previous misconceptions of man and woman fled in the wake of his blazing touch, and she welcomed the slow, sweet invasion.

She was so tight, Dix didn't want to move too fast lest he spill himself and end it all now. He wanted her to come with him on this maiden foray, not be left behind in pain and tears. "Am I hurting you?" he asked softly.

Katherine shook her head in the dark and whispered, "No." She had been told by her aunt that this joining would cause severe pain. Katherine felt discomfort for a moment, but in the excitement ripening all around it, it soon faded. Passion took hold once more. "I like this, Dixon," she whispered heatedly as she felt him throbbing within her with male life and vigor. "I truly like this. . . ."

She ran her hands over the magnificent chest, savoring his strength and the feel of his muscular arms. She leaned up to receive his kiss but paused and eased back as the euphoric stroking began. It was glorious, hot. There was no pain now, only the enticing rhythm he coaxed her to try.

For Dix, nothing in his past experience equaled the passion possessing him now. Her body was so attuned to his, it was as if they'd been lovers for a lifetime. Each and every nuance of her lush virgin's body drove him to seek that much more.

So, with that in mind, Dix took the time to teach her the joy to be found in passion, stroking her, loving her, and it didn't take her long to proceed to the head of the class.

When Katherine's bliss finally exploded, the force of it shook her so intensely that she clung to him like a raft in a storm. He was her refuge but also the source of her turbulent sea as his heated strokes increased, then quickened. Moments later passion broke over him like surf against the shore. Pulling her to him, he gripped her hips and let loose a soft, growling roar.

In the aftermath there was only silence.

They made sweet, lingering love a few more times that night, and for them both, nothing would ever be the same again.

Chapter 11

❧

Day 15. We are crossing the plains of Illinois. The monotony of daily routine is wearing.

Day 20. Four hours are spent ferrying the Mississippi into Missouri. Missouri at last!

Day 23. A three-day rain welcomed us into the state. Mud has slowed travel considerably. We are forced to halt numerous times to free wagons mired axle deep in the Missouri muck. Those not driving have to walk beside their teams to lighten the burden on the animals. We resemble an exotic tribe of mud people. Because of the adverse weather, we have only covered twenty-five miles in the past three days.

Day 26. Today is the Sabbath, and we do not travel. We give thanks that no one has contracted disease or suffered tragedy. We spend the day rearranging wagon loads and airing and straightening up the interiors.

Day 28. We have had a few mules stolen during the night's rain. The wagon master has instituted a night watch to keep an eye on our animals and belongings. The women each take a shift. Those lacking firearms skills are receiving training. Those who can't abide *weapons have armed themselves with cast iron skillets.*

Day 32. We have had the pleasure of meeting a trav-
eling troupe of actors who entertained us with skits and
songs in exchange for a meal. Their arrival has done
much to raise our spirits because many despair of ever
reaching our goal.

Day 35. We reached Kirksville, weary and dirty. The
mosquitoes at night are horrendous. Kansas City is a
mere one hundred and sixty miles away.

Day 37. Some of the caravan members are beginning
to grouse and are threatening to desert at the next de-
cent town, but most have their eyes set on meeting the
men awaiting them in Kansas City and are determined
to press on.

Day 40. We passed Indians on the road today. The
scout said they are being removed and relocated. They
were not the "dreaded savages" we've been led to pic-
ture. The slow-walking party consisted of elders, women,
and children. Many appeared weary, sick, and ill-fed.
They were under escort of Black soldiers from the Tenth
Cavalry.

Day 45. Kansas City is only a half day away! Hal-
lelujah!!

The wagon train came to a final halt at a farm outside
of town. The owner, Grace's cousin, waved them onto
his acreage with a welcoming grin. Katherine had never
been so glad to see a friendly face. It had taken over a
month to go from the outskirts of Chicago to Kansas
City, and as much as Katherine loved adventure, she
vowed never to travel by wagon ever again.

According to Grace's cousin, the grooms had come to
town the week before and were staying at various boardinghouses and hotels around the city. He sent one of his
sons into town to alert the men that the brides had ar-

rived safely. However, Grace insisted the women be given a few days to refresh themselves before meeting their prospective mates. Dresses needed unpacking and pressing, baths had to be taken, and hair needed coifing. Not a woman in the caravan wished to be seen as they appeared now, covered with the grime of the trail.

The excitement of arrival pushed aside weariness as the women hugged each other in celebration. They'd done it: traveled over five hundred miles with little to rely upon but themselves. Katherine could see the sense of accomplishment in their faces. In many ways they'd all been altered by the experience; most were stronger and more confident both inside and out. She hoped the grooms would appreciate women who had traveled across the country to be their mates and treat them with the respect they deserved.

She, too, had been changed by the experience. She was in love with Dixon Wildhorse. Though she knew it made no sense and that he likely did not share her feelings, there was nothing she could do about it. Katherine found the situation ironic. She'd sworn she would never expose her heart to a man because to do so would be to surrender herself and her dreams. Now she questioned that logic. Although she and Dix had only scratched the surface of what this marriage could become, she had the impression that he would not stifle her as some men were wont to do to their wives. She felt certain Dix would always let her speak her opinion, even if he didn't agree. He'd never intimated that being his wife precluded her continued work as a journalist and had given her the option of returning East if she desired. If one coupled all those things with his exquisite talent for loving, Katherine challenged any woman not to fall in love.

By evening, arrangements had been finalized for the brides to stay with members of the local A.M.E. church, whose parishioners had graciously offered places to bathe and sleep. Katherine made the rounds, saying good-bye to the women she'd come to regard as friends. She had a special hug for Loreli Winters and her wagon mate, Belle Carson. Belle's condition was quite obvious now, and Katherine hoped the young woman would find a man who would love both her and the unborn child.

Katherine then sought out Yancey Fitzgerald and wished the pretty widow luck in her quest. Katherine had one last rousing footrace with Yancey's young sons, and for the first time eight-year-old Whitney outran them all.

She left her good-byes to Grace for last. She would miss her a great deal. She and the hellion had shared many confidences and frustrations during their time on the road, and her companionship would be dearly missed.

She found Grace in the farmhouse. They embraced one another, and both stepped back with tears in their eyes. Grace would be going along to the colony with the brides, then return to her home in Chicago.

"I'll miss you, Grace Atwood."

"I'll miss you also, Katherine Wildhorse. How soon are you and Dix going on to Indian Territory?"

"Soon as we rest up a bit. We'll spend a few days in town and take a train after that."

"Promise me you'll write." Grace found a pen on her cousin's desk and scribbled down her address in Chicago. "I've added my cousin's address in the colony. I'll probably be there until spring."

"What about you and Blake?"

"I'm sure Jackson Blake will no longer be seeking my company, now that we're in the big city. He's probably appraising the town daughters even as we speak."

"Now, Grace."

She shrugged. "It's true. What would a man like Blake want with an opinionated, red-headed spinster?"

For a moment Grace looked sad, then seemed to regain her mood. "Enough about me. What about you and Dix; in love with him yet?"

Katherine nodded, grinning. "And as you said: stupidest, damnedest experience of my life."

Grace smiled. "Good for you. I knew it wouldn't take long."

"I've no idea if it's good at all. Things are fairly complicated."

"It will work out for the best, don't worry."

But what *was* "best"? Katherine wondered.

They spent a few more minutes talking, trying to stall their parting, but in the end both knew the time had come. Though they'd vowed to write, there was a good possibility that they would never lay eyes on each other again. Katherine sincerely hoped that would not be the case.

They shared a final, poignant hug. Then Katherine left to find Dix.

Dix and Blake were out in the pasture by the wagons, saying their own good-byes. "Well, Blake, thanks for quite a ride."

"I can't believe we made it, but we did. Thanks for the help. Are you heading back to the Territory?"

"In a few days. What about you? You going back East?"

"Hell, no. Five years of civilization is about all I can stand. Think I'll go back down to Texas and see about that bounty on my head."

"You serious?"

Blake nodded. "I want my badge back."

Blake had left Texas five years before to escape a trumped-up murder charge. It was difficult being a Black sheriff in a state filled with former rebs, especially when it came to arresting the son of an influential cattle baron on suspicion of rustling and murder. When Blake had come calling, the baron hadn't cottoned to the idea of a Black man wanting to jail his son, badge or no badge. He and his men had opened fire on Blake and his deputies. The gunfight resulted in the baron's death, and Blake had been charged with murder. He'd fled rather than take a chance on the reb version of justice.

Dix warned, "Things haven't gotten much better down there."

"I know, but I miss my home. A man can't hide out forever."

"Well, if you need my help, wire me."

"I will."

"Oh, and if you run across that bandit brother of yours, tell him if he ever sets foot in my town again, I'll arrest him on the spot. He had the women fighting in the streets over his favors by the time he left town."

Blake laughed. His baby brother, Griffin, was a true lady's man, but he was also a notorious outlaw. There were warrants for his arrest from Kansas to the Pacific. Some were legitimate, like those posted for the trains he kept robbing, but many of the charges were due to the young punks who kept challenging him everywhere in an effort to be known as the one who beat Griffin Blake to the draw. The challengers kept drawing, and Griff kept sending them to the undertaker's office. "Maybe he's found religion."

"And I can fly."

Dix and Blake had known one another since the war. Unlike some of the slave-holding members of the Five Civilized Tribes, Dix and the other Seminole men had fought on the side of the Union. At the time, both seventeen-year-olds worked together as members of a reconnaissance unit under the command of the master spy herself, General Harriet Tubman. The friendship continued after the surrender at Appomattox when Blake accompanied Dix back to Indian Territory and made it his home for ten years.

Blake asked, "Have you heard anything from our old friend, Chase Jefferson?"

"About a year ago. He's married now."

"Chase Jefferson is *married?!*" Chase Jefferson had also worked with General Tubman during the war.

"Yep, to a schoolteacher named Cara Lee. He's sheriff up in one of the colonies outside Nicodemus. Henry Adams is the name of the town I believe."

"That's amazing."

"I thought so, too. If we weren't so far south I'd swing up and see him, but I've already been away too long."

Blake shook his head again. "Chase married. I may have to ride up to this Henry Adams just to see how he looks being yoked to a schoolmarm."

Dix grinned. "You should talk. You're going to wind up yoked, too, if you're not careful."

"Meaning?"

"Meaning, you've been hot after the hellion since the day I arrived in camp."

Silence.

Dix smiled at the mild irritation on Blake's face.

Blake finally spoke. "Who'd've ever thought I'd want a bad-tempered, red-headed spinster? Certainly not me. I like cathouse women. No commitments, no problems. But this one . . . I want her so badly, I can't eat."

Dix chuckled.

Blake said, "Not funny, Dix. I don't even like short women."

"So, what are you going to do?"

"Hope it goes away. If it doesn't, she may wind up going back to Texas with me. What about you and Katherine? You've been fairly calf-eyed the whole trip yourself."

"Don't confuse my situation with yours, my friend. I can eat. Kate's a unique woman. A man would be proud to name her his wife, but we aren't going to fool ourselves into thinking we're in love. This is strictly an agreement. The fact that we enjoy each other makes it easier, but there're no ensnared emotions."

Blake uttered a skeptical, "Uh-huh."

"You doubt me?"

"Yes, I doubt you, I've seen you watching her, and you're as afflicted with female fever as I am. I'm just owning up to mine."

"Blake, I have never in my life fallen in love with a woman."

"There's a first time for everything, even for a Seminole like you."

Dix shook his head.

Blake grinned. "All right, don't believe me, but believe this: That woman of yours is going to have you so turned inside out, you, my brother, are not going to know up from down."

Dix replied confidently, "Put your money where your mouth is, Jackson Blake."

"Okay. Here's a ten-dollar gold piece that says she'll have you permanently calf-eyed before Christmas."

They were both smiling as they shook hands to seal the wager.

They spent a few more moments boasting over who would win, then time came for their final good-bye.

They embraced each other with friendship and sadness. Dix told him, "You know we can always use a good man in the Territory if you can't get that bounty cleared up.''

"I know."

Then Dix spied Katherine standing a bit away from them, waiting quietly.

Blake saw her also and said, "Take good care of yourself, Dix."

Dix said softly, "You, too."

Katherine and Dix drove the remaining few miles into town and parked their wagon outside one of the best Black hotels in the city. Katherine looked down at herself. Back at the farmhouse she'd done her best to remove the grime from her face and hands, but her trail-soiled clothes were the same ones she'd donned three days ago. She resembled a beggar. "Dix, this is a pretty fancy place."

"Just what we need, don't you think?"

"But I'm covered with mud. Will they give us a room?"

"I dare them not to," he told her pointedly.

Katherine smiled. Yep, she liked this man a lot.

Inside the elegant lobby, they crossed the thick carpets to the highly polished guest desk.

The short, dark-skinned uniformed man on duty took one look at them and, in a haughty voice, said, "I believe you folks should try Hattie's boardinghouse down the street."

Then he turned away and resumed putting what appeared to be messages and telegrams in the pigeonholes on the wall.

Katherine shared a pointed look with her husband.

Dix said softly, "Go and get your manager."

The man turned back, seeming surprised to find them still soiling the premises. "Hattie's is—"

"I'd like to speak to your boss."

"Oh, no," the man said with a chuckle. "My employer does not have the time—"

Dix calmly took hold of the man's shirtfront and dragged him very slowly across the desk. The man was gulping, wide-eyed, and a breath away when Dix drawled, "You must be hard of hearing. I said, get your boss."

"Okay, okay," he promised.

Dix let him go.

He returned moments later with three men. Katherine guessed the manager to be the one in the middle dressed in the suit. The two big men flanking him were undoubtedly members of the hotel's security force.

As the contingent neared, the clerk pointed, "There they are. As I said, they are not the type of guests we have here."

Dix ignored the thugs and spoke to the brown-skinned man in the suit. "Do you know the penalty for refusing to house a federal officer of the law?"

Dix took out his star and placed it on the desk.

The man stared at Dix, then stuttered, "Uh–uh, no, I don't."

The rude little clerk responded accusingly, "He never said anything about that!"

The manager shot him an angry look and said, "Shut up, Ben."

"The United States government can shut you down just like you're running a cathouse."

The manager stared daggers over at his employee, then looked back at Dix. "Who are you, sir?"

"Dixon Wildhorse, United States deputy marshal. This is my wife. She's a newspaperwoman. Works for Mr. Pulitzer."

The man paled visibly. When his shocked eyes met

Katherine's, she smiled and gave a little wave. This was the best bit of entertainment she'd witnessed since the itinerant group of actors they'd happened upon on the trail.

Dix said, "My wife and I just came off the road. We know we're dirty, but our gold is clean."

The manager once again turned irritated eyes on his clerk before saying, "Right this way, folks. Ben there takes himself a bit too seriously sometimes. As a show of apology for the appalling way you've been treated, I'll see to it that you get the best suite we have to offer. On the house, of course."

"That isn't necessary," Dix pointed out.

"No, Marshal, I insist."

So a few minutes later, the sullen clerk showed them up to the third floor and into the best suite in the house. The appointments were grand, the bed and other furnishings lavish. There was an attached bathing room, an outer sitting room, and windows large enough to offer an expansive view.

Ben told them frostily, "We call this the Frederick Douglass suite because he stayed here last year. We had the interior and the furnishings all redone for his visit. Please try and treat it with the reverence it deserves."

Dix, tired of his yapping, looked at him and promised coolly, "If I hear one more snippy remark, I'm going to treat you with the reverence *you* deserve."

Ben huffed out the door, muttering, "Barbarians," and slammed it as he exited.

Katherine shook her head. "I enjoyed the way you handled our arrival. I thought the manager would succumb to apoplexy when you told him who you were. Is there really a penalty for refusing a room to a marshal?"

Dix shrugged. "I've no idea."

Katherine chuckled. "You lied?"

"Suppose so. I've used it before. Always works."

"Dixon Wildhorse, you surprise me. You seem to take things so seriously most times. Never pegged you for a situational liar. That's more *my* bailiwick."

He grinned. "Whatever works."

Katherine was glad it had. The Frederick Douglass suite was fabulous, far grander than any room she'd ever stayed in before. The best part was knowing she'd be able to enjoy the surroundings for the next few days. "So, what shall we do first? Eat? See if there's a theater?"

"Wash."

She dropped her eyes in embarrassment. "Oh, right. I almost forgot. I feel as if I've been away from civilization for so long, I want to immerse myself in everything all at once."

Dix walked to the door. "I'm going to get the gear. I'll be right back."

"Will you have Ben send me up water for a bath?"

"Will do."

Dix stood at the door for a moment just taking in her tall presence. Even though she had a month of trail dust on her, she was still pretty as a sunrise.

"Something wrong?" she asked.

Dix shook himself. "No. I'll have the water sent."

After he exited, Katherine couldn't help but ponder why he'd been staring at her so intensely.

He returned a short while later with valises and his war bag holding his personal belongings. "The water's coming. I'm going to go and see if I can't find someone to buy the wagon and the horse. While I'm gone, don't open the door to anyone, and don't talk to strangers. The varmints here are a lot meaner and slicker than your back-East variety. Okay?"

"Dix, I doubt I will be in any danger."

"Okay?" he asked again as if she hadn't offered the reassurance.

"Okay," she said. "I'm just not accustomed to being coddled. I usually do a fairly decent job of looking after myself *by* myself."

"Well, that's fine, but everybody needs assistance now and again, even you, Warrior Woman. Remember, your name could've been Mrs. Rupert Samuels."

"Don't remind me. Your point is made. I will be careful, and I won't open the door."

"Good. I'll be back as soon as I can."

As he stood there, hand on the door, Katherine saw desire flare in his dark eyes, and her senses answered the gaze. The steady, unending pace of the wagon train journey had made a repeat of their lovemaking impossible. Did hoping to be intimate with him again make her brazen?

"Your need is showing, Mrs. Wildhorse. . . ."

Katherine tossed back saucily, "And so is yours, Marshal."

With a twinkle in his dark eyes he left.

It took an hour for the water to arrive, but Katherine didn't fuss. She used the first big bucket to wash away the grime, then let the water drain away. The other buckets had been saved to luxuriate in, so she poured them in and did just that. She could have soaked for an eternity, but when the water began to cool, she stepped out of the bathtub and dried off.

Katherine pulled clean clothing from one of the carpetbags and donned a crisp, but creased, white shirt and dark skirt. In the valise she found Sweetie Pie, the derringer given to her by Miss Sunshine. If Dix felt this place was so dangerous, she thought it best to keep

Sweetie Pie within ready reach, so she hid it beneath one of the bed pillows.

Katherine had just turned away from the bed when a knock sounded on the door. Remembering Dix's warning, Katherine asked, "Who's there?"

A man replied, "I've come to get the buckets, ma'am."

Relieved, Katherine unlocked the door. In a blink of an eye a large quilt was thrown over her head. She began to fight immediately, but the large covering muffled her screams and impeded any effective actions. While she struggled to free herself from the constricting folds, she was lifted onto a strong shoulder and carried away.

Her kidnapper didn't carry her very far. When Katherine was eased back to her feet, she was far too furious to be frightened when the quilt was taken away. She was in a smaller hotel room along with three of the dirtiest looking men she'd ever seen. They were in western garb—stained hats, stained and dirty shirts and trousers, mud-caked boots. She didn't recognize any of them. "What is the meaning of this?"

A man with hard eyes and a sly grin asked, "Is this her?"

"Pretty sure, Vern," one of the other men answered.

The one named Vern came over and took a slow tour around her, examining her from head to toe. He apparently approved of what he saw. "She ain't bad, is she boys?"

"No, she ain't, Vern, " one of the others laughed. "Mona's gonna hit the roof when Dix brings this one back."

Katherine stared. Mona? "You know my husband?"

"Sure do, which is why we got to get you back to your room before he knows you're gone. Where's the map?"

"What map?"

"The map your daddy, Bart, posted to you for safe-keeping?"

Her father?! Now what had he done, she thought wildly. "What is this map to?"

"A Texas gold mine."

"A Texas gold mine?! And you believed him? Surely you know my father is prone to exaggeration."

"We do, but we also know that sometimes he's telling the truth, and this may just be one of those times."

Katherine couldn't believe this situation and briefly wondered about the Territorial penalty for patricide. "My father never posted me a map. I've no idea what you're talking about."

"Quit stalling. Where is it?"

Before Katherine could reply, one of Vern's cohorts volunteered helpfully, "Maybe she already gave it to the marshal."

Vern snapped, "Shut up, Clyde!" Then he said to her, "Now, lady, I don't like hurting women, but I want that map."

He tried to appear menacing, and perhaps Katherine might have been intimidated, but she towered over him by a good five inches.

Vern asked, "Do you understand me?"

"Sir, I assure you, I would not lie to you about something that obviously means a great deal, so I repeat: I know nothing about a map."

The man standing next to Clyde said, "She's lying!"

"Shut up, Ned!"

Ned shut up.

Vern said, "Okay, lady, have a seat. Ned, get over here and tie her up. Clyde, go slip that note I wrote under the marshal's door."

Katherine asked, "What does the note say?"

"It's an invitation to a meeting tomorrow morning to discuss the map."

"Suppose he decides not to come?"

"Then we shoot you."

He gave her a lascivious grin, and for the first time Katherine felt a shiver of fear.

Dix returned late that night. It hadn't taken long to find a buyer for the Hiram Walker, but the new owner didn't have any coin on him; Dix rode with the man to his farm outside town so he could be paid in full.

He unlocked the door to the hotel room and entered the dark outer sitting room. Because there were no lamps lit, he assumed Katherine had gone to bed. He was admittedly disappointed; he'd hoped to share a big meal with her and then the big bed before calling an end to such a whirlwind day. *Oh, well,* he sighed to himself, *tomorrow.*

He removed his boots and tiptoed into the bedroom as quietly as possible. He'd grabbed a bath at a bathhouse down the street so there was no need to disturb her by bathing now. He began to unbutton his shirt, and called softly toward the bed, "Kate?"

When she failed to respond in the sleepy voice he'd become accustomed to hearing, he took a good look at the dark outline of the bed. The hair stood up on the back of his neck. He swiftly lit a lamp. The bed was empty. Where the hell was she? He went into the bathing room and found it as empty and silent as the rest of the suite. He stood there and thought a moment. The door had been locked. Had she gone out somewhere? If she had, he doubted that she would have gone without leaving word, so he spent a few moments searching the premises for a note of some kind. Nothing.

Telling himself it was too early to panic, he went down to the hotel's desk.

The uniformed man on duty was unfamiliar. Dix asked, "Where's Ben?"

"Gone home for the evening. May I help you, Marshal?"

"You know me?"

"Everyone in the place knows you, sir. You're a hero around here for the way you handled Ben. It's not often he gets flayed so publicly."

"Glad I could help. You haven't seen my wife have you?"

"Mrs. Wildhorse, no sir, I'm afraid I haven't. Have you tried the dining room?"

When his search there proved equally fruitless, he went back to the desk.

The clerk asked, "Not there?"

"No."

"You look worried, Marshal."

"I am. It isn't like her to take off this way. Where does our friend Ben live?"

"At the employee boardinghouse in back of the hotel."

"Can you get me somebody to take me there? He may know something."

"I'll take you myself."

Ben did not like being awakened. Dix had to shake him a couple times to make him open his eyes. When he looked up and saw Dix standing over him, his face soured. "What do you want? Some hay so you can bring your horse inside the suite for the night?"

Dix was too upset over Katherine to be polite. He grabbed Ben by his nightshirt and lifted him clear off the bed. "Have you seen my wife?"

"No," Ben snapped, then looked away from Dix's penetrating eyes.

Over the years Dix had been lied to by more thieves, murderers, and outlaws than he cared to count. Compared to them, Ben was a greenhorn amateur. "You're not telling me something, Ben. What is it?"

"I told you, I haven't seen her."

"Then do you know where she might be—and remember Ben, I'm normally a very patient man, but not when my wife is missing."

"You can't touch me, I know the law."

Angry, Dix threw him back on the bed, and when Ben bounced, Dix grabbed him by the ankles and held him upside down. He bounced his body up and down a few inches above the floor until Ben's nightshirt rolled down over his head, revealing his skinny little legs and the fact that Ben slept nude beneath his shirt. The bouncing continued, and Ben began to scream. The polite young man who'd escorted Dix to the room was laughing so hard, he was on the floor.

"Stop it!" Ben pleaded.

"Is your memory starting to come back?" Dix asked still dunking him up and down.

"Yes!" Ben squealed. "Yes! Oh, please!"

"Then talk."

"They said they were friends of yours!"

"Who?"

"Some men. Oh, let me down, my head's starting to spin!" he whined.

Dix took pity and tossed him back on the bed. He waited for Ben to pull himself together, then asked, "Now, who said they were friends of mine?"

"There were three of them. They said they'd heard you were in town and wanted to surprise you with a visit. They were so dirty, I never questioned their story.

After all, they did appear to be people you would know."

Dix ignored the dig. "What did they want?"

"Your room number, along with a room of their own."

"They're registered at the hotel?"

Ben nodded frostily.

"Under what name?"

"Morgan."

"Vernon Morgan?"

"I believe that is correct, yes."

Dix cursed silently. What in the hell was Vernon Morgan doing here? The men with him had to be his twin brothers, Clyde and Ned, because they always traveled as a trio. They were small-time bootleggers and rustlers from the Territory. "What's their room number?"

"Six. May I go back to sleep now?"

"Yes, you may. Thanks for the hospitality."

On the way back to the hotel, the young clerk said, "I sure do like the way you conduct an interrogation, Marshal. Ben was squealing like a pig."

"I'll need the key to room six."

"You shall have it."

Dix wondered if anyone knew or cared how tired he was. He'd reached Kansas City that morning after forty or so days on the road; then he'd driven the Hiram Walker out to a farm ten miles outside of the city. In reality, he was dead on his feet. He had planned to enjoy his wife's company and then sleep until noon tomorrow—not spend the night talking to squealing clerks and dealing with Territorial varmints like the Morgans. If no one knew the depth of his fatigue, the Morgans were about to find out.

Dix stormed into their room, snatched the sleeping

Vernon Morgan up off the floor, and stuck the Colt in his nostril. ''Where's my wife, Vern?''

Recognizing Dix, Vern squealed in fright, but he didn't move because of the cold pressure of the long-nosed Colt. ''Uh, how you doing, Dix?''

''I was doing fine until I came back and found my wife missing. Where is she?''

''She's . . . over there. We was just keeping her company until you got back.''

Dix kept his grasp on Vern and turned to survey the surroundings. By now the clerk had lit a lamp and was untying and ungagging a very furious Katherine. The twins, Ned and Clyde, were just now coming awake. They sat up sleepily in their bedrolls and looked around. Upon spotting Dix, both paled as if they'd seen a ghost.

''Evening, boys. Heard you were planning a surprise for me.''

Both quickly denied everything.

''Shut up!'' Vern yelled, still under the Colt. ''Just shut up!''

Katherine had by now been freed. She gave the clerk a curt nod of thanks, walked over to her husband, and said, ''Shoot him.''

''*Noooo!*'' Vernon screeched. ''This is all her daddy's fault!''

Confused, Dix turned to Katherine, who replied, ''My father has them believing I possess a map to a gold mine.''

Dix barked, ''Vern you caused me all this anxiety over a Bart Love lie? I should shoot you just for being so stupid. You know damn well Bart never tells the truth.'' Disgusted, Dix turned him loose.

''But, Marshal, he swore it existed.''

''So did that Spanish treasure he had you looking for last year. Vern, when are you going to learn?''

Clyde cut in, "I tried to tell him, but—"

Vern snapped, "Shut up!"

Clyde shut up.

Katherine firmly repeated her original request, "Shoot him, Dix. Now."

A small smile escaped his lips. "Are you okay?"

"No, I enjoyed having a smelly quilt thrown over my head and being abducted. I enjoyed it almost as much as being tied up for three hours. If you won't shoot them, then give me the Colt and I'll shoot him."

Dix shook his head and tried to suppress his grin. "If you shoot them here, you'll go to jail. How about I let you shoot them when we reach home?"

Vern stared from Katherine's angry countenance to Dix. "You aren't really going to let her shoot me, are you?"

"I don't know, Vern, she's pretty adamant. I'd rather have her mad at you than at me."

Katherine had spent the last three hours battling fears that she would be killed. Now that Dix had neutralized the situation, she was so mad at Vernon Morgan for putting her through such a frightening few hours, she couldn't see straight. She'd strangle her father with her bare hands when she reached Indian Territory. A gold mine! What would be next?

Dix turned away from his fire-breathing wife and told the Morgans, "If I were you, I'd head for home."

"Now?" Vern asked. "It's the middle of the night."

Dix remained silent.

Evidently, the Morgans knew Dix well enough to recognize his stance because they didn't argue further. Grumbling, they gathered their gear.

Ned said sullenly, "I still think she's lying."

Katherine fairly screeched at him, "I do not have a

map to a gold mine! There is no gold mine!''

Vernon Morgan didn't appear convinced.

A frustrated Katherine threw up her hands and stormed out.

Chapter 12

The Morgan brothers were escorted from the hotel by members of its security detail. Samuel Dennis, the young clerk who'd been at Dix's side all night, received a commendation from the manager for his assistance in rescuing Mrs. Wildhorse, plus a raise in position and pay. When everything was over, Dix and Katherine finally trudged up the three flights of stairs to their suite. Once inside, they fell atop the bed and were instantly asleep.

The next morning dawned sunny and bright. Dix and Katherine were treated to a sumptuous breakfast delivered by Samuel Dennis. He rolled in a cart filled with covered dishes, and mouth-watering scents permeated the room. As he set the table, Katherine stared in amazement at the amount of food: bacon and eggs, grits, ham, oatmeal, two kinds of stewed fruits, biscuits, corn fritters, jams, honey, marmalade, coffee, and tea. She looked to Dix, who appeared just as overwhelmed watching Samuel unearth fried potatoes, corn chowder, a baked hen, and a tall pitcher of lemonade.

As the young man continued to add more culinary delights to the already groaning table, Katherine asked with a chuckle, "Samuel, who is going to eat all this?"

"I tried to tell my mother it would take the two of you a month to eat so much, but she wouldn't listen."

Dix asked, "Your mother?"

Samuel nodded proudly. "She's head cook here. This is her way of saying thanks for getting me the raise in rank and pay. Now I can leave my other job down at Mr. Rice's stable and concentrate on my schoolwork. I'm studying to go back East to Howard College. I want to be a doctor someday."

Katherine smiled and Dix appeared pleased.

Dix said, "Tell your mama thank you for us. We'll try and do this justice."

Samuel began to roll the cart toward the door when Dix stopped him by saying, "Listen, if you find doctoring's not all it's cracked up to be, come on out to the Territory and be a deputy."

Samuel beamed. "You really mean that, Marshal?"

Dix nodded.

"Thanks!" he gushed and left them alone.

Katherine took her seat. "That was nice of you, Marshal."

"He's a nice kid. I hope the future gives him what he wants."

They spent the next few moments piling their plates with food. Everything tasted just as wonderful as it looked. Katherine still had no kind words for the Morgans, however. "You really should have let me shoot them, you know."

Dix's mustache lifted in a smile over his raised coffee cup. "No."

"I can't believe they came all this way just because they thought I had a map."

"The idea of gold makes people stupid sometimes,

and with Vernon and his brothers they wouldn't have to go too far.''

"That I believe, but who are they?''

"Penny-ante bootleggers. They rustle a few cows, rob a train or a post office now and again, but for the most part they're harmless. Vern fancies himself the brains of the bunch because he's the eldest. Clyde is the most likable, however, and the only one with a working brain. Ned is the one to watch. He's mean, selfish, always trying to show everybody how tough and smart he is.''

"So did you find the note they left?''

"What note?''

"Vern had Clyde slip a note beneath the door, informing you of a meeting they wanted to hold concerning the map.''

"Nope.''

Curious about it, however, Dix left the table to search around the doorway. When he returned, he said, "Nothing. Knowing them, though, they probably slipped it into the wrong room.''

Katherine would not have been surprised. Their plan to retrieve the map was not only filled with holes, it had not been very brilliantly conceived or carried out. Under further interrogation last night, the Morgans confessed to arriving in Kansas City about three weeks ago. It seems Bart had been caught cheating in a card game less than three days after his return from Chicago, and unlike most of the town's residents, Vernon had demanded satisfaction. As restitution and to appease Vern's anger, Bart offered him the map to a legendary Texas gold mine known as the Lost African mine. He then told Vern he'd posted the map to Katherine for safekeeping.

"Why would my father deliberately sic them on me?''

"Knowing your daddy, he probably didn't think they'd find us. This is a big city. He also knew I'd never let you come to harm even if they did, so Bart had nothing to be worried about.''

Her father's logic notwithstanding, Katherine planned on speaking with him the moment she returned. "If the Morgans know my father, why on earth would they believe him?''

"Because as Vern said, one day your pa just might be telling the truth."

Katherine thought that a possibility, but not a very large nor likely one. "Does this Lost African mine really exist?''

"No one's sure. The legend, which goes back to the forties, has it that a slave was sent by his Texan owner to round up some stray horses. The slave was gone longer than was expected, and when he finally returned, he was beaten for his tardiness. Now, supposedly the slave returned with two huge nuggets of gold but never had the chance to tell his master about the find because the master was too busy beating the man. Evidently someone else did see the gold, but when the master went to ask the slave about it, he was nowhere to be found. He'd run—taking the gold and the location of the mine with him.''

"Good for him. I take it the master never found him?''

"Never did, and he searched for years.''

Katherine thought it a great story. "And this is the map my father told the Morgans I had in my possession.''

"Yep," he replied. "Your pa can fool some of the folks in the Territory some of the time, but he can fool fools like Vern Morgan and his brothers all the time.''

Once Katherine finally had her fill of the hearty breakfast, she pushed back from the table. While Dix finished up, she walked over to the windows that looked down on the streets. Kansas City was a busy place. All manner of vehicles were traveling below: Conestogas, buckboards, carriages, and sumptuous private coaches. The city wasn't as large as the big cities back East, but with the wealth of people coming and going, she didn't believe it would be long before it would be.

The first thing she wanted to do was find a newspaper so she read about how the world had been spinning during their month on the trail. Her next task would be to search out a telegraph office and wire her whereabouts to Geoff in New York.

Katherine turned back to see that Dix had finished eating and was enjoying a cup of coffee. Over the raised cup, his eyes held hers, and all she could think about were his kisses and that just the sight of him made her senses warm. Last night he'd teased her about her need showing; she wondered if it was showing now.

"I never did say thanks for rescuing me last night, so, thank you," Katherine said warmly.

"Most lawmen are given a reward for such services."

She smiled at the playfulness in his eyes and asked, "Oh, really? And what kind of reward are you fishing for, Marshal?"

He didn't reply aloud, but his eyes told her quite plainly what he desired.

She crossed over to where he sat at the table and stopped close enough to feel his body's warmth mingling with her own. "Since I have no money . . . is there another way I might . . . reward you?"

She eased herself down onto his lap and draped her arms around his strong neck.

Dix was hard as iron. He looked into her eyes and said, "You seem to be doing pretty well without my prompting."

"Good . . . then, kiss me, lawman. . . ."

The kiss was sure and steamy. The touch of his mouth upon hers singed her like a too-hot stove. His kisses invited and beckoned as passion began to take hold.

She offered an invitation of her own in the parting of her lips and the nibbles she took. Beneath her hands the flesh of his strong arms flexed subtly, singeing her palms the way his kisses singed her lips. Leaving her mouth, Dix began to blaze a trail down the sensitive skin of her throat. He filled a hand with the sweet weight of her breast. She arched responsively, willingly. She now knew all about the parts between kissing and cleaving and brazenly wanted to be shown more.

Dix used slow hands to make her tremble, gasp, and blossom. Her eyes slid closed as his fingers teased her nipples into tight twin peaks. She was so ripe, he could hardly wait to explore the full measure of her passionate depths, leisurely and without interruption.

She held his glittering eyes as he slowly undid the buttons of her blouse. Her focus dissolved when his warm hands pulled down her camisole. Her eyes closed as his mouth covered her, and she crooned pleasurably.

The soft sound fueled Dix to extract as much intensity from this morning interlude as manly possible. He wanted her twisting and mindless by the time they ended; after all, this beautiful woman was his wife, and she deserved no less than pure bliss.

So, with an erotic expertise that had made Dixon Wildhorse a legend in the female parts of Indian Territory, he proceeded.

He treated her bared breasts first—nibbling, suckling, planting wet kisses on the silken golden undercurves. He brushed his lips over the ripe, bud-hard nipples, then the sensuous valley between, feeling her tremble, hearing her sigh. A few minutes later, he raised her skirts to expose her thighs to his touches, and his hand wandered wantonly outside her drawers. Her lovely legs parted willingly to his gentle command, letting him tease and circle. Desire had him so enthralled, he wanted to fill her right there and then, but he wanted something else first.

"Stand up a minute, sweetheart. . . ."

She was sprawled across his lap, blouse undone, skirt about her thighs. The way her hips were gently rising in response to his fingers upon the damp cotton shielding her heat made him think she hadn't heard. "Kate . . ."

Katherine didn't know why he was trying to make her talk. Every stroke and movement of his hands made the passion build like water backing up behind a dam. She felt so ripe with the intensity, she didn't want to try.

Dix lowered his head to once again greet her sablé-tipped nipples. Only when she crooned did he raise up. "Stand, *chica*," he whispered against her ear. "I want to hear you count for me. . . ."

Katherine could almost swear he'd said he wanted to hear her count, but she was certain her muddled senses hadn't heard him clearly. She stood anyway, barely sure of where she was or who she was. However, she did know that the man seated before her was Dix and that his hands had set her afire.

She trembled as he whispered instructions for her to raise up her skirt. When she complied, he slowly untied the strings of her drawers, then removed the undergarment. While she stood before him with her bunched up skirt, soaring on the passion beating through her like an African drum, he played, caressed, and enflamed her until she moaned in sensual delight. The far-off sounds of dishes being moved around drifted through her foggy state, but it did not intrude upon her passion. She had the vague sensation of being laid down on something hard, then realized she was on her back atop the linen-covered table.

He smiled sensually at the confusion on her face. When she held out her arms in welcome, he kissed her soundly. He stripped her of everything but her dark cotton stockings and garters. There, on the tabletop, in the Frederick Douglass suite, Katherine Wildhorse, her brown body ripening in the bright morning sunshine, moaned as her husband's hands once again raised her heat. It began anew, the burgeoning intensity, the burning kisses, the body-caressing passes of his possessive hands . . .

Then as his hands dallied between her thighs, making her flow hot, sweet, and free, he lowered his head and flicked his tongue against the spot he'd been ripening for his feast. She stiffened, then moaned as wild enchantment took hold.

"Count for me Katherine . . . let's see if you can make it to fifty."

She never knew such wanton kisses existed, never knew such carnal pleasuring could be had. Katherine couldn't count; she could barely breathe.

"Count for me. . . ." he whispered sensually, thickly.

Katherine replied softly, "One . . ."

His bold expertise made her purr.

"Two . . ."

He took her in fully, and she could count no more. His bold play took her over the edge, and the exploding pleasure shattered her like glass.

Pleased as only a male can be, Dix stood and watched his wife ride out her pleasure atop the fine linen table-cloth. The sun streaming in through the thin white curtains made her jewel-hard nipples that much more alluring. It spotlighted her trim waist, the dark hair at the V of her thighs, and her gorgeous long legs. This would be a morning he would never forget.

Katherine wouldn't, either. Nothing in her experience had ever prepared for such overwhelming sensations. Even as she regained her faculties and opened her eyes, she still throbbed and bloomed with the echoing heat. He stood above her, giving her that ought-to-be-patented ghost of a smile.

"You didn't count very high, *chica*. . . ."

As he spoke, his finger grazed across the swollen treasure between her thighs. She drew in a tight, moan-filled breath. "You are not . . . *ohhhh* . . . treating this room with the reverence it deserves. . . ."

He bent and touched his mouth heatedly to her damp gate. Her hips flew up off the table.

"But I am treating *you* with the reverence you deserve. . . ."

He treated her with *such* reverence that when he finally pulled her to him and joined his iron-hard heat to her own, Katherine groaned with delight. The initial feel of him entering her was so intense, she wanted to ask him to withdraw and enter her again, but to ask for such a thing would be shameless—too shameless even for the brazen woman she'd become as his wife.

The stroking was bliss, too, she admitted. The friction of his need against her own made her answer the strokes in a rhythm unique to the duet of love. She could feel the linen beneath her hips undulating in sensuous time. His eyes were hot, glittering with desire. She leaned up for his kiss, and he lowered his mouth to meet hers.

Dix thrust up gently as they shared the kiss, making her shimmer and tighten around his manhood even more. He had to pace himself lest he take her as quickly as his ardor demanded. Her intoxicating kisses in tandem with her temptress body made him want to toss aside husbandly considerations and ride her like the winds of a storm.

In the end he went slow, so slow she was gasping and rising and treating him to a most erotic tableau. Soon passion burst, and her keening cry of release filled the sun-bright room. A second later, unable to hold back, he stiffened as his own world exploded. He gripped her hips. Shuddering, he pumped out his essence with a raw-sounding roar. He would never get enough of her, he realized. Never.

In the aftermath, Katherine felt boneless. It had been such a dazzling feast, she could not move. "Remind me to be wary the next time you invite me to breakfast," she told him.

He gave her one last kiss. "And remind me to see how you taste with marmalade the next time I do. . . ."

His words and his kiss made a sensual ripple run through her. "I didn't get very far with my counting, did I?"

"No, you didn't. Isn't counting to fifty what your aunt told you to do?"

She nodded, remembering then that she'd told him of her aunt's advice on how to survive the marriage act. Her aunt couldn't have been more wrong.

Dix leaned over her and said, "Maybe next time you'll make it to ten."

She took his teasing with a smile. "You are too good for your own good, Dixon."

"And so are you, my Kate."

They spent the rest of the day tending to errands. Katherine found herself smiling up at him as they toured the streets and went in and out of stores. She felt like a grinning idiot at times, basking in his eyes. She tried to rein herself in from exhibiting such uncharacteristic behavior, then told herself that the breakfast she'd had this morning would make any woman giddy.

The trip to the telegraph office proved to be fruitful; not only were there messages for Dix, there were two for Katherine, as well. Both missives were from Geoff. The first one read:

Alerted by Sunshine. Glad you're safe. Bridegroom irate. Crying kidnap. On his way to you. Watch for Pinkertons. Be careful!

G.

The second one, dated just a week earlier, left her stunned:

Bad news. Paper about to close. T.F. and Rev. D. at odds. All agents terminated. Sorry. Wired your bank funds to Sunshine. She will relay. Stay safe.

G.

Katherine stared wide-eyed. She read the last telegram again, but the wording did not change. She had no job! After all she'd been through, she'd been terminated! For a moment she felt sick. She'd known that the owner, Mr. Fortune, and the Revered Derrick, an investor, hadn't seen eye to eye, but to close down the paper?!

Dix, standing beside her, saw the odd bleakness in her face and asked, ''What's wrong?''

Wordlessly, she handed him Geoff's messages.

She began to walk away, her thoughts on nothing but her dilemma. She didn't give a fig about Rupert or his Pinkertons. Good Lord, how was she going to support herself now? After a few steps, she sensed Dix striding silently beside her, but she didn't say anything all the way back to the hotel.

Dix's messages had been a bit less wrenching. The first one, dated three weeks ago, had been from his light horse deputy, Lyndon Green. Dix had wired Lyndon while on the trail of his Kansas City destination and the approximate date of arrival. The message warned Dix of the impending visit by the Morgan brothers. Dix kicked himself for not checking the telegraph office as soon as he and Katherine had arrived. Had he done so, he might have headed off the encounter with the threesome. The second note, from Sunshine, alerted him to funds on deposit for Katherine at one of the local Black banks from Kate's editor. Dix hoped the small boon would cheer her a bit.

She was standing before the window, looking out at the sunset. When he told her about the funds, she acknowledged him with a nod, then turned back. Dix wanted to fold her in his arms and keep her there until the sadness left her eyes. He did not enjoy seeing her this way—at all.

Katherine knew wallowing accomplished little if anything, but she indulged herself a few moments longer as she faced the truth. She would have to find other employment because she refused to go to her husband with her hand out in order to buy clothes, food, or ink for her pens. The money forwarded by Miss Sunshine amounted to all of her accumulated savings, but it would not see her through the winter. She hoped to wrangle another newspaper position but knew the calls for female agents were few and far between. If the situation became desperate, she could always fall back on her sewing talents or scrub floors or do whatever it took to keep herself afloat. She knew Dix would offer what help he could, but she wanted to be able to pay her own way. She'd never lived her life being beholden to anyone.

Finally, she turned to the silent man sitting in the chair and said, "I'm done."

"With what?"

"Wallowing. My aunt used to say, 'Ten minutes for joy and ten minutes to grieve.' That's all we're allowed because life goes on."

He looked over at the clock.

Following his eyes, Katherine said defensively, "I know. It's been two hours, not ten minutes, but it's the best I could do."

He shook his head with amusement, then stated, "That aunt of yours sounds as if she led a very timely life."

Katherine smiled. "The most punctual woman I've ever known."

"So Rupert's claiming I kidnapped you."

"According to Geoff."

"How in the world did you ever wind up going down the aisle with him?"

"Circumstances beyond my control. The way the plan was *supposed* to unfold, I was to masquerade as a seamstress and listen to the gossip of the Black elite and report back."

"So what when wrong?"

"Rupert. He came into the shop one day and became smitten. I was appalled, of course, and so was his dear mama, Pearl. Even though I tried to discourage him, he persisted in coming by the shop. He brought me presents every day for a week in an effort to convince me to dine with him. I finally agreed, hoping he would go away and leave me free to engineer his downfall.

"But he didn't, did he?"

"No. After the dinner came requests to accompany him to the theater, lectures, and visits to the local lending library. He began sending Frank or Joe with the carriage so I wouldn't have to walk to fittings. I admit he was witty, charming, and possessed the most impeccable manners, but he'd swindled a passel of people, and no amount of charm could make me look past that.''

"So why'd you agree to marriage?"

"At first his proposal knocked me for a loop. Rupert Samuels was the last man on earth I wished to spend my life with, but I had worked hard trying to expose him and his counterfeit stock scheme. The night I saw the plates in the safe set the pudding. The plates were all the authorities would need, but I had to remain in Rupert's life in order to gain access to them, so—"

"You agreed to marry him."

"I figured I'd take the plates and disappear long before the wedding date came around, but it took Geoff longer than we both imagined it would to find a cracksman who could open the safe."

She then related the tale of being discovered in the room along with her accomplice.

"I believe Frank and Joe killed that poor man."

Upon hearing the story, Dix tended to agree. "So now he wants you back."

"Only so he can lock me away in a sanitorium or kill me."

"Well, no one's going to do either, at least not as long as I'm standing. Rupert is welcome to come to the Territory, but he'll find we do things a bit different out West."

"Do you think he knows who you are?"

"I'm sure the helpful Miss Melinda told him all she knew."

Katherine had all but forgotten about the duplicitous Melinda. "I hope Rupert didn't give Miss Sunshine trouble."

"If he did, it didn't last long. Sunshine is a very influential woman, and her customers come from all levels of society. Rupert may be powerful in his Black circles, but Sunshine knows her share of well-heeled alligators, too. Her clientele could collectively crush Rupert both financially and physically, should she ask their assistance."

Katherine was relieved. She'd left a wake of troubles on the doorsteps of innocent folks when she fled Chicago, and she hadn't wanted Miss Sunshine added to their number. She still carried the guilt from the destruction of the dress shop and hoped poor Mrs. Tuttle had been able to set it to rights.

They had dinner in the suite, then went to bed. This was only the second day off the trail, and both needed resting up. Dix wanted nothing better than to make love to her once more, but he was certain she was sore, so he kissed her on the cheek and sought sleep instead.

Katherine was admittedly disappointed when he turned over. His kiss was sweet, but after that morning's breakfast, she didn't want sweet; she wanted passion and heat. She scolded herself for being such a shameless glutton, then closed her eyes.

Sleep didn't come peacefully. She dreamed of the Morgan brothers, of Rupert, Frank, and Joe. They were all chasing her, and Dix was nowhere to be seen.

Her tossing and turning woke Dix around four. Since she was also snoring, he didn't see himself falling back to sleep anytime soon, so he left the bed quietly to go stand by the window. The moon was up, illuminating the night so brilliantly that he could almost make out the features on the faces of two men as they crossed the street and came toward the hotel. Both were muscular and short of stature, and the longer he watched the more convinced he became of their identity: Rupert's employees, Frank and Joe. He cursed silently. No doubt they had come to get back Katherine, and frankly, he was getting fairly tired of folks trying to steal his woman.

With an exasperated sigh, he drew on his trousers and took a seat, his rifle lying across his lap.

A short time later, Dix listened to them scratching at the lock. He wondered how long it had taken them to make their way back to Chicago after the last encounter. It couldn't've been an easy task, having to travel covered in honey and feathers.

Their key finally sprang the lock. Dix raised his rifle. When the door opened wide enough to let a sliver of the hallway light slide in, Dix fired. The shot shattered against the door, the sound almost masking the terrified yells of Frank and Joe, who hit the floor almost instantaneously. They tried to scramble to their feet, but by then, Dix was already on them. "You boys aren't going to leave so soon. Come on in and sit awhile."

A light flared to life, and Dix said to his wife, "Thanks for the light. Sorry I woke you up."

"Apology accepted," she said, moving now to his side. In her hand was the cocked Sweetie Pie. She overlooked her husband's amusement at the sight of Sweetie Pie and instead asked, "These two never learn, do they?"

"Doesn't seem like."

Neither Frank nor his buddy Joe appeared pleased. Just like last time, Dix was always one step ahead.

"What do you think we ought to do with them?" Katherine asked. "I've really been itching to try out Sweetie Pie."

Dix chuckled. "No."

"Please?"

"No."

"Oh, all right. What do you propose?"

"I think I want their clothes."

"Really?"

Dix nodded.

Frank and Joe looked so mad, steam should have been rolling from their ears.

"Strip, boys."

They hesitated at first, so Dix fired another shot over their heads, winging the wainscoting above the door. They frantically began removing belts and undoing shirt buttons. Once they were reduced to wearing nothing but their drawers, Dix smiled coldly and said, "Kate, go and get their things."

Kate bundled everything in her arms and waited for further instructions.

"Open the window and toss it all outside."

Though both men protested, their clothing was flung down to the street, ripe pickings for any vagrants who might come across them.

Dix was about to say something else when Ben the clerk came rushing in. His eyes widened when he saw the gun and widened even further at the appearance of the men facing the gun.

He gasped, "What is going on? Someone said they heard shooting."

"Ben, want you to meet Frank and Joe. Say hi, boys."

They didn't.

"Caught them stealing into my room. Lots of rats in your hotel, Ben."

Ben's eyes widened with outrage when he spied the bullet holes. "I thought I told you to treat this room with reverence! Aren't those bullet holes?"

"Nope, prairie dogs made them. Now, go get the authorities."

Ben appeared as if he would much rather discuss the

damage to the Frederick Douglass suite, so Dix growled, "Go and get the authorities before I have to bounce you again."

Katherine stared at her husband. *Bounce him again?* She had no idea what he might be alluding to, but Ben seemed to know because he left the room fairly running.

The local constables came and questioned everyone. When Dix showed them his papers and star, they were quite astonished.

"You're a *real* deputy marshal?" one of the constables asked.

Dix nodded emotionlessly.

The other constable, who introduced himself as Gordon, grinned, "That's damn impressive. I knew they had some of your kind keeping the law out West but never met one. Welcome to Kansas City, Marshal Wildhorse."

Both men seemed so awed by Dix, Katherine had to suppress a smile.

"Thank you," Dix replied. "These men broke into our room."

Constable Gordon said, "Well, we can't have that, now, can we? Trash like this'll make folks not want to visit our fair city." He then looked them up and down. "I like the way they're dressed, though. Were they dressed this way when they came in?"

Katherine lied baldly, "Yes."

He took up a position a breath away from Frank's ear and bellowed, "*Did you think the marshal's room was the whorehouse?!*"

Both men jumped at least a foot in the air, and Katherine almost felt sorry for them. Almost.

Gordon told his partner, "Get them out of here."

He then wished Dix and Katherine a pleasant stay and left them alone with Ben.

Ben began to fuss almost immediately. "Who's going to pay for this damage."

"Send me the bill. Good night."

"But—"

"Good night."

The next morning, they withdrew Katherine's small nest egg from the bank and boarded the Kansas Pacific for the train ride west to Oklahoma.

Chapter 13

Katherine had wanted to stay in Kansas City a bit longer but agreed with Dix that heading out might be best. They had no way of determining where Rupert and his minions might show up next time, but if and when they did, Dix wanted the confrontation to take place on the familiar ground of Indian Territory. To pass the time on the sixty-odd-mile trip to Topeka where they would change trains, Dix told her more of the triumphs and tragedies of the Black Seminoles.

The Black-Seminole alliance fought on after the 1814 destruction of Fort Negro. In spite of the ten thousand soldiers the United States sent to bring them to heel, they refused to surrender. They survived Andrew Jackson's vengeful burning of their cities, falsely worded treaties, and even the death and subsequent beheading of the great war chief Osceola. But they couldn't survive time nor a United States government intent upon usurping their lands. The country had changed; slavery was now the fuel that made America run. Southern slave owners feared that the free Black villages in Seminole Florida would tempt their own human property to flee and so wanted the villages destroyed and the Blacks reenslaved. America's White population was expanding across the continent under the banner of Manifest Destiny. Settlers in Florida were clamoring for the fertile land upon which the Blacks and Seminoles grew rice, orchards of wild oranges, tended their cattle, and sheltered their families. Even after one-sided treaties herded the members of the alliance into parts of Florida so desolate the land would not sustain crops, the government continued to allow settlers to steal treaty-protected land.

The alliance fought bravely for over thirty years. John Horse, leader of the Black Seminoles, finally surrendered in 1838 because of growing losses and the starvation his people faced. The U.S. Cavalry captured Seminole Chief Coatoochee, called Wild Cat by the soldiers, three years later. The Second Seminole War officially lasted seven years and cost the United States government 40 million dollars. Fifteen hundred American soldiers lost their lives.

In Topeka, Dix and Katherine switched trains. The Topeka–Santa Fe would take them as far as Wichita. From there they'd ride the Missouri, Kansas, and Texas Railroad down into Indian Territory.

With their tickets in hand, Dix and Katherine approached the Topeka–Santa Fe platform, then stood in line with the other passengers. When they reached the conductor, the man asked, ''Where do you two think you're going?''

Dix answered coolly, ''Indian Territory.''

The conductor looked them up and down. ''Name?''

''Dixon Wildhorse.''

The man's face brightened immediately. ''*The* Dixon Wildhorse, that Seminole marshal?''

Dix nodded tightly.

''Me and my family owe you a heap for putting a

stop to those train robberies last year. Them outlaws nearly killed my brother-in-law during one of their boardings.''

''Just doing my job.''

''Well, you did a damn fine one. Heard you caught the gang hiding out in the Territory.''

''Yes.''

The man's grin stretched from ear to ear. ''I'll have to tell everybody I met you, they're going to be green jealous. It's an honor to take your ticket. This here your missus?''

''Yes.''

''She's a tall drink of water. If you need any help turning on the spigots, you just let me know.'' He gave Dix an exaggerated wink.

Katherine's lips curled with distaste.

Dix appeared as impassive as stone.

The conductor tore their tickets in half, then pointed down the tracks. ''Injuns and Blacks in that back car. You two have a nice journey. I can't wait to get home and tell the wife I met you both.''

As Katherine and Dix headed back up the track, they could hear the conductor further extolling his good fortune at meeting them to the other passengers in line.

Katherine said bitterly, ''You do a 'damn fine' job, but 'Injuns and Blacks' get to ride jim crow.''

Dix replied, ''It's part of the so-called civilization being brought west by the homesteaders. It's never been real good for us out here, but most folks tended to judge you on your word and how good a job you could do. That's changing.''

As Katherine and Dix made their way down the graveled edge of the tracks, she could see the passengers inside gazing down on their progress. She didn't acknowledge them, and neither did Dix.

Fifteen Black and Indian passengers rode the 134 miles to Wichita in the cattle car.

In Wichita, they rented themselves a place to sleep at a local boardinghouse. After dinner, Dix escorted her back to their room.

It was a sharp contrast to the elegant confines of the Frederick Douglass suite in Kansas City. This room had a bed, a small writing desk with a lamp, a wardrobe, and a screen to hide the chamber pot. It was clean, however.

As Katherine lit the lamp and drew down the lone window shade, Dix strapped on his gun and said, "I'm going over to the telegraph office. You should stay put until I get back."

After riding in a cattle car for the past two days, Katherine had no desire to be cooped up. "I'll go with you."

"No."

"What do you mean, no?"

"It isn't safe."

"I can look out for myself."

"No."

"You're coddling me. I'm not accustomed to being coddled."

"I'm aware of that, but you're not going. This isn't Chicago, and it isn't New York. The streets of Wichita at night can be dangerous."

"So, I'll bring Sweetie Pie along."

"That gun couldn't wound a tree frog."

She put her hands on her hips and chuckled. "I don't care. I'm coming along. So unless you plan on tying me to the bedpost, we may as well end this discussion."

"Does that usually work with that Geoff friend of yours?"

"Does what usually work?"

"Your Warrior Woman ultimatums?" he asked quietly.

"Most times, yes," she replied.

He walked over and stood close enough for her to feel his body's warmth. She began to tremble as he slowly lowered his head and touched his mouth to hers. "I'm not Geoff," he whispered. "What I say, goes."

The sweetness of the kiss dampened her urge to sock him for uttering such male nonsense, but knowing him, she was certain there'd be another opportunity—probably soon. "You know I can't let you order me around this way . . . ohhh . . ."

The moan slid out because he'd opened her blouse and was now settling hot fiery kisses on the sensitive tops of her breasts. His big hands dragged her camisole down and bared the golden prizes to his eyes. "An obedient wife will always be rewarded, *chica*. . . ."

He bestowed his reward upon each sable nipple, and her soft groans of pleasure floated on the room's silence. While his mouth continued to tantalize her, he lazily raised her skirt, then circled the bunched-up fabric over her hips, legs, and the backs of her thighs. Her thighs parted shamelessly, delightedly, letting his lingering touches convey their hot-handed welcome.

He brushed his mouth across her ear. "I love making you bloom and flow. . . ."

His fingers were wanton bliss. His kisses sure, possessive. Katherine now understood the power of passion. And because she did, she slowly ran her hand over the hard length of him. She'd no idea if proper wives were allowed to be active participants in lovemaking, and she didn't care. She enjoyed watching his eyes close as her hand continued its fiery movements. She wanted him to be dazzled by her caresses. "May I touch you?" she asked in a voice softened by her desire.

"Anywhere . . . and anytime you like. . . ."

They both undressed, and she was again struck by his virile beauty. Power called from every muscle and sinew. The granite shoulders and muscular legs gleamed seductively in the pale light of the lamp.

For his part, Dix wondered if a more magnificent woman had ever been created. She was gorgeously made. Her beautiful mouth fit his perfectly. Just the sight of her silken brown legs made him ache to feel them surround him. Even if they remained lovers for a lifetime, he'd go to his grave having never gotten enough of her lush, ripe breasts and those sweetly flaring hips. Wordlessly, he carried her over to the bed and set her on top of the thin mattress. Before he could join her, she reached up and surrounded him with a possessive hand making Dix sigh with pleasure.

He was warm, hard, and soft in Katherine's hand. She whispered, "You feel like velvet. . . ." Then she lowered her head. When he groaned pleasurably, she smiled. She treated him to the same erotic tribute he'd paid her back in Kansas City. She had no idea if proper wives loved their husbands this way, but again she didn't care. All she cared about was dazzling him, melting him, and from the way his eyes were closed and the short gasps he uttered, she supposed she was doing a bang-up job.

A short while later, Dix eased her away and reversed the tables. His revenge was sweet and slow, so much so that when her release came, she had to muffle her screams against his shoulder. Dix, stroking her hard and fast, shattered only a moment behind her.

In the silent aftermath, Katherine turned her head to her husband beside her. She met the twinkle in his eyes and said, "You look entirely too pleased with yourself, Dixon."

"That's because I'm entirely too pleased with you."

He rolled closer, then ran the pad of his thumb over her nipple. It budded almost instantly, "Never thought you'd be this passionate."

"Never knew I was."

"Then I've done you a service."

"Your modesty is astounding." She leaned up and touched her lips to his. "I like you anyway, though." When the kiss ended, she asked, "Is this how you plan to end all of our disagreements?"

He flicked his tongue over her ear. "Since I rarely change my mind, this is as good a way as any. . . ."

"Then prepare for a rough ride, Marshal," she promised, seeking his kiss again. "I will not be so distracted again."

He met her kiss and whispered, "You're on."

In the end, he washed up in the communal bath down the hall and left her in the room to await his return.

There had been no messages waiting for them at the Wichita telegraph office. The next morning they boarded the Missouri, Kansas, and Texas Railroad for the final leg of the journey. There were no jim crow problems on the MK&T. With the government still restricting travel into the Territory by White settlers, the only regular passengers were Indians and Blacks. It was one of the main reasons the railroads were agitating on the side of those who wanted to make Oklahoma a state and let in the settlers. They made little profit hauling nothing but freight and Indians. Dix, seated next to his sleeping wife, hoped they'd have to haul nothing but freight and Indians until the mountains fell. How much more would the tribes be forced to surrender? The Chickasaw Nation once covered land south from the mouth of the Ohio River, across western Kentucky to Tennessee, and down into central Mississippi. The Creek claimed millions of

acres in what is now known as Georgia and Alabama
until they were broken at Horseshoe Bend by the forces
of Andrew Jackson in 1814. When Jackson negated the
articles of the Treaty of Ghent and illegally confiscated
the land of the Cherokee, the Cherokee Nation took their
case all the way to the Supreme Court. Although the
Court ruled in favor of the tribe, the government in
Georgia ignored the edict, and President Andrew Jackson did, too. The land was confiscated, and the Cherokee
were evicted by 7,000 U.S. troops. Five million acres
were taken from the Seminole, who in turn were offered
land not only barren and stormswept, but lay within territory already claimed by their enemies, the Creek. After
the Civil War, the government punished the tribes because some supported the Confederacy. Some of the
tribes had held slaves before the removal and continued
the practice after arriving in Indian Territory. Many
Seminoles, both Native and Black, fought for the Union,
but no distinctions were made by the U.S. All treaties
were negated, payments for land in the East were
stopped, and the land in Indian Territory was divvied up
again to incorporate tribes being removed from the
plains.

The five tribes were designated as "civilized" by
their steps toward civilized life and customs as determined by the United States government, a government
that in Dix's humble opinion had never been civil in
return. In compensation for the millions upon millions
of acres usurped, the land designated as Indian Territory
covered roughly 74,000 square miles.

But the Territory was home. The open land, the open
sky, the clean crispness of the air had been dearly missed
these past few months. Back east, the big cities always
made him feel constricted, caged in, like maybe wearing
a too-small suit. Out here he could stretch out, relax,

breathe. It felt good to be going home. He looked down at Katherine and again wondered how she'd feel about living out here. He realized he had grown attached to her, sentiments he felt he could not have. Keeping the peace was all he knew, and having a woman share his name would not alter his commitment to justice, nor change how he did his job. It surprised him how much he enjoyed her company, and he halfway wished the relationship could blossom; but once they set foot in the Seminole Nation, there'd be no more flower bringing or time for playful interludes. Although a portion of himself disagreed, the rational part thought this for the best. Getting back to work would help restore the distance he felt he needed to maintain. Having her on his mind could prove to be a fatal distraction in his oftentimes volatile occupation. He needed to be clearheaded and dispassionate when on the job. He didn't want to be thinking about her kisses while tracking outlaws or in a gun fight with a gang of bootleggers. In the end, he doubted she would stay, and like him would probably welcome a cooling down of their budding relationship for that reason alone.

In 1850, Tullahassee became the first all-Black town in Indian Territory. The year 1869 saw the founding of three more: North Folk Colored, Arkansas Colored, and Canadian. Gibson Station followed in 1880. Wewoka, where Dix and Katherine were headed, served as county seat of the Seminole Nation. It also held the distinction of being the village where Black Seminole Chief John Horse and many of his people settled after their removal from Florida. Dix lived three miles away in a Black Seminole settlement known as Nero, named for one of the old Black Seminole chiefs.

When the train reached the Wewoka station, a small

brass band greeted the return of the marshal and his wife. Word had it that the new Mrs. Wildhorse was Bart Love's daughter and that old Bart had lost her to the marshal in a card game. Of course, since Bart never told the truth, folks didn't know what to believe, so they turned out in force to welcome them home and see the new missus for themselves.

Katherine grasped Dix's offered hand as she stepped out of the car and onto the platform. She grinned at the sight and sounds of the lustily playing band and wished she were cleaner and better dressed. People began to applaud, and she looked up at Dix. He didn't appear particularly pleased by all the fanfare but stayed at her side. She spotted her father pushing his way through the crowd. He gave her a hug, which she returned in earnest, thankful that none of his pranks had gotten him killed. She did promise herself to speak to him later about his mischief making.

Dix took Katherine into the crowd and introduced her around. She met townspeople, business owners, and Seminoles both Black and Native. She brightened particularly when introduced to the local newspaper owner but had no opportunity to ask about employment because of the chaotic nature of the festivities and demands of those who wanted to shake her hand. She and Dix received numerous invitations to dinner, but Katherine noticed that Dix made no formal acceptances, so she didn't either. In all, the welcoming lasted about thirty minutes, and when it ended she accompanied Dix over to the marshal's office.

Inside she was introduced to Lyndon Green. He was Dix's right hand and a light horse policeman. Dix had explained to her that the light horse were the mounted police of the Territory. They dispensed tribal justice. Green gave her a polite, tight nod, but his dark eyes appeared cold and resentful. Katherine knew right away that the young policeman did not like her. Having never been one to shy away from confrontation, she asked plainly, "Have I offended you in some way, Officer Green?"

Her frankness didn't appear to bother him. "No, ma'am. Why do you ask?"

"You look as if I'm an enemy."

"You just may be," he said.

Without another word, he picked up his hat from the desk and left the office.

Astonished, Katherine looked to Dix for an explanation. Dix, by now seated behind the desk in the chair Green had vacated, glanced up from a pile of stacked mail and said to her, "He wanted me to marry his sister."

At first, Katherine didn't know how to reply to that or how the information made her feel. "What did the sister want?"

"The same thing," he said without raising his eyes from whatever he was reading.

"I see."

He looked up then as if to gauge her reaction. "I believe it's better you hear it from me, rather than the gossips around here."

Katherine couldn't argue with his logic. She did wonder how many other women's hearts had been broken by their marriage, though. She wanted to believe Lyndon Green's sister would be the only one, but she knew better. His handsomeness would make him quite a catch. Undoubtedly women all over the Territory had taken to their beds upon hearing the news that Dix had gotten himself a wife.

He told her, "Why don't you have a seat. Let me

glance through these warrants and then we'll ride to my *chickee*."

"And that is—what?"

"My house."

"Ah." Katherine took a seat. She felt very unsure and out of her element for now. In a matter of hours the Dix she thought she knew seemed to have withdrawn behind the marshal persona. She'd noticed the subtle changes during the last leg of the train ride. He'd been no less gentlemanly or polite, but there was something different in his eyes when he looked at her, almost as if he were a stranger. He hadn't touched her or kissed her since the night in Wichita. For reasons unknown to her there was a distance between them now, and it blew across her heart like a cold wind. Their relationship had gotten off to a fairly decent start, considering the circumstances. She'd hoped they would come to his home and continue to learn the ways of each other. But obviously he had no such aspirations. She remembered what he'd said in the beginning—he had no interest in love. He wanted a child, not her heart. Well, it was too late. She'd already given him her heart and, foolish woman that she was, had no idea how to take it back.

Katherine sat there for over an hour while he went over the warrants. When he was done, he set them aside and stood. "Can you ride a horse?"

"No." His answering look made her slightly defensive. "I'm a city girl. Why would I know how to ride?"

"You're going to have to learn."

"I agree, as long as the lessons do not start today. Who's Mona?"

The question seemed to catch him off guard. "She's my housekeeper. How do you know her name?"

"The Morgans. The night we met, Vernon said Mona

was going to hit the roof when you brought me home. Will she?''

''Probably.''

''Does she do more than keep your house?''

Dix looked over at his plainspeaking wife and told her the truth. ''She did in the past.''

Katherine did not doubt his veracity. ''I can't wait to meet her.''

She meant no such thing, and Dix knew it.

Mona met them at the door and gave Dix a long welcome-home hug. She was much shorter than Katherine, possessed an exotic, mixed race face, and a head of fine black hair that rippled to her hips.

When the welcome ended, Dix turned and said, ''Katherine, this is Mona Blackfeather. Mona, my wife, Katherine.''

''Pleased to meet you,'' Mona replied, smiling, ''Welcome to the Seminole Nation.''

Katherine was a bit surprised at the woman's friendliness. ''Why, thank you.''

''The Morgans said you were beautiful.'' Mona added, looking Katherine up and down. ''You chose well, Dix,'' she said approvingly.

They were then ushered into the house Katherine would now call home, which was much larger than it appeared from the outside and spread out ranch style over one level. In the front room were a comfortable sofa and chairs covered with patterned throws. The wood floors gleamed. On the mantle above the big fireplace were framed photographs and a beautiful basket. There were no fancy curtains or lace doilies beneath the lamps. No woman lived here. This was the house of a man.

In the kitchen, Mona fed them a savory meal of beans

and bread. It was the best food Katherine had tasted since leaving St. Louis.

"You're a very good cook, Mona," Katherine told her genuinely.

"Thank you. Do you enjoy cooking?"

"No."

Mona held Katherine's eyes, and Katherine swore the woman smiled inwardly as she said, "Well, since Dix loves to eat, we'll find a way to keep him fed."

Katherine met Dix's impassive eyes across the table, but neither said anything.

When the meal concluded, Dix stood and excused himself. "I have to go to work."

Katherine had not expected to be set aside so quickly, but she would not fuss, especially not in front of the housekeeper. "I'll see you later, then."

"More likely the morning. I left a lot brewing."

"I understand."

Dix's hand ached to caress her cheek in good-bye, but he was supposed to be keeping her at arm's length, not pulling her *into* his arms. He turned and left without a word.

After Katherine heard the screen door close, she got up from the table and went to stand at the open window in the front room. She could see him saddling a big chestnut horse. As he mounted, Mona hurried out the front door, calling for him to wait. Katherine could not hear what they were saying at first but then clearly heard Mona call, "I will tell her!" as he rode away.

When Mona came back to the house, she showed Katherine into the room that would be hers. The room was small, the walls bare. There was a wardrobe and a standing mirror. The bed looked comfortable enough, but for some reason Katherine did not picture Dix sleeping there.

She turned to Mona and asked. "Is this where Dix sleeps?"

Mona shook her head. "No, his room is in the other wing. He thought you might be more comfortable here. He comes in late many nights and does not wish to disturb you."

"I see," was all Katherine said in response. She'd become accustomed to his late arrivals. They hadn't slept apart since the night of their marriage. How could he think she would be more comfortable so far away? It was obvious that he found this arrangement more suitable, so it was just one more thing with which she would have to learn to live.

Mona interrupted her thoughts by asking, "Are the rest of your belongings arriving later?"

"This is all I own," Katherine said referring to the worn carpetbag at her feet. Inside it held her wedding dress, her meager cache of clothing. And Sweetie Pie.

"Dix is a fairly important man in these parts. You ought to get some clothes."

"I'll do that," Katherine promised, trying not to be offended. "So, where do you live?"

"Here."

Katherine barely managed to mask her surprise. "Well, isn't that convenient. Where's your room?"

"In the far wing, by the stables."

"I see. Well, thank you for everything. All I need now is a hot bath. It's been an exhausting trip. If you'll just point me to the pump and some buckets—"

"You just relax. I'll heat up some water; it'll be ready in no time."

"Mona, you don't have to wait on me—"

"I know. Consider this my wedding gift."

Katherine grinned. "Okay, I accept."

"Good. Come help me drag a tub in here, and I'll set the water to boil."

As Dix rode back into town, he wondered about Mona. She'd accepted the introduction of Katherine without a peep, which wasn't like her. She had one of the most volatile tempers in the Nation, and she had been brought before the tribal justices more than once because of it. She was of African-Choctaw ancestry and had been his housekeeper on and off during the past three years. He'd sought solace in her bed a few times in the beginning, but only a few. Her possessive ways quickly drove him out of her bed, and he eventually had to let her go. He took her back into his employ a few months before his departure east because she needed the money to help put food on the table for herself and her six-year-old son, Clint. Since Dix hadn't seen hide nor hair of the youngster today, he could only assume he'd been left with some relative somewhere—again.

He set aside thoughts of Mona to dwell on Katherine instead. He didn't like the idea but in the end knew separate rooms would be best. Many times after being on the trail for days and weeks at a time he would fall into bed fully clothed, smelling of gun powder, blood, and horse. This way she wouldn't be subjected to that. Admittedly he would miss her softness beside him at night. He'd grown accustomed to her warmth mingling with his, the smells of her and the sounds of her snoring, but this would go a long way toward encouraging the distance he thought necessary.

Indian Territory covered 74,000 square miles and was under the jurisdiction of the United States Court at Fort Smith, Arkansas. It was the largest criminal court in the country, a district court with circuit court powers. It administered the law in sixteen western Arkansas counties and for the Five Civilized Tribes. Officially there were five federal lawmen for the Creek and Cherokee Nations; five assigned to the Choctaw; and two for the Chickasaw. Dix and his supervising marshal, the great Bass Reeves, kept the law in the Seminole Nation and were also assigned to the Creek and Chickasaw. Each Nation also had their own light horsemen and their own councils of justice. Overseeing all this was Judge Isaac Charles Parker, known to the criminal element as the "Hanging Judge" of Fort Smith. The reputation was well earned. He believed certainty of punishment to be the only sure way to prevent crime, and his zealous practice of that philosophy sent shivers up the spines of those who came before his bench. Over his eleven-year judicial tenure, Judge Parker tried over thirteen thousand cases and convicted over eight thousand criminals. He ran his court six days a week, nine hours a day. More than eight-five percent of the cases before him were for crimes committed in the Territory.

However, with so few men to cover so much territory, the lawmen were always behind. Dix was especially behind. He'd been away almost eight weeks. On his desk were at least one hundred warrants needing serving, on everything from bootlegging to horse theft to murder. It would take him months to serve all the warrants—providing the wanted individuals could even be found. There were many areas of the Territory that were isolated and unpopulated, perfect places for the wanted to hide. Many criminals hightailed it down to Texas or up into Kansas to escape the long arm of Judge Parker's jurisdiction. Dix did not relish having to search them out. Those served would have to be arrested and hauled up to Fort Smith, a long and oftentimes dangerous trip.

However bounty hunting and the payments it generated supplemented his marshal's income of $125 a month. Escorting a load of sixteen or seventeen prisoners to Fort Smith could result in fees and expense money equaling $900. Being a marshal was hard, oftentimes thankless work, but it could also be quite lucrative if a man could stay alive long enough to be paid.

At his desk, Dix separated the new warrants from the old. Some of the old were for crimes committed as recently as last year or as long ago as ten. Many of the new were for repeat offenders, like Dick Glass, the African-Creek outlaw, while others were for faces or names Dix had never seen before. Most of the Whites were wanted for bringing in whiskey, a violation of the Trade and Intercourse Act, which forbade the importing of liquor into the Territory. Bootlegging was a profitable and thriving enterprise. The illegal intoxicants could bring a profit as high as four dollars a gallon, and with law enforcement stretched so thin, the liquor merchants ran a fairly good chance of operating their businesses without interference.

Dix didn't return home until the wee hours of the morning. Before heading to his bed, he stood in the door of Katherine's room and watched her sleep. Staying away from her might be more difficult than he'd first imagined, he realized. Right now, he wanted nothing more than to awaken her gently and let her know he'd returned so he could hear her sleepy voice of recognition and share a brief kiss. But he didn't. Instead, he forced himself away from her door and made the silent walk to his own.

Yes, he told himself, a lot more difficult than he imagined.

Chapter 14

By the time Katherine awoke the next morning, Dix had already left for town. She swallowed her disappointment and ate the breakfast Mona set before her without comment. Katherine longed to discuss her concerns about Dix with someone who knew him well, but she wasn't desperate enough to seek advice from his former lover. At least not yet.

However, she did seek Mona's advice on where she might find someone to coif her hair. Supplied with a name and directions, Katherine took the buggy and drove the road into town.

Driving the buggy seemed like child's play after handling the Hiram Walker. Thoughts of the schooner made her think about Grace and the brides. She wondered how they were faring and hoped Grace had found more happiness with Jackson Blake than she was now finding with Dix.

She rolled into the main part of town a short while later. She'd been unable to get a good look at Wewoka's layout yesterday due to all the excitement, but today she could. There were all manner of vehicles and conveyances parked alongside the wooden boardwalks. Main

Street had quite a few businesses, and many people of all races were frequenting them. She passed the general store, a millinery shop, and a blacksmith establishment; a newspaper office, a few boardinghouses, and a barber shop. There were two churches—one A.M.E., one Baptist. The marshal's office sat next to the bank. She didn't see her husband, but the big chestnut horse he'd been riding yesterday was tied to the post outside. Katherine didn't stop. She had no intentions of chasing after him. When Dixon Wildhorse wanted her company, he'd let her know. Right now she planned on getting her hair done.

The woman to do it was Vera Landry, and she did so at her house just outside of town. Katherine could not help but be impressed by the beautiful gardens surrounding the large log cabin. There were barns out back and a corral filled with huge hogs. Like Dix's home, this one was also built on one level, ranch style.

The short, brown woman who greeted Katherine's knock stepped to the screened doorway drying her hands on a small towel. "May I help you?"

"I was told you do hair."

"Sure do, but I've never seen you before."

"No, I'm new here. I'm married to the marshal."

"Oh, you're Kate! Come in darlin', I'm Vera."

As Vera took Katherine into her airy kitchen, Katherine felt right at home.

Vera said contritely, "I'm sorry I missed the welcome yesterday, but I was doing the heads of those Logan twins. How was the trip out?"

Vera was married to Solomon Landry, the present owner of the general store, Katherine soon learned. She was African-Cherokee and had taught at the Cherokee school for girls for many years until her recent retirement.

"What did you teach?" Katherine asked while Vera gently washed Katherine's hair.

"Classical literature."

"Really? What is your favorite work?"

"I love the Greek comedies."

Katherine was properly impressed. Greek comedies were not a subject Katherine could intelligently discuss, however, so she moved the conversation elsewhere. "How long have you lived in the Seminole Nation?"

"Just the five years I've been married to Solomon. Lived in the Cherokee Nation most of my life."

"You two haven't been married long, then?"

"No, we haven't, but we've been friends for many, many years. You and the marshal haven't been married very long, either."

"No, we haven't."

" Don't mean to speak out of turn, but I'm surprised he married anyone."

Katherine chuckled. "Why?"

"He's already married to that badge and has been since his grandfather was killed by horse thieves, a few years after the war. When the light horse couldn't find the murderers, Dix did. Tracked them for three weeks. Brought them in and stood them before the council."

"What did the council do?"

"Found them guilty. The council gave them time to put their affairs in order; then the light horse took them out to the tree, pinned the white heart on their chests, and executed them."

Katherine stared wide-eyed.

Vera said, "Seminole justice is fair, swift, and sometimes severe because they still cling to some of the old ways. For minor first offenses, you get twenty-five lashes across the bare back with a six-foot hickory stick. The second time the lashes are doubled. Convicted murderers are taken to the Execution Tree outside of town. They are blindfolded, a white paper heart is placed over the heart, and two light horsemen are selected to act as the firing squad.''

''My goodness.''

''Such justice applies only to members of the tribe. Nontribal members are tried in Judge Parker's court up at Fort Smith.''

''So, you how long have you known Dix?''

''Since he was a baby. His grandfather and my father were friends.''

''What was he like growing up?''

''No different than the other children his age. Oh, maybe a head taller than some, but the Seminole men tend to run tall.''

''Does he have any other family?''

''No, his parents were killed during the Seminole exodus to Mexico in '49.''

''What exodus?''

''Some of the Seminoles under Wild Cat and John Horse left the Territory in '49 after the Creeks and slave catchers attacked some of the other Black towns outside Wewoka. The slave catchers had promised the Creek one hundred dollars for every Black they could capture. They managed to kidnap a number of men, women, and children and sold them away. The Seminole were outraged by this and by the fact that the Territory land they'd been given after the Florida surrender was inside the Creek Nation, which essentially placed them under Creek control. Wild Cat and the Black Chief John Horse decided their people would be safer in Mexico, so in the fall of '49 they left.''

''Did the government sanction their actions?''

''Of course not, but they escaped anyway. Two hundred Blacks, Seminoles, and a handful of Cherokees loaded all their possessions on wagons, gathered their families, and left. They battled Comanches, Creeks, and bands of slave catchers, but made it across the Rio Grande. The Mexican government gave them land and guaranteed their freedom; in exchange, the Blacks and Seminoles promised to use their formidable fighting skills to keep Mexico's border safe from marauding Indians and renegade Americans.''

"So what happened to Dix's parents?''

"They were among one of the other groups that struck out later to join the new colony in Mexico. Few made it. One band met up with Comanches, and all were killed except two little girls. Another band of Blacks led by Jim Bowlegs were captured by Creeks. On the return trek bitter fighting broke out between the opposing forces, and lives on both sides were lost, Dix's parents among them. Dix was but a babe at the time. One of the women kept him safe until they returned to the Territory. She gave him over to his grandfather who'd stayed behind with the old chiefs.''

"So did the ones in Mexico ever return here?''

"Some returned after Wild Cat died from smallpox in '57, others after the war. Many of the Blacks never came back, though. They stayed in Mexico, although one group is now living in west Texas from what I hear.''

Katherine thought about how such a life must have shaped Dix. "Do you really believe he is married to the law?''

"Yep. I believe he sees his job as a way of honoring Ino, his grandfather's, memory. Ino was the only family he'd had his whole life, and Dixon truly loved the old man. Solomon says that when Dix rode off to find Ino's killers, he left as an angry, grief-driven boy. But when he returned, he came back a stoic, impassive man and has been that way ever since. He doesn't socialize very much, he doesn't joke, and wastes no time on frivolity. Keeping the peace is his life and what he does best. He's tracked men down into Mexico and up into Canada. If the Territory had more officers like him and Marshal Bass Reeves, all this wildness would stop. Every time you look around there are horse thefts and bank robberies, people stabbing their neighbors or strangers because everyone has had too much Muskogee water—''

"What on earth is that?"

"Liquor. It's illegal in the Territory, but the law is no deterrent and neither is the three hundred dollar fine. Some of us ladies have been trying to get the border saloons closed, but we haven't been very successful.'' She then added sagely, "If it were our people selling illegal liquor to the Whites, the Cavalry would be here to remove us before the sun set.''

Katherine replied knowingly, "But because it is the other way around, nothing can be done.''

"Exactly, but what can you expect when there are only two hundred lawmen to cover the whole of the Territory. The light horse have had *their* horses stolen on occasion. Can you believe it, stealing a policeman's horse?''

"Sounds a bit like my father and Dix's cows.''

Vera shook her head. "Your father is one of a kind. Had it not been for Dix, Bart would be before Judge Parker and in the penitentiary right now.''

"He said he thought Dix was dead.''

"Well, some of us did, too. It's happened before. Have Dix show you the Muskogee newspaper article that printed his obituary last year. He was gone for almost a full season, chasing some train bandits who fled to Mexico. Brought them back along with three wanted bootleggers. Your daddy was lucky he had you to barter. Some here wanted him lynched.''

"To whom did he sell the cows?"

"The government."

"The United States government?"

"Yep. An agent came through wanting to buy cattle. Your father told him he had some for sale and sold him Dix's herd."

"Didn't anyone try to stop the sale?"

"No one knew Bart had done something so outrageous, and the soldiers headed the herd out at night."

"Why?"

"Moving stock during the day leaves you vulnerable to rustlers. They'll follow the herd and cut out the stragglers. Because Dix's chickee sits off by itself, the herd had been gone for a couple days before anyone noticed anything amiss."

Katherine thought it a miracle her father hadn't been sent to prison. "Dix couldn't get his cows returned?"

"The government slaughtered them and sold the meat to the Indian Agency at Muskogee. For them it appeared to be a legitimate sale. The U.S. government is the King of the Twisted Tongue, but not even they would suspect someone of trying to sell someone else's cattle."

"Until they met my father."

"Until they met your father."

Vera dried Katherine's hair and oiled it with a light, fragrant pomade made from the oils of orange and lemon. "That feels and smells wonderful," Katherine said with a sigh.

"Why, thank you, I make it myself. Solomon has Seminole relatives in Florida, and they ship him fruit every year. Women out here swear by my oils."

Katherine understood their loyalty. Once Vera had finished with her irons and curlers, Katherine felt and looked like a new woman.

She looked at herself approvingly in the mirror. "How much do I owe you?"

"It's on me."

"Vera, I can't possibly—"

"Yes, you can. It's my welcome to the Nation," the older woman insisted. "Now, how about some lunch?"

Katherine agreed and sat down to a glorious meal of ham sandwiches made on thick brown bread.

Vera smiled. "You should have tasted my hams before the war. Now, that meat would melt in your mouth. So tell me, what did Mona say when Dix brought you in?"

Katherine smiled at the change in subject. "She was very kind."

"Mona, kind? Those words rarely go together. She can cook like nobody's business, but there isn't a husband in the Territory safe from her."

"Really?"

"Really. She has the morals of a black widow. If she was kind, she's up to something, believe me."

Katherine shrugged. "I've no complaints so far."

"Well, keep an eye on her."

They spent the rest of the afternoon chatting and getting to know one another. Katherine told her of her newspaper aspirations. To her surprise, Vera's first husband had run a territorial newspaper before passing away five years before.

Vera said, "In fact the newspaper here is printed on the equipment my husband once owned. Merle Gleason bought it from me at auction when my husband, Black Cat, died."

"Do you think Mr. Gleason will employ me?"

"Far as I know, he's never had a woman work for him before—but then again, no woman has ever asked before. He can be temperamental, though; remember that if you go and speak with him.''

After lunch, they took their glasses of lemonade out onto the porch. Vera asked, ''So tell me, how does it feel to be married to the Territory's most eligible bachelor?''

''I'm not sure, really. I fought the idea of this marriage tooth and nail at first, but he was so understanding and easy to know. I thought we'd made a good beginning, considering the circumstances, but now I don't know.''

Katherine wanted to talk to someone about the changes she'd sensed in her husband since his return, but she didn't know Vera well enough to be burdening her with her problems. After all, the whole thing could just be her imagination. They'd been back in town only a day, and he had much to catch up on. Katherine looked over to find Vera watching her intently.

Vera said, ''Give him time. He's a good man, but to insure he doesn't forget you, how about we go by Solomon's store and see what came in on the train yesterday? You look like you could use a bit of shopping.''

Katherine's wardrobe was dreadfully lacking. ''Mona suggested I improve my wardrobe, but I doubt there will be anything suitable for someone as tall as me.''

''Probably not, but part of the joy of shopping is in the hunt,'' she offered dramatically. ''So, shall we go?''

Katherine bowed. ''Lead the way.''

Katherine had a good time with Vera, and while her husband's store had nothing suitable, he did have some nice bolts of fabric. Katherine purchased as much as she thought she could afford, then set the fabrics on the counter so that Mr. Landry could cut them to the lengths needed. She turned to go look at the selection of threads available when the sight of Dix watching her from the doorway froze her in her tracks. Even though his features were unreadable, the veiled heat behind the hat-shrouded eyes touched her like a hand, setting off her own desires. She finally nodded tightly, uncertain how she should react to him, and he touched his hat politely in return.

He entered the store slowly, his presence filling the interior. He looked every bit the lawman with the gun belt on his hip. The heeled boots made him appear that much taller, and the closer his steps brought him to her, the faster her heart beat.

"Afternoon, Kate."

She had to fight to hold onto her distance as the familiar, low voice washed over her senses. "Hello Mr. Wildhorse, how are you?"

"Fine. Lyndon said he saw you ride into town. What're you buying?"

"Dress fabrics."

Vera and her husband, Solomon, were standing behind the counter looking on. There were only a few other customers inside, and they appeared to be watching with great interest, as well. Dix gave them all a pointed look, and they briskly returned to whatever they'd been doing.

He turned his eyes back to his wife. "Is this going to be enough fabric for your needs?"

"Probably not, but this is what I can afford."

"I make a good wage, Katherine; get what you need."

"I have what I need. Thank you, though."

She felt the tension rise off his body and mingle with her own as she looked over the assortment of threads available. She picked up a few spools she thought would go well with the colors of the fabrics she'd chosen.

Keeping her tone light, she asked, "Will you be joining me for supper?"

"Probably not. I have to go into Pottawatomie Territory and serve a warrant. May not get back until morning if the man's not where he's supposed to be."

"I see," she said with a false brightness. She looked up into his eyes and said softly, "Then have a safe trip."

She took her threads and left him standing there.

She tried to ignore his presence while she and Vera finished shopping, but it was hard to do because his dark gaze followed her every move. She wanted to take him by the lapels and drag him someplace where they could speak privately, but in the end he merely nodded her way and left.

On the way back, Vera told Katherine, "I've never seen him watch a woman the way he did you in the store."

"He's probably trying to figure out how soon he can send me back to Chicago."

"No, my dear. I believe you're mistaken."

"Why?"

"It just isn't like him. All the other customers noticed it, too. The Dixon Wildhorse who left here to track your father has never been observed paying that much attention to any female. Why do you think half the female population around here had their caps set after him? It was because no woman seemed able to move him. A few of them are going to be real displeased, knowing a city woman saddled him, arranged marriage or not."

Katherine thought back on Dix's behavior toward her. "So are you saying he's not a man to carry a woman across a threshold?"

"No, he isn't."

"He carried me."

"Dix carried you over a threshold?!"

"It was a tent, mind you, but a threshold, nonetheless."

Vera simply stared, then replied, "Amazing."

The knowledge that he'd never shown his tender side to any other woman gladdened her heart, but it didn't make his current distance any more understandable. She very much wanted to talk with him, but since he was heading out to serve a warrant, any discussion would have to wait until his return.

Katherine spent the next two days sewing at Vera's house and meeting the women who stopped by to have their hair done. Most were married and so had no bone to pick with her over saddling Dix, but a few of the younger women—in particular, the beautiful African-Chickasaw Hannah Green, sister of light horseman Lyndon Green—greeted the introduction to Katherine frostily. Katherine didn't care. Dix had married *her,* and if Hannah and her cohorts didn't care for the idea, there wasn't much they could do about it.

The other women were friendly and open. Katherine met Candace Taylor, wife of the town's banker; Lydia Craig, the spinster milliner, who loaned Katherine her brand-spanking-new Howe sewing machine; Alfreda Lane, telegraph operator and wife of the A.M.E. minister; and Silken Way, a self proclaimed *nymph du pavé* from one of the border saloons.

At the look of confusion on Katherine's face, Silken, a plain-faced, brown-skinned woman originally from Mississippi, smiled and said, "A *nymph du pavé* is a streetwalker, honey, a sporting woman."

Katherine blinked with astonishment.

Silken explained, "Miss Vera's one of the few women who don't mind my occupation."

Vera smiled. "Sure don't—though I do wish you'd try other work."

Silken looked amused, but didn't reply.

Katherine was able to squeeze two new dresses, a blouse, and a skirt out of the fabric she'd purchased. Dix had been gone three days and she missed him sorely, but Katherine had never been a woman to mope. Instead she donned one of her new dresses, pulled on a pair of gloves, grabbed a handbag, and drove into town to do some banking.

Having grown up so independently, the last thing she expected was to have the bank refuse to give her an account without authorization from her husband.

"Mr. Taylor, I don't mean any disrespect but that is ridiculous," she told the banker.

"No, it is our policy. Wives must have approval," Arnold Taylor explained.

"So you don't do business with widows or unmarried ladies?"

"Yes, we do, but seeing as you are neither, you need the marshal's approval."

Katherine's lip curled at the stupidity of this injustice, but she asked calmly, "Is there another bank nearby?"

"No. Even if there were, they'd tell you the same thing."

"Thank you for your time, sir."

"Welcome to the Nation, Mrs. Wildhorse. When the marshal returns, my bank will be more than happy to take your business."

Katherine nodded and left.

Since the marshal's office was right next door she stopped inside.

A male voice hailed her as soon she entered. "Well,

hello, Mrs. Wildhorse. I see you made it here in one piece."

Katherine looked past the sullen-faced Lyndon Green seated at the desk and over to the man in the small lockup. It was Clyde Morgan—the lone Morgan sibling with a brain, according to Dix. He was smiling at her with such enthusiasm, she couldn't suppress a smiling reply. "Hello, Mr. Morgan. I see you made it back also."

"Yep. Got caught bootlegging, though."

Lyndon Green drawled, "Again."

Clyde ignored Green and sighed, "You sure are pretty, Mrs. Marshal."

Katherine shook her head. "Thank you, Clyde." She then turned her attention to Green. "Has the marshal returned?"

"Nope."

"Do you have an inkling as to when he might?"

"Nope."

"I met your sister the other day, Lyndon."

"She told me."

Katherine did not want to be at odds with this young man whom Dix obviously trusted so much. She truly wanted them to get along. "So are you going to stay mad at me forever?"

He shrugged.

"I would like for us to be friends."

He held her eyes for a moment, then looked away. "I'll tell the marshal you came looking for him."

"Thank you, Lyndon. Good-bye, Mr. Morgan."

Now doubly frustrated, Katherine left the office.

She stopped in at the telegraph office. The operator, Alfreda Lane, greeted Katherine with a smile. Alfreda was in the process of taking down a message, so Katherine waited patiently until the clicking ceased and Alfreda had finished her transcribing.

"There's a message over there for you in the marshal's box," Alfreda pointed out.

Katherine sifted through telegrams alerting Dix to warrants and court dates until she found the one sent to her. It was from Geoff. He had signed on with a new paper in Boston and wanted her to send him any stories she might have on the brides' trek or events in the Territory. Katherine was near ecstatic at the good news. He didn't have much to offer in the way of payment, but it would be ample enough that she wouldn't have to apply to her husband every time she needed funds.

Alfreda must have seen the happiness on Katherine's face because she asked, "Good news then?"

"Extremely! I've been offered a job of sorts. An editor friend back east wants me to send him some pieces on the Territory."

"That *is* good news. Congratulations."

Katherine left the telegraph office in high spirits. A visit to her father's boardinghouse didn't even deflate her. His landlady, a formidably sized woman named Dahlia Hurd, informed Katherine that Bart had gone up to visit a lady friend in a town near Tiger Creek, north of Wewoka, and he'd be home next week. The landlady also informed Katherine that Bart owed a month's back rent. Katherine, who had no intentions of paying off yet another of her father's debts, assured the woman he'd undoubtedly take care of the obligation to her upon his return. The landlady looked skeptical, and Katherine had no difficulty imagining why.

The person named in the warrant, Mico Parker, had lit out, according to his wife, Faith. Dix followed his trail up into the Kickapoo lands but lost it at the Canadian River. Since Dix hadn't outfitted himself for an extended journey, he turned back. He was confident that Mico would come home in a week or so. The man was so crazy in love with his wife, he'd never be away from her for very long. He was also crazy jealous, which was why the warrant had been sworn out on him. He was wanted for assault on one of his neighbors. The bruised victim swore he hadn't looked upon Faith with anything other than respect. Dix tended to believe him, especially after the questioning of Faith corroborated the neighbor's side. Although Mico never took out his anger on his wife or children, Faith was beginning to lose patience with her husband's aggressive devotions. He'd been arrested four times in the last two years because of his jealousy. She spoke of leaving him and taking her children to her mother's home over in the Creek Nation.

Dix doubted he would ever go to such extremes over Katherine, but he now better understood those who committed crimes of passion. He didn't hold them in any higher regard, but he now knew how emotions could influence the actions of men and women. He had only to look at his own situation. Riding the trail back to the Seminole Nation, Dix admitted that his plan to keep his wife at arm's length wasn't working out as he'd envisioned. He was as close to miserable as he'd ever been over a woman. He dreamed of her at night, and daydreamed about her all day. He wanted her so bad he ached. If he were this calf-sick after less than a week, what would he be like in a month's time? He'd always been in control of his life, his feelings, his desires. Katherine had changed all that. She had affected him from the first moment he saw her standing in her wedding dress in the parlor of Rupert Samuels's home. He should've headed for the hills while he still had the chance, but those cinnamon-colored eyes had snared him nearly immediately. That was how he felt—as if he'd inadvertently stepped into a rabbit snare and couldn't shake himself loose. It wasn't a terrible feeling nor was there pain, but the snare had him, and he couldn't get free. Did he even want to be free? Not really. He relished her company and her Warrior Woman ways. She had a gift for giving and receiving pleasure he'd come to savor. No, they weren't in love, but who was to say they couldn't enjoy one another until she decided to head back East?

Dix saw the abandoned cabin where he planned on spending the night up ahead. As he bedded down beneath the stars shining through the hole in the shack's roof, he vowed that tomorrow night his wife would be sleeping at his side. Distance be damned.

Katherine had planned to spend the day working on some articles for Geoff. In order to begin, though, she had to get her pens, ink, and journals from the trunk in Dix's room. However, when she found the door to Dix's room locked, she went to Mona for the key. Mona was out throwing feed to the chickens in the coop behind the house.

"Mona, I need the key to Dix's room."

"Why?"

Katherine didn't feel she had to explain her actions to the housekeeper, but in the efforts of peace said calmly, "I need some things from one of the trunks."

Mona stood there with the feed bowl on her hip and observed Katherine a moment, then said, "Come with me."

"You can simply give me the key; you don't have to stop what you're doing."

"It is no trouble."

So Katherine entered her husband's room for the first

time. The expansiveness of the space took her breath away. It was almost as spacious as the Frederick Douglass suite back in Kansas City. Large windows let in the light and breeze. The entrance area seemed to be used as a sitting room of sorts. It was furnished with a sofa, some lamps, and two comfortable-looking upholstered chairs. There was a huge tanned skin stretched out above a large stone hearth. The walls on both sides of the hearth were covered with shelves of books.

Katherine also noted the gleaming wooden floors as she followed Mona farther inside. The part of the room she entered next seemed to be an addition, projecting from the other room like the top of the letter T. The far-right end held another window, nearby which sat a large bathing tub and a small table piled with clean towels. The far-left end held his bed, which was big enough to hold a man of Dix's size quite easily. It was enclosed by yards of finely woven netting that flowed down from the canopy above. Katherine couldn't help imagining how it would be to make love with Dix inside the shadowy confines. She could almost hear the soft whisper of the fabric rustling in the night breeze.

Remembering that she wasn't here to dwell on such things, she dragged her attention back to Mona and found her watching her with cool eyes.

Mona pointed and said, "The trunk is there."

Katherine found her things with little difficulty. Closing it, she stood and took one last wistful look around at his room and his things, then exited. She may have imagined it, but she could've sworn there was a gleam of satisfaction in Mona's eyes. Later that afternoon, Vera and Alfreda dropped in to invite Katherine to dine with them and attend the monthly meeting of the Morning Dew Woman's Society. Katherine knew from Dix's history lessons that Morning Dew had been the Black wife of Osceola. She'd given him four children only to be stolen from him and sold into slavery. Katherine hoped the meeting might supply her with information for a story, so she grabbed her writing gear and joined them.

As Vera drove the road to town, she explained, ''We call ourselves Dewies for short.''

Alberta chimed in, ''The men call us the Trouble Do-ers.''

Katherine chuckled, asking, ''And are you?''

''Damn right we are,'' Vera confessed with pride. ''We used to be content to sew for refugees and collect what we could for the orphans, but lately we've taken on a cause that has made us very unpopular. Whiskey.''

Alberta added in a serious tone. ''The spirit sellers are undermining the nations. Families are starving because their government scrip is being traded under the table for spirits. People are losing their land, having been swindled out of it while intoxicated. My husband has preached many a sermon on it, but those who need to hear are not the parishioners. The ones who need to hear are those throwing their lives away in the border sa-loons.''

Katherine could feel the sincerity and determination in the voice of the reverend's wife. ''So what have you done?''

''Every Wednesday night for the past three weeks, we and women from the bordering nations have marched in front of the saloons, hoping our presence will deter some of the trade.''

''Has it?''

Alfreda confessed, ''Not as much as we'd hoped.''

Vera declared, ''But we're not giving up—at least not yet.''

After dinner, fifteen women drove to the border of the Seminole Nation. They were joined by twenty-five women from other tribes and towns, the best turnout yet, according to the very pleased Vera. The Wewoka contingent included the cool Miss Hannah Green and her equally frosty mother, Ruth.

The strip of squalid border-town saloons were a stark contrast to the well-kept parts of the Nation Katherine had seen. The places were squat cabins constructed of ill-fitted logs and looked as if they'd been thrown up overnight. Tucked in among the saloons were gambling dens and houses of ill-repute. Roaming the area were men of all races, a few women, horses, and stray dogs. Because the owners had complained previously about the women's harassment of their establishments, two light horsemen were on hand to make sure things didn't get out of hand. The women were shown the imaginary line that represented the boundary of the Seminole Nation and were instructed by the policeman not to cross it or risk jail. The women heard them out respectfully, then began their march. They carried placards denouncing the saloons and their illegal offerings.

It didn't take long for an opposing crowd to gather. The heckling began almost immediately.

"Go home you biddies!"

"Where are your husbands? Can't the Seminole control their women?!"

"Any you ladies want a drink?"

That last comment drew gales of laughter, but the women marched on, singing their hymns. Katherine spent her time both marching and talking to some of the women about why they'd join the Dewies in this particular fight. The answers were varied, but many had relatives whose lives were being ruined by liquor.

Alfreda began sermonizing to the men on the wages of sin and drunkenness, imploring those with children to give thought to their youngsters' welfare. In a loud voice she asked, "Don't you wish for your children to grow up with dignity and pride? They cannot if their parents squander their lives on Muskogee water."

She was roundly booed.

Alfreda continued her speech. Out of nowhere, a peach pit hit one of the placards. Stones and clods of brick-hard dirt followed, making one woman cry out as she was cut on the cheek by a flying stone. The women continued to sing loudly even as they ducked beneath the hail of objects now raining down from their opponents. Katherine was hit once in the face, then in the arm. When she was struck again, this time right between the eyes, the blood she wiped away with her fingers made her mad. She became even angrier when she saw the man responsible laughing and pointing his finger her way. Grabbing the placard from Hannah Green, she marched across the imaginary line and brought it down on top of his head. In the silence that descended over the gathering, she tossed the busted stick at the feet of the mounted and stunned light horseman and crossed back into the Seminole Nation.

The policeman yelled, "Hey, you can't do that!"

"Then I suppose you will have to arrest me," she snapped angrily.

So he did.

As soon as Dix rode up to his office, he knew something must have happened because there were all manner of vehicles parked out front. Inside he found the place filled with many of the town fathers. They were arguing so loudly, Dix had to shout for quiet. Once he had everyone's attention, he quietly asked Lyndon, "What the hell is going on in here?"

"Your wife's been arrested."

"Do tell."

"Along with Miss Vera; Hannah, my mother; Mrs. Lane, the reverend's wife; Mr. Taylor's wife; and a passel of other ladies."

Dix passed a hand over his weary eyes. Katherine had been in town less than a week, and she was already making trouble. She'd been so tame and even-tempered on the trail he'd forgotten how much hell she could raise when left to her own devices. "So, where are they?"

"Light horse has them in the border town lockup. The ladies were marching in front of the saloons."

Dix sighed.

"Light horse said you'll have to come get your wife personally. It seems the man she assaulted was Boyd Donovan."

Donovan owned most of the business on the border. He'd been a thorn in Dix's side for nearly three years now. Dix knew he was bringing in illegal whiskey, but so far he'd been far too slippery to catch. Dix hoped Katherine had walloped him good and hard. "What did she assault him with?"

"A sign. The report I got said he needed three stitches."

So she had walloped him good, Dix thought. "I'll go get the bunch of them."

Banker Taylor said, "Marshal, we can't have your wife leading the women in this town astray. We're aware that she's from back east, but out here we don't like women rabble-rousers. Do we, boys?"

A resounding "no" echoed around the room.

Dix looked around at all the determined faces and said, "Mr. Taylor, where was your wife last Wednesday night?"

Everyone in attendance knew the answer to the question. Taylor dropped his eyes.

Dix singled out a few more men. "What about you,

Mr. Green? Where were your wife and Hannah? How about your wife, Reverend?''

Each man knew that on Wednesday night last, their wives and daughters were exactly where they'd been tonight, marching in front of the border town saloons.

Dix spoke directly to the banker, since he had a habit of leading contingents like this. "In light of the answer to my question, who's leading whom?"

Dix didn't expect an answer, and he didn't receive one. "Come on, Lyndon. The rest of you go on home or wait over at Solomon's store. I'll be back directly."

They all left quickly.

Dix and Lyndon mounted up and rode off toward the border.

Chapter 15

~~OO~~

When Dix and Lyndon entered the border's jailhouse, the women descended upon them like jays on corn, all talking at once, each trying to tell him her side of the story. They were raising so much cain and fussing so fiercely, Dix couldn't understand a word. The light horseman on duty, a Creek freedman named Harry Lake, stood up from behind his desk and shouted over the din, "Evenin', Dix, Lyndon."

Dix spotted Katherine on a bench seated next to Hannah Green. The small bandage on her forehead grabbed his attention first. Ignoring everyone else for a moment, Dix picked his way through the ladies and walked over to his wife. He hunkered down before her, well aware that every person in the place was watching. His concerned gaze swept her face. "Did Donovan harm you?"

"Not as badly as I harmed him."

Dix smiled. She looked like she'd been in a brawl. Her hair was mussed, her clothes covered with dust. He slowly ran his thumb across her dirt-smudged cheek, then leaned forward and gently touched his lips to her forehead above the bandage. "I'll have you out of here in a second."

As he made his way back to the desk, Katherine sat there more than a bit amazed by his overt expression of his regard. She hadn't seen this side of him since coming to town.

Hannah, seated beside Katherine, said, "You win, Katherine. He certainly never looked at me that way."

Katherine met her eyes.

"I mean it. When I found out he married you, it never crossed my mind he would be in love with you—"

"He isn't . . ."

"Shh!" Hannah snapped like royalty scolding a servant. Katherine shhed.

Hannah continued, "I was angry because I felt that if he had to marry someone he didn't love, he may as well have married me."

Katherine thought she understood the woman's logic, but she wasn't sure.

The beautiful Hannah went on, "So, since Dix loves you, I suppose we will have to be friends."

Katherine nodded, more out of surprise than anything else.

The ladies had once again surrounded Dix, vying for his attention to tell him what had transpired earlier that evening. He finally turned and said, "Ladies, please, let Harry tell me how his men saw it first. You will be heard next, you have my word."

There was a lot of grumbling, but they finally quieted down.

Harry told Dix what happened up to the point when Katherine laid Donovan flat with Hannah's sign. He didn't get a chance to go on because Vera cut in angrily, "Katherine was bleeding, for heaven's sake. Your men should have stepped in when the stones first began to fly. Instead they did nothing."

Harry conceded, "You're right, Miss Vera, and I've

spoken to the young man about what he should have done. He said things happened so fast, he was caught flat-footed—but did you have to make things worse by getting yourself arrested, too?"

"Yes," came her proudly spoken answer. "If he was going to arrest Katherine, the least I could do was get arrested with her."

"So what did you get arrested for, Miss Vera?" Dix asked even while he feared the answer.

"Inciting to riot. When Donovan finally regained his senses after being bashed over the head, he rushed across the line with hell in his eyes. He was going to hurt Katherine, Dix, so I whacked him across the knees with my sign."

Harry interjected dryly, "When he went down, the other ladies joined in and used their signs to beat him like an old rug, according to my men."

"He deserved it," Candace Taylor offered pointedly. "I'll bet he'll think twice before he assaults another bunch of defenseless women."

The room echoed with "Amens."

Dix thought Donovan would, too. He also thought that the word "defenseless" had no business being in any sentence describing this particular tribe of women.

"How much is Kate's fine?" he asked Harry.

"She really is your wife, then?"

"Yes," Dix replied without hesitation.

"Congratulations, Marshal, got yourself a real thunderbolt in that one. Her fine's twenty-five dollars. The others can go on home. I'm charging them with simple assault under extenuating circumstances."

Lake then looked them over and said, "Ladies, I'm letting you off with just a warning this time, but I do not want to see any of you in my jail again. Do I make myself clear?"

They grumbled that they understood.

Dix thanked Harry, then turned to the Dewies and said, "Let's go, ladies."

The ladies climbed into their vehicles, and Katherine was about to join Vera in her buggy when Dix rode up.

"Ride with me," he invited.

Katherine hesitated a moment—but only because of the sweet weakness in her knees. "I'd like that," she confessed.

He helped her up, set her in front of him, then headed his horse toward home.

Once he'd placed a fair amount of distance between themselves and the other rigs, he eased the horse back to a canter. The feel of Katherine's softness against him filled his parched soul like a desert rain. Her nearness brought him a contentedness he'd missed.

Katherine asked softly, "Are you mad at me for getting myself arrested?"

"The marshal's wife is not supposed to be arrested."

She turned to get a look at his face, and asked innocently, "Really?"

"Really."

"I'll reimburse you the amount of my fine."

"You bet you will."

She smiled and turned back. His chest was solid, yet comforting. Being encircled in his arms made her want to nestle like a kitten.

"Are you squirming around like that for a reason?" he asked.

She grinned provocatively and said, "Maybe." Katherine leaned back against his chest again. She, too, was content. It was a beautiful starry night, she was with the man she loved, and at this moment it mattered little that he did not share her feelings. "I've missed you," she confessed.

Plainspoken as ever, Dix thought to himself.

She then asked, "Was it something I said or did to make you avoid me like the pox?"

"No, it's my own doing. I've never had a woman in my life. I needed to think about which road I wanted to take."

"I see," she said quietly, although she didn't really see at all.

"I've missed you, too, Kate."

It was not something she'd expected to hear. She turned to look up into his face. His eyes were shrouded by the hat and the velvet night, but the desire burned like a beacon.

He reined the horse to a halt.

The kiss that followed was as natural as night following day—but far more passionate. The time they'd been apart showed in the fervid touches of their lips, the possessive way their hands roamed, and in the sighs of pleasure they both gave. He wanted her and she wanted him.

"Kate . . ." he whispered against her ear. "My own, sweet Kate . . ."

His lips found hers again, coaxing, inviting, charming. She returned his passion in kind. Under the black night they reacquainted themselves with the scents, tastes and feel of each other. Her lips were even riper than he remembered and twice as intoxicating. He'd gone without her kisses for nearly a week, and he would make sure it would never happen again.

The intimacy of the moment was dashed by the sound of wheels rattling on the road behind them. It was the Dewies.

Even as he continued to nibble at his wife's luscious lower lip, Dix raised the reins and kneed the horse forward. The poor animal didn't know which way to head, however, because the man with the reins in his hands couldn't keep his mind on the road or his hands off of his wife.

He whispered thickly against her throat. "We're going to wind up in a gopher hole if you don't let me guide the reins."

In reply, Katherine kissed him so passionately, the reins melted from his hands. He pulled her up against him and gave her a taste of her own medicine, then whispered heatedly, "Just wait until I get you home. . . ."

But when he rode up to the house, there were horses tied up outside, along with two buggies. As he dismounted and helped Katherine down, he recognized two of the horses: the big sorrel belonged to Marshal Bass Reeves; the paint stallion beside it had to be Sam Sixkiller's. Sixkiller headed the light horse agency in Muskogee. Dix wondered what had brought them out here in the middle of the night.

Katherine said, "Looks as if we have guests."

Guests indeed! In his front room stood Reeves, Sixkiller, Rupert Samuels, of all people, and Judge Parker from the courthouse at Fort Smith. Standing next to the judge was his Black bailiff, George S. Winston.

Sixkiller and Reeves gave Dix no indication as to what this might be about. Dix pointedly ignored the well dressed and impatient Rupert and approached the judge seated on the sofa.

"Judge Parker, how are you this evening, sir?"

Parker stood. "I'm fine, Dix. How are you?"

"No complaints, sir."

Rupert snapped, "You know him?"

"Yep, and for quite a while. The marshal is one of the three finest lawmen in my jurisdiction. Sixkiller and Reeves are the other two."

Rupert did not appear pleased.

Dix knew better than to press the judge for an explanation of his presence. Parker did things in his own time and in his own way. Dix looked across the room at Katherine, standing in the doorway.

"Judge, I want you to meet my wife."

Katherine stepped forward. The lawmen touched their hats politely as she passed them, and she nodded in reply.

As she passed Rupert, he drawled, "Rustic life must appeal to you, Katherine. You look like you've been wrestling with pigs."

She ignored his nasty remark, choosing to concentrate on the matter at hand. She hadn't an inkling as to what this might be about, either, but she knew how to play situations by ear very well.

Dix said, "Kate, this is Judge Parker from the court at Fort Smith, Arkansas. Judge, my wife, Katherine Wildhorse."

"Pleased to meet you, sir."

The judge's eyes smiled. "Pleased to meet you, too, Mrs. Wildhorse. Heard you had a run-in with Donovan over on the border tonight."

"Yes, sir."

"Heard he lost."

Katherine's smile peeked out. "You heard correctly, sir."

The judge turned to Dix and said, "She's glorious, Dixon."

Parker then looked over at the glowering Rupert. "Mrs. Wildhorse, do you know that man over there?"

"Yes. His name is Rupert Samuels. I was to marry him."

Rupert's cool eyes met her frosty ones.

The judge asked, "So why didn't you?"

"I found I had a prior commitment."

"What type of prior commitment?"

"My father had already promised my hand to the marshal."

"And you were not aware of this at the time."

"No, sir."

Dix could see the bailiff, Winston, recording the responses. The judge was conducting court, Dix realized.

The judge turned to Dix and said, "Mr. Samuels wants you arrested for kidnapping. Says you stole his bride."

"I admit it may have looked that way, your honor, but his hired help wouldn't let me in the place so I could talk with her."

"Well, he's got some pretty powerful friends, and they've sent me many letters and telegrams demanding you be arrested, too."

Rupert looked smug.

The judge didn't appear pleased by Rupert's demeanor. He asked, "Mr. Samuels, do you have a Frank Lester and a Joe Prock in your employ? And before you say something you may regret, know that this is a federal court proceeding. Lying will get you tossed in prison."

Rupert's eyes narrowed. "This isn't a court of law."

The judge contradicted him. "Since I'm the judge, court is where I say it is, Mr. Samuels. Shall I fine you for contempt to prove my point?"

No longer looking smug, Rupert looked downright uncomfortable. "'No, your honor."

"Excellent. Now, your answer to my question?"

"Yes, they are my employees."

"Did you know they were caught trespassing in a hotel room in Kansas City that was occupied by the marshal and his wife?"

Katherine's eyes went to Dix. How had the judge known that?

"Yes, sir, but I was under the impression that Katherine was being held against her will. I sent them to rescue her," Rupert answered.

The judge asked Katherine, "Were you being held against your will?"

"No," she replied truthfully.

"Are you being held against your will now?"

She looked over at her handsome, marshal husband and replied, "No."

The judge smiled. "So, now that we've established that the marshal's wife is not in any danger, Mr. Samuels, I'd like to get back to your two employees, Mr. Lester and Mr. Prock. Now, you say you sent them to Kansas to rescue Mrs. Wildhorse because you thought she was in danger, am I correct?"

"Correct."

"The night your men were caught trespassing at Miss Sunshine's brothel, did they not tell you then that Mrs. Wildhorse was in no danger?"

The question seemed to catch Rupert by such surprise, Katherine thought for a moment his eyes were going to pop from his head. He began to stammer unintelligibly.

Judge Parker waved him to silence. "That's what I thought."

He directed his next question at Katherine, "My reports on you say you're a newspaperwoman."

Katherine nodded.

"And the lawman in me says that Mr. Samuels wants you back for another reason. Am I correct."

Katherine looked to Dix. He nodded.

"Correct."

"Are those wants tied to something this court might take an interest in?"

She thought about Rupert's counterfeit stocks and all

the people he'd swindled. "Yes, sir, but I lack tangible proof."

"I see." Parker observed Samuels briefly, then turned back to Katherine. "Well, if and when you acquire tangible proof, the court would like it forwarded to our attention."

"It will be my pleasure."

"Then, by the power vested in me by the federal government, I declare the Samuels petition for the arrest of Dixon Wildhorse null and void. Court closed."

Rupert fumed. "This can't be legal!"

The judge shrugged. "Believe what you like, but there are no appeals from my decisions. Only person to ever intervene in one of my judgments was the president of the United States—and he did it only once."

Rupert gave Katherine one last look that was filled with anger, then stormed out, announcing he would wait for the judge in the buggy.

After his exit the tension seemed to leave the room, and the remaining occupants relaxed a bit. Katherine tried to apologize for her disheveled appearance but the men would hear none of it. In fact, they laughingly congratulated her on besting the bootlegger Donovan.

Soon Dix was escorting them to the door. Judge Parker picked up Katherine's hand and gallantly brought it to his lips. "Lovely lady, if there is ever anything this court can do for you, please do not hesitate to ask."

"Thank you, Judge."

Dix walked them outside into the night. Katherine, standing on the porch, could see the dark outline of Rupert's body as he sat holding the reins of his fancy buggy. Judge Parker had put him on notice and in his place; she hoped he'd have sense enough to go back to Chicago and leave her alone.

Suddenly, Mona stepped out onto the porch at Katherine's side. Katherine wondered if the housekeeper had been watching the proceedings from the kitchen.

Mona asked, "Is he really as wealthy as he appears?"

Katherine observed her a moment, then said, "Yes, but he's also a snake."

"He's a handsome one."

"Yes, but he's still a snake."

"Then why were you going to marry him?"

"It was a ruse, nothing more."

"I don't believe you. A man that handsome and wealthy . . . a woman would be a fool to toss him away."

"Well, go and introduce yourself. I'm certain he'd be pleased to make your acquaintance."

Katherine's sarcasm was wasted on Mona. To her utter surprise, the young woman stepped down off the porch and began walking in Rupert's direction.

"Mona!" Katherine cried, but her call was ignored.

While everyone stared on curiously, Mona climbed up into Rupert's buggy. Katherine had no idea what their short conversation entailed, but when Rupert guided his team back out toward the road, Mona was cuddled against his side.

On the heels of that surprising event, the others departed, leaving Katherine and Dix alone under the night sky.

"It's been quite the night," she said to him standing at her side.

"Yes, it has."

Without warning, he scooped her up and headed back into the house. She laughed aloud as he carried her around to his wing. At the door of his bedroom, he turned the knob, but the door wouldn't open.

Katherine said, "It's locked."

"I can see that, but why, is my question."

"I was under the impression you wanted it so." Looking up into his face she told him of her sole venture into his room and how she'd had to go to Mona for the key. "She opened the door, then stood and watched me like a hawk the whole time I was inside. I thought maybe it had something to do with you not wanting me in there. Especially since you wanted separate beds."

"I didn't want separate beds. That was *your* preference."

Katherine stared dumbfounded a moment, then said, "Dixon, the first evening we were here, Mona told me that you said *you* thought I'd be more comfortable sleeping elsewhere."

"Mona approached me and said you *wanted* to sleep elsewhere."

Katherine shook her head. "I wanted no such thing."

"And neither did I."

Dix's desire unfurled upon learning the truth. He could barely wait to welcome her to his bed. "I suppose I'll have to fire her for this. . . ."

Katherine could feel her own desire begin to blossom under his longing eyes. "If you don't, I will."

He leaned down and kissed her, a promise of the passion to come. He left her lips with great reluctance, then slowly set her on her feet.

"The room's back door is probably open. Come with me." He led her outside and around to the back of the house and found he was correct. The room's large interior was shadowy and silent. They spent the next few moments sharing kisses, until, breathless, Katherine brushed her mouth across his and whispered, "I need to wash up. . . ."

Equally breathless, Dix murmured, "I'll meet you out by the pump."

Katherine hastened to her room and disrobed. She

covered her bareness with one of the thin wrappers given to her by Miss Sunshine, grabbed her toiletries, and went out to meet Dix at the pump.

He was already there and washing. His nudity drew her eyes as always because he was so magnificently made and virile. She mused that one day, Lord willing, she would have sons just as handsome.

When it was her turn to wash, she shyly dropped the robe and moved to the pump. He stood off to the side drying himself, but his eyes charted her every move. Katherine had never washed under the scrutiny of a man's hot gaze before, and at first she felt very self-conscious, but as the soap and water began to cleanse away the dust, dirt, and perspiration of the day, she gave less concern to Dix and more attention to the joy of being clean again.

His hands sliding up her wet back came as a pleasant surprise. When they eased around and cupped her breasts she melted with a sigh. He lazily kissed the back of her neck, her shoulders, and the indentation of her spine, going lower until he was on his knees. He gently turned her and brushed his cheek over the damp, clean hair at the apex of her thighs. While she fought to breathe over the rising, throbbing heat, he touched his lips to the tiny circle of her navel, tracing a bold finger over the soft bud of flesh that made her woman. His caresses awakened her slowly, wholly, until her legs parted. His touches were a carnal, sensual branding. Panting from the glory of it all, she stood above him, head back, nipples glass hard, and allowed herself to be audaciously loved under the star-bright indigo sky. Too soon, release crackled through her like lightning, shattering her body and her soul, forcing her to scream his name into the July night.

Later in his bed, they came together with an urgency

fueled by long-starved passion. The feel of him filling her made her hips rise to offer him more, and he took all she gave—plying her breasts, kissing her mouth, making her gasp and croon.

He wanted to prolong the moments and make love to her until the sun rose, but she was too tight, her beauty too lush. He had no defense when the release shuddered over him, so he rode the buffeting wave and roared out her name.

In the silent aftermath, Dix lay on his side, propped on an elbow, slowly gifting her mouth with soft, passionate kisses. "I did miss you. . . ."

"You didn't act that way."

"That day in Solomon's store, I wanted to place you on the counter and take you then and there. It wouldn't've looked good."

She turned over on her stomach and raised up so they would be eye to eye. "Where are we headed, you and I?"

Plainspoken as always, he thought to himself. He kissed her again, then slowly pulled away from her beautiful full mouth. As he spoke, his hand moved over the rising curve of her hips. "We know there is no love in what we have. I told you in the beginning I didn't expect love, just your nearness. For me, that can be enough; neither of us should pretend emotions we don't feel." He cupped her cheek. "Let's just enjoy each other."

For the first time in her life, Katherine did not reply plainly because telling him of her love would accomplish nothing. She was a realist; he did not love her. The last thing she wanted would be for him to keep her at his side out of some misguided sense of obligation simply because she'd foolishly revealed her true feelings. If they ever decided to go their separate ways, no one need know she would be leaving with a broken heart.

"You're right. Why not just enjoy what each day brings and leave the rest to the future."

Dix thought she sounded a bit too bright when she spoke. He wished he had a lamp lit so he could see her features. He knew her well enough now to recognize the different tones and inflections of her voice, and something wasn't right. He reached out and gently pulled her body atop him. "Did I say something you don't agree with?"

Katherine leaned down and kissed him soundly. "Nope."

She sought to distract him and thereby distract herself from the tiny ache in her heart. "You know, I've never lain atop a man quite this way before."

"I should hope not."

She giggled and felt his manhood rising and ripening between their bodies. "You seem to like having me up here."

He whispered pointedly. "I seem to like having you anywhere . . . anytime."

To prove his point, he showed her the wonders of making love astride and the unique pleasure it could bring a woman. He also tutored her in a few other wonders that left her sated, breathless, and liquid, like when he had her kneel and face the big wooden headboard at the top of the bed.

"Let's see if you like this . . ." he murmured.

Katherine thought her desire had been drained, depleted by all the loving that had gone before, but the moment he knelt behind her and fit himself snugly against her back like a hot, male spoon, the embers of her passion flared to life once more. He grazed his mouth across the edge of her neck and shoulder, then bit her gently. His hands slid up and down her arms, relearning her, exploring her, then savored the luscious globes of her breasts. The meandering kisses on her neck and shoulders continued as he coaxed, teased, and circled her nipples until they stood up ripe and sweet. His large hand roamed possessively over the flat golden plane of her belly and brushed across the soft texture of her dark triangle. It dipped lower, boldly testing her readiness.

The stroking fingers brazenly added to her bliss and she arched for more. His slow hands filled her with such dizzying delight, it made her reach back and capture his splendid maleness in her warm hand. She stroked him, setting off a languid rhythm that caused him to drop his head back and close his eyes. When he felt himself on the edge, he pulled away. To repay her for her sensual boldness, Dix slid a finger over the damp, swollen entrance to his paradise and told her gruffly. "Open these beautiful legs. . . ."

She did and he slowly pushed his manhood into the tight, flushed cove of her warmth. His thrusts were at first controlled, even, but as she began to sensually ebb and flow to the age-old rhythm, the feel of her surrounding him soon rendered control unattainable. His thrusting became more ardent and impassioned. Their positioning offered him uninhibited access to all the places he'd tutored so delightfully in the past. He played her skillfully, lustfully, and when she couldn't bear the intensity any longer, she screamed her release. Gripping her hips, he shattered too.

Dawn was peeking over the horizon by the time they finally went to sleep. He pulled her in against him and covered them both with the thin white sheet. Katherine closed her eyes, knowing she would love this man for the rest of her life.

Chapter 16

〜〜⟧◯◯⟦〜〜

The next morning Mona entered the room holding a tray with Dix's breakfast. She set the tray on a table beside the bed, then pulled back the canopy netting. Her surprise at meeting Katherine's smug eyes would have been comical had Katherine not wanted to shake the housekeeper silly for her role in keeping her and Dix apart.

Mona asked sharply, "What are you doing in here?"

"Sharing my husband's bed."

Dix, who lay propped up on an elbow with his lower body concealed by the sheet, seemed more interested in tracing his finger lightly down the structure of Katherine's spine than talking with the startled Mona. However, he did manage to pull himself away from the alluring texture of his wife's satiny brown skin long enough to say, "Mona, you need to find another place to work."

"Why?"

Katherine made it simple: "You're fired."

Mona looked between them with fiery black eyes. "Why?"

Dix replied easily, "For meddling. Neither of us wanted separate rooms."

Mona argued, "This woman is not worthy of you, Dix. She can't even cook."

"She has other talents."

Katherine peered back over her shoulder at him, pleased with his answer.

Mona's lip curled in anger. "Then I hope you and your useless beanpole of a woman will be happy. I've gained a new protector, anyway. Rupert has promised to buy me the world. Of course, he is not as skillful a lover as you, Dix, but then few men are."

If she had intended for her remarks to be a reminder to Katherine that Dix had once been her lover, she succeeded. Katherine told her coolly, "Move your things out by sunset, or I'll give them away to the nearest mission."

Mona turned outraged eyes to Dix, seemingly waiting for him to contradict Katherine's edict, but it never came. "You heard the lady."

The housekeeper turned and marched out.

After the echoes of Mona's door slamming faded, Katherine said, "Did she not believe me when I told her about Rupert?"

"Evidently she wants to see for herself. After all, would you take advice from a beanpole of a woman who can't even cook?"

Katherine punched him playfully.

He grimaced exaggeratedly, then pulled over the tray of food, and he and Katherine shared a breakfast of thick slabs of bacon, eggs, and biscuits.

When they were through, she lay on her back looking up at the netting overhead. He lay silent at her side. She asked him, "So, how many other women am I going to have to fight off before my claim is recognized?"

He smiled. "Oh, I don't know . . . fifty, sixty more."

"You are kidding me, of course?"

"Yes, but now maybe you understand why I chose you blind. Wife pickings are pretty slim around here."

"What was wrong with Hannah?"

"Entirely too spoiled. I didn't want a woman I'd have to drag away from the mirror seventy-five times a day."

"There was no one else?"

"Not any one who moved me. I called on two women in Chicago while tracking your father. I'd been given their names by Miss Vera. She knew their parents from her younger days and thought the daughters might be suitable. The first one was such a tiny little thing, I was afraid of turning around and stepping on her."

Katherine grinned. "And the other?"

"When I informed her of my Black Seminole heritage and that, if we married, our home would be in Indian Territory, she got up and left me sitting in the parlor. Her mama came in a short while later and said her daughter wanted nothing to do with a heathen redskin, then politely showed me the door."

"How bigoted and rude."

"I thought so, too, but had one of those women agreed to be my wife, I might not have discovered you."

"Would that have been so bad?"

"Maybe not, if they could cook."

Katherine growled in mock offense and pounded him across the chest with a bed pillow. "Wretched man!"

A shriek of laughter followed as he dragged her beneath him and tried to wrestle the down-filled weapon from her grasp. She fought to maintain control even as he rolled her all over the bed. Her laughter filled the room as the battle went on. She pounded him, he tickled her. The spirited play tumbled them both off the bed.

Katherine screamed with hilarity as they landed on the floor.

He pulled her onto his lap and held her while they both laughed and fought to catch their breath. Her joy made Dix's heart swell and for a brief moment he wondered what would become of his heart if she ever decided to return east.

Katherine quieted upon seeing the sudden seriousness in his eyes. "What's wrong?"

"Nothing," he lied. He moved the pad of his thumb over her cheek, then raised her chin. "Just kiss me. . . ."

Later that day, Katherine posted her wagon-train journal off to Geoff. She also included a short letter to catch him up on the whirlwind events in her life and to inform him of Judge Parker's interest in Rupert's counterfeit stock scheme. Afterward she walked over to the office of the town's newspaper in hopes of wrangling some work. In talking with Vera the other day about her deceased husband's paper, Katherine had been surprised to learn that Territorial newspapers had a long and rich tradition. The *Cherokee Phoenix* had begun publishing in both Cherokee and English back in 1828 in Georgia. In 1835, Georgia's governor took issue with the paper's views and used the state militia to close it down. True to its name, however, the *Phoenix* rose again after the Cherokee removal west. Also serving the tribal nations were the *Cherokee Advocate*, the *Chickasaw Enterprise*, and the *Indian Journal*.

The local paper in town was known as the *Herald*; the owner was a Mr. Merle Gleason. The smell of the ink filled her nostrils as soon as she entered the establishment and brought with it memories of other newspapers she'd worked for in the past.

A man's impatient voice broke her reverie. "Can I help you?"

Katherine met the eyes of a man not much taller than herself. He was bright skinned, balding and had graying muttonchops accenting his cheeks. His apron and hands were ink stained.

"My name is Katherine Wildhorse. I'm a journalist seeking employment."

"You're the marshal's wife."

"Yes."

He looked her up and down. Katherine had purposefully donned the best of her skirts and blouses. She hadn't had an opportunity to make herself any walking suits since her arrival, but she hoped he would judge her on her credentials and not her clothing.

"You have any previous experience?"

"I was a journalist for Mr. T. Thomas Fortune's *Globe* back East."

He seemed grudgingly impressed. "Fortune's a lion. Heard rumors that the *Globe*'s being closed."

Katherine nodded. "There's been friction between Mr. Fortune and one of the investors."

"Pity."

"So, may I apply for employment with your publication?"

"Nope."

"May I ask why not?"

"Don't employ females."

Katherine stared, stunned. It took her a moment to find her voice, and when she did, she asked, "And your reason is . . . ?"

He shrugged. "I just don't—all women want to write about is them getting the vote."

"That is a legitimate political stance, Mr. Gleason, but not all women write exclusively about the vote.

Take, for instance, Miss Ida Wells down in Memphis.
There are nearly two hundred Black newspapers in this
country, and a good many of them carry her columns.
She writes literary review, religious pieces. Did you see
her piece last year in the Memphis religious weekly, *The
Living Way*?''

''No.''

''Then you don't know that Miss Wells sued the
Chesapeake & Ohio Railroad for forcibly evicting her
from a first-class seat. She chronicled the whole experience in *The Living Way*. She won a five-hundred-dollar
judgment. Women journalists are doing more than
clamoring for the vote, Mr. Gleason, they're helping the
race.''

''Doesn't change my mind.''

''Fine,'' Katherine said behind gritted teeth. ''I shall
return tomorrow and see if you have changed your mind
by then.''

''Won't make no difference. I'm not hiring a
woman.''

In spite of his declaration, Katherine returned to the
paper's office every day for a week, and every day he
said no.

Finally she decided to stop being polite. The next day,
bright and early, she showed up outside his establishment with a placard on a stick that read, GLEASON UN-
FAIR TO WOMEN.

When he came to open up for the day, there she was,
marching back and forth in front of his door. He asked
that she leave and she refused. ''I will cease my protest
when you give me a legitimate reason for not employing
me. Until then . . .'' Leaving her sentence unfinished,
she resumed her pacing.

''You can't do this.''

Katherine ignored him.

Some of the other businessmen were also opening up for the day. Seeing Katherine parading back and forth in front of the newspaper office carrying a sign drew them over to satisfy their curiosity.

The well-dressed banker, Arnold Taylor asked, "What's she doing, Merle?"

Merle grumbled, "She says she's picketing me."

"Why?"

"Read the sign."

"You tell her to go home?"

"Yep."

"You tell her she can't do this?"

"Yep, but she's one of them newfangled back-East women. They don't listen to men."

Soon, the other men were throwing in their two cents on the vagaries of back-East women. Katherine kept right on parading.

By now, the small crowd of business owners had drawn a slightly larger crowd of townspeople. When word spread to them about what Katherine was up to, a man yelled, "Is she really a newspaperwoman, Merle?"

"Says she is."

Someone else pointed out, "But she's Bart Love's daughter. Next she'll be claiming she's the Queen Of Sheba!"

That got a few laughs.

A woman seated on a buckboard yelled, "How come you won't hire her, Merle?"

"Because it's my paper, and I don't hire females."

"Makes sense!" a man told the crowd.

The woman countered, "No, it doesn't." She then called out to Katherine, "Honey when you finish with Merle, go down to Solomon's store. See if you can make him hire a woman clerk. We've been trying for ten years.'' Then she drove away.

Katherine wondered if these men knew of the gains women had made both before and after the war. There were now large numbers of female physicians, lawyers, and business owners. Women of all races and creeds, from all levels of society, were starting to leave the confines of their homes in search of something more meaningful in their lives than the day's wash. Obviously these men did not know, she answered herself. If they did, she wouldn't be protesting.

Across the street, Lyndon Green drew back the window shade of the marshal's office and looked over at the commotion in front of the newspaper office. ''Marshal, you should maybe come see this.''

Dix looked up from the report he was sending to Judge Parker concerning Rupert Samuels's stock certificates and asked, ''What should I see?''

''Your wife. She's got a sign, and she's walking back and forth in front of the newspaper.''

Dix came out from behind the desk. He went to the door and stood in the opening. At the sight of his wife, he sighed. He knew about her quest for a job on the paper. He'd even encouraged her as much as he could, but after a week of Merle telling her no, Dix had mistakenly assumed she'd given up. Clearly, she had not.

Dix caught the grin on Lyndon's face and asked, ''What's so funny?''

''Just wondering what you're going to do with her, that's all. She's not real tamed, is she?''

''No, she is not. I'll be back.''

Dix had to admit he liked his untamed woman, but the look on Merle Gleason's face as Dix made his way through the crowd indicated he did not share that view.

Gleason spied Dix and said, "Finally! Marshal, please, take your wife home."

Dix took in the determined set of her beautiful face and knew evicting her from the premises would not be as easy as Merle assumed. He took a moment to disperse the members of the crowd and sent them on their way. Once they were gone, he asked Gleason, "Why don't you just hire her, Merle? I'll vouch for her credentials."

"I don't care if she has a note from Osceola himself. This is my paper, and I hire whom I like, when I like."

Katherine's jaw tightened on the heels of his words, but she said nothing. She let her sign express her sentiments.

Dix knew Merle Gleason to be one of the most stubborn men in the nation. He also knew how stubborn Katherine could be. Trying to get Gleason to see reason, he said, "Merle, we all know this is just the type of thing to polarize a town. Miss Vera and the Dewies are sure to take up the fight if this doesn't get settled, and then all hell is going to break loose."

Gleason said, "I don't care, Marshal. If the men around here knew how to control their women, there'd be no such things as Dewies."

Dix sighed with frustration. "Okay, Merle."

He walked over to his wife. "Kate, I'm going to have to ask you to leave Merle's door."

"Am I violating some law?"

"Probably."

She stopped. "What do you mean, probably?"

He shrugged. "For sure you're trespassing."

"This is a public walk."

"True, but unless you wanted to be publicly walked to jail, Mrs. Wildhorse, I suggest you heed my advice."

"You would arrest me?"

"Yep."

"Then take me away, Marshal, because I am not abandoning my protest willingly."

Dix took her to jail, posted her bond, then escorted her home.

The next morning, Katherine disregarded the previous day's arrest and once again took up her march outside the newspaper office. To her delight, Miss Vera and the banker's wife, Candace Taylor, were on hand to lend support and carry signs of their own.

Because Dix had gone up to Tiger Creek to investigate a swindler and was therefore out of town, not only did the women picket the newspaper, they moved up the street to picket Solomon Landry's general store about his staunch refusal to hire a female clerk. The ladies wanted a woman's presence when they needed help ordering undergarments from the catalogs or when they came in to purchase their female preventives and other intimate items. Solomon or his sixteen-year old nephew, Peter, the store's only other clerk, simply would not do. In the past, Solomon had been able to stave off the women's request for a female clerk simply by agreeing to look into the matter—and then doing nothing when the heat cooled. Not even his wife, Vera, had been able to sway him. But now they were going to put his feet to the fire and not let up until he relented.

Solomon was a short, round, bear of a man. He came barreling out of the entrance as soon as the women began their slow paced, silent parade.

"What are you doing here?"

Vera answered, "Picketing you, Solomon. Hire a female clerk and we'll go away."

"Vera, I promise I will take it under consideration. Now, go on back and pester Merle. You ladies are bad for business."

"No," Candace Taylor stated. "This is the 1880's, and some men in this town will listen to their livestock before they listen to their wives. It's going to stop. Give us a clerk, Sol, and we'll leave you in peace."

Solomon appealed to Vera. "You're my wife. How can you do this to your husband?"

"Sol, when I come to this store, do I ever ask you to give me an item free of charge?"

"No."

"Have I ever spent anything other than my own money?"

"No."

"Exactly. When I enter your store, I enter and leave as a paying customer. I spend a lot of my money in your place, Solomon. I would hate to think this loyal customer will be forced to take her considerable business elsewhere, all because of backward practices."

"Is that a threat, Vera?"

"No, lamb, that's a promise."

Solomon stormed back inside the store.

Vera smiled. "He'll come around. He loves profit almost as much as he loves me."

When Dix returned to town around noon two days later, his slow ride down Main Street showed him women carrying signs not only in front of Gleason's paper but also the general store and the bank. He estimated there were at least thirty of them, all chanting and marching around. Reporters, vehicles, and crowds of gawkers filled the street and boardwalks, and some enterprising kids had set up a lemonade stand. The atmosphere mirrored a holiday. For the first time as a lawman, Dix wished he'd chosen another occupation. He didn't relish getting in the middle of this. Where, he wondered with irritation, was Lyndon Green, and how had this gotten so out of hand?

Trailing on the horse behind him was the Tiger Creek swindler. The arrest had been fairly routine. As Dix dismounted in front of the marshal's office, the prisoner said, "Oh, come on now, Dix, not the poky. Can't I just go on home?"

"No, Bart, you can't just go home."

Bart Love had been up to his old tricks. He'd somehow convinced a group of Brits touring the Territory that he'd been given a divine gift for finding gold. He'd taken them out to Tiger Creek, muttered some mumbojumbo, then led the group to his "latest, miraculous find." Bart had salted the spot with gold coins prior to the visit of course, but the tourists hadn't known. Bart repeated the act two more times over as many days, and each time the amount of gold coins found increased. The Brits were impressed, convinced they were indeed in divine company. When Bart humbly confessed that he needed investors to be able to travel to other places where gold lay hidden, they jumped at the chance to invest in him for a percentage of the finds. After being given close to two thousand dollars by his new partners, Bart, of course, disappeared. Dix tracked him to Donovan's place on the border.

Now, as Dix ushered him into the cell, he found a note left by Lyndon on his desk. There'd been a train robbery up near Violet Springs, and he'd gone to help with the investigation.

Bart called, "Dix, how is this going to look, me in the poky? You're married to my Katherine."

"Yep, Bart, I am. I'm married to Katherine, not to you." He closed, then locked, the cell's wooden door. "Be back later."

Out on the street, the air echoed with the noise of all

the goings-on and faint strains of chanting, marching women. Arnold Taylor suddenly appeared at his side, saying, "Marshal, I demand you do something about this. These women are taking over the town."

Dix, who hadn't slowed his steps, asked, "Is your wife involved?"

"Yes," came the tightly spoken answer. "It's as if they are all deaf."

"If Merle hadn't been so deaf in the beginning, none of this would be happening."

"Merle has a right—"

"Now who's being deaf?"

Taylor sputtered, "I want those females moved away from my bank."

"Why did *you* become a target?"

"They want me to allow married ladies to open their own accounts."

"You have a problem with that, I take it?"

"Why, yes, I—"

"The world is changing, Mr. Taylor. If my wife's any indication, pretty soon women are going to be running the train, and if you don't get on board or get out of the way, they're going to steamroll right over you."

"So you're on their side?"

"I'm the marshal; I don't take sides. I'm simply saying read the smoke. Being deaf is not a solution."

Taylor disagreed. "This is a man's world, Marshal, and these women have to be shown their place."

"Remember you said that, Mr. Taylor."

At the bank, Dix asked the women to disperse, but they kept right on singing and marching, so he placed all eight of them under arrest, including the banker's wife, Candace.

Dix did the same thing down at the general store, where Vera Landry was heading up a troop of twelve to protest. In the midst of the arrest a reporter rushed up to Dix wanting a quote for his daily, but the marshal's glare of displeasure made the man back away hastily.

Katherine was marching in front of the newspaper office when she spotted her husband coming up the boardwalk. He did not appear to be pleased. Katherine felt a bit guilty for putting him in the middle, but getting Gleason and the other town fathers to relent had become very important, not only to Katherine but to the other women, as well. Times were changing, and this town would have to change, too. The women weren't asking for the world, just a female store clerk, the right to bank, and a chance to work at the newspaper.

Dix looked at his lovely, trouble-making wife, and in spite of all the cain she'd been raising, he didn't want to do anything to her except carry her off to his bed. He doubted the business owners would approve of such dereliction of duty, however, so he had to do his job.

"Afternoon, Kate," he said as she passed by him.

She stepped out of the line, but the others, including Hannah Green and her mother, Ruth, kept up the pace.

"Afternoon, Marshal. Glad to see you made it back safely. Did you find the swindler?"

"Yes, it was your father."

Katherine groaned aloud. "What was he doing this time?"

He gave her a quick rundown on Bart's activities, adding, "He's over in the jail."

"I'll post his bond. Send him on home."

"So who's going to post *your* bond?"

"My very intelligent and supportive husband?"

He gave her a hint of a grin. "I'll get my reimbursement later."

He then yelled to the other marchers. "Okay, ladies,

parade yourselves over to my office. You're all under arrest.''

An hour later, all the paperwork had been processed, but some of the husbands, including Arnold Taylor, refused to post bond. Ruth Green, one of the richest women in the Territory, covered the bail of the women whose men refused to do so. Then Dix sent everyone home.

That evening, while the town fathers were sitting in Wilbur Bigelow's barbershop extolling their victory over the women, their wives and daughters were at Vera's house plotting their next move.

Candace Taylor stood and said, ''I would like to thank Katherine for being the impetus to this battle. Without her, we'd be still sitting around grumbling instead of acting.'' She began to applaud, and the twenty-five women in the room enthusiastically joined in.

The attention embarrassed Katherine a bit, but she was glad the women were trying to control their own lives.

Candace said, ''I personally will be withdrawing my share of my husband's account first thing in the morning. I suggest you ladies do the same.''

Lydia Craig, the spinster milliner said, ''What if we are refused?''

''If Arnold refuses, he'll have to answer to me.''

Ruth Green said, ''Why can't we open our own bank? Other women have.''

Katherine thought that to be an excellent idea. ''But where would it be?''

''In my kitchen, if necessary. I will wire my barrister in Boston tomorrow and have him investigate the legalalities. Until then, I agree with Candace. Let's withdraw our funds. Maybe affecting the bank's profits will change some minds.''

*   *   *

When Arnold Taylor opened the bank the next morning, he was pleased to see all the women lined up outside. They appeared to be orderly—they were not carrying signs—so he assumed they'd been taught a lesson and were there on banking business.

That assumption faded as Ruth Green stepped to his desk and informed him she'd come to withdraw all her funds.

Banker Taylor began to choke. He finally croaked, "But that's over—"

"I know how much it is, Arnold," she said, smiling serenely. "Hannah and I came with satchels."

He stared around at the other women, then addressed Ruth, "Does your husband know about this?"

"It is my money, Arnold, not his."

Katherine was standing off to the side, writing about the confrontation. She thought the battle they were waging would be of great interest to many female readers back East.

"You'll need your husband's approval."

"I am the eldest daughter of a Cherokee chief. I do not need his approval or yours, Arnold Taylor. Shall I call for a tribal council to settle this?"

He visibly blanched. "Ruth, if I give you what you're asking, I'll have to close my doors."

She didn't waver.

Vera told him, "We're all here to withdraw our funds, Arnold, so start counting."

Arnold snapped, "I will not bow to this intimidation. You ladies will have to leave."

No one moved.

"Either leave or I'll go and get the marshal."

The ladies stood firm.

His wife said reasonably, "We are here to conduct business, sweetheart. We're not breaking any laws."

"Don't you sweetheart me, Candace Taylor. You're a traitor to me and our marriage."

Candace smiled and said, "I love the way your eyes flash when you're angry with me, Arnold."

He stared at her as if she'd grown another head. "I'll be bringing back the marshal."

The banker tried, but Dix refused to intervene. His explanation echoed what Candace had said earlier. "They're not breaking any laws, Mr. Taylor. There's nothing on the books saying a woman can't withdraw money, especially since you've never limited their privileges before."

"But they want to take out *everything!*"

Dix shrugged. "Sounds like you need to draw up a treaty."

"No. I refuse to be steamrollered."

"Suit yourself. Let me know when they break the law."

As the banker huffed out, Dix shook his head, wondering what it would take for men like Arnold Taylor to admit times were changing. Dix saw no problem with the women's campaign; many of the women in the Territory headed up their tribes, and many controlled the finances. He saw nothing wrong with females having a say in what was theirs. The settlers were bringing to the west their own American ideal of a woman's place in society, though, and shortsighted men of all races had come to embrace that ideal. At one time, he, too, thought a woman had a distinct place in life—until he married Katherine. Now he knew better.

And he didn't mind that she was a nontraditional woman. Being with her meant never having a dull day, he was finding. He wanted sons, but he wanted daughters now, too; little warrior women to follow in the steps of their crusading mother.

*   *   *

Because the banker didn't know what else to do, when he returned, he announced the bank would be closing for the day.

His wife, Candace, said, "Closing the bank is not a solution, Arnold."

"Yes, it is. Now, all of you, out!"

Vera remarked, "Ladies, you know, suddenly my old bones are pretty tired. I think I'll take a seat."

Following her cue, women all over the bank began to sit. When the chairs were filled, they sat on the floor.

They looked up at Taylor, who looked ready to explode. He snapped, "Everyone will have to leave the premises."

No one moved.

"Okay, I'm giving you thirty seconds."

He picked up his pocket watch and peered at it with irritation. When the time had elapsed, he said coolly, "Fine. You ladies want to stay in the bank, you're welcome to stay here until I reopen tomorrow."

He walked to the back entrance and put on the padlock. He then proceeded to the front door. "This is your last chance."

Vera sent the women with babies home, but the remaining eight stayed, and Taylor locked them in.

Inside the marshal's office, Taylor gleefully related his besting of the women until Dix asked him, "How are you going to get them out of there?"

"What do you mean?"

"Think, man. Suppose they decide to stay in there indefinitely?"

"They won't," he replied confidently, then added fearfully, "Will they?"

"You tell me, Mr. Taylor."

"They have to come out eventually. I can't conduct business if they don't."

"Too bad you didn't think of that twenty minutes ago before you locked them inside."

Taylor asked, "So what are you going to do?"

"You tell me."

"You cannot just let them squat in my bank. Aren't you the law?"

"Yes, I am, and as the law, I'm going up to Muskogee for a deposition. I'll be back maybe tomorrow."

"But, what about my bank?!"

"I'll go over and talk to them, but if you can't negotiate a treaty, guess it'll have to wait until I get back."

Inside the bank, Vera looked at her troops and said, "Well, ladies, he's locked us in. Now what?"

Candace said, "I say we stay here a while; let him stew."

Someone else pointed out, "But we can't stay here without food and supplies."

Katherine walked over to the padlock on the inside of the back door and asked Candace, "You wouldn't by chance have the key to this lock."

"Nope."

"Not to worry."

Katherine went into her handbag and withdrew her lock picks. She held them up for all to see and smiled. Fascinated, the other ladies gathered around her as she worked. A minute later, it opened.

Vera said, impressed, "My, my, my. Aren't you handy to have around!"

Suddenly, Dix was standing outside the bank window and rapping on the fancy glass pane. Katherine motioned for him to go around to the back of the building, and he complied.

Inside he found the room filled with women. Candace

Taylor was seated at her husband's desk, surrounded by Vera and the others.

Katherine greeted his entrance. "Good morning, Marshal."

"What are you ladies up to now?"

She replied. "Well, we aren't real sure, but Mr. Taylor seems to have given us a golden opportunity, so we aim to take advantage."

"How so?"

Vera said, "We're going to live here a few days. We're putting together a list of the supplies we'll need."

"Ladies you can't squat in the bank."

Candace disagreed. "Sure, we can. Especially since Arnold locked us in. This was his idea, not ours."

Dix had to admit she was correct. "I'm going to have to arrest you when I return."

Katherine asked, "When will that be?"

"Hopefully tomorrow. The deposition is up in Muskogee."

Dix wanted to kiss her good-bye very much, but with all the onlookers decided it wouldn't do. "I'll see you in a few days, Katherine."

"Keep yourself safe."

"You, too. And, ladies, try to have the town still standing when I return. Okay?"

When they assured him it would be so, he tipped his hat and strode out.

By midafternoon, the women had their bunker nicely stocked with water, food, and sewing. The men were all huddled down at Solomon's store, plotting a counter strategy, and therefore had no idea the women were using the back door to slip in and out. By the time they were alerted, the women were hunkered down ready for a siege. They piled furniture up against the doors, snapped the padlock, and took turns keeping watch at the window.

In late afternoon, Arnold Taylor and a contingent of town fathers descended upon the bank. Since the women refused to remove the barricade in front of the door, the men were reduced to shouting through the big plate-glass window.

Because of its muffling effects, their voices had none of the impact they hoped. In fact, to the ladies inside they sounded downright silly, especially the very over-wrought banker.

Katherine said, "Candace, your poor husband is going to explode if you don't go out and talk to him."

"Let him yell a bit longer. I love him dearly, but it's time he learned that this town is going forward, whether he likes it or not."

Vera walked to the window and shouted to her husband, "Don't you have a store to run, Solomon?"

Solomon's muffled voice came through the glass. No one understood a word he said.

Frustrated, the men left.

"You know, ladies," Vera pointed out, "this siege reminds me of my favorite Greek comedy, *Lysistrata*. It was written in 411 B.C. by the great comedic playwright Aristophanes." She explained further, "It's about a group of women who are trying to put an end to the Athenian wars. Lysistrata is the women's leader. At one point during the story, the women hole up in the Acropolis, just as we are holed up here. The men refuse to take them seriously until the women withhold the one thing men love more than anything—more than profit or themselves or making war."

Hannah looked confused. "And that is?"

"Lovemaking."

Hannah's eyes widened with shock. Katherine

grinned; so did Candace Taylor and the reverend's wife, Alfreda Lane.

Ruth Green asked, "Do you have this play at home, Vera?"

"Certainly. Be happy to lend it to you whenever you like. In the story, the men tried bullying, yelling, and everything else, but the women had the power and eventually prevailed."

Katherine could see the wheels turning in Candace Taylor's well coifed-head, for she commented, "You know, I might like to read that also, Vera."

Katherine asked, "Candace, what are you thinking?"

The banker's wife wiggled her delicate eyebrows. "What do you think I'm thinking?"

They all laughed and agreed to revisit the novel plan of Lysistrata at a later time if the men continued to refuse the women's demands.

That evening, as the women ate a simple dinner of fruit and ham, Hannah Green, on watch at the front window, alerted them to the approach of the men.

"They have what looks to be a tree riding in the bed of Father's wagon."

All the ladies came to the window, and sure enough, a small company of men were escorting a wagon being driven by Mr. Green.

Katherine asked, "What do you suppose they are doing?"

Vera replied, "Something foolish, I'll wager."

They all watched and waited as the men struggled to remove what appeared to be a very large and very long tree section. It had to be at least nine feet in length by Katherine's estimation, and it must have weighed a ton because it took eight men to lift it. Once they got it free of the bed, they staggered their way toward the front of the bank.

Alfreda said, "I do believe they are going to try and use that as a battering ram."

"Only if they can carry it this far."

Candace noted, "Arnold's back's been paining him for at least ten years. He'll be flat in bed until Christmas behind this nonsense."

The men were weaving back and forth because of the tree's extreme weight, their exertion and strain evident in their faces.

Vera stood there, shaking her head. "Will wonders never cease."

Candace said, "You know, ladies, it will be terribly ironic if that tree ends up coming through Arnold's prized window instead."

The men halted about six or seven feet from the entrance, and the banker began to shout ultimatums. He couldn't shout very loudly because holding up his side of the tree seemed to be sapping most of his strength.

Ruth Green remarked, "I assume he's shouting for us to leave."

Candace replied, "I suppose he is, but who really knows? He could be inviting us to a bonfire, for all we can tell."

Even though she knew he couldn't hear her, she shouted back, "Speak up, darling! We can't understand you!"

Katherine watched the men trying to keep the weight evenly distributed and asked dryly, "Is this town always this exciting?"

Alfreda quipped, "It wasn't before you came, dear."

"Uh oh, here they come. Back away from the glass," Vera warned

The men were trying for a running start, but the crushing weight of the tree kept them from achieving any type of speed. They sort of wove their way toward their goal, only to have someone slip on a lump of horse pie and send the whole battalion into chaos. Just as Candace predicted, the tree came crashing through the bank's fancy plate-glass window. No one inside was hurt. The ladies stepped around the shattered glass and the huge tree now resting both inside and out of what used to be Banker Taylor's front window. The shattered glass offered them a clear outlet to the angry argument going on in front of the bank.

Evidently, the idea of the battering ram had been Merle Gleason's idea, and Arnold Taylor was holding the newspaperman directly responsible for the debacle and the damage. The newspaperman growled back that it was Taylor's fault, saying that had he been able to control his wife, none of this would have been necessary. The banker took immediate offense and punched Gleason square in the nose. Gleason punched him back, and pretty soon all of the men were arguing and punching one another in the middle of the street.

Katherine shook her head at their antics.

Vera intoned dryly, "So much for solidarity."

The next morning, Arnold Taylor surrendered. He tacked a notice to the boards he'd nailed up over what was once the fanciest glass window in the Territory.

It read:

From this day forward,
ALL bank services will be offered to ALL women.

The next day, Solomon Landry surrendered as well. The sign he posted read:

Looking to hire FEMALE clerk.
Inquire within.

The reports Katherine had been sending back East on the Dewies campaign were being well received, according to Geoff's telegraphs. Even though the pay was dismal, more than a dozen Black eastern papers had added her columns to their pages; of course, they still believed the writings had been penned by a man, but Katherine refused to fret over the deception. She was working again and that mattered the most.

With all that in mind, she made sure she accurately transcribed the battering-ram incident for use in her next installment.

Chapter 17

The only goal left for the Dewies to accomplish involved moving the stubborn, and now black-eyed, Merle Gleason. Unlike his former companions banker Arnold Taylor and store owner Solomon Landry, Gleason refused to capitulate, thereby placing Katherine no closer to working for him than she had when all the hubbub had begun.

Dix rode back into town two days after the battering-ram fiasco. Even though dusk had fallen, he had no trouble spotting the boarded-up front window of the bank. Slowing the horses' pace a bit, he assessed the damage. When he entered his office, Lyndon Green filled him in on just how the window had been shattered. Once Dix had stopped laughing, Lyndon told him of the subsequent surrender of the banker and Solomon Landry.

Dix was glad to hear someone had finally come to his senses. "What about Merle?"

"Won't budge. Says he'll close down the paper first before he gives your wife a job."

Dix sighed. "So what are the women doing now?"

"Plotting."

"What do you mean, plotting?"

"Plotting. My father says they're up to something. Says he can smell it."

The deposition up in Muskogee had taken much longer than Dix had anticipated, and all he wanted to do now was to go home, take a hot bath, and make slow love to his wife. He had no desire to hear about plots, mainly because Lyndon's father was probably correct in his assessment. "I'm going. I'll see you in the morning."

When Dix got home, he dropped his gear by the front door and called his wife's name. When Katherine came out of the kitchen, he greeted her welcoming smile with one of his own. "Miss me?" he asked.

"Tremendously."

He held out his arms. "Then come and greet me properly."

"I'd love to, Dixon, but I can't."

He surveyed her face, his arms dropping slowly. "Are you angry with me?"

"Oh, no!" she denied hastily. "It's nothing like that."

"Then what is it?"

"The Dewies have all taken a vow that there will be no kissing or cleaving until Merle Gleason agrees to hire a qualified female."

"*What?!*"

"Pressure has to be brought to bear, or nothing will change here."

"Katherine, this is not going to go over well."

"I agree, but it's the only weapon we have left. If it'll make you feel any better, three quarters of the women in the Nation have agreed to participate. All the men will be in the same boat. It seems the women here in Wewoka are not the only ones who've been going up against male brick walls, so they've joined on to try and make changes in their towns, also.''

"How long do you think this will last?"

She shrugged. "You'll have to ask Mr. Gleason."

Dix was at a loss for words for a few moments. "Whose idea was this?"

"Initially a Greek playwright named Aristophanes. We used his play *Lysistrata* as a model for our campaign." She took a few minutes to explain the story to him. When she was finished, she asked, "I think it's a marvelous idea, don't you?"

"No."

"Why not?"

"Because I am a man, Katherine Wildhorse—*your* man. What am I supposed to do when the urge to make love to you comes over me?"

She dropped her eyes to hide her amusement. "I don't know."

"You're determined to keep your vow?"

"Yes."

"Then know this: I will not play fair."

"Meaning?"

"I'm going to do everything in my power to make you willingly break that vow. You enjoy passion, Kate, and I know how needy you can become."

Katherine could not deny her body's response to his sensual words. "I do believe you are challenging me, Marshal."

He came nearer and, looking right into her eyes said, "No, *chica,* I'm promising."

His aura shimmered around her like heat on the horizon.

She managed to say, "Under the circumstances, I believe I should sleep in the other room."

"I'd rather have you in bed beside me, but that's your choice."

Katherine knew weaning herself from him would not be easy; she had no inkling it would turn out to be so hard.

He reached out and slowly, very slowly, traced his thumb over the line of her sultry bottom lip. He asked her quietly, "Is touching you one of the things I'm not supposed to do . . . ?"

She was being held prisoner by his panther-black eyes. "Yes . . ." Her lip was trembling under his lazy stroking.

"I should stop then, I suppose," he whispered huskily.

"Yes, you should."

He reluctantly withdrew his touch, leaving her bereft.

"I believe I'm going to enjoy playing this game, *chica*," he told her.

"You're supposed to be taking this seriously."

"All I've been thinking about since I left town has been coming home and taking you seriously—so seriously, folks would hear you in Kansas City."

Her heart pounding, she said, "That isn't what I meant."

"It's what I meant. How long can you hold out, Kate?"

"Long enough."

He gave her that ghost of a smile. "We'll see."

The men, Dix included, were convinced that the ladies were just fooling. After all, everyone knew that a married man had certain unalienable rights when it came to the bedroom. But the women were serious.

As the first few days passed, many of the men came home to find their sleeping arrangements drastically altered. Wives had moved to spare bedrooms, barns, and even tents they erected out doors. Some of the ladies chose a different tack: They went off to pay extended visits to their mothers and sisters, leaving their husbands to handle the day-to-day chores and the caring of the children. Very few homes went unaffected. Women all over the Territory took up the Dewies' gauntlet and used it to bar their bedroom doors.

By the end of the first week, the campaign began to take its toll. There were condemning editorials in the papers. Broadsides were posted on buildings, denouncing the women as troublemakers. The bootlegger Donovan was in an uproar because the whores in some of the border cribs had joined the Dewies' fight in an attempt to have their wages and working conditions bettered. Men all over the Territory were angrily demanding that the authorities do something, but as Dix pointed out to Arnold Taylor, there was nothing the law could do. The feuding was a domestic matter between a husband and his wife. Being the deputy marshal did not give Dix the power to force the women to share their husbands' beds; hell, he couldn't even convince his own wife, and all the ancestors knew he'd been trying.

At dinner that evening, Dix looked up from his plate and said to Katherine, ''The Dewies have got folks pretty riled up over this whole thing.''

''If Merle Gleason weren't so stubborn, none of this would have been necessary.''

''For the good of everybody involved, why don't you back off a little and let Merle breathe a bit?''

''No,'' she said offensively.

''I don't want anybody getting hurt, especially you. I'm the law around here.''

''Then as the law, you ought to be supporting our goal.''

"As the law, I have to take everybody's welfare into consideration, not just that of my hell-raising wife."

"Well, your hell-raising wife is going to continue to raise hell, whether you care for it or not."

"You've got a stubborn streak in you a mile wide."

"Thank you very much," she said sweetly.

"You know, the Reverend Mr. Lane is sleeping in his barn."

She nodded. "At last night's prayer meeting, he called our pledge blasphemous. When Alfreda pointed out that slave owners said the same thing about abolition, he got angry, went home, and moved into the barn."

"See, this is what I mean. They've been married as long as I've been alive—and now he's sleeping in the barn?"

"You act as if this were all my fault, and it's not."

"This did all start when you picketed Merle's newspaper."

"What other recourse did I have? Should I have waited until hell froze?"

They were both angry now.

Katherine continued, "You knew when you married me that I was not meek and biddable. If it's anyone's fault, it is yours for bringing me here!" She pushed her chair back from the table and left the kitchen.

Alone in her room, Katherine paced back and forth, trying to let go of her anger. She understood his position, but the goals of the women far outweighed the men's whining. All they wanted to do was place blame rather than deal with the underlying problem. It was the nineteenth century, for heaven's sake. Sooner or later women were going to get the vote and take their rightful place in this country, whether these men around here cared for the idea or not.

In the days that followed, Katherine had very little to

say to her husband, as did he to her—both seemed to prefer it that way. In church on Sunday, the men sat on one side of the aisle and the women on the other. The Reverend Mr. Lane gave a decidedly one-sided sermon on why females were created *after* man and of a woman's role in her husband's life. When the service concluded, none of the women left the church feeling particularly uplifted.

It was nearly dusk by the time Dix made his way to Donovan's saloon. At his entrance, the piano player's hands froze above his keys, and the previously raucous room became tomb silent. Dix looked around. He'd been out serving warrants all day, and this was his last stop. The man he was looking for was wanted for horse theft. Dix didn't see him among the patrons, and he turned to leave when Donovan's voice rang out. "Well, what brings you here, Marshal? Hiding from your wife?"

Dix heard a few snickers but didn't move.

"Hear she's got you so dick whipped, you even do the cooking."

When Dix slowly turned back around, the little piano player took one look at the marshal's deadly calm face and grabbed up his music, hightailing it out the door. A few of the other patrons hastily followed suit.

Dix walked over to the table where Donovan was sitting. He had just about had it. Katherine had plunged him in the middle of this mess, and he did not like it. He especially didn't cotton to having his manhood questioned by a drunken, fat-bellied pimp because of it.

He leaned down to Donovan and in a voice barely above a whisper said, "I can either whip your ass or close this hole down. Take your pick, because those are your choices."

Donovan snarled, "Why don't you use that on your wife?"

The lawman exploded his fist into the other man's face. The force of the blow knocked Donovan backward out of his chair, and Dix waited to see if the man was stupid enough to get up and challenge him, but he did not.

Dix left. He had planned on spending the night in one of the abandoned shacks along the trail because he had more warrants to serve the next day; instead, he headed the horse toward home.

When he entered, the house was so dark and quiet, he thought at first that Katherine was asleep. Moving quietly, he went to her door and opened it noiselessly. Moonlight streamed across her empty bed. Had she spent the night with Miss Vera? He went to see if she'd left a note in the kitchen. Not finding one, he made his way around to his side of the house. The sound of her humming floated on the silence. He realized she was in his room, and the knowledge made him smile for the first time in days. Walking in the door, he found a very nude Katherine standing in the big bathing tub. She almost jumped to the ceiling when she saw him stride in.

"My, my," he offered up appreciatively. He eased his gear to the floor and closed the door behind him.

At his startling entrance, Katherine had snatched up her wash cloth in an instinctive move and continued to hold it against her bosom as he made his way to the tub.

Dix stopped at the edge and turned glowing eyes on her glistening gold beauty. "You make quite a sight, Mrs. Wildhorse."

The cloth only covered a portion of her breasts, leaving one of her nipples sensually exposed along with the rest of her tall, lush body. Dix ran a lazy finger over the dark jewel, saying quietly, "You need a larger cloth . . ."

Katherine tried to remain unmoved by his sweet play, but it took less than a breath for her nipple to ripen to his slow command.

In contrast to his actions, he whispered, "I forgot . . . I'm not supposed to be doing this, am I . . . ?"

He drew a line down through the soap covering her belly, then continued the line back up to her breast. He circled her nipple only long enough for her eyes to slide closed, then asked, "Are you ready to be rinsed?"

Katherine nodded—or at least she thought she did—and a moment later he gently poured the water from the waiting bucket down over her body. He repeated the rinsing with the second bucket she'd placed by the tub. Now soap free, she let herself be wrapped in a large drying sheet and be helped to step out.

The heat in his eyes could have warmed a three-room house during a Chicago winter, and because that heat threatened to send her and the sheet up in flames, she said hastily, "I–I must go. Thank you for your help."

He nodded and drawled, "Anytime." He then added, "You're welcome to stay."

She searched his dark eyes a moment before asking quietly, "Are we still fighting?"

A small smile lifted his mustache. "Only if you wish it."

"I don't," she confessed truthfully. She'd missed him.

He reached out and stroked her cheek. "Then we agree." He'd missed her.

"I'm not going to abandon my pledge."

"I know."

Katherine looked up at the tall man she'd come to

love so passionately and said, "I'll see you in the morning."

"You won't stay?"

She shook her head no. "If I do, I'll break my vow."

Dix grinned. "And we can't have that, now, can we?"

"No, we can't, at least not yet . . ." She winked at him saucily, then left him alone.

Dix lay in bed, listening to the songs of the night. He'd much rather have been listening to the songs his wife sang when he made love to her, but that privilege lay stuck behind Merle Gleason's stubborn attitude.

He thought back upon her in his tub. He didn't even have to close his eyes to conjure up how absolutely fetching she'd looked standing nude in the candlelight. He'd had to dig deep in order to find the discipline he needed to keep his hands from touching her. The memories made his manhood rise, and he groaned inwardly. He didn't know how much longer he could stay celibate; every time he laid eyes on her, he wanted her nude and in his bed. If the Dewies didn't break soon, the men in the Territory were going to run Merle out of town on a rail—and Dix would be leading the mob.

In Aristophanes' play, the character Lysistrata urges her troops to wear comely clothes and splash on alluring perfumes in order to push the Athenian and Spartan men over the edge. Vera Landry encouraged her forces to do the same. From all the reports given at the Dewies nightly meetings, it appeared the women had the men on the run, and in an effort to give the ladies an opportunity to exercise their charms to the fullest, Vera decided to throw a party.

Katherine spent a full week creating the dress she planned on wearing. She hoped the suit Dix decided to wear had pockets because he would need someplace to hold his eyes after they popped out of his head. To her critical gaze, the gown rivaled the beauty of her wedding dress. The overdress of topaz-colored brocaded silk fell in heavy folds in the front and looped up at the sides to reveal a finer silk underdress. The bottom of the gown was trimmed with lace-edged scallops while the neckline left her throat and the caps of her shoulders bare.

It would be a dress to tempt the most disciplined of men, and her husband deserved a bit of humbling after the heated skirmishes he'd been waging the past few days against her Dewie vow. Although the women had agreed not to be moved by their husbands' advances, Katherine had not been married to Dix long enough to be able to keep her barricades in place.

As a consequence, trying to stay true to her pledge was akin to walking on a rocky beach. When he wasn't softly brushing his lips across her neck then slipping away before she could protest, he was watching her with those glittering, veiled eyes. He had only to look at her across the kitchen table and her need would rise.

So now, as she sat putting the final touches on her dress, Katherine couldn't wait to wear her creation and treat Dixon Wildhorse to a dose of his own medicine.

Meanwhile, Dix stood in the front parlor, waiting for his wife to make her entrance. He'd never been one for parties; however, he knew his wife enjoyed socializing.

Bringing her joy of a different sort seized his thoughts, though, as she slowly entered the room. He couldn't decide which was more beautiful, the brocaded topaz-colored gown or the polished-bronze woman wearing it. She moved like a tall queen. The crowns of her breasts rose sumptuously above the straight-lined bodice, and the silk dress rustled bewitchingly as she neared. There were gloves on her arms and soft curls around her face. The thin gold chain around her neck drew his eyes to the lovely column of her neck. Her loveliness made him pledge to make Merle Gleason surrender first thing in the morning. Dix refused to endure another celibate night.

"You look lovely, Katherine."

"Thank you, and I couldn't ask for a more handsome escort." She enjoyed his appreciative stare. It made her feel like a sumptuous dessert. Gleason had better surrender soon, because Katherine doubted her ability to resist her husband for very much longer.

The road leading to the Landry home was choked with vehicles. Dix let Katherine out at the door, then drove off to find a spot to park the buggy. He returned a short while later and escorted her inside. Katherine assumed the town's quarreling had been temporarily set aside for this occasion.

However, her assumption proved wrong. As soon as the welcoming died down, the men retreated to one side of the beautifully decorated barn, and the women congregated on the other. Between the two forces stood the lavishly set buffet table. At the other end of the barn, a five piece band began to play a lively tune.

The music gave the setting a festive air in spite of the feud. The women visited and gossiped while the men grumbled and shot daggers over at their wives.

Dix stood on the side with the men and watched his wife with glowing eyes. Every now and then she would glance his way, and he made no effort to mask his desire. A few times she let him see her own unveiled need, and it took all of his will not to march across the room and carry her off.

The Reverend Mr. Lane appeared at Dix's side and said, "This is probably harder on you than any of us—you being newly married and all."

Dix chuckled softly. "I've had snake bites that felt better."

"I certainly miss my Alfreda," he confessed wistfully. "You know, the only way out of this mess is for Merle to just give in."

The men around them all agreed.

Without taking his eyes off of his wife, Dix vowed, "I plan on taking care of Merle first thing in the morning."

The reverend looked up at the marshal and declared, "Hallelujah! Lord knows I'm tired of sleeping in the barn."

"In the meantime, I think I want to dance with my wife."

The reverend stared. "Dixon, I've known you all your life. Since when did you start dancing?"

"Since I found the right partner."

When Dix stepped out onto the floor and began walking toward his wife, the musicians stopped. Voices quieted. Everybody stared. Dix extended his hand to Katherine. She placed her hand in his without hesitation and let him lead her out onto the empty floor.

The musicians began a slow, beautiful tune played on a Mexican guitar. As Dix expertly moved her around, Katherine was surprised at how well he danced. "I thought Blake said you couldn't dance?"

"He said I didn't dance, not couldn't. There's a difference."

Having her so close reminded Dix how long it had been since their last kiss. He ran his gaze over the tempting crests of her breasts. "Be glad there's a lot of people in here."

"Why?"

"Because if we were alone, I'd already be undressing you. . . ."

Her passion flared. "I took a vow, remember?"

"If I get you alone tonight, you're not going to re-member your name, let alone that vow."

The heat in his black eyes told her he meant every word, and it made her heart pound. She wondered how much the Dewies would fine her if she succumbed right there on the dance floor.

At the end of their dance, he escorted her back to her spot among the ladies and retreated to the line of males. Katherine could see Vera over by the musicians dis-cussing something with them. When she returned, an-other tantalizing melody rose over the room, and she told her troops, "I've instructed the band to play soft and sweet for a while; let's see how the men like it. Shall we go ask them to dance, ladies?"

The men didn't stand a chance. They'd been deprived of their wives' companionship for over two weeks. Every woman had dressed especially alluringly that eve-ning, and the hunger in the men's eyes was quite evident as the women approached. The wives offered soundless invitations, and not a man refused.

The initial dance melted into a second dance and then a third and a fourth. Over the course of the evening the air became charged, volatile. One could sense the bur-geoning heat in the way the men held their wives and the way the women responded with longing looks and parted lips.

Katherine herself was not immune. Dix's hand upon her back seemed to be burning through the fabric of her dress.

She told him plainly, "I want to go home, Dixon."

"And do what?"

"I've a sudden need to count."

He grinned down into her liquid eyes. "As I remem-ber, you can't count very high."

"Maybe you can help me."

"We can't leave yet; it's still early."

"I think we'll be forgiven."

"What about your vow?"

"In the spirit of fair play, you'll have to promise to speak with Gleason."

"You have my word." He didn't tell her he'd already planned to do just that.

When the music ended, he took her hand and led her out into the night.

Dix brought the buggy to a halt in front of the porch. He looked over at his beautifully gowned wife and said, "Well, we're here."

Beneath the halfshell canopy of the buggy, Katherine held his eyes. Without a word she leaned near and kissed him softly. It was the only invitation he seemed to require because he pulled her across the worn leather seat and into his arms. He plundered her mouth deliciously, tempting her further with tiny, little licks from the tip of his tongue. She trembled as he stole heated, long snatches of sweetness from her lips.

"I've missed you," he whispered thickly.

His hands were making large warm circles over her silk covered back. Her perfume filled his nostrils, and the effect hardened his manhood like iron. Off in the distance, thunder rumbled. She stiffened, then drew away. He waited, wondering how she would react.

The last thing Katherine wanted was to end this interlude, but the approaching storm awakened her wariness. Passion had a firmer grip, however, and it was to it that she surrendered.

"Make me forget about the storm. . . ."

He lowered his mouth to hers, intent upon fulfilling her wish.

Carrying her in his arms, Dix stepped up on the porch and set her on her feet. Thunder rumbled once more, and he used the power of his kiss to befuddle her fears.

The wind rose, softly rustling the silk dress. Dix rustled it further as he pushed it above to her hips and boldly explored. He recaptured her mouth, nibbling as she sighed.

Katherine began to lose all sense of time and place; his hands, so deliciously slow, were hot, possessive. She uttered not a peep of protest when he undid the strings of her drawers. He took them from her soundlessly, then delicately teased the bareness left behind.

"You can start counting . . ." he informed her softly.

Katherine trembled in reaction to the thick timbre of his voice and to the cajoling of his meandering hand. "One . . ."

He slid a finger into the damp silk between her thighs. Her flesh rippled around him; he kissed her, her reward for being so ripe with pleasure.

"Two . . ." she breathed.

He withdrew from her honey-filled gate, then grazed a knuckle over the berried bud before letting her dress whisper down again.

"Three . . ." he said huskily.

The thunder sounded louder, nearer. Had she not been so overwhelmed by him freeing her breasts from her gown, she might have given way to her anxiety. But she was too busy swooning. He brushed her skirts up her thighs once more, seemingly unable to keep his hands from her sheltered secrets, and pleasured her until her legs parted wantonly. The winds of the approaching storm played over her damp nipples and her scandalously bared limbs, but she stood there on the porch, shuddering as he ran his hands over her without inhibition.

When he dropped to his knees and placed his kiss above each of the garters anchoring her stockings, her croon rose on the night. He filled his hands with silken hips and brought her forward to claim his prize. He teased and dallied until her legs parted in shameless, greedy welcome.

"So beautiful . . ." he breathed.

He loved her in earnest then, nibbling, circling, plying the hidden bud with such erotic expertise, it didn't take long for completion to shatter her and send her senses soaring.

By now the storm was almost upon them, and it had begun to rain. Her fears demanded that she go inside, but the woman in her did not want to part from him for even a moment.

When he suggested she might be more comfortable in a bed, she kissed him deeply and told him plainly, "No. Here. From now on, I want storms to remind me of you . . . us."

So Dixon Wildhorse removed his wife's fancy gown and made love to her on the front porch amid the wind and the thunder and the warm, cleansing rain. He drank the beaded water from her breasts and throat and filled his hands with her rain-slick hips. He spread his suit coat on the porch and took her there. As he drove her to new heights, he kissed the raindrops from her eyes and watched ecstasy crackle over her like lightning. His own release soon followed, resonating through his being like ground-shaking thunder.

The next morning, the Dewies gathered in the basement of the church. Most of the women at last night's party were in attendance, and all looked tired.

Once everyone was settled, Vera Landry asked, "How many of you broke your vow last night?"

A hush settled over the room. Katherine looked around and spied many guilty-looking faces. She felt relieved knowing she hadn't been the only weak sister, but she doubted anyone would confess unless she went first, so she raised her hand.

Vera acknowledged Katherine's declaration of guilt by saying sadly, "Oh, Katherine, not you?"

"I'm afraid so," she replied. "I'd like to say it was not my fault, but I'd be lying."

A few giggles met the statement. Katherine dropped her head to hide her smile.

Vera said, "Well, I slipped, too. Solomon and I have not slept apart since we married five years ago. It like to killed us both."

Laughs greeted Vera's admission. Soon more and more women were stepping forward to confess. A newlywed woman from Muskogee drew the most mock derision for admitting she hadn't lasted one night. Women all over the room threw their bonnets at her as punishment.

It took the ladies a moment to notice Dix standing in the doorway. Katherine wondered how long he'd been there and how much he'd heard.

Vera motioned him on in. "Good morning, Marshal. How may we help you?"

Dix strode farther into the room, silently greeted his wife, then said, "Come to deliver a truce from the men."

Everyone viewed him excitedly.

Vera stated, "We're listening."

"Merle says he'll hire Kate if you ladies will call off your campaign."

A buzz went through the room.

Katherine wanted to know, "What made him change his mind?"

"A bit of pressure in the right place" was all Dix was willing to admit. He planned to tell her later that the truce came about only when Arnold Taylor threatened to call in Merle's note to the bank if he didn't end the feud.

"So, ladies, I guess you won."

Cheering voices filled the room as the celebration began. They'd won!

Dix held Katherine's eyes. She smiled and mouthed a silent thank you.

He touched his hat and departed.

Katherine reported to work bright and early the next day.

"Good morning, Mr. Gleason," she said cheerily upon entering his small office. The familiar smell of the ink filled her with happiness.

He didn't respond. Instead, he walked over to his desk and began to write something on a piece of paper. Without looking up, he told her, "Want you to go out to the Dickey place and talk to the woman there. Heard she just received some type of fancy dress from back East."

He handed Katherine a crudely drawn map.

Confused, she asked, "Why is this dress important enough to write about?"

"It isn't, but it's the kind of items you females like to know about."

At first Katherine was certain he was pulling her leg, but when she realized he was quite serious, she fought to keep her temper under control. "Mr. Gleason, surely, there is a more worthy subject for me to pursue."

"Nope," he replied easily. He then took his seat behind the desk and smiled smugly as he picked up his coffee cup and took a sip.

Katherine refused to rise to the bait. "Fine," she said coolly. "I will go and see Mrs. Dickey."

"Before you go, just so you'll know: The paper here's not real big—one sometimes two pages. I don't know when I'll have the space to print what you write, but I'll pay you for it just as soon as I do."

Katherine was furious when she left. She was still fuming when she ran into Dix a few moments later. He was just stepping out of the barbershop, and she was on her way to the livery to retrieve her buggy. It took him only an instant to gauge her mood. "What rocker rolled over your tail?"

She didn't tell him about Gleason's patronizing assignment because she didn't want to be accused of whining. "Nothing's wrong. I'm on my way to get the buggy. I have to find the Dickey place."

"What's there?"

"A dress."

"A dress?"

"Yes, a dress. I must go."

"I'll send Lyndon with you."

"Dix, I don't need an escort."

"No, but you might need protection."

She conceded that point. "Well, tell him to be ready. I won't wait."

He placed a hand on her arm as she began to walk away. "Are you sure you're okay?"

"Sure," she lied. She leaned up and kissed him on the cheek, much to the amusement of the people passing by on the boardwalk. "I'll be back as soon as I'm able."

As it turned out, even though Lyndon was silent for most of their journey, Katherine wound up being grateful for the company. Merle Gleason had misdrawn the map.

Lyndon looked it over and asked quizzically, ''Who did you say drew this?''

''Mr. Gleason.''

''Well, following this would've had you out in the middle of nowhere. Mr. Gleason knows the Territory better than most folks. What could he have been thinking?''

Katherine had a fairly good idea, but she kept the speculation to herself.

With Lyndon driving, they finally arrived at the Dickey home. Mrs. Dickey hadn't had a dress shipped from back East in two years.

Katherine wanted to stake Merle Gleason in the middle of the road and run a herd of cattle over him. He'd not only sent her on a wild goose chase, he'd tried to get her lost. She didn't envision him changing, either. If she continued to work for him, he'd run her ragged investigating quilting bees, wedding receptions, and piano recitals and undoubtedly would not print a word she wrote. This had happened before when she first began pursuing her career as a journalist. She'd worked for a paper in New York edited by a man harboring the same prejudices as Gleason. For eight months he seemed determined to break her spirit and enthusiasm because, as he put it, she should be home having babies, not writing. He never printed anything she wrote and like Gleason assigned her items with little value. Back then she'd had youth and stubbornness on her side, and she'd been naive enough to believe that if she didn't grumble or whine, her hard work would eventually win him over. It didn't. He died during her ninth month on the job, and she was let go when the next editor came aboard because he couldn't justify paying a woman who had never written anything worthy enough to reach print. She was as angry now as she was then.

Lyndon's voice drew her attention when he said, "You know, my sister, Hannah, is thinking about going away to school because of you."

Katherine said, "I'm sorry, but I had nothing to do with it."

He chuckled. "No, it isn't a bad thing. The family's happy."

Katherine brightened. "Oh, well, good. But how am I involved in her decision?"

"She wants to be a career woman like you."

"Why?"

"Because the marshal is in love with you."

"No, he isn't."

"Yes, he is. I've known him a lot longer than you. He's in love. Hannah thinks it's because you're smart."

"Hannah is smart."

"I know, but she didn't think having smarts meant anything. People have been telling her all her life how beautiful she is, so she thought that was all she had to be. When the marshal brought you home, she was not pleased."

"Neither were you, as I remember."

He looked embarrassed for a moment. "My apologies. You broke my sister's heart. I didn't want to like you out of loyalty to her."

Katherine smiled. "I understand."

"But I do like you now, Mrs. Wildhorse."

"I'm glad Lyndon. Do me a favor and promise me you won't tell the marshal about the map."

"Why not? He'll want to know."

"I don't want him to think I'm whining."

"You're not whining. Mr. Gleason could've been responsible for you getting hurt."

"But I wasn't hurt, thanks to you."

"The marshal's going to find out eventually. Always

does. He'll kill me if he learns I knew about this and didn't tell him. I'd rather he kill Mr. Gleason.''

He then looked over at her and asked, ''Do you love the marshal?''

Katherine nodded. ''I do, but despite what you believe, I don't think he shares my feelings.''

''Pardon me, but you must be blind.''

Katherine chuckled. ''What am I not seeing, Lyndon?''

''The way he looks at you, the way he talks about you all the time.''

''That doesn't necessarily mean he loves me.''

''Yes, it does. He's never looked at a woman the way he does you. He has never ever, *ever* danced with anybody, but he did with you a few nights ago. My mother said she almost fell over.''

''The marshal and I get along fairly well, I admit, and he seems to enjoy my company. I don't think his feelings run any deeper than that, however.''

He observed her. ''You really don't understand, do you?''

Surprised by his sage tone, she replied, ''I guess I don't.''

''Well, he's not going to say it, but he loves you.''

Katherine didn't know what to say.

Chapter 18

That night as Katherine lay in bed next to her sleeping husband, she thought about her conversation with Lyndon. Did Dix really love her? She harbored doubts, but her doubts seemed to be at odds with the rest of the folks in town. Vera had said he loved her, Hannah had said he loved her, and now, Lyndon. She freely admitted they had known her husband much longer than she—but love? Their marriage had evolved into something very special, mostly because Dix had turned out to be a very special man. Had someone told her that day in Rupert Samuels's parlor that the dark-skinned giant at the center of the fight would eventually be her husband and lover, she'd've said, "Hogwash!"

But she wasn't saying hogwash now. She loved him and wanted to be at his side for the rest of her life. She wanted to give him daughters and sons and make love to him every sunrise. He was her shelter from the storm, her lover, her protective topaz. To have him declare his love for her would certainly make her glad. If he never did, so be it; she was certain he'd continue to treat her tenderly. She didn't need more.

Dix waited over a week for Katherine to say something to him about the misdrawn map. Lyndon had spilled the beans immediately upon his return to town, but she never said a word. Even so, Dix had a few choice words with Merle, who chalked the whole thing up to a simple misunderstanding. He promised the angry Dix it would never happen again.

Dix didn't want her working for someone so petty, but knew he'd never be able to convince her to quit without her threatening him with Sweetie Pie, so he kept his opinion to himself.

He finally broke through the ice that night. They were sitting on the porch watching the stars come out when she said quietly, "I won't be working for Mr. Gleason any longer."

"No?" he asked, hoping his voice didn't reveal his elation.

"No, and you don't have to sound so elated by the news. I know you've wanted me to leave his employment." With a smile on her face she looked over at him sitting in the dark.

"You know me well. You shouldn't have to work for someone so filled with spite," he confessed. "What made you fold?"

"The fact that he will never change, and I refuse to waste my talents on the drivel he wants me to report on. Another day of his snide comments and I'd be arrested for assault."

"Why didn't you tell me about the map he drew?"

"I didn't want to complain, especially after all the town went through so I could gain the position in the first place."

He replied, "Under the circumstances I think folks would've understood."

"Well, I didn't see it that way. Besides, you've a lot more important matters to handle. I can't come running to you every time I fall and skin my knee.''

"But you can, Kate. Anytime."

"You're a very decent man, Dixon Wildhorse."

"We make a good pair."

She rested her back against the porch column and sighed contentedly.

His voice came out of the night. "So, do you like it here?"

"It's the most exciting place I've ever been in in my life."

"It wasn't before you came to town."

"Oh, now you're going to lay it all at my door?"

He smiled. He had no idea he'd come to value her companionship so highly. He could no longer fathom waking up without her at his side. Her smile buoyed his days, and her kisses inflamed his nights. He'd grown accustomed to her scents, the way she walked, and her crusading independence. She was one of a kind, his Kate, and he wanted her beside him for a lifetime.

She asked then, "What are the winters like here?"

"Sometimes brutal, sometimes mild."

"That could be a description of the land."

"I suppose it could be."

Katherine had come to appreciate this wild, untamed place. The beautiful, unspoiled openness and the clear, pure air filled one with purpose and energy. She now understood why people were drawn to the West. Out here, the land led you to believe anything was possible and anything could be achieved if you just went after it. "Do you know what would be wonderful?"

"No, what?"

"If I could start my own paper."

"What's stopping you?"

"Money for a press."

"I can loan you the funds."

"No."

"Why not?"

"Suppose I can't pay you back?"

"We can talk about that if and when the time comes."

The offer tempted her mightily, but she said, "No. I'll come up with something."

As the heat of August gave way to the fickle winds of September, Katherine continued to send columns back East. Her articles had drawn a modicum of praise from a few editors, but none offered her full-time employment.

Her father had managed to stay out of jail these past six weeks, and he and she spent time building a relationship they'd never had. He told her stories of her mother and his family; they shared dinners, and played many rounds of checkers. Bart Love provided the last link to her mother, and in spite of his penchant for flim-flam, Katherine found that she loved him very much.

During the second week of September, Katherine was driving down the road toward town to have lunch with Vera. The land between Dix's *chickee* and town was open and flat as a plain, except for a series of hills in the distance that held the area's only trees. As she drove past the small rise, shots rang out. She nearly broke her neck diving out of the rig. Seeking safety down by the wheels, she crouched still as a statue waiting for the assault to continue. Two more bullets hit the side of the buggy, making her jump with fright. Then, came silence. She didn't dare move for fear of drawing more fire, but she really wanted to leave this place. She waited for what seemed hours, then, keeping her head low, slowly peeked around. The surrounding silence seemed as loud as her breathing. No more shots greeted her, nor did she see anyone. She very cautiously retook her seat, slapped the reins across the team, and hightailed it into town.

Her first stop was the marshal's office. Dix was not pleased to hear her news. He asked her a million questions about the location, what she'd seen, and what she heard. She couldn't offer much information other than the basic facts and that she'd been scared half to death.

"Until I find out what's going on, I don't want you out on the road alone," Dix declared.

Katherine didn't want to agree, but since he was more knowledgeable in situations such as this, she deferred to his judgment. He then sent Lyndon out to the spot where the shooting had occurred to look for any clues the sniper might have left behind.

After Lyndon's exit, Dix took Katherine in his arms. For a moment silence reigned as they savored one another's nearness. He wanted to know, "Are you certain you're okay?"

"I'm still shaking a bit, but I'll be fine."

"I'd cut out my heart if anything happened to you."

Katherine looked up at him in surprise. "Dixon?" Had she heard him correctly?

His eyes locked with hers but he didn't reply. Instead, he pulled her close again and folded her back against his chest, kissing the top of her head and holding her as if he never wanted to let her go. She held on to him just as tightly.

Because it was Dix's turn to work the late shift he refused to let her go home alone. He insisted that she stay in town at Dahlia Hurd's boardinghouse, and she didn't argue. He escorted her there and secured her a room.

Inside, Katherine looked around at the small well-kept room with its small bed and dresser. The bed would've never held the two of them, so she thought it was for the best that her husband had to work that night.

For Dix's part, Katherine's story about the sniper had shaken him to his soul, and he did not want her out of his sight. He wished he could stash her in a pocket so he'd be assured of her safety, though that obviously wasn't possible. He took solace in the knowledge that at Mrs. Hurd's, Katherine would be close by.

"I need to go and see if Lyndon found anything. You're sure you're okay now?"

His protectiveness was touching. "Yes, Marshal, I'm fine."

He did not want to leave her but had to if he wanted to catch the person responsible.

She asked the question paramount in her mind. "Who would want to shoot me?"

He shrugged. "No idea, but believe me, I'll find out."

She came over and stood close enough to place her hand on his chest. "You will be careful?"

He raised her hand and pressed his lips tenderly to the center of her palm. "Always . . ."

She leaned up to give him a kiss good-bye. "Come back later if you can."

He nodded, kissed her one last time, and departed.

Lyndon Green returned to town later with no clues. The gunman, whoever it was, had covered his exit well by using a branch to brush away the tracks. Lyndon followed the distinctive swath through the dust for more than a mile, but the trail petered out once the soil became rocky.

Lyndon said, "Whoever it was, he was pretty brazen shooting at her like that in broad daylight."

Dix thought so, too. "It's either someone so mad they didn't care or somebody so stupid they didn't know any better. Either way, the person is dangerous."

"But why would someone want to shoot her?"

"Who knows?"

"She hasn't been here long enough to rile anybody that much, has she?"

"Well, let's see. There's the bootlegger, Donovan; Rupert Samuels, who last I heard was up in Creek country with Mona; Merle Gleason; and half the men in the Seminole Nation. Some of them are still pretty sore over her part in the Dewie rebellion."

"Short list, huh?"

"Very short," Dix drawled, "but I plan on whittling it down—quickly."

"Want me to alert Sixkiller in Muskogee?"

Dix nodded. "Wire Bass Reeves and Judge Parker, too. Both will want to know."

Lyndon grabbed his hat and headed out for the telegraph office.

Alone now, Dix puzzled over the near shooting of his wife. The more he mused over it, the angrier he became. She could have been killed. Whoever was responsible would pay—and pay dearly.

Katherine finally made it to Vera's the next afternoon. Vera, like everyone else in the Territory, had heard about the sniper attack. She and Katherine spent a few moments discussing it, then changed the conversation to Katherine's search for another position. She'd sent letters outlining her credentials to the other papers in the Territory but so far had received no reply.

Katherine said, "If I had the money for the press, I'd start my own."

"Well, when you do, you won't have to worry about paper. I've tons of it out in the dugout behind the house."

Surprised, Katherine asked to see it.

"The paper's in here," she said gesturing to an

earthen mound that appeared to be a small hill. Katherine had heard about dugouts but had never seen one.

Vera pulled open the wooden door built into the hillside. Inside it was dark, and patches of cobwebs draped the entrance. Vera lit a lantern. The earthen ceiling was far too low for Katherine to stand upright, so she stooped and went inside. As she peered around, she noted that the place appeared to be fairly clean. Five big barrels stood against the wall.

It took only a short while to roll the large cooper's barrels out of the dark and into the fall sunshine. When they'd completed the task, they both took a moment to rid their hair and clothing of cobwebs and shook their hems free of soil.

Only two of the five barrels of paper hadn't been damaged by dampness, rodents, or insects. Katherine was pleased to find even a portion of the stock useable.

Vera said, "Take as much as you need. I've no use for it, as you can see. When Black Cat died and Merle took over his equipment, he refused to buy the paper. Said I was charging too dear a price."

"How much do you want for it?"

"Not a dime. I'll consider it an investment."

Katherine started to argue, but the displeased look on Vera's face prompted her to forget about a price and instead say, "Thank you."

She wasted little time driving her precious paper home. She planned on publishing such an excellent newspaper, everyone in the Territory would want to read it. Merle Gleason refused to carry any papers from back East, but Katherine planned on wrangling as many subscriptions to other papers as could be managed. Granted, she had no presses, print devils, or field stringers, but she had determination—and now she had paper. It was a start.

Vera had suggested Katherine talk to Arnold Taylor about loaning her the capital for presses. Now, at their meeting, the banker listened sympathetically, but since she had no ready cash or collateral, he couldn't take the risk. Katherine didn't argue; she knew the state of her finances. Were she in Taylor's shoes, she would do the same. He suggested she have her husband sign for the loan, but Katherine disagreed. If this were going to be her paper, she'd have to find a way to publish it on her own.

A few days later Katherine ran into Merle Gleason as he was coming out of the general store. The smug smile on his face had become a permanent fixture since the day she quit working for him.

"Well, well, well. How's the newspaper business, Mrs. Wildhorse? Hear you're having trouble raising the money to buy a press. Maybe you ought to have the children at the school hand letter your newspaper. I'm pretty sure they'd do a bang-up job."

His chuckle made Katherine's lip curl. She longed to tell him what she thought he ought to do with himself, but didn't; such a reply would be neither polite nor ladylike. She replied instead, "I'll keep your suggestion in mind, Mr. Gleason."

Still grinning, he said, "You do that."

His mocking presence stayed with her for the remainder of the day. Everywhere her mind turned, his smarmy face appeared. The urge to make him eat his hat burned hotly within her, but without presses she couldn't compete. His taunting suggestion that she hand letter her paper made her fume even more until she remembered something. One of the elder *Globe* editors had once mentioned a paper he'd seen in the eastern part of Michigan. The Michigan paper didn't have a press, either, but made up for the lack of one by doing just as Gleason had suggested: The editor encouraged the citizenry and folks traveling through the small town to pen any news they'd heard or seen on large pieces of paper. He then posted the paper for everyone's perusal. News was added or deleted as space allowed, and the unique concept proved fairly successful. Katherine could not think of any reason why the idea could not be duplicated here in Nero. In fact, she'd be willing to bet her neighbors would get a kick out of such an undertaking.

Her first item of business was to find a place to house her paper. Vera convinced her husband to lease Katherine an empty storeroom built on to the back of his store. Katherine thought the place ideal, even though it was small and she would not be facing Main Street. However, it had more than enough room for her purposes. It also had its own door, which meant folks wouldn't have to cut through Solomon's business to reach her.

She published the first edition two days later. Thanks to Alfreda Lane's tireless expertise on the telegraph, Katherine, via Geoff on the other end, was able to print items of importance from back East. Of particular interest was one about John R. Lynch, a former Black congressman from Mississippi. He'd been elected the temporary chairman of the Republican convention—the first Black ever to preside over the proceedings of an American political party. During the convention, the Republican incumbent president, Chester Arthur, lost the nomination to James G. Blaine. Blaine's opponent in the upcoming election would be the Democrat, Grover Cleveland. If elected, Cleveland would be the first Democratic president since the Civil War.

In the meantime, Dix had been in the saddle for four days, chasing information on the person or persons responsible for shooting at his wife—and he'd not been polite. He'd roused drunks in the border towns, questioned whores in their cribs, and harassed bootleggers all over the Nation in his search for a lead. Word got around that Wildhorse was in an unusually vile mood, and the number of people he placed under arrest and the many fines and citations he issued confirmed it. The fines on Donovan's operations alone totaled over three hundred dollars. He fined him for everything from selling liquor to youngsters to having dirty glasses behind the bar. When Donovan protested, Dix fined him another fifty dollars for interfering with an officer of the law. In the four days he'd been criss-crossing the Nation, he'd given the criminal element fits. Everyone wanted the perpetrator found because they knew there'd be no peace until then.

When Dix dragged himself home that evening, he found his wife at the kitchen table, scribbling on large flats of paper. She looked up and gave him a welcoming smile when he entered. "Hello. Did you find anything?"

"No. Did you take any vows while I was gone?"

Grinning, she shook her head.

"Good, then come greet me properly. . . ."

She walked to him slowly, her eyes saucy, her walk enticing, and draped her arms dramatically around his neck. She lowered his head and gifted him with a kiss that could've meited snow on a Boston roof. Slowly easing her lips from his, she asked huskily, "How's that?"

His mustache lifted with his smile. "Not bad, but I'd like a second opinion."

"Greedy man."

She gave him one, then another, and then another.

As Dix surfaced from the haze brought on by her welcome, he murmured against her lips, "Excellent . . ."

They kissed until they'd had enough; then he scanned

her face. "Anybody take pot shots at you while I was gone?"

"Just Gleason, but he doesn't count. I did start my paper while you were out chasing outlaws though."

"Really?"

She told him the story and showed him the papers she was lettering. He sat down to read some of her columns, then pulled her down onto his lap.

Katherine admitted, "I don't have a name for it yet. Candace Taylor suggested I have a contest. We both agree it might spark interest."

"You might be right. Why won't you let me buy you a press?"

"Because," she said softly, "I want to do it this way."

He kissed her forehead. "You are such a stubborn woman."

"True, but think how boring life would be if I said yes to everything."

"Think how peaceful things would be."

She punched him playfully and he made an exaggerated groan.

Later, as they lay in bed, Katherine asked him about his search.

"Turned up nothing substantial."

"Were you able to locate Rupert?"

"Didn't see him, but rumor has it he and Mona are up visiting her relatives over in the Creek Nation. Rumor also has it that he's been wiped out financially. Seems Judge Parker quietly poked under some rocks and found a few snakes. There's a bunch of indictments waiting both in Chicago and Baltimore with Rupert's name on them."

"For the counterfeit stocks?"

"That and a Back to Africa scheme."

Across the nation many Black leaders were discussing

the idea of emigrating back to Mother Africa. The idea was not new; the debate had been going on since the end of the Revolutionary War. Those who opted to leave America in those early days had settled in places like Sierra Leone and Liberia. Lately the debate had increased tenfold because of the violent disenfranchisement going on in the South.

"What did Rupert do?" Katherine asked.

"Sold a bunch of folks tickets to Liberia on an uncertified ship. It sank in the Atlantic about fifty miles off the coast of Maryland, and ten people died, including three children."

"So is he under arrest?"

"Soon as the law finds him. The Maryland authorities have already jailed two of his three partners."

"Do you think he's the one behind the sniper?"

"Could be. We'll know soon, I'm pretty sure."

"You sound fairly confident."

"I am. Everyone knows how unhappy I am about having my wife used as a target." He reached over and pulled her close. "I don't want anything to happen to you. Not many women will let me make love to them on the porch in a rainstorm."

She grinned. "You're right, so treat me like the treasure I am."

"Always . . ." he whispered, kissing her softly.

A heartbeat later he was asleep.

Katherine's paper became the talk of the Territory. By the end of September, folks were driving down from as far away as Tahlequah in the Cherokee Nation just to get a look at it. It had been christened the *Nero Bulletin*, a name submitted by Lyndon Green.

The name lacked the style Katherine had envisioned, but it turned out to be the appropriate one. Her news items were indeed posted like bulletins. In addition to the information brought in by travelers and the tele-graph, she tacked up posters featuring wanted outlaws and notices to the tribes from the federal government. She charged folks a penny a read. Some folks stayed all day, debating and drinking coffee. Even the other estab-lished papers began taking an interest. They sent re-porters to interview her and printed stories about her paper in their own dailies and weeklies. She displayed those articles on the walls of the store room, as well.

At breakfast a few mornings later, Dix informed Kath-erine that he'd be gone for a few days in order to serve a warrant on a man up near Turkey Creek, northwest of Wewoka. When Katherine asked to accompany him, he said no.

Katherine, seated across the kitchen table, replied eas-ily, "I think my readers would like to know how a mar-shal goes about his job. I won't interfere in any way."

"No."

"Why not?"

"It's too dangerous."

"What's this man wanted for?"

"Murder."

"Oh. I see."

"Killed his brother-in-law over a keg of Muskogee water."

Katherine shook her head sadly. The illegal "intro-ducing" had not ceased. She and the Dewies continued to march every Wednesday evening down by the border town saloons in an effort to try and bring about a change. "Has the man taken flight?"

"I'm not sure."

"I'd still like to go."

"No."

"Dix—"

"No. I'll have enough to worry about without having to look out for you."

"I'll look out for myself."

He got up from the table, and she followed him out to the front room. "I insist we discuss this. I wouldn't go along as your wife, but as a member of the press."

"You can be part of the President's entourage as far as I'm concerned, but you're not going. If something happened to you, I'd never forgive myself."

"Please, please, please! I won't complain, I won't talk when I'm not supposed to, I'll keep my head down, and I'll do everything you ask, I promise."

He shook his head at her singular pleading and proclaimed softy, "You wheedle well, woman."

She asked in a hesitant voice, "Does that mean I can go?"

In reality, Dix didn't really want to be separated from her again. Over the past month or so, he'd spent more time away from her than with her. During the wagon train trip and on their train ride to Wewoka, he'd grown accustomed to constantly having her by his side. Coming home and having to resume his duties as marshal had made the closeness hard to maintain. He freely admitted missing it. "Yes, you can go. But . . ."

"But what?"

"If you step out of line for even an instant, I'll take you across my knee."

Katherine wiggled her eyebrows suggestively. "Take me across your knee and do *what,* Marshal?"

"Just go get your gear, brazen woman."

Katherine left the room, the happiest editor in the Territory.

Dix's decision to allow her to accompany him earned him a visit from a very angry Merle Gleason later that day in town. He stormed into Dix's office and snapped,

"Are you really allowing your wife to accompany you on an arrest?"

"Why?"

"Because if one member of the press is going along, I demand to be included also."

Dix looked him up and down. "No."

"What do you mean, no?"

"It's just going to be me and my wife."

"That is unfair, Marshal."

"No, it isn't. This is a wedding trip, Merle. Kate and I never got to have one. I want to show her the countryside before winter closes us down."

"But I heard—"

"You heard wrong. Anything else?"

Gleason stormed out.

Lyndon said, "He really doesn't like your wife, does he?"

"Nope." Dix had no idea how he'd found out about the trip. He was certain Kate hadn't revealed the information. She'd balk at telling Gleason the time of day. He supposed it was just another benefit of living in a small town where there were no such things as secrets.

"How about you?"

Dix's face mirrored his confusion. "What?"

"Do you like your wife?"

"Yes."

"Do you love her?"

Dix scanned the young light horseman's face. "Why are you asking me these questions?"

"Because she loves you, and I want to know if you love her."

"Kate doesn't love me."

"Sure she does. She told me so."

Dix stared. "Why would she tell you something like that?"

Lyndon shrugged. "I asked her. So, do you love her?"

Dix didn't answer. Instead, he walked over to the window and looked out over the comings and goings of the vehicles and people on the street. The silence lengthened.

Lyndon said, "I know you pretty well, Marshal, so I'm going to take that as a yes. You should tell her, you know."

"Since when did you become so wise?"

"It's from listening to my mother and the other ladies. My mother had Miss Vera and some of the Dewies over for dinner last evening. They were discussing the two of you."

"And what was the consensus?"

"The consensus was that you should tell her you love her. The women around here admire her a lot."

Dix did, too, but he'd never even hoped she would love him. Lyndon had to be mistaken. "I think you're wrong, kid."

"About what?"

"Her loving me."

"Nope. I told you, she said so herself."

"I still think you're wrong."

Dix left the office a while later and rode out to Vera's. She was out in her front yard, tending her garden. She stood and smiled as he tied up his horse to her post. "Afternoon, Dixon. What brings you out to see this old woman?"

Dixon liked Vera Landry, always had. Her father and his grandfather had come west together. He'd known her virtually his whole life, and he considered her to be as wise as she was unconventional. "I need to talk to you."

She invited him into the house. He waved off her

gesture to take a seat and went and stood at the window with his back to her instead.

"When you stand like that, I know something's bothering you," she said. "Your father, Ruffin, stood that way, too."

Dix had been a babe when his parents were killed during the Seminole Exodus, and he did not remember either of them. Every now and then Vera would mention how he favored Ruffin Wildhorse in some way, and the knowledge always touched his heart. "It's about Katherine."

"What about her?"

"Lyndon says she loves me."

"Is that a problem?"

He shook his head. "No. I just find it hard to believe is all."

"Why, don't you think she's capable of love?"

"Of course she is, but me?"

"Why not you? You are as handsome as you are honorable. Do you love her?"

"I'm pretty sure I do. Have for a while."

"You haven't told her, I take it."

"Nope."

"Well, no time like the present. The two of you should use the ride to Turtle Creek to talk and set things straight. You don't want her thinking you don't love her and have her head back East, do you?"

"No."

"Then tell her."

Dix turned and asked, "Is there anybody in town who *doesn't* know Kate and I are heading for Turtle Creek?"

"Not that I'm aware of."

He chuckled and shook his head. Then he turned serious. "Thanks for the advice, Vera."

"You've always been the son I never had, Dixon.

From the day I cared for you on the trek back to the Territory after your parents died, I've considered you the child of my heart. Tell Katherine of your love. You deserve the happiness she will bring you.''

He walked over and kissed her on the cheek. ''I will. Thank you. Don't wreck my town while I'm gone, okay?''

She smiled but made no promises.

Chapter 19

Dix and Katherine headed out for Turtle Creek early the next morning. Katherine had learned to ride over the summer, thanks to the tutelage of the Dewies, but she'd never ridden very far. She definitely never spent four hours in the saddle. As the day lengthened, her bottom, back, and shoulders stung from the strain and exertion, but she kept her pains to herself because she had promised not to complain.

Dix didn't realize how much she was suffering until they stopped to rest late in the day. He noticed how slow she seemed to be dismounting and the hobbling walk she affected once she did.

"Are you okay?"

"No, but I promised I wouldn't complain."

She very gingerly lowered herself atop a conveniently placed boulder. Her bottom complained about having to sit on something so hard, but Katherine didn't mind because, blessedly, the rock was stationary.

"Why didn't you tell me earlier?"

"I already told you. I promised I wouldn't complain."

He took the canteen from his saddle and handed it to

her. She took a few long draws, then gushed out a thanks as she handed the container back.

"I ought to take you over my knee for being so close-mouthed. We've a few more miles until we stop for the night. Are you able to ride?"

"No. Just go on without me and come get me on your way back."

"I'm tempted, believe me."

She cut him an angry look.

He asked her, "Why are you so stubborn? We could've stopped hours ago."

She could feel her temper sliding up. "I'm female; it's in my blood."

"You're exasperating."

"You're no model of sweetness and light, either."

He shook his head, then spoke softly, "You're turning me inside out, you know that?"

She looked into his unveiled eyes and replied just as softly, "I'll take that as a compliment. . . ."

Dix knew that in about a half a second he was going to pull her into his arms and make love to her right out there in the open if they didn't get a move on. He loved her all right, as dearly as his people loved freedom. "You can ride with me the rest of the way. Let me transfer some of the gear."

She waited while he went about the task. His softly spoken declaration of her effect on his life still echoed inside. Once again she found herself wondering if those who claimed Dix loved her were correct.

Katherine rode the remainder of the day's miles cushioned against Dix's broad chest. He kept the horse at a slow pace, mindful of her aches and pains. When he halted in front of what appeared to be an abandoned shack, she tilted her head back to see his face and asked, "Is this where we're staying the night?"

"Yep. Are you complaining?"

She hastily shook her head no.

"Good."

Once he'd lit a lantern and she had the opportunity to look around the inside of the shack, Katherine decided it wasn't so bad. There was a partial roof, a relatively clean dirt floor, the listing remains of a fireplace, and no furniture. "Lovely accommodations, Marshal."

"Glad you like it."

"Reminds me of the Frederick Douglass suite in a way."

"I thought it might."

She grinned. He did, too.

He went out to retrieve their bedrolls and the cooking utensils. They built a fire in the broken-down grate and heated up some stew they'd brought along. Silence settled between them as they sat on a tarp and ate the meal, but each time Katherine glanced up, he seemed to be watching her intently.

She ate two helpings. When she finished, she tried to stand but found it near impossible; her muscles had tightened considerably over the course of the evening. It hurt to move, and the pains were reminiscent of the ones she'd suffered during the first few days in camp with the brides.

Dix stated the obvious. "You are in bad shape, aren't you?"

"I feel like I'm back with the brides and just learning how to drive the teams."

The salve she'd been given by Loreli Winter had helped immensely back then. Luckily she still had the tin and had packed it with the things she'd brought on this trip.

Dusk had now fallen. While Katherine struggled to remove her boots, Dix took advantage of the fading light to search for more wood for their fire. He returned a short time later, his arms filled with branches and twigs, and laid the bundle next to the grate. She was rubbing the ointment on her tired arms and wrists.

"Can you do my shoulders, please?" she asked.

He tossed some of the wood into the fire and knelt behind her on the tarp. She had trouble undoing the buttons of her blouse, so he helped. She slowly shrugged the garment off her shoulders. Beneath the shirt she wore a plain camisole. Dix made himself look away from the beauty of her golden breasts shimmering temptingly behind the thin cloth. He mentally forced his manhood down and his mind back on her request.

Fighting his rising desire, Dix applied the sweet-scented salve to the firm, soft flesh of her shoulders. He kneaded gently. Her reaction melted him like ice on a stove. "Don't do that," he warned.

"What?" she asked dreamily. His hands felt like heaven.

"Purr like I'm pleasuring you . . ."

"It's how I feel. You have wonderful hands. . . ."

He eased the bottom of her camisole free of her skirt's waistband and slid his massaging hands up inside so he could minister to her bare back. His hands ached to feel the velvet weight of her breasts against his palms, but now was not the time. When he finished with her back, arms, and shoulders, he whispered, "Lie down a moment."

She didn't have to be asked twice. She felt weightless, content; she'd do anything to keep him from withdrawing his soothing touches. She stretched out on her stomach. He gently eased her skirt up and began to slowly manipulate the tight muscles in the backs of her thighs and legs.

The sight of her gorgeous legs displayed for his eyes

alone played havoc with his barely manageable manhood. Touching her did not help. He imagined her bottom could use a bit of salving, too, after being in the saddle all day, but he was hesitant. He couldn't offer her relief without removing her drawers—and if he did, all hell was liable to break loose.

She unwittingly made the decision for him by saying in a hushed voice, "Hold on, let me pull down my drawers so you can do my poor bottom."

As she raised her hips a bit to accomplish the task, Dix looked on with glowing eyes. He didn't think her bottom "poor" at all. He found it rich, lush, and highly arousing. He had to once again force himself to remember he was supposed to be helping her, not filling her with his flaring need.

Her hips in his hands were as pliant as exotic fruit. Careful to keep to the task and not touch her where he wanted to the most, he concentrated on making her feel better. He refused to deny his eyes the sights, though no man alive could overlook her long legs and the shadowy secrets they sheltered.

His lulling touch had such an effect on Katherine, she didn't realize she'd fallen asleep until she awakened the next morning to the sunshine streaming in through the shack's partial roof.

When they headed out after breakfast, Katherine felt much better. Loreli's salve had rescued her from pain once again. Loreli's salve *and* Dix's hands she added knowingly. His touch could charm the bark off of trees.

The man Dix had come to serve the warrant on could not be found, nor could any of his family. Still mounted, Katherine scanned the collection of dilapidated wagons circled beneath a thin bower of trees and said, "Surely, he and his family did not live out in the open like this."

Dix nodded grimly.

It was little more than a campsite to Katherine's eyes. When Dix dismounted, she followed and joined him in surveying what they could of the unorthodox home. Katherine spied thin, soiled pallets beneath a few of the wagons. She imagined them to be sleeping places. Someone had erected a tattered tarp over a portion of the area as a sort of makeshift roof. She doubted it offered much protection from inclement weather. "How do they survive?"

"They just do. Some corn's planted over there that's been harvested. They've fresh water from the creek over there. Looks like they were here a while. Squatters probably. Indian Territory is still closed to settlers, but it hasn't stopped folks from slipping in and setting up illegal homesteads."

"Where would they have gone?"

"South; west, maybe. Someplace warm, certainly. No one can live this way once winter hits. The warrant probably made them pull up stakes."

Katherine wondered about a family having to live under such abject poverty. Were there children, a wife? Dix said one member of the family had murdered another over whiskey. Had the awful circumstances of a life such as this forced them into drink as a way to escape the painful reality of a day-to-day existence? She thought about the monetary wealth of people like Rupert Samuels and others of all races across the country. How could such abundance co-exist alongside such indigence? In Rupert's case, she thought he should be made to give every cent he had to the nearest mission; folks shouldn't be forced to live this way, squatters or not.

Dix spent a few more moments walking through the site. He turned over pieces of rusted machinery, fingered a worn bridle, and used the toe of his boot to break down the ash in a fire pit.

Katherine walked off a ways, scanning the area beyond the wagons. Her steps and breathing halted as she spied a tiny cross at the base of a nearby tree. The cross had been made from two sticks lashed together with dark thread. Coming closer she knelt to read the marker, which was nothing more than a weathered square of wood. Someone had carved into the face:

RACHEL. BORN SEPTEMBER 12 1884.
DIED SEPTEMBER 14 1884.
PLEASE PLACE FLOWERS ON HER GRAVE.

Katherine realized sadly that there had been a woman here, a woman who'd had to bury her child. The poignant plea for flowers tugged at Katherine's heart. How awful it must have been to lay a two-day-old daughter to rest and have to leave her in a place you might never be able to revisit ever again. It would have broken Katherine's heart. She didn't realize she was crying until she tasted the tears on her lips. Katherine had no flowers to give to the babe, but she took off her mother's topaz. Using her hands and a sharp stick, she dug down into the grave a short distance, then placed the pendant inside. It had kept Katherine safe all these many years; it could certainly do the same for the soul of a defenseless infant. Katherine didn't think her mother would mind. Wiping away her tears, she repacked the dirt and stood.

Dix had been watching silently. He held out his arms, and she let herself be held close. "There's a two-day-old baby girl buried over there," she whispered through the lump in her throat. "Two days old, Dixon!"

He held her tighter and felt her grief bring tears to his own eyes. "You did a good thing, giving up your stone.

How about we gather some rocks to place on top so the grave won't be disturbed?''

They spent time gathering rocks both large and small and placing them over the mound of dirt. When they were both satisfied that the vault of rocks looked sturdy enough to keep the tiny remains safe from predators, Katherine reverently repositioned the cross and marker. She offered up a silent prayer. Holding her hand, Dix silently did the same.

They rode out a short while later. Although Katherine left with a heavy heart, she vowed to visit Rachel's grave again, bringing flowers.

The baby's grave floated through Katherine's mind for the rest of the day. Dix seemed subdued also, but she didn't question his mood, just as he didn't question hers.

They made camp later that afternoon near another abandoned shack on Tiger Creek. She left their small campsite to walk along the creek's edge. As she walked, she thought about her future, her children. If she were ever blessed with a child, she now knew she would never abandon it. When she and Dix had first agreed to marry, she'd been perfectly willing to give birth and then turn the child over to its father. She hadn't been around many infants and had never felt the power of new life until today. Seeing that grave had had a profound effect upon her, and she didn't know the reason why. Katherine had never been a mystical person, but it almost seemed as if she'd been given the spirits of that baby and its grieving mother, and it had become her fate to bring them a restful peace. She knew it sounded silly, but having a child of her own made her believe that they would find that peace. The wild, sometimes unforgiving Territory had claimed one child, Rachel; Katherine wanted to bring her own baby into the world to even the balance.

But even had she not discovered the grave, her desire to live here and raise her children under this endless sky had been mounting since the day she stepped off the train in Wewoka. She'd come to love both her husband and the harsh yet beautiful country he called home. She hadn't heard the hustle and bustle of a big city in months and found she didn't miss the noise or the hectic pace. She'd come to appreciate the silence her husband obviously enjoyed, and she considered that a major accomplishment, knowing how much she enjoyed talking. She had also never experienced the warm feel of a small town. The folks of Wewoka had taken her into their lives and didn't care that she'd brought chaos along for the ride. If she were to ever move back East, how on earth would she get along without the Dewies or Vera's unique hair oils? If she were to go, she would probably even miss old sour-faced Merle Gleason.

All in all, she supposed she'd come to a decision. She wouldn't be going back East, no matter what the future held. This was her home, and if Dix didn't care to continue the marriage, she could live with that, too. But she and her child were going to be together.

He came up behind her then and gently wrapped his arms around her waist. She leaned back against his chest and savored being held. She then said softly, ''I've come to a decision.''

Dix stiffened slightly in response to her serious-sounding tone. ''What decision is that?''

''I'm staying here in the Territory whether you like it or not.''

He relaxed. ''Plainspoken as usual.''

Katherine waited for him to respond, steeling her heart to stave off the pain of what might come next.

He told her just as plainly, "Good, because I planned on keeping you here, even if I had to tie you to the porch."

She leaned her head back and echoed, "Tie me to the porch?"

"Yep."

She scanned his eyes, saw the seriousness there, and shook her head. "You western men," she said, chuckling softly.

"I love you, Katherine. I'm not letting you go. . . ."

"Good thing I've decided to stay, then, I suppose . . . I love you, too."

His declaration of love filled her with as much bliss as the kiss they then shared. It was a kiss of commitment, passion, and love. When they finally eased their lips apart she looked up at his handsome dark face and asked, "Do you really love me?"

"Nope. I was lying."

She punched him playfully. He groaned loudly. "Yes, I love you—more than anything in this world, I'm thinking. Shall I tell you every day so you'll believe me?"

"Only if I can tell you the same."

He nodded. "We have a deal."

Dix had never known he had a playful side until Katherine entered his life, but he found himself enjoying their easy and oftentimes spirited banter. He looked forward to a long married life filled with spirited conversation and lovemaking on the front porch.

For dinner they pan-fried the perch Dix caught from the creek. It was so tasty, Katherine declared, "I'm never going to learn to cook if I can eat food prepared like this."

"You're going to have to learn sooner or later, you know."

"I know, but you are so much better at it than I am."

"Spoiled woman."

"It's your own fault."

He drank his coffee and observed her over his cup. "I never understood men who spoiled their women."

"Now you do?"

"Now I do."

The sun died in a fiery haze that took Katherine's breath away. While she stood marveling, Dix hauled their gear over to the shack for the night's stay. When she finally walked the short distance back to the shack, she noticed him peering at its door. "Is something wrong?" she asked.

"I'm not sure. When I passed through here about a month ago, this door wasn't here."

"I don't understand."

"There are abandoned and broken-down places like this all over the Territory. Folks use them for overnighting sometimes and know what type of condition each one is in. I've slept here many times over the years. There hasn't been a door here since '82."

"Do you suppose someone is now living here?"

"Doesn't look like it inside. Looks just as empty as it did the last time I was here."

Katherine scanned the brand-new hinges and the fresh wood of the door. "It doesn't appear to have been up for very long. You can still see the oil on the hinges."

Dix nodded. He'd seen the oil himself and was impressed that she had noticed. "So, if you were a deputy, what would be your thought on this? What's this all mean?" Dix already had a theory. Knowing she had a quick brain, he wanted to see if she'd come up with a comparable scenario.

Katherine glanced at the door again. "Was it locked or no when you first found it."

"Unlocked."

She thought it over a bit longer, then said, "Now, granted, I'm no deputy marshal, but I think something is hidden inside."

"Why?"

"You said there was no door before, but there is now. The only reason someone would put a door on a place like this would be to keep something safe."

"Very good, but why isn't the door locked?"

That question was harder to answer. "Maybe what was hidden is no longer here? I don't know."

"You'd make a pretty good deputy. I believe you've figured it out for the most part. There probably is something being hid here from time to time, and I'll bet it's whiskey. Has to be somebody new to the area, though. This shack isn't as far off the trail as it might seem. People use this shack all the time because the roof is in good shape and there's water nearby."

But inside they found nothing.

Katherine was a bit disappointed, but then she supposed she should've been glad, for if anything illegal had been found, she and Dix would probably have had to head back home so that he could dispense the necessary justice. This way, she could have his dark handsomeness all to herself. With the thought of him in mind, she asked, "I'd like to bathe. Do you think it'll be safe?"

"Probably, although I can't vouch for your safety from your husband."

She grinned and said, "I think I can handle him."

So Katherine and Dix went down to the bank of the dark creek and washed themselves clean. The water was cold as would be expected in early October, but the past week of unusually balmy weather kept it from being as cold as it could have been.

When they finished, they each wrapped themselves in

a drying flannel and dashed back to the cabin, where Dix had prepared a fire before their leaving. Upon their return they found it roaring, and because the roof was intact, heat filled the place.

Katherine donned a long-sleeved gown and slipped on a warm robe. He pulled on a clean shirt and pants. He then retrieved a large blanket-sized skin from his gear and spread it out before the fire. Next came another large covering of about the same dimensions, which had a soft, furry underside. He placed it atop the first skin. He added a bed sheet and another fur-backed quilt.

He had a compelling light in his eyes as he held out his hand and said, "Come join me."

She didn't hesitate but came to him on legs that shook and with her heart pounding in her chest. That he loved her still amazed her to no end. He was handsome, caring, and passionate; no woman could ask for more.

His hand cupped her face gently, then held it there as he kissed her deeply. Her eyes slid closed in reaction to the sweet power he made flow, and she slid her arms around his waist to get closer and receive more. They stood before the fire in the dark room and cast erotic shadows on the walls as they pleasured each other with slow-roaming hands and kisses that drew sighs. The kisses became more languid and prolonged as they warmed to this most ancient of dances. He ran his hands over her breasts and the alluring curve of her hips. She was deliciously bare beneath her gown, and he savored the boon lustily. A few hot moments later, he tossed her gown aside.

Katherine stood before the fire nude and proud as a queen. She let him fill his eyes with dark-tipped breasts and bronzed hips and rode the power only a woman can know. Before Dix had come into her life, she'd never considered herself beautiful; but being before him now, wearing nothing but the rings in her ears, she could not help but feel that way. His eyes said so, as did his splendidly ready manhood.

He had her kneel before the hearth with her back to him, then fit his naked heat behind her. His hands moved to answer the tempting call of her breasts, then down to the small bud at the base of her still-damp triangle. He played until she arched her back sinuously and groaned from the glory of it all. Only then did he join his flesh to hers.

Katherine had always treasured the initial sweet invasion, and tonight was no exception. Feeling him pulsing so masculinely within her almost sent her over the edge.

He began to stroke her with a lazy rhythm that she answered gladly. His hands teased the nubbins of her breasts. They were already berried like the sweet succulent fruit he considered them to be but he couldn't stop touching her. He pleasured her with slow, hot circles of his hands, roaming high on her body at first, and then low. He dallied on the low passes even as he kept up the lulling rhythm.

Katherine could see the red haze of the fire from behind her closed lids and could feel the heat licking sensually over the front of her body. His caressing hands and his wanton stroking were just as hot.

Soon passion set off its own flames, and his thrusts became deeper and less controlled as they soared on the erotic madness of making love. He guided her hips to his increasing pace and she began to croon. Her desire climbed and she curved forward just a bit, shamelessly answering his male call. It was Dix's turn to groan then, and to reward her for such uninhibited response, he slid his hand around to the tiny kernel of flesh that made her woman and sent her straight to paradise. As the completion shuddered over her, Dix's began to roar. He rode out his own explosive end, thrusting possessively, mindlessly, until only the silence remained.

Later that night, Dix awakened to the sound of voices outside. It helped to be a light sleeper in his line of work, and he'd been easily awakened since childhood. The faint voices he'd heard seemed to be coming from down by the creek bank. He looked down at Katherine asleep beside him. She was snoring so peacefully that he hated to wake her up, but he had to because he'd no idea who or what they might be facing.

He roused her gently but firmly. When she opened her eyes, he told her, "Get dressed as quickly as you can. Sounds like we have guests."

She groaned but got herself up and moving. Pulling on her gown, she asked crossly, "Why do people keep visiting us in the middle of the night?"

He shrugged, smiling, as he quickly pulled on his pants and shirt, then instructed, "I want you to get over there behind that saddle. If any shooting starts, keep your head down."

The fire had burned down to embers, which Dix doused with water from his canteen. He didn't want its light to alert those approaching that the shack was occupied. The horses had been tied up out back, facing the road. The horses would be discovered eventually, but he hoped not before he had a chance to figure out what was going on.

It was now black as pitch inside the shack. With the fire gone, there was no light or heat to counteract the chilly October breeze drifting through the paneless square that served as the only window. Behind the saddle, Katherine shivered inside her robe. She wished the nocturnal visitors would hurry up and show themselves or move along. She wanted to crawl back under the warm furs and return to sleep.

She soon got her wish. The door opened, revealing the faint light of the quarter moon and the outlines of two men. They were carrying what appeared to be crates. By the sound of their harsh breathing and the slow steps they were taking, the crates must have been heavy.

Dix let them get all the way inside before he called out, "Deputy Marshal. Do not move. Do not take your hands off those crates."

The men froze in their bent over positions.

Dix quickly lit the lamp he'd positioned at his side. When the light flared, it showed the startled faces of Frank and Joe, Rupert's men.

Dix asked, "What is it with you two?" The thugs uttered sharp curses as Dix stepped out from behind the door with his Colt drawn. "This is the third time."

"We didn't know you was here," Frank protested glumly. Katherine came out from behind the saddle and stalked back to the bedroll. She groused, "I can't believe I had to get up for them. Just shoot them Dix, and we can both get back to sleep."

She crawled back beneath the furs, confident her husband could handle this situation without her assistance

Frank and Joe were still holding the crates. The strain on their faces was hard to miss. Dix drawled, "Those things look pretty heavy. Go ahead and put them down. Easy now," he warned.

Once the men had complied, neither could mask their relief.

"So, what's inside? I'm sure I already know, but humor me."

"We don't know," Frank lied angrily.

Katherine quipped, "You would think they'd be more

truthful. After all, you could arrange for them to be in the penitentiary for the rest of their lives.''

''True,'' Dix replied. ''Unless you gentlemen speak up, I'll be adding a charge of lying to a federal officer to the charges you're going to get for whatever is in those boxes.''

When neither Frank nor Joe spoke, Dix asked Katherine, ''Would you get those bracelets out of my war bag, please?''

She fished out the handcuffs. ''Shall I put them on them?''

''Just toss them to them. I don't want you getting too close.'' Dix didn't want them to do something stupid like grab her and attempt to use her release as leverage for their own. He'd have to shoot them for sure then.

Katherine tossed over the handcuffs.

Dix instructed them to chain themselves together at the wrists. They balked at first, but when the lawman raised his Colt, they grudgingly complied.

''Kate, fetch the ropes on the saddle, please.'' He then said to his prisoners, ''Kate's going to come over there and tie you up. If you touch her or even look at her, this Colt's going to bark lead. Understand?''

They nodded angrily.

''Don't even breathe hard, gentlemen,'' he warned again. Then he said, ''Go ahead, Katherine.''

Following Dix's instructions, they stood side by side as Katherine wound the thick rope around their arms and chests like they were an odd sort of top. Around she went, pulling tight as she'd learned to do with the ropes on a schooner's canvas, then tying the ends securely with a complicated knot. Next, Dix had her bind Frank's left leg to Joe's right.

When Katherine was finished, she stood back to view her handiwork. Their arms were secured to their sides by the rope wound around their chests, and because of the way their inner legs were joined, they were going to have to coordinate their movements to walk with any success.

Now that they'd been neutralized, Dix relit the fire, lit another lantern, and walked over to the boxes. Using the blade of the stout knife he took from the sheath on his belt, he pried out the nails sealing the tops. The first one he opened held bottles of illegal whiskey, just as he'd suspected. The contents of the other made him turn on them and ask sharply, "Where'd you get this crate?"

It was filled with medical supplies. The outside of the box bore the words FEDERAL GOVERNMENT ISSUE. MEDICAL SUPPLIES. CHILDREN. It had been slated for the children on one of the government reserves. Dix had seen many just like it.

Neither Frank nor Joe answered.

"Judge Parker is going to send you away for the rest of your thieving lives," he pronounced roughly.

Katherine came over and examined the contents: specially packaged vaccines, fever medicines, plasters, blankets, and bandages. It appeared as if Rupert hadn't been content with hauling in the profits from illegal liquor sales, he was also trying to turn a profit on sick children. Katherine looked over at the two in disgust. She was outraged because she knew how the People were suffering on the reserves; everyone in the Territories knew. The government continued to herd the tribes like cattle, forcing them to live in squalor and poverty, while missionaries and agents got fat off bribes and skimming profits from the illegal trafficking of beef and other goods. The People's customs were being taken away, deemed inciting and pagan by governing wages. The nonothings in Washington were even passing legislation that made many aspects of tribal life and culture illegal.

Being removed from their ancestral lands had severed their ties to the flora and fauna they'd used for healing. Now their children and elders had to rely on government medicine, only to have villains like Rupert and his ilk deprive them of that, as well.

She snapped, "How can you live with yourselves knowing that children probably died because you stole their medicine? Frank, you and I have spoken about your two sons in Baltimore. What if this vaccine had been needed by them?"

He wouldn't meet her eyes.

"Can Rupert be paying you so much that you can do this to needy little ones and still sleep at night?"

Dix looked on silently.

She walked over and stood before the decidedly unhappy Frank and went on softly, "My husband and I came across a grave yesterday of a two-day-old baby girl. I don't know how she died, but what if the medicine you've been pilfering could have saved her life? How old are your sons, Frank? Didn't you once tell me they were nine and six? Suppose your eldest had died at two days because someone had stolen medicine that would have let him live. How would you feel?"

She didn't expect a reply, and she didn't receive one. "As I said, I hope Rupert is paying you a pretty penny now, because you're not going to be able to spend a cent of it in hell."

Dix then hustled them outside. They fell twice before figuring out how to walk. Dix had them sit with their backs against the shack's broken-down well pump. He used his last length of rope to lash them to the pump's shaft and left them there.

Come daylight, Dix found a small flatbed boat resting on the creek's bank. Atop it were another two boxes of liquor and one holding more medical supplies. Dix knew that neither Frank nor Joe were bright enough to pull off such smuggling on their own; Rupert or someone like him had to be running the show.

Because Frank and Joe had come by boat, they had no horses to ride back to Wewoka and jail. Dix tied them to the pack mule's rein and made them walk most of the first day. The bound prisoners had a very difficult time finding their rhythm at first and kept falling and being dragged behind the mule. The first time it occurred, Dix heard them yelling, and he looked back and saw their dilemma.

Katherine looked back, too. "They seem to be having problems," she noted easily.

Dix straightened and said, "Yep, seems like it."

He let them be dragged a good half mile before stopping. It happened again and again, and finally Dix had had enough. Dismounting, he drawled, "We'll never get home at this rate."

So he undid the rope joining their legs, then remounted and pushed ahead.

About ten miles outside of Wewoka, Dix stopped at the house of a light horseman he knew and borrowed a buckboard and team. He put his trussed-up prisoners in the back, tied the horses to the back of the wagon, then he and Katherine took seats up front and struck out for home.

Chapter 20

⟨∿⟩☉☉⟨∿⟩

When they finally reached town, Dix locked Frank and Joe in the small cell behind the wooden door, gave the keys over to Lyndon Green, and drove himself and Katherine home.

That night as they lay in bed, Dix held his wife close and said into the dark, "You make a pretty decent deputy, Kate. I could see Frank shrinking right before my eyes when you laid into him about the medicine."

"Well, thank you, he deserved it."

Dix traced a finger over her bare shoulder. "He may be the likeliest of the two to give us the information we need to catch his boss. I want you to visit him a few times over the next couple of days and see if we can't play upon that guilt you put in him."

"If you think it might help, I'd be glad to."

The next day, Dix sent Lyndon back to the shack on Tiger Creek to retrieve the crates. When he got there, the boxes of liquor were gone, but the medical supplies were right where Dix said they would be.

The days and nights grew colder as autumn came into its own. Folks were gearing up for the coming of winter and the upcoming local and national elections. Territorial newspapers including Katherine's were filled with editorial opinions on which way the country should be going and which candidates merited support. The Black papers were, of course, debating these same issues in another voice, a voice that called for the Redemptionists in the south to allow Black voters to exercise their dearly won right to the ballot box and for the federal government to make sure they did.

Since U.S. marshals were appointed to their posts, Dix didn't have to run for re-election. Katherine did not endorse her father's campaign, however. He was running for the county's cattle commission, of all things. In her editorial she noted that she loved her father but would not support electing a fox to guard the chickens. He sulked for a few days over her words, but she was confident he would get over it and resume playing checkers with her.

On election day, November 4, 1884, Americans went to the booths and voted in Grover Cleveland, the former governor of the state of New York, as the twenty-second president of the United States. He would be the first Democratic president since the swearing in of James Buchanan in 1856. Considering the volatile conditions in the South and the previous year's ruling by the Supreme Court that gutted the postwar Civil Rights Act, thereby legalizing jim crow, the Black Republican electorate did not view the Cleveland victory as a step forward for the nation.

A week after the election, Frank and Joe were still in jail. Ned Morgan was also enjoying the marshal's hospitality, having been caught "introducing." He spent the first few days boasting about being broken out of jail by his brothers, but after five days of confinement, he began to sulk. Unlike earlier in the summer when brother Clyde had been jailed, Vernon, the oldest Morgan, had not come in to post bail.

As Dix had asked, Katherine stopped in a few times to visit with Frank, but he wouldn't speak with her. It didn't matter because the warrants for Rupert's arrest had finally arrived from the sovereign state of Maryland, giving Dix the legal right to track Samuels down.

The next morning, Dix was seated in the office going over some wanted posters when he came across one for Jackson Blake's baby brother, Griffin. It seems Griff and his gang had robbed a train up in Kansas—again—and the authorities were looking for the handsome outlaw— again. Dix said to the empty office, "Probably hiding beneath some woman's bed."

Griffin did have a way with ladies. In fact, if Dix remembered correctly, two females had helped break him out of a Reno jail the year before. Dix set the notice on Griffin Blake with the others on the stack and picked up the next poster, only to hear a commotion going on behind the cell door. He pulled his Colt and went to investigate.

Twisting the key in the padlock, he pulled the door open. "What's going on in here?"

Ned Morgan snarled from within his cell, "They've been arguing and fighting like two old women. I demand to be moved to another jail."

Dix ignored him. In the other cell, Frank and Joe were shooting daggers at each other. Frank's eye was swelling, and he looked like he'd been punched. Joe was wiping blood from his bleeding nose.

Frank announced, "I want out of here, Marshal—"

"Shut your mouth!" Joe demanded and jumped on him. The two rolled around as they fought within the small confines of the cell.

Dix barked, "Settle down!"

When they ignored him, he waited. For a moment it was hard to determine who had the upper hand. A few moments later, Frank felled his cohort with a blow that left him dazed and then staggered over to the bars.

Breathing hard, he told Dix, "I'll tell you whatever you want to know! Just send me home. I'll stand trial and do whatever, but I want out. I hate this place."

Having recovered, Joe sat upon the cot and wiped the blood from his mouth. "You're a damn traitor, Frank! A goddamn traitor!"

Frank turned and snapped, "Samuels ain't gonna get us out of here! He and that Blackfeather woman are probably off drinking champagne someplace while we're in here rotting away. We ain't been paid in weeks."

Dix drawled, "And you probably won't be, ever. Your boss is wanted back East on murder charges."

Dix noted the surprised look on Joe's face and asked, "You didn't know? I'd think after all you've done for him, he would've told you."

Joe didn't answer.

"All his money has been seized and sealed. He can't pay himself now, let alone expendable help."

"See?" Frank exclaimed to his companion. "This sea is getting too deep for me to swim in. I don't mind roughing folks up or applying the screws, but when you killed that man we caught with Miss Katherine the night she broke into the safe, I ain't felt right since."

Joe sneered, "Liar. The only reason you ain't felt right is because we ain't been paid."

Dix didn't care about Frank's motivation; all he wanted was information on Rupert and his operation. "So how is Mona Blackfeather involved?"

Joe snapped, "Don't tell him!"

Frank spoke anyway. "She tells Rupert about shipments, where he can hide them, who wants to buy. Draws him maps.''

''Where's she getting her information, do you know?''

''The big bootlegger, Donovan. I think she must be sharing her favors with him, if you get my meaning.''

Dix knew with a fair amount of certainty that if Mona was using her wiles on Donovan to obtain information on his shipments so Samuels could steal them, Donovan would have them both killed if he ever found out.

''Where are they holed up?''

''Up in the Creek Nation. I couldn't tell you exactly where, though. I'm still learning my way around this godawful country. The Blackfeather woman draws me a map, I go do the job, I follow it back.''

Dix nodded.

Joe said nastily, ''Frank, when Mr. Samuels gets here, I'll be sure to tell him you spilled the beans.''

Frank shot back, ''He ain't coming! How many times do I have to say it?! He ain't coming!''

Frank was wrong.

Three days later, eight masked men descended upon the Wewoka jail at a little past noon. Lyndon Green, in the office playing checkers with Bart Love, didn't stand a chance of holding them off. Dix came running out of the telegraph office on the heels of the explosion and got there just in time to see the gang riding away, hard. They'd used dynamite to blow out the back wall. Many people were already inside the collapsed structure, tossing aside the chunks of brick and metal in an effort to find Lyndon. Katherine was one of them. As folks searched frantically, Dix joined in, harshly calling the young peace officer's name. Dix prayed as he'd never done before.

The prayers weren't answered. They found the young

light horseman beneath the rubble, dead. Beside him lay
Bart Love, clutching the remnant of a checkerboard in
his lifeless hand.

The town's undertaker took the bodies away while
Dix consoled his wife. He didn't want to leave her alone,
but he had to round up a posse and go after the killers.

"I'm coming with you," she said angrily through her
grief.

"You have to stay here."

"The hell I do! I'm going!"

He didn't have time to argue, so he left her standing
in the street. While the hastily gathered posse stormed
off down the road. Katherine began running toward the
store to retrieve her buggy when Ruth and Hannah
Green came barreling around the corner in Ruth's expensive and well-sprung rig. Ruth dragged the team to
a halt, and Hannah yelled, "Get in, Katherine! Get in!"

Katherine hesitated for only a moment, then quickly
hiked up her skirt and climbed aboard.

Ruth got the team underway almost immediately.

"Where are we going!" Katherine yelled as she hung
on.

Ruth yelled angrily, "After the cowards who killed
my son!"

While Ruth pushed her rig to its limits on the open
road, Hannah told Katherine, "We passed the gang
while we were driving into town. They came thundering
toward us like demons. Of course, at the time, we'd no
idea what they'd done. Mother simply pulled to the side
and they rode past. A couple of the riders were barely
in their saddles. They looked hurt, but they went by so
quickly it was hard to be sure. Oh, and Mona Blackfeather was one of the riders. I know it was her because
she looked me straight in the face. She looked terrified."

Katherine noted, "She has a reason to."

There were tears in the eyes of the Green women as the horses' hooves continued to eat up the miles. They had lost both son and brother. Katherine was certain their pain echoed her own.

After Ruth tired, Hannah took over the driving from her mother and drove them the rest of the way. They caught up with the posse an hour out. The men were all dismounted when they arrived.

A grim Dix walked over to their rig and said, "Clyde Morgan says they're holed up in a shack at the foot of those hills. You're all welcome to stay, but keep out of the way."

Katherine nodded at him, her thanks shining in her tear-bright eyes.

Dix turned to go back, but Hannah stopped him before he could leave and told him what she'd related to Katherine about seeing the gang ride by. "A couple of them appeared injured."

"Probably from the blast," Dix replied. "And Mona was with them, you say?"

Hannah nodded.

He shook his head. He then looked at Ruth, sitting so still in the buggy. When she met his eyes she began to cry silent tears. Her grief over losing her son seemed to have aged her. Dix took her hand and held it tight. "I'm so, so sorry."

She nodded, then whispered, "I know. You loved him, too."

And Dix had.

"You made my son into a fine light horseman, Dixon. He died doing what he did best, and he died with honor. I've already wired my husband to return from his trip to Houston." Her tears began anew.

Hannah put an arm around her mother and said softly, "You know Lyn wouldn't want us crying this way."

Ruth wiped at her eyes. "No, he would not. He would want us to find his killers and bring them to justice."

"And that's what I plan to do," Dix told her. He then turned to his wife and took her hand. "Come walk with me."

They walked silently together then halted a short distance down the road. "Are you okay?" he asked quietly.

"No."

He gazed down into her red, swollen eyes. "They won't get away. I give you my word."

"I don't doubt that." She then added, "Papa and I were just getting to know one another. It's so unfair, is all."

He took her into his arms and held her tight. "I love you, Katherine," he whispered.

"I love you, too. . . ."

For a few more moments they stood there, letting their love salve their grief.

Finally she leaned back and said, "You need to get back to your posse."

"Rupert and Mona aren't going anywhere."

"Still, you've a job to do. As much as I would love to be held all night, you're needed back there."

He kissed her dusty forehead. "Anybody ever tell you that you make a good marshal's wife?"

She gave him a watery smile.

He left her then to go and do his job.

The shack was in a valley among some trees below the road, and the posse had surrounded the place. When Dix rejoined the men, Arnold Taylor asked, "How're we going to get them out of there? They're yelling that they're not coming out."

"We wait," Dix informed him.

"How long?"

"As long as it takes."

Dix and a few members of the posse dug in for the night. The Greens, Katherine, and the rest of the men went back to town. Katherine vowed to return after burying her father the next day. Lyndon would be laid to rest upon his father's return from Houston. Both families had to make arrangements with the town undertaker before they could go home.

The Reverend Mr. Lane conducted Bart's burial at the Nero A.M.E. church. A good portion of the town showed up to offer their condolences to Katherine and pay their last respects. Dix, dressed in a somber black suit, quietly slipped into the seat next to her just as the service began. Katherine thought he wouldn't be able to attend because of the siege at the shack, but he had come. There were more than enough men at the site to keep an eye on things, he explained to her. Having him at her side made her grief easier to bear.

After returning from the cemetery, Katherine, with the help of some of the Dewies, went over to her father's room and packed up his belongings. When they were done, they loaded the two boxes in the back of Katherine's buggy, and she drove home.

She spent the day grieving and didn't get back out to the shack until the next day.

The situation had not changed in her absence. Rupert and his companions still refused to come out.

While Katherine waited with everyone else for the situation to come to a head, she chronicled the account of the standoff for her own paper and the ones that carried her work back East. She began the story with Frank and Joe's original arrest at Tiger Creek, then brought the readers up to date. To add more flavor, she talked to the posse members to get their thoughts and opinions.

Clyde Morgan turned out to be an interesting subject.

For the first time, Katherine learned that his brother Vernon, in addition to the escaped Ned, was also in the shack.

Katherine wrote quickly to keep pace with his words as he said, "Mona Blackfeather came out to the house the other day and asked if we wanted to break Ned out of jail. She said a man she knew had some friends in the same jail, and he'd pay good money if we helped free them."

Katherine, seated on a flat rock, looked up and asked, "Did you agree?"

"I didn't agree to anything because I know Mona. She's been no good since we were in primary school. Vernon agreed, though. Said he felt bad about Ned being in jail and us not having the money to post bail. Believe me, Mrs. Marshal, I felt bad, too—but not bad enough to sign on with Mona Blackfeather. I told Vernon to tell her no, but he wouldn't listen to me."

Clyde continued, telling Katherine how Mona rounded out the gang by recruiting men she knew up in the Creek Nation to help and how they'd been using the shack as their base of operations.

"According to what Mona told Vernon, they were supposed to head back up into the Creek lands after the job. I figure somebody in there is hurt bad if they had to hightail it here to the shack, instead."

Katherine asked, "What will it take to make your brothers surrender?"

Clyde shrugged. "Both of them are pretty hardheaded. Who knows? Maybe the marshal should put a snake in there," he said with a chuckle.

He must have interpreted her look of confusion because he explained, "Vernon's scared to death of them. I remember one time when we were young, he made me mad over something or other, so I threw a snake into the privy with him. He came tearing out of there like a bat outta hell. Had his pants still down around his ankles. I can still see it. I laughed so hard, thought I'd bust a gut.''

Katherine found his wide grin infectious.

"Teased him about it for at least a year.''

Katherine spent a few more minutes talking with Clyde, then excused herself to continue her rounds.

The legendary lawmen Bass Reeves and Sam Sixkiller rode into the posse's camp that same afternoon, bringing with them sixteen light horsemen from across the Nations. They'd come to assist with the siege and to offer their condolences to Katherine for the loss of her father and to Dix for the loss of Lyndon Green.

Bass said to Katherine, "That pappy of yours was one of a kind.''

She nodded. "He truly was.''

The siege began its third day with Mona Blackfeather stepping out onto the porch bright and early that morning. She shouted, "I'm folding, Dix! Don't shoot! Me and the Creeks are coming out!''

She held her hands up in the air and was soon joined by five men. The posse trained their weapons on Mona and her companions as they slowly walked up the rise. When they reached the top, all were taken into custody, tied up, and placed in a wagon to await transport.

Dix questioned Mona as she sat waiting. "What made you come out?''

"You ever been locked up with those Morgans?''

Blessedly, Dix had not.

Mona hadn't enjoyed it at all. "Arguing, fussing— Vern screaming 'Shut up!' at Ned a million times a day. Made me insane.''

"What about Rupert?''

"He was almost as useless as Vern and Ned. He had so much potential, Dix, but could not take orders—especially from a woman. He knew absolutely nothing about smuggling whiskey but began second guessing me from the start."

"Whose idea was it to use the dynamite?"

"His. He'd never held a stick in his life. Had never even seen one except in the newspapers. Damn near blew us all up."

Dix told her emotionlessly, "The blast killed Lyndon and Bart Love."

She stiffened and searched his face as if seeking truth. She brought her hands to her mouth. "Good lord!" She met his eyes again. "Not Lyndon?"

"Yes, Lyndon."

She looked away, seemingly unable to answer. Then she said, "I would have never harmed Lyndon. I don't get along with Hannah, but I liked her brother. In fact, I was the first woman he ever slept with."

Dix sighed tiredly. "They're going to hang you, Mona."

She met his eyes. "I know." She stared off into the distance as if contemplating her future.

He asked her quietly, "Who's injured inside the shack?"

"Joe and Frank. Both were hurt by the explosion. Frank's pretty bad. Ned's arm is broken."

"Those men need a doctor."

"I know, but Rupert doesn't seem to care. He has Vern and Ned convinced he's going to be able to find a way out of this. I told him you'd never allow it, but as I said, he has a hard time listening to me. Oh, and, Dix, it was me who shot at your wife that day on the road. Rupert and I just wanted to scare her some."

Dix shook his head. He then questioned her a few

moments more. When he felt he'd gotten all the information she had to offer, he signaled the wagon's driver to head out. The prisoners were being taken straight to Judge Parker's court at Fort Smith, Arkansas. To make certain the journey would be trouble free, Sixkiller sent along an escort of four Creek light horsemen.

Mona's eyes held Dix's as the wagon rolled away. He knew it would probably be the last time.

That evening as Katherine sat with her husband and the other marshals around the fire, eating and trying to stay warm, she listened to the conversations flowing around her.

Dix said, "According to Mona, their rations should be pretty well finished. I know how much Vernon likes to eat. He won't hold out more than a day or two, once he gets hungry."

Katherine quipped, "And according to his brother, Clyde, if you put a snake in there, Vernon'll come out quicker still."

The men stared curiously, so Katherine related the snake story she'd been told. Everyone laughed at the anecdote. Then Dix, Sixkiller, and Bass looked at each other and smiled.

Sometimes the Territory's marshals had to use unorthodox ways to obtain arrests. Bass Reeves had once lain facedown in a weed-filled ditch by the road and snagged his wanted man as the man rode by. Dix had once set fire to an old wagon and sent it barreling down on the hideout of some outlaws he'd been asked to bring in. The burning wagon hit the old shack, coming to rest against the wall with the only window, and the outlaws were smoked out like a hive of honeybees. Many creative solutions had been applied over the years, but none of the lawmen had ever employed snakes.

       *   *   *

That next afternoon, Katherine drove out to the siege site and noticed the posse's numbers appeared to have thinned. When she found her husband, she asked him about it.

"Has something happened? Did all the light horsemen go home?"

"Nope. They're out snake hunting."

"Snake hunting?"

"After you left last night, Sixkiller, Bass, and I got to talking. Clyde's snake idea seemed like a good one, so we're going to try it. Granted, it's a little late in the year—most snakes are probably already winter sleeping—but we sent the light horsemen out early this morning anyway to see what they could find."

Katherine shook her head, finding the tale absolutely amazing.

The light horsemen did not return until late that evening, but they did not return empty-handed. They'd captured only venomless reptiles as instructed and brought them into camp in a large burlap bag. Katherine took a peek inside. The writhing mass of snakes resembled the head of the Medusa. She shuddered and backed away.

The next morning at first light, Dix grabbed the tied-up bag and began making his way down the hill. Ned Morgan, who'd apparently had the night watch, was asleep on the ground in front of the door. Dix shook his head at Ned's vigilance as he tiptoed by him. Behind Dix, Bass Reeves clamped a hand over Ned's mouth. As Ned opened his startled eyes, Bass stuck his Colt in his face and signaled for him to remain quiet. Ned complied, swiftly nodding his head, intimating that he understood. Bass escorted him back up the hill. A smiling Dix slipped around the side of the weathered wooden shack and out of sight.

Katherine watched Ned be led away to the transport

wagon by one of the light horsemen. The Morgan brother looked decidedly unhappy.

Back down at the shack, Dix slid up against the wall that had the only window and peered inside. He could see Frank lying in a corner. He appeared dead. Joe did, too. Both men had their heads and parts of their faces wrapped with blood-soaked bandages. The tarps they were lying on showed blood pooled beneath their still bodies.

Rupert was asleep in a bedroll in the middle of the room. Vernon slept in a bedroll a bit away.

Dix knelt and untied the rope around the lip of the bag. The snakes had been kept relatively warm by the fire last night. The temperature this morning was a bit brisk. Once the snakes were freed, they'd instinctively seek warmth, which is exactly what Dix wanted them to do. Moving carefully and quietly, Dix shook the reptiles out of the bag, and they coiled at the base of the shack's foundation. The wood there had rotted in many spots leaving wide gaps. The openings were more than adequate for ground slithering reptiles to slide through, and once they were out of the bag, they did just that.

A satisfied Dix quickly picked his way back up the hill. Then he and everyone else in the posse settled back to wait.

It took about an hour to know whether the plan had worked. When the sound of Vernon Morgan screaming at the top of his lungs pierced the early-morning silence, everyone knew it had. Vernon continued to scream and gunshots began as a counterpoint. Seconds later, Vernon came charging out of the shack, stumbling and falling and running, as he tried to hold up his pants and put distance between himself and the snake-infested shack. He ran right into the hands of the light horsemen waiting outside the door. Rupert, who came barreling out behind him, did the same.

The posse up on the hill laughed until they cried. Neither Vernon nor the angry Rupert seemed to enjoy being the butt of their humor, but there was nothing they could do about it as they were led away.

Inside the shack, they confirmed that Frank was dead. Joe died later, on the operating table of the local doctor.

Rupert's capture went a long ways toward easing the grief of Katherine and Lyndon Green's family. It would not bring the two men back to the people who loved them best, but justice had been served.

A few days later, Katherine received a telegram from Geoff that made her crow so joyfully, the folks reading the news on her walls turned and stared. It read:

Good News! T.T. Fortune starting new paper named *New York Freeman*. Will you accept agent position? G.

Katherine ran all the way to the telegraph office, yelling and waving Geoff's message as she did. She had Alfreda wire Geoff back immediately with a one word reply:

YES!!

Thanksgiving arrived on the fourth Thursday of November. Everyone in town knew of Katherine's nonexistent cooking skills, so Vera took pity on Dix and invited the marshal and his wife to share dinner with her and Solomon.

On the ride home, Katherine snuggled against her husband as he guided the team through the night. Never in her wildest dreams had she imagined she would be destined to live in such a raucous and untamed land. She'd been forced into marriage, spent over a month trekking across country with mail-order brides, and had buried her father. But out of that last bit of sadness had come joy. Yesterday the town midwife confirmed what Katherine had suspected: She and Dix were going to have a child. She hadn't yet mentioned anything to him for fear of being wrong. Now, riding along in the dark with only the lantern on the buggy to light the way, she breathed in the clean, crisp night air and thought the time was right.

"Do you know how to prepare baby food?"

He had such a puzzled look on his dark face, she couldn't help but smile.

He asked, "Why?"

"Because one of us is going to need to know. Our child will need to be fed."

He dragged back on the reins and stopped the buggy. He studied her face in the lantern's pale glow. "What do you mean, our child is going to need to be fed?" Then as if a light had gone on in his head, his eyes widened. *"Are you having a baby?!"*

"Nope. *We're* having a baby."

He was so excited and elated that he pulled her across the seat and spiritedly rocked her back and forth, his heart pounding with joy. "That's wonderful news! Wonderful news!"

When he finally let her go, they grinned at each other like simpletons.

Katherine then reached out a gloved hand and placed it against his cheek. She spoke from the heart. "I will never love anyone as much as I do you. . . ."

He turned his lips to her hand and placed a kiss in the palm. "I should hope not."

Grinning, she punched him in the shoulder, then settled in against it for the rest of the ride home.

Author's Note

I do hope you enjoyed this rousing tale of the Wild West. I've always wanted to write a shoot-'em-up, as my late grandfather called westerns, and I had a great time.

Katherine's father, Bart, is based in part on a true con man of the west, Ben Hodges. Hodges was a card cheat, a fast talker, and a rustler. He was buried in 1929, the same year his old friend Wyatt Earp was interred. Frederick Douglass was this nation's first Black U.S. marshal, appointed by President Rutherford B. Hayes in 1877. The first Black man commissioned as deputy marshal in the West was the famous Bass Reeves. The true exploits of Black lawmen like Reeves and Zeke Miller are finally being rediscovered. For more on these men and the other historical aspects of *Topaz*, please look for the books and articles I've cited below.

Buckmaster, Henrietta. *Seminole Wars*. New York: Macmillan, 1966.

Burton, Arthur T. *Black, Red, and Deadly*. Austin, Texas: Eakin Press, 1991.

Dann, Martin E., Ed. *Black Press 1827–1890*. New York: Putnam, 1971.

Katz, William Loren. *Black Indians: A Hidden Heritage*. New York: Atheneum/Macmillan Co., 1986.

Katz, William Loren. *Black West*. Garden City, New York: Anchor Books, 1973.

McReynolds, Edwin C. *Seminoles*. Norman, Okla.: University of Oklahoma Press, 1957.

Schlissel, Lillian. *Women's Diaries of the Westward Journey*. New York: Schocken Books, 1982.

Thybony, Scott. "The Black Seminole: A Tradition of Courage." *Smithsonian*, vol. 22, no. 5 (August 1991).

Littlefield, Daniel, Jr. and Lonnie E. Underhill. "Negro Marshals in the Indian Territory." *Journal of Negro History* 56 (April 1971).

Jeltz, Wyatt F. "The Relations of Negroes and Choctaws and Chickasaw Indians." *Journal of Negro History* 33 (January 1948).

Mooney, Charles. "Bass Reeves, Black Deputy U.S. Marshal." *Real West* (July 1976).

Porter, Kenneth Wiggins. "Negroes and Indians on the Texas Frontier, 1836–1876." *Journal of Negro History* (October 1956).

In closing, I want to say thanks to everyone who has written to me offering prayers, blessings, and words of support, especially Patti Aden and the good folks in Gothenburg, Nebraska. All of you, no matter where you are, fill my heart. Until next time. Peace.

Avon Romances—
the best in exceptional authors
and unforgettable novels!

Avon Romantic Treasures

*Unforgettable, enthralling love stories,
sparkling with passion and adventure
from Romance's bestselling authors*

LADY OF WINTER *by Emma Merritt*
77985-4/$5.99 US/$7.99 Can

SILVER MOON SONG *by Genell Dellin*
78602-8/$5.99 US/$7.99 Can

FIRE HAWK'S BRIDE *by Judith E. French*
78745-8/$5.99 US/$7.99 Can

WANTED ACROSS TIME *by Eugenia Riley*
78909-4/$5.99 US/$7.99 Can

EVERYTHING AND THE MOON *by Julia Quinn*
78933-7/$5.99 US/$7.99 Can

BEAST *by Judith Ivory*
78644-3/$5.99 US/$7.99 Can

HIS FORBIDDEN TOUCH *by Shelley Thacker*
78120-4/$5.99 US/$7.99 Can

LYON'S GIFT *by Tanya Anne Crosby*
78571-4/$5.99 US/$7.99 Can

Discover Contemporary Romances
at Their Sizzling Hot Best
from Avon Books

RYAN'S RETURN   *by Barbara Freethy*
78531-5/$5.99 US/$7.99 Can

CATCH ME IF YOU CAN   *by Jillian Karr*
77876-9/$5.99 US/$7.99 Can

WINNING WAYS   *by Barbara Boswell*
72743-9/$5.99 US/$7.99 Can

CARRIED AWAY   *by Sue Civil-Brown*
72774-9/$5.99 US/$7.99 Can

**LOVE IN A
SMALL TOWN**   *by Curtiss Ann Matlock*
78107-7/$5.99 US/$7.99 Can

HEAVEN KNOWS BEST   *by Nikki Holiday*
78797-0/$5.99 US/$7.99 Can

FOREVER ENCHANTED   *by Maggie Shayne*
78746-6/$5.99 US/$7.99 Can